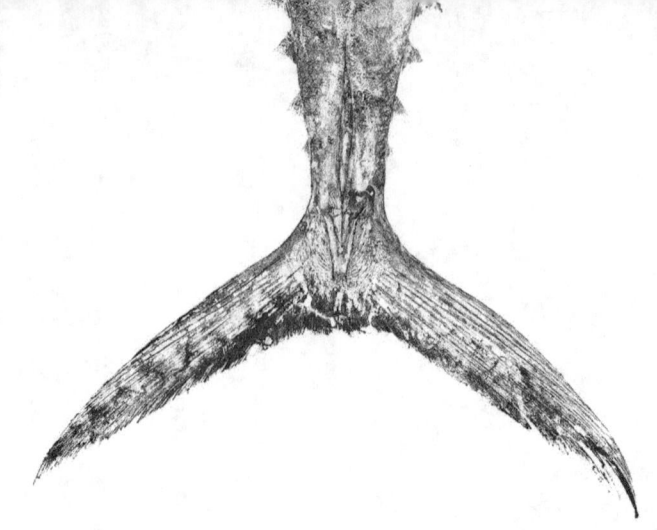

Sleepingfish issue XX

ISBN 978-1-940853-20-8

Edited by Garielle Lutz + Cal A. Mari.

Dedicated to the dead before us.

Published by Calamari Archive, Ink.
NY, NY

http://www.calamaripress.com

CONTENTS

All other design elements + interstitial images by Cal A. Mari, or from specified Calamari publications. The images on pages 5, 6 + 67 were made in collaboration w/ OpenAI's DALL·E text-to-image generator.

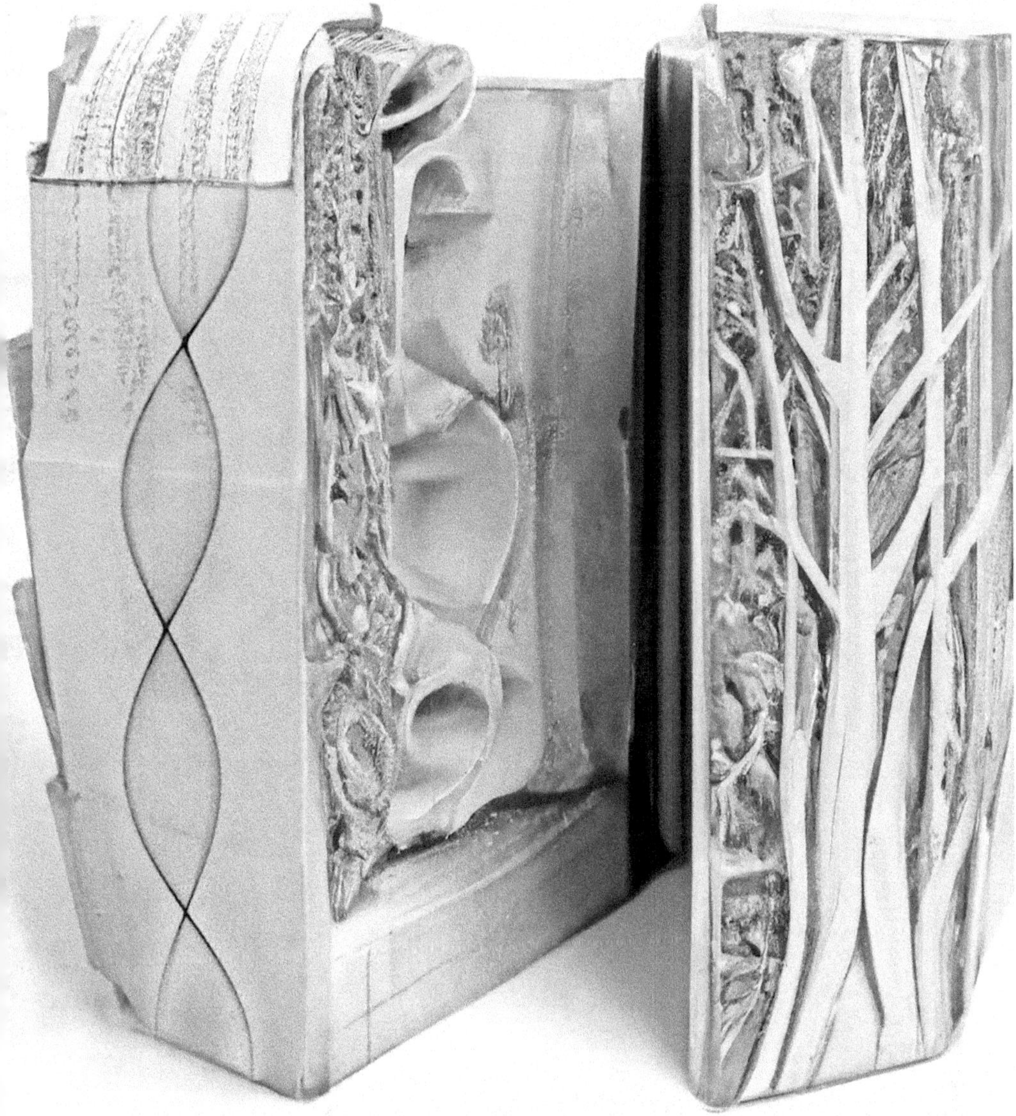

LES COMMENÇANTS (1986)

p. 37 / Chapitre IV
L'ONDE-COMMENCE

...

...

...

L'Onde-Commence est l'ensemble des éléments qui instituent l'emprise commenciale et servent l'exploit.

LES ÉLÉMENTS DE L'ONDE-COMMENCE
On distingue les éléments corporels et les éléments incorporels.

Éléments corporels. — Constituent les éléments corporels tout ce qui collabore à l'exploit (corps propre, site géo-politique, archives impubliées, allusions plus ou moins opaques, mobilier commencial intime et stock des récits hors dim. garnissant le magazin).

Éléments incorporels. — Ce sont :
Les *faux mais*, c'est-à-dire l'ensemble des personnes qui ont l'habitude de s'adresser à l'Onde-Commence (incurieux profession- nels & pseudo-foule, promenés, incités & provocables, mutateurs amuïssants, êtres chers, spectres normaux & enseignes). C'est l'élément le plus important, celui sans lequel l'Onde-Commence ne saurait qu'apparaître sans exister. Sa valeur dépend du rapport faire-valoir sur affaires-values et des connivences reliables.
Le *suivant* attend que le Commençant commence par prendre sa suite.
Ennemi & Promeneur. Ils sont en même temps partout et extrê- mement rares. Le Promeneur est un Commençant inconnu ou en-deçà de l'exploit, à force d'assister à ce qui commence il s'intéresse à ce qui finit, risquant lui-même le principal à tout coup. L'Ennemi est trop puissant pour commencer, malgré lui il achève, voire empêche tout commencement ; il ignore le Promeneur ou il le flatte.
Le *choc* & le *stigmate* : non commercial ou *mondre* dont on a donné plus haut les caractéristiques. Il faut savoir qu'en cas de vent, le mondre peut suivre sans effacement, avec ou sans inter- férence ; mais alors, mention doit être faite du *suivant* (appelé parfois, bien inutilement, poursuivant).
Les *bérets* d'intention : le béret est un titre délivré par la Garniture à l'auteur d'une intention ou d'un découvert pour assurer son exploit exclusif et signer son souffle pendant la durée d'un cer- tain nombre de termes, années fames ou infames.

p. 37 / Chapter IV
THE COMMENCE-WAVE

...

...

...

The Commence-Wave is the set of elements that establish the commencial hold and serve the deed.

ELEMENTS OF THE COMMENCE-WAVE
A distinction is made between corporeal elements and incorporeal elements.

Corporeal elements. — Anything that participates in the deed is considered a corporeal element (body proper, geopolitical site, unpubliced archives, more or less opaque allusions, cozy commencial furnishings and stock of outsized fictions compounding the store).

Incorporeal elements. — These are:
The *false fiends*, that is to say all persons used to addressing the Commence-Wave (incurious professionals & pseudo-mob, taken round, incited & excitable, mutators growing mute, loved ones, typical specters & signs). This is the most important element, the one without which the Commence-Wave could only appear yet not exist. Its value depends on the relationship between stooge value over business value and collusions one can link.
The *follower* waits for the Commencer to commence following his suite.
Enemy & Walker. They are at the same time everywhere and extremely rare. The Walker is an unknown Commencer or falls short of the deed by witnessing what commences his interest in what ends, risking the essential at every turn. The Enemy is too strong to commence; despite himself he curtails, even prevents, all commencing; he ignores the Walker or he flatters him.
The *shock* & the *stigma*: not commencial or *mortel*, the characteristics of which are given above. It should be noted that in case of wind, the mortel can follow without expungement, with or without intrusion; yet in this case the *follower* must be mentioned (sometimes, quite needlessly, called pursuer).
The *berets* of intent: the beret is a certificate issued by the Garnison to the author of an intent or an overdraft to ensure his exclusive deed and enroll his spirit for the duration of a certain number of terms, noble or ignoble years.

Les *licences* : autorisations données pour exercer une emprise commenciale ou une industrie indéterminée au titulaire d'un béret d'intention. (v.d. silences)

Le droit à l'*ennuit* (ou droit de bâiller) : un des éléments les plus importants de l'onde-commence, car les *faux-mais* s'attardent très souvent sur un sujet déterminé. L'ennuit est le ras-compte de célébration cloacale plus ou moins « vaste ».

Le droit de *plonger* (ou droit à la baille) afin d'entretenir le cours de l'événement ou la cour des faux mais (noyer la fin dans le début) ; pratique indécise, laissée à l'appréciation corpide.

L'ennuit est dit « commercial » quand il émane d'un lieu prospère où commence à se faire sentir l'onde-commence. Elle bouleverse d'emblée l'industrie et l'artifice.

Il est dit « écrit » quand il est conçu pour une durée déterminée. Il est appelé « location orale » quand il est conclu sans mention de durée.

Le prix de l'ennuit, c'est-à-dire la *louange*, est déterminée au moment du conte entre les *faux mais*, ou par décision judiciaire en cas de recommencement, si l'exploit sombre dans l'indifférence.

M.V.
Le Guide des Commençants

p-o = peut.on

– Un bon commençant est content de son métier, pourrait-on dire. Mais qu'est-ce qu'un « bon » commençant, et peut-on parler de métier puisqu'un métier implique un résultat ou quelque efficacité universellement constatable ?

Il est clair qu'un commençant ne peut non plus se définir par le nombre de ses adeptes, on n'adhère qu'aux fins et aux projets, pas au commencement en tant que tel.

termes

se complaire : chercher l'achèvement dans le commencement.
SYN : *ABOUTIR* FAM : *SOMBRER*

rechancer : action de la Battante.

commence
LE = le fait d'avoir commencé
LA = l'exploit de commencer

Permits: authorizations given to exert a commencial hold or unspecified business for the bearer of a beret of intent (v.d., silences).

The right to *ennuit* (or right to yawn): one of the most important elements of the commence-wave, since *false-fiends* quite often drag out certain subjects. Ennuit is the recount-down of more or less "endless" cloacal celebration.

The right to *dive* (or right to splash) so as to maintain the course of the ending or the court of false fiends (to drown the end in the beginning)— uncertain practice given to corpid appraisal.

Ennuit is said to be "commencial" when it stems from a propitious place in which the commence-wave commences to make itself felt. Straightaway it shakes up business and artifice.

It is said to be "written" when it is conceived to last a certain duration. It is called "oral leasing" when it's settled without reference to duration.

The prize of the ennuit, that is to say *praise*, is determined during the recounting between *false fiends*, or by judicial decision in the event of a restart, if the deed succumbs to indifference.

M.V.
The Commencer's Guide

c-o = can.one

– A good commencer is pleased with his craft, one could say. But what is a "good" commencer, and can one speak of a craft since a craft implies a result or some universally observable efficiency?

It is clear that a commencer cannot be defined by the number of his followers either; one only accedes to the ends and to the plans, not to the commencement as such.

terms

indulge: to seek completion in the commencement.
SYN: *ATTAIN* FAM: *SINK*

rechance: action of the Fighter.

commence
HIS = the fact of having commenced
HER = the deed of commencing

décisif
la rencontre avec
l'expérience
le noir

La Battante

Tout individu, Français ou Étranger, exerçant en France un Commerce de débuts, une Entreprise de détails, une Industrie d'origines, une Agence d'oublis, une profession fondamenteuse ou un métier inchoatif se trouve, en cas d'achèvement prévu par l'Ode des marques, assujetti à rebut avec la Battante.

La Battante est normalement contactée au profit d'une communauté locale finisseuse dès que le commençant atteint le sommet d'une phase inconsidérée. Ce contact personnel ne vaut que pour qui s'est complu. La Battante relance l'exploit, retarde la chute, sanctionne sévèrement les attitudes dilatoires. Elle annule momentanément le *principe fictif des commençants*. Elle renverse la nostalgie, recharge le but, épuise les faux-fuyants, écarte les aboutissants, elle rechance.

Un *rechancé* doit absolument tout oublier sinon il ne commence plus, se demande comment commencer, on dit qu'il recommence.

La commence est égale au *principe fictif* multiplié par 85, lequel varie selon les communes et les années.

76 ↓
Contrat de gag

Le gag est en général destitué par le *commençant* afin de provoquer l'avance. La Semblante Bank la garantit par le Fonds Sérieux et la mise en alerte des sourdes échonomiques & trous habitués (*seth*).

On émet un vent valable (ou croyable quelconque) sous le nez du Reveneur intéressé au début.

Le Commençant vise à ne pas finir, il entretient donc les *seth* entre but et début (il les débute, dit-on), entre fin et faim, par le drame *obséquieux* de sa faintise, allusion permanente au mouvement. (On connait certains proverbes platement cyniques : plutôt recul modifiant le souffle qu'une tension invisible ; son propre pas menace qui n'en montre pas son lendemain.)

Le crédit accordé au Commençant par le Reveneur est quasi nul, en tout cas pas plus grand que celui apporté spontanément par le regard de n'importe quel spectateur fortuit : sans compétence

conclusive
the encounter with
the experience
black

The Fighter

Any individual, French or Foreign, exercising in France a Commerce of Starts, a Business of Details, an Industry of Origins, an Agency of Oversights, a fundamentous profession or an inchoative craft is, in the event of completion foreseen by the Ode of Signs, subject to disposal through the Fighter.

The Fighter is normally contacted on behalf of a local finishing community as soon as the commencer attains the peak of a rash phase. This personal contact applies only to those who have indulged.

The Fighter resumes the deed, delays the ending, severely sanctions stalling attitudes. She temporarily invalidates the *fictitious principle of commencers*. She drives back nostalgia, recharges the goal, wears down prevaricators, discards the outcomers—she rechances.

The *rechanced* must completely forget everything, otherwise they no longer commence, wonder how to commence; one says that they start over.

The commence is equal to the *fictitious principle* multiplied by 85, which varies according to boroughs and years.

76 ↓

Gag contract

The gag is generally removed by the *commencer* in order to produce the advance. The Semblant Bank secures this through the Serious Funds and the echonomic surd alert & regular deficits (*sard*).

A good (or any likely) wind is released under the nose of the Reverser involved at the outset.

The Commencer intends not to finish, so he maintains the *sard* between outset and object (he out*sets* them, it is said), between want and wane, through the *obsequious* drama of his pretense, a standing allusion to movement. (We know certain plainly cynical proverbs: better to retreat and temper the spirit than feel an invisible strain; one's own step endangers when it shows not its sequel.)

The credit extended to the Commencer by the Reverser is almost null, in any case no greater than that given spontaneously by the glance of any chance spectator: without particular skill. A truly competent Reverser

particulière. Un Reveneur réellement compétent se fie d'ailleurs autant à l'attitude des spectateurs fortuits (qu'il doit alors personnellement surprendre — encore que là aussi de nouvelles compétences se soient développées — ce qui le place au rang de tout le monde et au rôle de n'importe qui) qu'aux échonomes de la Semblante Bank et aux veneurs du Fonds Sérieux.

Par défaut de commencement, au cas où le commençant aboutirait trop vite, voire en cas de butées trop maladroites, rebutements continuels, pseudo-rebut, le Reveneur doit adresser une signification au commençant. L'un et l'autre ont alors le statut : le commençant est déchu en Commenceur, le Reveneur institué Revenant. Une semaine après le Revenant peut faire procéder à la restauration publique du gag — lequel devient Gage — autorisant le Revenant à effacer ses propres anciens débuts *en en finissant avec* l'éternel commenceur qu'il peut utiliser à toutes fins jusqu'à le faire simplement disparaître.

distraction
inadvertance
négligence
[désenchantement]
Reveneur ≠ Souveneur

Débuts et *Détails*
Rebuts et *faiblesses*
Oublis et *buts*

also relies as much on the attitude of chance spectators (whom he must then personally entrap—although here too new skills have been developed—which places him in the rank of everyone else and in the role of anyone) as on the echonomers of the Semblant Bank and the hunters of the Serious Funds.

By default of commencement, in case the commencer attains too quickly, or even in the event of too clunky stops, continual rejections, pseudo-rejection, the Reverser must send notice to the commencer. Both then know their status: the commencer is demoted to Commencor, the Reverser is established as Revenant. A week later the Revenant can proceed with the public restoration of the gag—which becomes Guarantee—authorizing the Revenant to expunge his own former starts *by putting an end to them with* the eternal commencor, whom he can use for all purposes until making him simply disappear.

distraction
inadvertence
neglect
[disenchantment]
Reverser ≠ Rememberer

Debuts and *Details*
Rejections and *failings*
Oversights and *ends*

On Artmaking

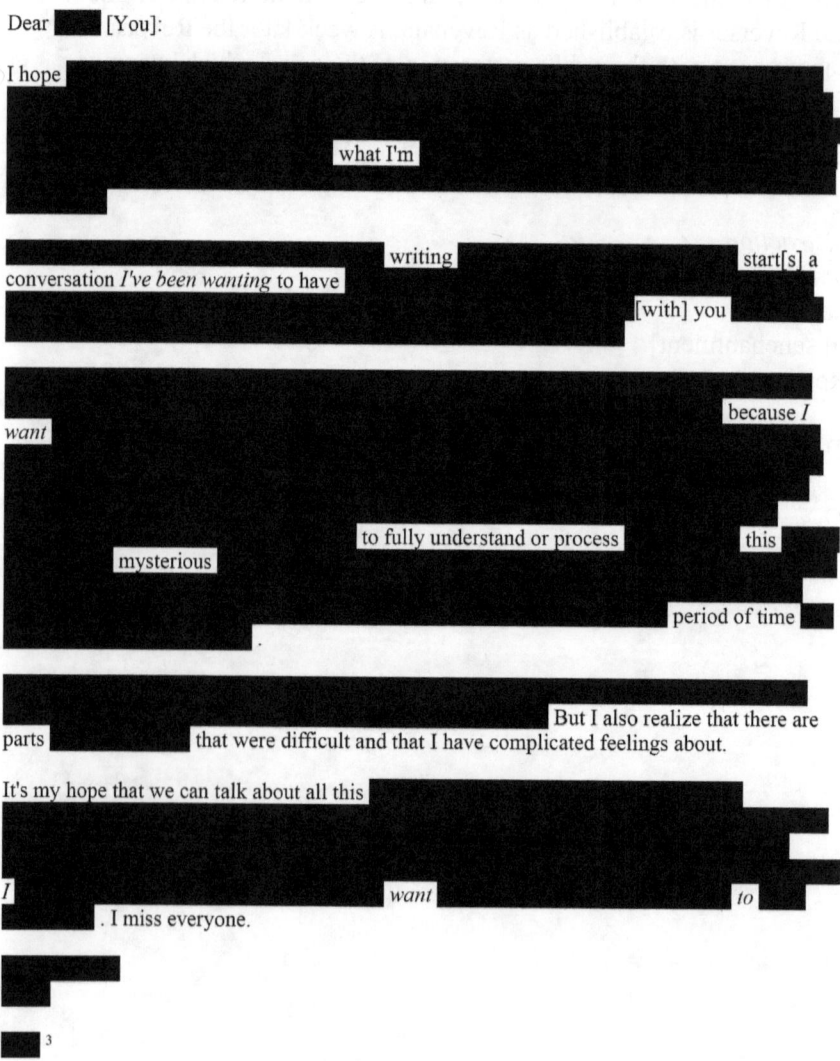

Dear ████ [You]:

I hope

what I'm

writing start[s] a
conversation *I've been wanting* to have
[with] you

because *I*

want

to fully understand or process this

mysterious

period of time

.

But I also realize that there are
parts that were difficult and that I have complicated feelings about.

It's my hope that we can talk about all this

I *want* *to*
. I miss everyone.

3

Emilio Carrero

Dear ███████ [You]:

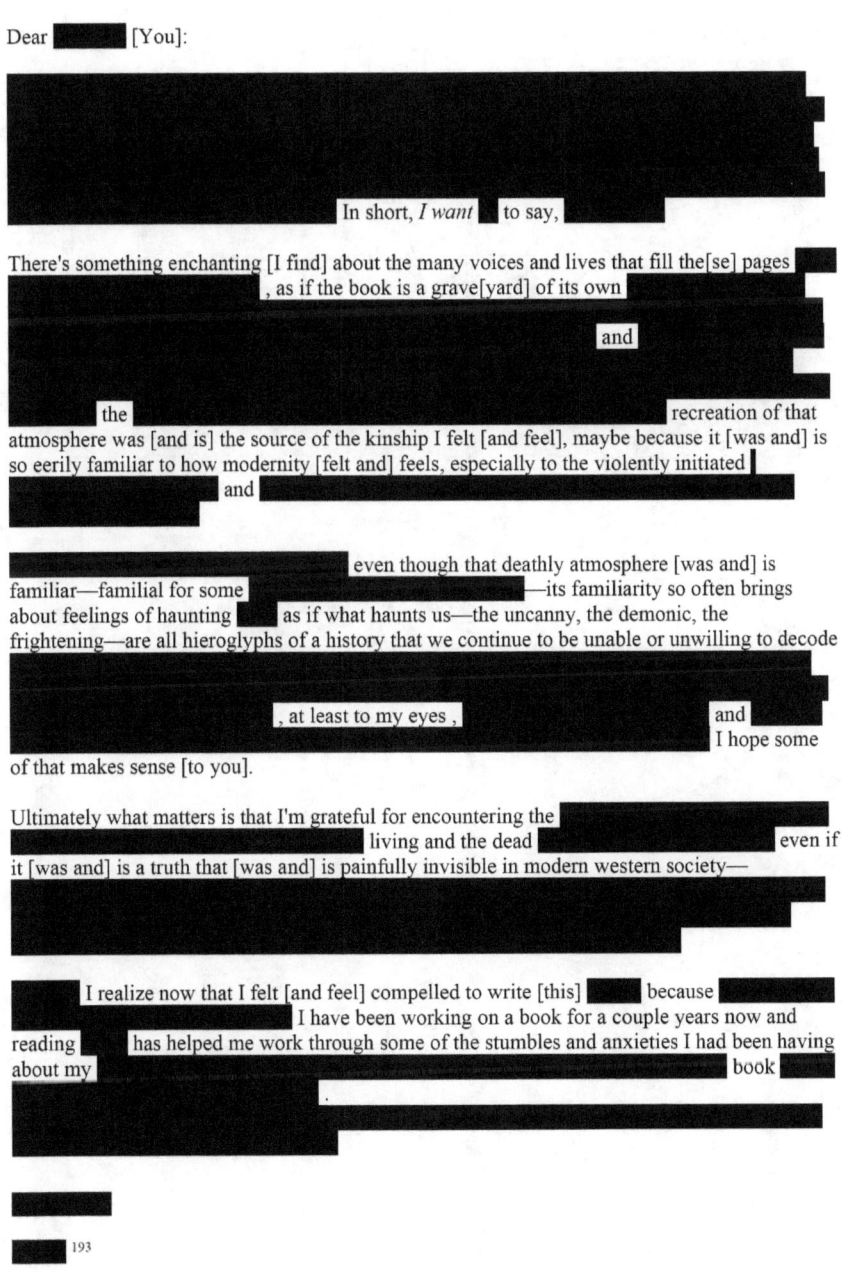

In short, *I want* to say,

There's something enchanting [I find] about the many voices and lives that fill the[se] pages ████ , as if the book is a grave[yard] of its own

and

the ███████████████████ recreation of that atmosphere was [and is] the source of the kinship I felt [and feel], maybe because it [was and] is so eerily familiar to how modernity [felt and] feels, especially to the violently initiated ████████████ and ██████████████████

██████████████ even though that deathly atmosphere [was and] is familiar—familial for some ████████████████ —its familiarity so often brings about feelings of haunting ████ as if what haunts us—the uncanny, the demonic, the frightening—are all hieroglyphs of a history that we continue to be unable or unwilling to decode

██████████████ , at least to my eyes , ██████ and ████
I hope some of that makes sense [to you].

Ultimately what matters is that I'm grateful for encountering the ██████████ ███████████ living and the dead ████████████ even if it [was and] is a truth that [was and] is painfully invisible in modern western society—

████ I realize now that I felt [and feel] compelled to write [this] ████ because ████████ ██████ I have been working on a book for a couple years now and reading ████ has helped me work through some of the stumbles and anxieties I had been having about my ██████████████████████████ book ████

███████
████ 193

---

³ Anonymous. Personal letter (2019).

¹⁹³ Anonymous. Personal letter (2020).

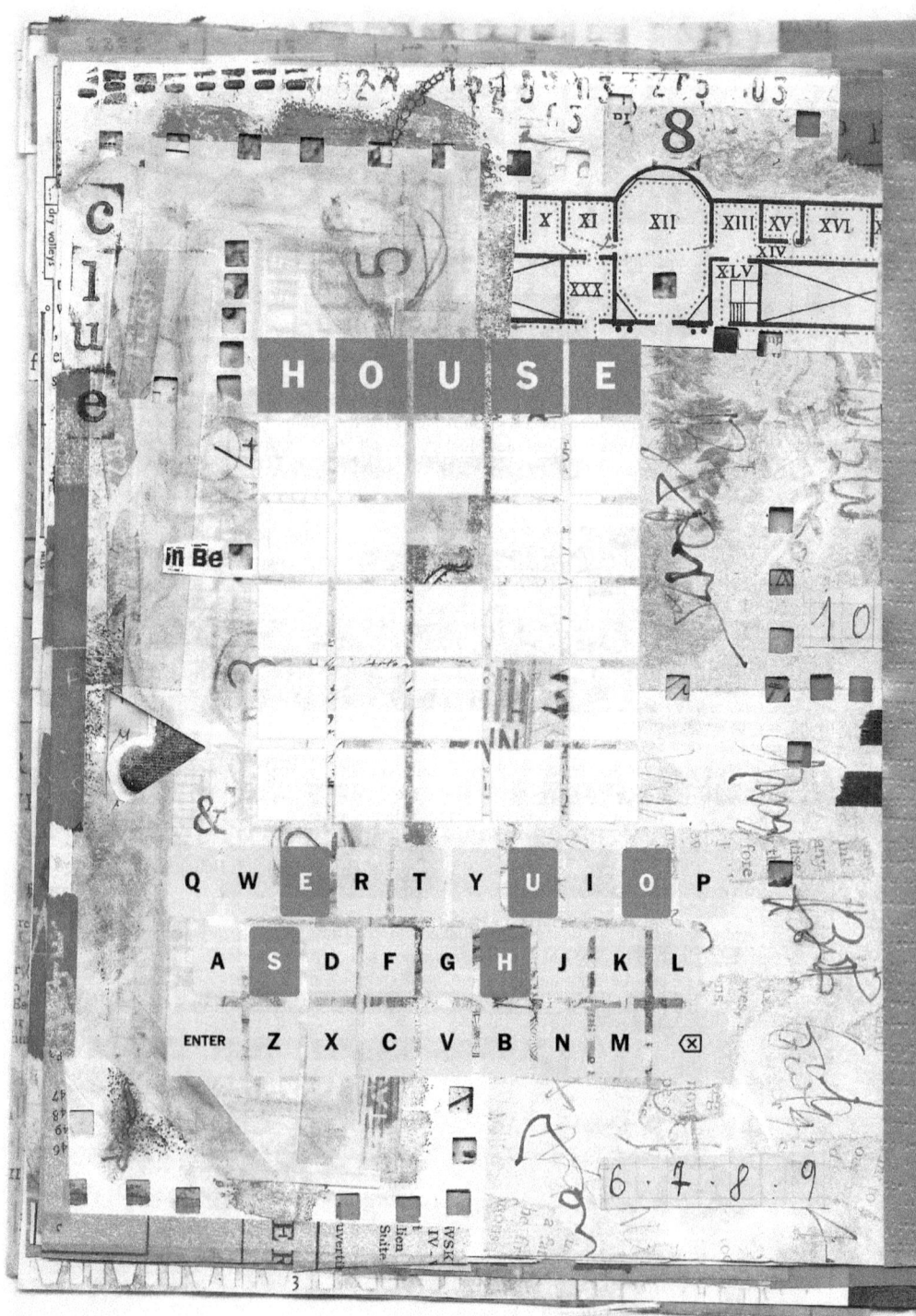

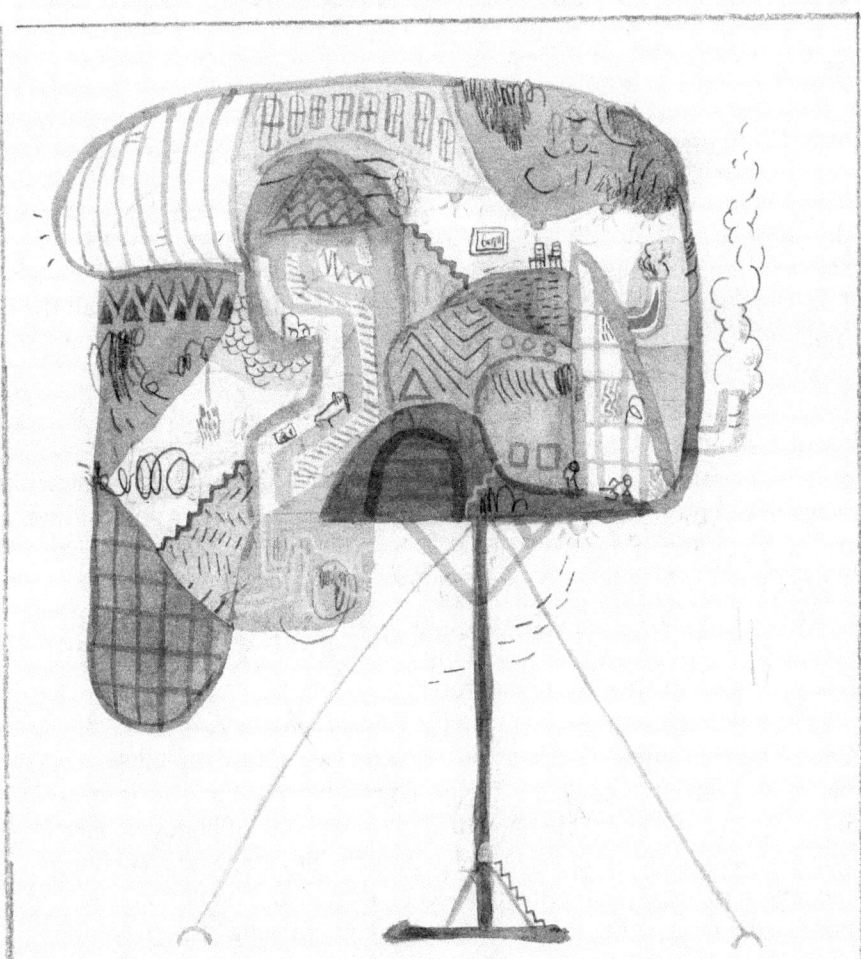

THE HOUSE IS THE SKIN OF THE MACHINE.
YOU MAKE A MISTAKE IN THE ENGINE ROOM.
MIST WRECKS THE MOUTHING PLATFORM. THE
UPPER HALLWAY GOES CROOKED. YOUR PART-
NER PERFORMS YOUR DEATH, REPEATEDLY CO-
LLAPSING IN THE LIVING ROOM.

A Letter to the People-Eating Buildings

Dear Buildings,

There're so many of you I don't even know where to begin. The directory has a complete list, over 7000 high-rises and among these, 50 are skyscrapers. The city has sent it to us ever since the plague began. Every resident received a copy either in email or in paper form of all the buildings in the city. There's no map, however. Only your names and numbers in bullet points listing your addresses.

But by now, we know it's not going to help. Where you are, how clean or tall or new or well-maintained, doesn't matter when you are hungry. People have gone in and out of your worst ramshackle and vandalized ones, such as those in district T, where the city's poorest live, treading your eerie stairwells and dark hallways without any mishaps. Plaza Florence is as busy as ever, business as usual selling cheap electronics and bootleg perfumes in the basement. It is a lottery world we live in now, ever since the case of the Lins a year ago, on September 9. They were eaten alive by a hotel room.

That was the best hotel in the city. Named *The Paradise*, it's 36 floors and was built in 2009, a posh, grand place with chandeliers and ballrooms, the city's pride and jewel. They'd been banking on it for income, advertising widely abroad as the ideal hotel of honeymooners' dreams, running promotions and changing themes alongside receiving important visitors. I still remember when it opened. The fanfare and pomp, streaming confetti and a marching band playing "Seven Nation Army" and "Eye of the Tiger," the vainglorious speeches from the city officials. They cut the ribbon at the prime hour, hand in hand with a pair of golden scissors and a celebrity. The celebrity wore a shimmering green suit and sang a number of pop songs, then he got into his sleek black car and was chauffeured away. The cameras were in love with him, flashing busily.

But ever since the incident, the unfathomable, insoluble case of the Lins, the first people ever to be eaten by our city's buildings, *The Paradise* has been lying in a dying slump, on the verge of bankruptcy, waiting for the Christmases and New Years to come around and to forget the horror. It's probably not going to work, people are going to remember it for a long time. The Lins, now dead, were a newly married couple. They'd flown in from afar for their honeymoon, expecting to enjoy the city's parks, zoos, and casinos, according to the newspapers, which had tried to downplay their deaths until the gory photographs of their corpses (certified genuine) blew up on the internet. Whoever found them dead, the housekeeper or the bellboy (identity protected), was haunted by the Lins. And of course, dear Buildings, you must know better than anyone else what happened. Their bodies were half-swallowed by the ceiling, legs dangling and heads protruding into the floor above (room 989, vacant then), dead in ways impossible for any human to have been the murderer.

Case after case blew up like land mines in the city after that. *The Paradise* was glad to get the heat off them, after months of interrogations from the police and the Department of Buildings about the safety of the construction and grade of plaster and paint the hotel used. Guests of that time period were indignant that they'd been staying on the same floor and not informed of the quiet murder ("It could have easily been us!"). The case busied the hotel's board of directors, who had to pacify the bad press, the families of the deceased, shedding public tears for their unborn grandchildren. A free year's stay at *The Paradise* couldn't placate them of course, they'd never visit our city again, and the cost of the deaths amounted to a million. Relations between cities soured. Investigations led nowhere. The police were unable to find a culprit to pin the blame on, or any leads that the couple had offended someone angry enough to shove their heads so brutally into the ceiling.

The internet speculated. It was truly humanly impossible. Completely bizarre, when the extra key cards to the Lins' room and 989, kept with the receptionists, were checked and proven not used, and only the Lins had access to their room. If there'd been a murderer, he or she or they would have had to prepare quite a bit beforehand, get access to 989, drill holes, and lower ropes to lynch the couple; then seal the cement around their necks. A whole lot of work. But 989 had last been occupied only some days before the couple checked in. The housekeeper who did the final cleaning was interrogated and passed the lie-detector test, said she'd left the room intact, clean, no holes on the carpeted floor. She swore on her mother's grave. No one was known to enter the room after that, unless the murderers had the wherewithal to climb through the sealed windows.

Accusations that the city loved foreigners' meat went out. It was soon disproved as bizarre new supernatural cases flowered: Local man dead in a government building, one leg eaten by a hungry staircase, his other foot chewed off with only the toe bones left. The staircase had opened like a mouth with sharp teeth, said the coroner and the building inspector. In Mint Towers the elevator swallowed a security guard, descending deep into the building's bowels and resurfacing with the skeleton one morning. He was last seen only three hours before by his frightened colleague, who immediately tendered his resignation, and in such a short time who had the powers to strip a man's flesh so cleanly and leave only a skeleton behind? Which acid corroded his organs so fast, if not those from your strange guts and bowels? A prostitute got trapped in a wall of a high-rise block numbered 29, the imprint of her face and breasts molded into the plaster left for identification, mouth opened in a half scream before the kill set her still and shut her eyes (photographs posted). Her soul is said to be flattened, and by now, you have the reputation of being versatile, elastic, stretchable when you wish, without cracking up.

I don't expect you, Buildings, to read this. After all, you're inhuman and concrete, full of bricks and pipework, dangerous asbestos, your wiring mysterious and faulty. The architects have absconded and I don't know where to mail this, or if you can understand human English, even though the directory signboards inside you are written in our alphabet. Some people claim that you have sight. They've grown obsessed with you, climbing up your rooftops and camping out there, watching you day and night with binoculars and recording you on videocams to discover your routines. They say that when your windows glint at a particular angle, a distorted amber slant, it means you're looking for your next meal. I don't know if that's true, or if it's just a widespread rumor. Our city has certainly gone mad, on the brink of a breakdown, some choosing to be homeless and sleeping out on the streets, afraid of their own houses (all murders have been in high-rises so far). There's daily chatter on TVs and radios and the internet about demolishing you, though no one has made the move yet except for cordoning off the culpable buildings. Many have migrated but just as many stay, going to work as usual and pretending the hunger in you doesn't exist, since nobody knows where or whom you'll devour next. There're 5 million of us and the odds are spread out. Every day is a matter of lottery. We know we might die the next time we step into a building, but that ultimately isn't too different from being hit by a car or a bus, and we can only go on living till we run out of luck.

So I am here now by lamplight, writing to you in my lazy handwriting, on my desk at home. I live on Marigold Street, house 27, as you know. My mother has been crying inconsolably since last night. I wish she'd stop. Her cries are as disturbing as out-of-tune violins. My sister has been out since yesterday morning and she hasn't come home or called. Her boyfriend, whom my mother hates, isn't picking up the phone. Right now we don't know if they're taking advantage of our city's chaotic plague to elope, or if they're already a part of your meal plan, lunch or supper. All these eaten people are really just news until someone I know intimately—her name's Jerry, with whom I exchanged dolls, and subsequently music, books, high heels, tank tops, lipsticks, and lately secrets from Mom (she might be pregnant)—doesn't come back. We can't call the police. She hasn't been gone for 72 hours yet. But I doubt they'll do anything about it. They've been so busy and relaxed at the same time, ever since it's been out in the open that our murderers are voracious buildings, unsure of their duties. Heck, the police might be eaten next. And who knows how many cases are unreported, people eaten by a storeroom or a toilet bowl? That's why I decided to write to you, since you're organic and alive. Some mercy and a sign, maybe an exceptionally lit building, would be appreciated; if by any chance you might change your mind and release Jerry, choose someone else. She's only 90 pounds, just so you know. Becoming a beauty, but that's not important to you. It's just not that satisfying to eat her, compared to my obese and obnoxious boss, who lives in the condominium on West End Street, apartment 16. He'd be perfect for you. He's bacon-fed. You could, alternatively, have me as a sacrifice, but my mom would be just as sad. I've been her only guiding light and home, as she put it, ever since this whole mess began. Just give me a sign, will you? Some clue as to where Jerry is, or what I should bring as an offering of exchange. I'll come get her, or her corpse, I promise.

Yours truly,
Francine

[from Blake Butler's *EVER* (2009)]

EVICTION

We still inhabited houses—walled, rectilinear, recognizable—but we struggled to sever our attachment to all that we owned. Treating objects with scorn, dismantling tables and chairs, eating meals from the bowls of our palms. We awaited our eviction with certainty, trying to predict the spaces we'd be forced to occupy, the structures we'd have to build. We studied the chambered towers of termite mounds. Contemplated the mole rat's darkened den. We revised our notions of shelter, constructing nests from shed cells and hair, weaving split ends into thread and then testing its tensile strength and stretch. We fashioned air pockets around ourselves shaped solely from mucus and breath. At night, we rubbed against each other in a futile effort to form callouses and carapaces, to transmute our skin into scale, our hair into hide. We knew, even then, that we were too soft. I would awaken to discover you scarring yourself, scoring the undersides of your arms, the insides of your thighs, extinguishing matches with your tongue. You began to taste charred, but that only increased my appetite. While you slept, I prowled your tunnels and openings—assessing their porousness. Their potential for expansion, defense. I closed off certain orifices, reinforced others with a sealant of saliva and secretions. I waited for you to harden around me, then I shaped your body into a suitable home.

LOVER MAN

Cesious strobe, my green pith has
embered.

Bala Krishna balances a jade ball in dancing
posture.

He kicks it into your eye socket: my heart which
rocks

green cradle is a kevel on
land, so

how come you don't croon
back

at this pyretic
sweetness?

How come my legs are lonely and
vaulted?

How come when you thumb my ruddy
cheek

I hear nothing but my dumb pulse
gabbling?

Green cathexis shaking me
down

like a gypsy
moth.

MILK

Day begins with milk for Mother. She rouses me out of bed, the windowpane iced above my head, beside my head his empty pillow wedded to the cold. Mother's sour breath heats my cheek. Only fresh milk will soothe her poor belly. Do not dally.

I walk out half-awake into a city shameful with night lights this early. Snow is this city's soil. My wool coat is worn to windows, and I draw it round me to lean against black skirts of snow. I wait for the bus. Sometimes the stars are still about. One, two, three, blink, but they move too fast to be stars—count airplanes, landing and launching at the airport close by.

Milk for Mother is two buses and a train. Our kind is used to the long road, Mother says. Shop owners around here sell us spoiled milk. The fresh stuff they keep in the backroom for their own kind.

I wait for the second bus that takes me to this city's edge. Here, the snow is orderly and still white but will dirty soon enough against buildings that tilt and sink into soil. Next the train stops in a place outside the city where snow only whitens as it falls. Where milk never spoils in market aisles of thin women toting bottles for milk so mild it can fertile the cow.

Care to sample our camel, almond, or dandelion milk? Good for the complexion.

Thank you, no, just this milk Mother likes. Could I have a lid, I forgot mine?

The frosty blue eyes gleam. Absolutely, but our milk is so wholesome, we could not possibly loan.

In line behind me, women spoiling with choices swear they hear the cow low. I don't know. Not a coin to spare for a lid. I cover the bottle with my palm. What if milk spills?

The milk is only as fresh as the distance back to her. One block longer, and Mother says the milk will do her no good. Better the taste of my palm in the milk than no milk at all.

Milk laps up along the lip of the bottle. I lick it off. More milk will surely spill with the tilting of this bus. The other rider—him, with gold wings on his cap—he watches me balance my bottle with no lid. Will he give me a knock, a kick, even a "Pardon me"? See any milk spill?

Even a drop Mother would miss. Mother sips milk from a cup she likes for its littleness, parched lips sipping over a bowl to catch spills. The glass fogs with her breath as she licks the cup dry.

Mother, it is only milk.

The bus jolts and swerves. Has the driver been sipping from her own bottle this morning? I try steadying the milk at my chest, but it dots my skirt in slow beads. This is no way to carry milk. More drops fall. Pale streaks divvying my stockings snagged and starting to run. Him, the other rider, yes, he sees this, too. The gold wings, the stitched-tight suit, bright with brass says he pilots a plane, but his eyes are on the milk on the run. Does his mouth want to catch the milk, suck it up through the mesh?

Here comes my stop. Milk, hold on. I rise from the bench, my hands rising with the bottle. No spill, not another drop. The man sees how I rise, and I am caught by his smile, his smile for me. The bus lurches, long honk. I fly forward—the bottle slips from my hands—my eyelids pressed shut against the smash of glass. The sound of shattering drowned in the screech of brakes. A hand on my shoulder, I shrug it off without a look back.

The doors closing.

Racing down the bus steps and hitting the street before trouble can hit me from the back, picturing milk running down the bus aisle, the bottle lost. What a mess.

End of the block before I think of the man on the bus. This is how it is when I think of a man—it is thigh, the hidden hair, what is in between. This and not this, but what is not this, biology, yes, makes flurries in my head. No time for such thoughts in rushing to be here, to be there.

God forgive.

Where was the time for his grave? With the first snow, where was I? Forgetful, that was what my husband called me. He joked that I would forget to place his stone—I suppose the dying like their jokes. But I placed the stone our kind is allowed, always the first to be buried by snow.

Is it just snow that buries the stone?

It is milk for Mother.

I dally before a shopwindow edged in black snow to study the sun-curled advertisement for milk bottles on the cheap. Do I buy a new bottle, take the buses back to the train to the fresh milk, again? In the reflection, the man swings into the window, crossing the street I just rushed up. This is not the first I have seen of those wings on his pilot's cap—he often watches me board the bus. This is the first he has followed me off.

Anyone who comes after my kind does not mean well. Keep walking. The snow, this city's soil, has iced, snapping at my heels. His boots snap right behind. Closer, he comes.

Mother is only this far. The entry light in our building is feeble but not enough to hide the wood rot of the doorframe. The door wheezes shut behind me. Whoosh, it opens again. He pulls the cold air to him. I grab the handle and pull it back closed. Between the door and the jamb, he thrusts the bottle—my bottle, unbroken. An ice-milk lid spits from the bottle's mouth. I grab the bottle before more milk spills. The man lets go, watching as I unbutton my coat, tuck the bottle against my chest to keep it warm—little ice slivers are something Mother dislikes. He lifts off his cap, his hair the white of winterish woods, hands whiter than his shirtsleeves unbuttoning my coat, opening the cold, worn wool dissolving in his hands. Milk spills. His hands cover mine, the icy milk sliding over fingers, brightening pink, iceless now, warming under his hands covering my belly, milk hot, rivering between the bone of my hip and the bank of his thumb, fingers and thumb rerouting milk, steaming milk, and the bottle I cannot any longer hold goes down and I let it and it hits hollowed bottomed echo round round to go still.

This is milk for Mother.

I drop to my knees, pooling the spilled milk with my palms. He stands back, breathless. I wring out the milk from my soaked skirt back into the bottle. My hands shake. The milk runs every which way. He snatches my skirt and grips the wet wool like a teat, shooting milk into the bottle to a drop.

Mother opens our apartment door. On her forefinger dangles the lid I forgot. I reach up to unbutton my coat, and her fingers flap down to the next button. She separates my coat and looks in at the bottle held at my chest.

If drops of milk were coins, she would count them. Her fingers pinch the soggy wool and draw the bottle out from my coat, eyes tracing the milk streaks down my chest. If this milk's soured, she will know against what skin.

Your coat is sopped, she says. Toss the thing already. You wear it like a shroud.

She raises the bottle to the light. Black flecks spin in the white. Her eyes slide over me but only so I will step aside and she can reach into the cupboard. Milk sheets her teeth as she sips from her cup. But she is not sipping as she usually would. She gulps the milk, gulping as if her last. The smack of her tongue tasting for what is off. A drop runs over her lip.

Wipe your mouth, Mother.

Sour milk is the taste of women with only their mothers to feed. I step into the toilet to rinse my chest, roll off my stockings, hang them over the tub. I push open the window beside the sink and snow sweeps in, swooshing the white water dripping from the stocking's toes. How they kick.

From the window I see his shadow. Then I see him and the way his cap tips back. How youthful the set of a cap makes a man. But it is still morning, and shouldn't mornings be without shadows?

The pilot stands across the street, in front of what is now deep-below snow and fenced. He looks up at me in my window.

A look with no story, maybe a beginning.

Let it spill over us, heat up our skin, boil over with biology. For this is how it is with a man, and to think of a man in any other way is to say, yes. Since yes is a thing of flight—and planes might be stars, after all, suspended high on the air, where everything is left behind, even biology, the very thing that launched you and, yes, to hold you together, aloft.

Until you land.

Down onto this city's soil, black snow below snow—more than my hands can clear. I look back at the pilot and I see what it is behind him, this thing I took for shadow but now I see is stone.

Mother knocks on the door. There was not enough milk. She needs more to settle the belly. Needs it now.

How can that man stand looking up at a woman who carries duty in a bottle of milk?

But still now, look!

Gold wings rising, gathering loft—

Mother shoves into my hands the empty bottle, the lid, shoves me back out the door. I launch down the stars—one, two, three—

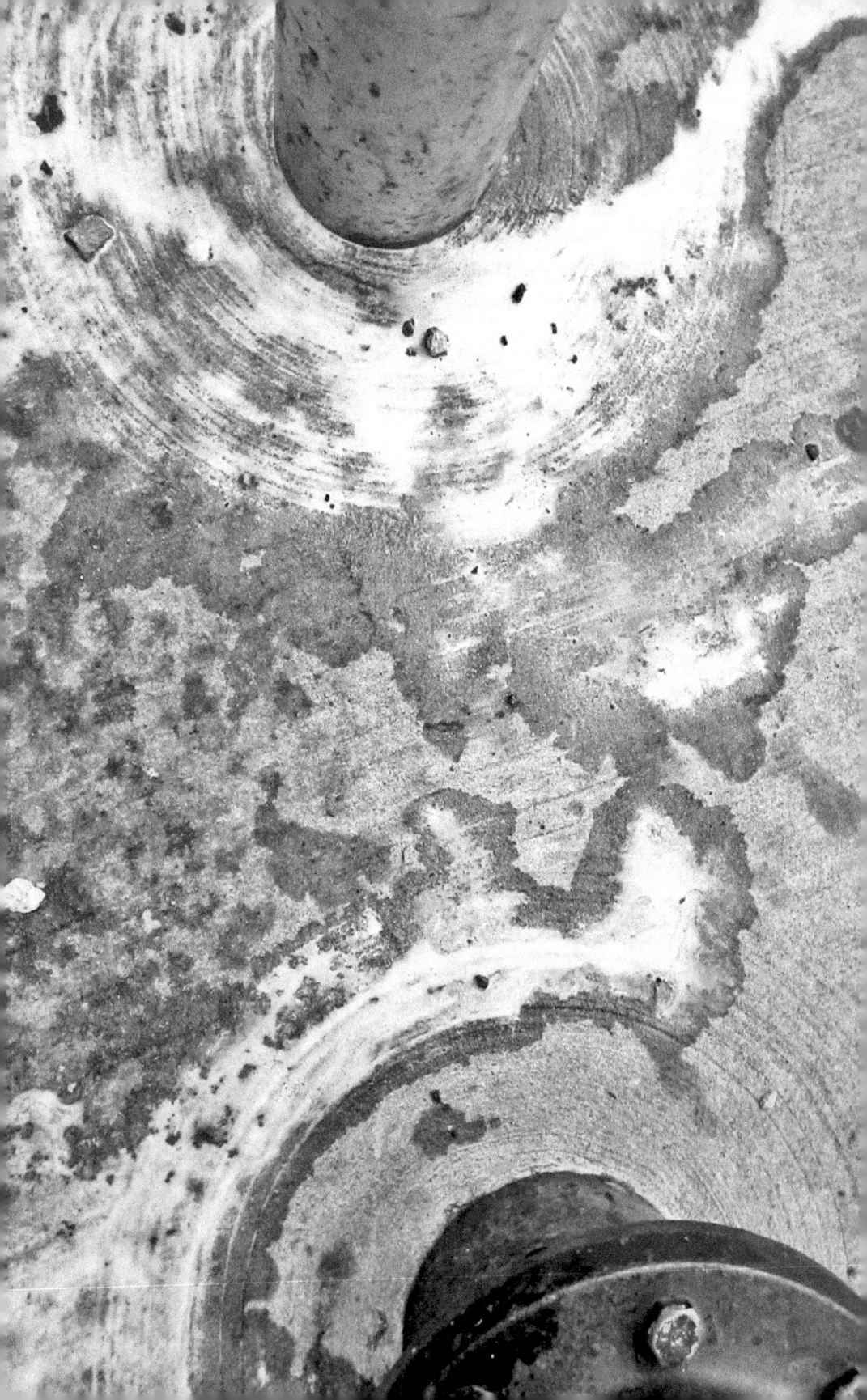

Ask for Milk

It wasn't often, but when it was, the mother hid her babies where she hid her knives. In the barn the babies lay in hay and their noses got used to the smell of cow shit. The mother, through the barn door, would feel the knives press against her backside more when she was walking down the steps than on the path through the field. When she touched each cow, they would turn to where she was going, an attempt to intimidate.

A lone man would be better than two, but a group would let her leave it to luck. This time, she met a single man, who didn't open the gate and didn't hop the fence. They met there at the edge of where the cows go, and she did what she always did when she met a man: she checked the fingers for signs of marriage, and she checked the heels for how they might have healed years after being sliced by a rock. Marriage only meant they'd have to sleep next to a woman when at night they had to think of all the things that men do. Scars at the heels meant the knives were in her hands.

Most men who stopped would want just water, but some asked for milk. Regardless of what they wanted to drink they'd only get water. For this man, she turned her back and walked to the well since the milk was too far to go. Before he tried to follow her, he saw the knives where she tied her apron and he stayed by the fence until he'd be back out on his way.

On the steps of the barn door, she watched out over the field. The man finished a well bucket of water and waved to her thank you from the gate. In a semicircle, the cows protected her just in case. Her knives were at her feet, clean and sharp for next time.

The mother pictured the man walking fast through the forest and holding his piss for as long as he could. She took off her apron and balled it up, propped it behind her neck when she let her head fall at the threshold of the door.

The daughter in the barn was pouring hay on her brother. From the doorway, looking behind her upside down, the mother couldn't tell if the daughter was calling it a blanket or calling it dirt. She knew both words and what they were, and her brother knew none. The mother walked in and whispered to her daughter to be gentle with him. The daughter brought her body next to his and put her arm around his chest. His heart beat into her elbow and she asked her mother if she could copy her, so that their heartbeats could keep going between them and she'd be in the middle. The mother said that she could, and they all held hands and the mother watched for how far fingernails grow between times strangers come for milk.

BREAD DISH

I am sorry,
Did I nail your head?
I'm sorry.
Did you think it was promising
To walk inside my kitchen?
There are loose planks instead of pavement
You should have known I couldn't be reliable.

I am sorry,
Did I really forget to wash your dishes?
However I bought bread.
We could have that for dinner.
With some salt or something.

I am sorry,
I forgot you don't like bread.
Should I feed you with sponges instead?
Or a different plate of salt?
Does that sound good?
I am sorry.

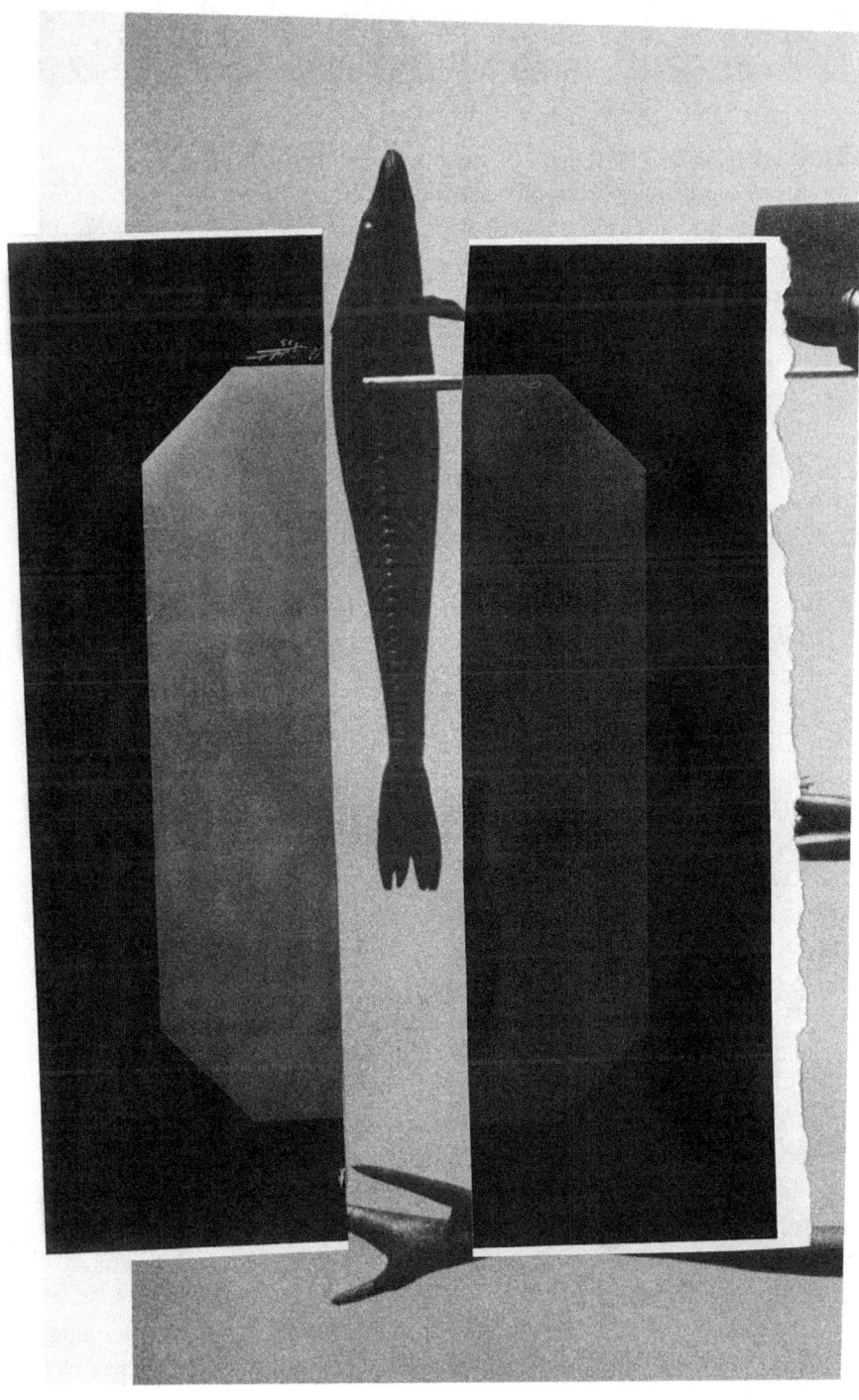

Carla Rak

THINGS LIKE THIS EXIST

The pigs howled like dogs, and the dogs disappeared in the field to run circles in the black, where the season's first traveler stood next to a few small trees and a wire fence, where he wouldn't hear my uncle, who'd snuck into the barn to sit on chewy piles, abuse himself, and cry. My uncle said the concrete plant ruined his gut, but he had always been like that. Ever since I could remember he had nursed himself to tears. I stepped out onto the front step, out into the cold, and waved at the traveler making his way toward me.

And he waved back.

Once inside, the traveler brushed ice from his hair while I babied his boots and bag. He had a helpless arm, a sally hairdo, and a deep, creasy face, the only part undressed from the wetted golden-brown stuff he wore head to foot. I showed him where he'd sleep, asked him what he needed, told him I felt like I'd seen him somewhere before.

"Where?" the traveler said. He goose-stepped closer. "Boy, where've you seen me?"

"I don't know," I said.

"But you've seen me?" the traveler said. "You know that?"

"I've seen you," I said. "I know that."

I laughed.

He didn't.

I was reminded of when I was a little boy and scared other people, other children especially, who irritated me like insects. My work has always absorbed all of who I am, everything I think and do. I've never kidded around.

"Tell me." The traveler lowered his voice, looked around the place, at the corners and countertops. "Boy, how long have you been here?"

"Since six," I said.

"And you're a man now," the traveler said.

I busied myself with the starts of old breakfast and lunch, while the traveler unwrapped liquor from fancy paper. I tried to focus on each task and topic. Dishing the stringy mess of sides. Business and piano music. Weather talk. I took my time with my answers. I had to stick up for myself on the inside first.

We talked like this for some time, until the wind broke, and we heard the pigs wolfing around their pen, and my uncle out there, spanking them, ruthlessly.

Chelsea Hogue

Out there, every day was the same. It was me, my uncle, down on his knees, with his hand pressed to a pig's swollen back. Come over and feel what I'm feeling, my uncle would say, and the pig's stain would quiver obediently under his hand. My uncle could touch each pig behind the ear. We both could. The two of us moving together, working, wordlessly, pushing the pigs to another paddock, my uncle made me learn how to call to them, and what to think, and he was right. They just boom, boom, boom, they came to us, even when they were new and little, their ears transparent as flower petals.

When my uncle entered, his pants were already loosened. He let his stink blow over the room. The traveler's nostrils filled and flexed. I breathed daggers through my mouth, and my uncle's lips burned back in goofy rictus.

"All right," my uncle said, pointing at the traveler. "Let's get on with it."

The traveler nodded. He used bread and sauce to map where he'd been and who he met. He looked at my uncle, at his belt buckle jingling. "These are the mountains," the traveler said, pointing to a knot in the wood. "And this is the top of the arête. Over here is the ocean," he said. "You ever been?"

My uncle wiped the ocean off the table. Far away, he had nursery features, but up close you could see fat, pissy eyes. Around his fingers were bites. Weekly, I gathered handfuls of the shriveled rags my uncle dabbed at himself, and in the backyard, with a lot of effort, I buried them in frozen ground. There were days, weeks even, that I believed my uncle was getting better, until he, once again, selected mouse droppings, one by one with a licked finger, and deposited them in the kitchen sink. It was during those weeks of better that my uncle's room would still smell dank, but not fishy, a smell that was pure, appetizing even, which led me to believe my uncle could control and wield what he was, until he grew tired of my relaxation, and it started all over again.

My uncle sat himself in a corner and pretended to read, pulling on his tight polo shirt, waiting to hear a nasty joke, until he eventually fell asleep, until his sort of soft felt hat fell off his head and woke him. He didn't bother to pick it up, gave out no night-nights as he slowly walked himself upstairs, and as he did, I turned to face the wall so I wouldn't have to see the spot that had grown on the seat of his pants.

"You know what you need?" the traveler whispered and rubbed his fingers together. "Quick cash. You get me?"

I did but downplayed it. With only his little finger, the traveler took a ring of loopy red onion from the plate and brought it to his mouth, while I chewed nervously on quarter-sized tablets. The traveler put his bad arm on the table and told me to give it a swift rub where the ridges peaked. I felt stones move beneath my fingers.

He lit me a cigarette off his and the ember took enormous bites out of the paper. The traveler's mouth was red with bacteria, and his eyes were watchful, like a rodent's, which I trusted, the prehistoric wisdom I saw there. I felt like he must've known why we were made this way because he saw it all happen. In the beginning.

The traveler pushed the dog's head from his lap and put a doll on the table.

"Go ahead," he said, "open her."

He winked, pushing her close. "But don't tear the buttons off her dress."

The doll was heavy and ugly, and her hair was matted to her head. I didn't want to touch her, but carefully undid the ties to her dress anyway. I pushed it down to her hips, and found the bump for the latch there, tiny, nearly hidden, and picked at it, but the dress was still too tight. I pushed it down some more and then took it off all the way, and she was naked, little lines drawn where her privates would be but no detail.

"Open her," the traveler said.

I did all I was asked. I unhooked the sticky gold latch and looked right inside of her, deep inside her big chest, at a wadded-up bill and a piece of paper that read: *He the metal, She the stone, Cherished secretly alone.* Blood was in the traveler's cheeks; he opened his own small, personal purse and told me to take another.

"For what?" I said, but my hand had already found and held the purse's bunch.

"For work," the traveler said, "for pleasure."

At that point I could still dream, endlessly, about leaving this place, riding into town and meeting my friend, the traveler, on his big gray horse, the one with a thin beard that needs brushing, and finding a girl there I could kiss and hold until I felt better.

For a while, we sat in silence together, and I imagined the next morning, watching the dogs bolt past the traveler's horse, down the path, peeing across thin snow, and waiting there in the upstairs window, until I could no longer see the rings of sunlight on the traveler's calf coat and hair, until he disappeared around the mountain, the hundreds of hiding places that shut our eastern view.

I wanted to throw up.

I couldn't sleep that night. I walked around the house until the sun began to show, until I found myself in the small room where we jar food to keep away the mice, with my pants pulled down yea enough, roughly yanking at what had been held up all day, until the traveler's doll, heavy and big-size, unscrewed the hinges on the door and began viciously popping me on the thigh, her braids swinging back and forth. She tugged my pants down the rest of the way, making all kinds of adjustments, until her pink face emerged again, sad, strong, and melted down my thighs. "Oh no, I've got something on you!" I wiped furiously. Although it was, mostly, really, all over me.

"Boy," I said. I could do the traveler's voice deep in my stomach. "Boy, which song is that you sing?"

There was only one that moved me to tears.

MEMORY MOUNTAIN

You don't want to go all the way up the mountain. Go-hards tend to make that mistake. But go-hards aren't the type of people that keep her advice. She knows this.

You want to take it easy up the mountain. Her place isn't on the steep path. There's a nice little alcove where the tree line takes a break, and the cabin is right there. She knows where to begin based on how sweaty you are.

She'll offer you a drink. It's different for everybody. Sometimes it's loose-leaf tea. Sometimes it's a minerally French red. Sometimes it's a regional soft drink that fizzes you with so much sentimentality you start reminiscing about perfect Saturday mornings you never had.

Then she'll tell you a secret about life that will change your world.

She asks that you don't write the secret down. You can if you want, but once you try to record the advice you've already lost it—not all of it, but trust me, it's a fundamental mistake.

The secret she told me was something like "Presence is an infinite present, and don't try so hard." I typed it into my phone, but something happened when I upgraded and I can't find the note anymore.

You'd think she'd be a stickler about phones but she's not a stickler about anything.

Are you sure she's not up there anymore?

I've heard some big shots say that they've visited her. So maybe she's gotten too popular. She might have moved somewhere else, but she's not hiding. She's not a hider. She's too beyond to hide.

My husband went to see her once. He wasn't my husband then. He started becoming my husband when I found out he'd seen her too.

"Seen her," isn't the right way to describe it. You're definitely around her for a few minutes but it doesn't feel real. Sometimes I can't tell if I dreamed the meeting or if I really went to see her. If it was a dream, I wouldn't feel so bad about forgetting exactly what she said. I try to remember. I picture myself in the cabin years ago, but I can't see it. I don't really remember what she looks like, or what drink she gave me.

I remember the drinks she gave other people.

    She told my husband, "Listen for the whisper, be informed by pain. Hold on to no parcel, and you will find your lane."

Now come to think of it, you kind of look like her.

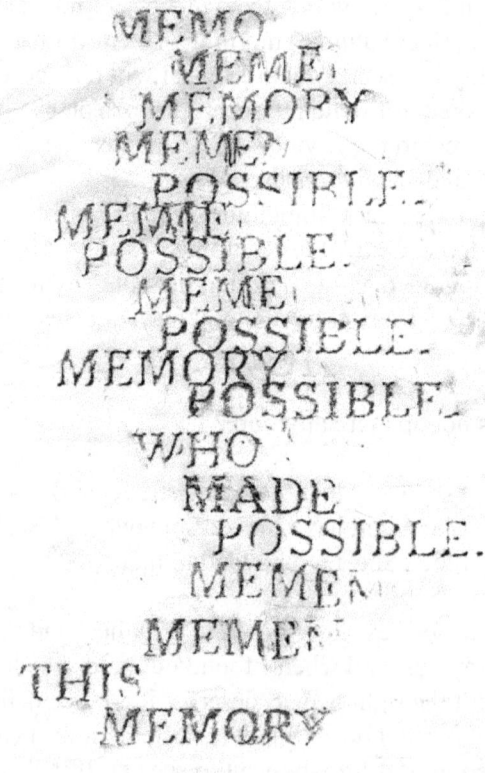

       Bobby Crace

THE LEMON WIFE

Ever headed home from somewhere? A real shame when you get there.
A few steps in, lift your head, really smell the air in there? And it smells
awful, and it doesn't smell at all, and then you know you are not enough
of an oozing, aching body to musk up even a box-bare rented room? So you
take up smoking, you smoke for the smell, but then you cannot smell—not
even smoke, specifically not smoke—because you smoke too much?
Ever get home from somewhere, from the drugstore, say, and take off
your shoes and get in bed and stay there? Stay stiff and twitch, you feel
like waiting, teeth-gritted visceral waiting, tense like for the phone to
ring? But you do not own a phone, or if you do, you can never remember
the number fast enough when it is asked for? You sequence the numbers
wrong, you mix the ones and sevens, or you say—not even numbers—
you say letters, you spell things, make words to assemble, but no one
assembles the words you are making, and no one is listening, and no one
even asked?

Ever love them anyway? Ever remember to love someone anyway? Ever
love the woman at the drugstore, by the hand soap at the drugstore, and
love her for touching with her short soft hands only the soaps with citrus
scent? No vague citrus, either. Not even lemon straight, but lemon-lime
or mandarin or lemon-melon-mint? You love how she touches the bottles,
how she turns them in her short soft hands. Later in bed you pretend she
is alone with you somewhere, that you share soap at a sink there, and you
smell her hands after, and you smell your hands after, and it is the same
smell, and you love her?

Ever wake and find her, still and tense, in the bed where you were
pretending? Find that now it is her bed, find that now you are her
husband, already you are husband to this hand-soap woman? And she
has been your wife awhile, and waiting in the bed awhile, for you to do
something aboard her? About her? You cannot figure what. And now she
is angry, she has been waiting enough already, and she has been wedded
enough already, and her hips are spreading now and messy, and you
never want to smell her hands, and when you do, you smell them and
smell nothing, you get nothing from them, you can smell nothing at all,
because you smoke too much?

Ever wonder where the scent went so quickly? Wonder was it lost over time, in the end, all in one, at the start, at the drugstore? At the second you met the woman with the soap, learned her name and followed her along: to the birthmarks, the lapsing hygiene, the crippled way at writing cramped, left-handed notes she could not mean, notes that thank you for things you never did, full of names you cannot face and places no one has heard of?

What if, at the store that day, you had gamely passed? Surveyed her turning the citrus soap, studied the poise of her short soft hands? Maybe, in passing, you slipped the hard side of your hand barely by her skirt, just at the high hem, and skimmed—maybe, barely—the soft back of one bare leg? And if you had the need, if you really did need more, you could have circled the store until you saw which soap she settled on, and settled yourself the same. You could have had the secret, the same-smelling hands, but none of the rest, none of the wife—just the hard side, the soft leg, and hand soap to wash with alone.

Ever sleep alone? And then wake, and then see, so suddenly, how always, how altogether, how all throughout the whole of it you must have been alone, because you are still in bed—but your shoes are on? And you do not have an angry wife, a lemon wife, or any kind otherwise; you cannot be a husband, even, because you are not a man. A woman then! And enough already.

Ever smoke too much in bed, at ease while you do because your shoes are on? Almost as though, should you fall asleep smoking, and you must wake up to flee the fire, it will be all right—because the shoes? And while you smoke in bed you pretend it, you start to pray it, even, that you will fall asleep smoking, that the sheets will catch, that you will smell no smoke and the show will end then, will burn to the end then, shoes and all the rest?

Ever only learned you were asleep from waking, waking with your shoes on, alone and in ashes and maybe you should go somewhere? Just somewhere? Just go somewhere. Just go.

[*Note: "The Lemon Wife" appeared previously in Sleepingfish issue 8.]

A HOUSE OPERATES WITHIN THE HOUSE AUTO-
NOMOUSLY. A PSYCHOLOGICAL DIAGRAM EMER-
GES. THROUGH THE WINDOW, A SMALLER
VERSION OF YOURSELF FALLS DRAMATICALLY.
THE RUNGS OF THE TINY LADDER PULSE. THE
REFRIGERATOR HANGS OPEN. YOU FLAIL
FOR YOURSELF, IN MINIATURE.

BORIS IN BED

I am only supposed to pass through this city's airport to transit to my final destination. But my first flight is delayed. After I miss my connecting flight, I am provided with vouchers for a cab ride and a night at a hotel.

In the hotel, I can't go to sleep. I shut the thick curtains. I roll in the bed and keep looking at my watch.

Time doesn't pass.

I contemplate calling Tara, but change my mind after.

It has been Tara's idea, this trip. I am not sure how it all started.

For a while, I resisted the idea. We often talked about how we needed change.

But why not adopt a dog? Why not just take a leave from our jobs? Why not travel together?

Eventually, each of us came up with a list of destinations we weren't supposed to tell each other. We would both start the trip on the same day.

I had my doubts, but I played along.

Both of us quit our jobs. The balance in our bank accounts would give us a year for traveling.

I wonder where she is now. Still on the plane? Already at her first destination?

I put on my jacket and leave the hotel room.

I'd first arrived in this city from my country. I lived here alone, walking through a landscape of concrete by the sea, staying in a dim room with a window opening to a gray sky.

I'd first come here with a large suitcase. I'd packed everything that had mattered: Tara's letters, tiny sculptures she had made, a notebook we'd written in each time we'd slept together. My mother had added other things to the suitcase. Pots and pans. Wool pants I never ended up wearing.

Later on, I used the same suitcase to buy groceries. Boris, my roommate, showed me how it was done. In the store, people stared at us with surprise as we slid our large suitcases behind us.

There is no one behind the reception desk at the hotel. After walking for several blocks, I find myself in a different neighborhood—garbage piled on the pavement, dilapidated shops with rusted fences, half-asleep figures in ragged sleeping bags.

I change my route, walk back past the hotel, past the bridge, until I am in front of my former apartment.

Boris had come from a village with a name that made me think of the name of a bird. The village had many small rivers where Boris used to fish. One day, Boris took me along on a fishing trip. We took the bus to a village and from there we walked for an hour to get to the river. Boris had his fishing rod with him and I had my camera. The sun, then, was finally shining after several weeks. I didn't like to take photos of rivers and lakes. I didn't like to take portraits of people. I took photos of feet instead—in boots or bare.

Boris didn't catch any fish.

The sun was going down and we didn't talk much on our way back.

Standing in front of the apartment, I picture the hallways, the room with two single beds—the brownish carpet with cigarette burns.

Across from the building, there is still the liquor store where I used to buy my liquor. We used to make our own wine back home and I hadn't drunk any other type. I'd read the names of different wines in books: Shiraz, sherry, port. My first time at the store, I'd looked for those names and picked a cheap sherry. I didn't know that it was going to be sweet. It didn't taste like wine to me.

Boris liked it, maybe because it was sweet. For a year, we only drank sherry until it made us sick, and we moved on to other cheap wines.

When I left my country and Tara to come live in this city years ago, we'd said we would not call each other, but just write. Tara and I were both the kind of people that could write better than talk. Instead, Tara called me and left several messages as soon as I'd gotten here. Her voice was like a sad cry of a bird in the morning. I called her back that day and other days and we talked for hours, and I didn't leave my bed except to buy bread.

I read a book about a man who wore his dead wife's underpants. I asked Tara to send me her underpants, but she didn't agree to that.

I don't know when Tara called to tell me she'd met someone. I was looking for scissors in a drawer as I was talking to her, and I found a package of condoms and blue bottles of pills.

By then, Boris had dropped his courses, but still worked at the butcher shop. I'd never seen Boris bring home any girls.

I told Tara this.

What do you think he does with the condoms then? Tara asked.

Once, I entered the apartment and found Boris sitting under the kitchen table. His eyes were red.

I poured water in a tall glass and gave it to Boris. Boris drank the water, but stayed under the table.

In my bed that night, I thought about the blue bottles of pills.

I recognize other familiar stores on the streets, all of them closed now. I see a bar that I used to go to when I used to live here.

No one is inside. I sit at the counter, remember the bartender. I look at my watch again, count the hours left until my flight.

The bartender doesn't seem to recognize me. It has been more than ten years. The pool table is still broken. The liquor bottles on the top shelf are covered in dust. The bartender drags his left foot on the floor as he walks.

Once, I came back to my apartment drunk from this bar, and Boris was on top of a woman on a sleeping bag spread out on the floor.

I went inside the bathroom and lay there inside the empty tub. I waited there until they were done.

When I came out, the woman was still there. She approached me and grabbed my penis.

Do you want to go, too?

Boris had shaved his beard and had red lipstick smeared on his face. A blanket was wrapped around his waist.

The woman had large brown eyes. I could smell her floral perfume mixed with the smell of her sweat.

Call me if you want, she said.

I pay for my drink and leave the bar. I walk faster to go back to the hotel, to take a shower, and to get to the airport in time. The sky has turned gray. More cars are on the streets. I pass by the public hospital where Boris spent a month in the psychiatric ward.

Babak Lakghomi

It was right before being hospitalized that Boris had left a raw beef liver on the kitchen table.

I'd been away for the weekend and I came back home to the smell, blood on the table, Boris in bed.

After they took Boris, I called Tara and we talked like we used to, like before she had met someone new.

Soon after Tara and I decided to get back together, Boris was fired from the butcher shop. Then Tara and I both moved to where we've lived together since.

After I left the city, I didn't hear from Boris for a while, until I heard that he'd gone back to his village.

Back in the airport, I pass by the arrival section and look at the people waiting. I remember the day I met Tara in an airport after two years. Every time the glass doors slid apart, my heart beat faster. I waited there for an hour until Tara finally arrived. She had lost a lot of weight, and for the first days her body felt like the body of another woman.

As my plane takes off, I watch the tall concrete buildings give way to small villages and lakes. I picture Boris in his boots deep into the water, the wind on his face, his fishing rod in his hands.

DIVINATIONS

artifacts | from *Codex Mojaodicus* book fourth

wan   howling beat | Oxomoco & Cipactonal

tú   Xóchitl's night axe | belly broken open

tree   owl | ¡tecolooo! ¡tecolooo!

for   frog

fi   towering menace Tezcatlipochx & four streams of
                    sangre

seeks   Cuitlapanton's panza

sayven   cuerpo penca-wrapped for La Muerte

eh eet   nixtamal in the pot

ni   ancestor drinks deep in agave dreams sees prophetic
                    visions of generations

River of Selves*

here.
look here, xagi.
the river is not water.
xagi stand on the bank. the bank makes river river, xagi.
here, this river is not with water.
here, this river is flowing stone, xagi.
this river leaks from a mountain.
a mountain of stone falling.
dim your eyes, xagi. dim your eyes to its sound.
here, the river is louder, xagi.
louder is the grinding, it doesn't make small.
it doesn't make small the stone.
the river is pushed, xagi.
the river is pulled downstream.
something does it upstream, xagi.
stand on the bank, see.
there is no water, xagi.
stones don't move like water.
stones make locks.
stones get stuck. roll and go, xagi.
stones get stuck and go.
here, from the bank xagi see the flow.
the river is lit in matchlight.
the river it flickers.
dim your eyes, xagi.
the sound is thicker.
the stones move. fire illuminates.
something does it, xagi.
something not here.
something upstream is time, unrun.
time is pushing the mountain, xagi.
the mountain is dying, xagi.
look.
this river of stone is drying.
this river has a long way to go.
xagi stand on the bank and see.

widen your eyes, xagi.
the stone is changing. the sound is changing, xagi.
hold your breath, xagi. ask.
is the mountain dead?
shout from the bank, xagi. look.
the river is not stone.
xagi stand on the bank.
look.
here, the river is a river of eggs.
tumbling like stone, xagi.
eggs don't make as much sound. look.
here, in each egg is a self. this is the river of selves, xagi.
careful. don't step in.
without will, xagi lose all self.
look.
here the banks are full-up with selves.
a gathering of xagi.
this is the river of selflessness.

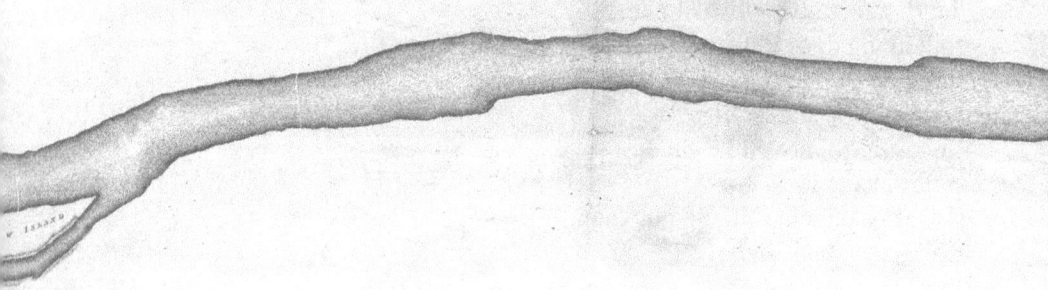

* *"River of Selves" and subsequent pieces from this series on pages 134, 174, 189, and 218 are from* **a few fading fables of Xagi** *(as transcribed from the Arif Bey tapes).*

Translator's note: An obvious linguistic clue to follow is the treatment of the kinship term "xagi" as both singular and plural. This ambiguity leads to the use of the same mode in verb conjugation for the 3rd-person plural (they) when talking "about" someones and 2nd-person singular (you) when talking "to" someone. We might call these two modes "narrative" and "instructive," respectively.

On the face of it, the term "xagi" seems like a figure of speech that emphasizes the address. However, the same term is used to denote kinship, proper. "Xagi" are all that are present, all that are existent during the time of the speech. So far as we understand, and the equivalency algorithms on Simon2 support this, speakers of xagi refer to each other as "xagi," they address each other as "xagi," and they also "call" all entities currently in existence, xagi."

THE STURGEON

We found the sturgeon washed up dead
on the shore of what we call the Black Lagoon.
The dogs sniffed at the scale-less carcass
before running off through the stunted scrub brush
that grew up from soil laced with molten slag.
Only the bottom half of this fish had been picked at by gulls
to get at what was left inside it. I set my hand
on its hard, bony head. Even the dead
are worthy of such tenderness. Words are one thing.
I want to believe that somewhere in the sky
there was at least one winged god
watching. A bird that would later remember
what it saw and put me into its song.

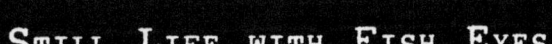

STILL LIFE WITH FISH EYES

The dead fish on the shore
feeds the bird that eats it.
The bird begins at the eyes,
then it moves to the body,
the flesh already beginning
to lose any memory of water.
Later the bird, full-bellied, will fly,
and the fish will see the sky
in ways it could never imagine.

ON A ROCK IN THE SEA

The tips of your claws shed skin and your intestines regret the fish eyes that slipped down your throat. The sea looks dark today. The tired sounds of arm strokes announce no excitement. Wounds on knees burn with the salt. If you were alive, you'd know how to seal it all up.

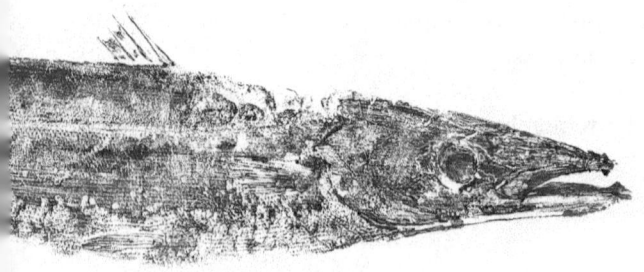

PREEMPTIVE DECAPITATION

One of the women who lived on top of the hill came running down holding a child in her arms. She had almost decapitated him by mistake, she said. She needed to stitch his head back in place. I sat there looking at her young naked feet and the way they rushed down the path, hitting each step with a thump. I could tell her son was already dead. She had gotten rid of him herself because she knew what was coming.

THE ARMCHAIRS GLINT AND YAWN IN THE
ABDOMEN. THE FACTORY ROOM REFILLS WITH
BLOOD. SMOKE SEEPS FROM THE WINDOWS.
A CLAW-FOOTED DEVICE IMAGINES THE HOUSE
IN RETROGRADE, UNTIL IT ISN'T A HOUSE
ANYMORE, THE OCCUPANTS ERASED: A
SIMULATION FOR EXTINCTION.

Sexless Morning from the Tally Call of a Rooster

The shrill paean of the
rooster

on a morning unsettled as
this

to
proceed

from the tumult of
yesterday

but symbol not an eye onto his
plume.

Keep your immanence your ashy tears and your
own

       mercenary
       fingers

out of his
feathers.

He does not call out the
grim

census of all your men gone;

he
dreams

of wheat or maize heaped at his
feet

and don't care
none

what the vulture
eat.

EXCERPT FROM *THE MOONS*

A classic Chinese math problem:

Some rabbits and roosters are locked in the same cage, and together they have 35 heads and 94 feet. How many rabbits are in the cage, and how many roosters?

A math/psychology problem I once encountered, approached by a college student doing research:

Imagine a family of a father, a mother, a 4-year-old son, a 16-year-old son, a 10-year-old daughter, and a 12-year-old daughter. If they only have 1 bed, how will you arrange them from the outermost to the innermost? Increase the number of their beds to 2, 3, 4, 5. Which ones should be sharing the same bed and why?

In the end my father got full marks for math and logic. He is proud of it and likes to give examples. He'll say, "It was something like, the person living in the house that is not white does not wear a green tie," though he's never recalled a problem in whole. Again and again he was refused a student visa because he didn't have enough funding. My mother says he felt so angry and disappointed. "Ever since then," she says, "he has not taken his work seriously again, not even for 1 day."

The 1st time my father went to visit my mother's parents, my grandmother told him, "My daughter is a shapeshifter. If you marry her, you will need to bear with it for maybe the rest of your life." He said, "But I don't feel that way." Then they got married. Now sometimes when they have a fight and my mother accidentally turns into a dragon, in his frustration my father still says, "Your mother warned me you were like this, and I didn't believe her!" Then he will try and fail to transform into a tiger because we moved years ago and the changing table is gone and without it, he can't shift shapes. He can no longer beat the dragon with pillows and blankets and my help.

Why write out an equation when we can easily count the heads of the animals, given that rabbits look quite distinct from roosters? Maybe we can't because instead of rabbits and roosters in the cage there are multiple fathers and multiple copies of me, which are rabbits and roosters that look very much alike and impossible to tell apart. Together with my mother, who is a dragon and an angel and a shapeshifter, we have 36 to 38 heads, 96 to 102 feet, and some 50 wings. How can we be arranged on 1 to 2 beds and lie still enough to sleep every night? We would shift shift

shift, brushing against each other, breaking extra arms and legs, leaving bruises on anonymous skin.

While she was pregnant with me, my mother was a baby-changing table. Planted inside the womb, an embryo goes through different stages, evolving and eventually getting rid of gill slits—growing into and out of being a fish. I was an unexpected baby. When she first conceived she didn't know it and went to ride a horse in Inner Mongolia, drinking rice wine with shepherds. She only became aware of me after she came back and started to bleed. I could still have been a fish. Had this embryo failed to make it through, it would have flowed out of her body and she would know what it feels like to eject a fish egg. But it stayed and shifted and shifted on its changing table. If I ever have kids, it would be hard to resist the temptation to scare them in the following way: Place them on my stomach and tell them it is a baby-changing table capable of changing them back into fishes if I please because we have all been fishes and they are still inside us, we are neither here nor there, we are somewhere in the middle, swaying left to right, up and down, like riding your mother's belly, like riding a horse, a train, a table, a body, anything. Everything around you is a blur, everyone faceless, boundaries shaken loose and thrown into midair. You were a fish and when you were a fish you were also inside me sharing my boundaries so I had gill slits and I was a fish too. I hope you enjoyed it.

During the month when my mother almost lost her embryo, she was always lying in bed, her whole body still. Now that she was a table, she must do as a table would do: stay flat and open and wait for something else to occupy her. My father fed her soup. Strictly speaking they were not yet mother and father and they had considered getting rid of it, seeing that a baby would be a heavy burden they were not prepared to carry and already it had caused her to bleed, trapped at home, half paralyzed, forbidden to move. Eventually the embryo stabilized and my father got better at cooking. They both grew heavier, drinking the same soup.

I want to know the shape of my mother's desire, and maybe my father's as well. Only then would it be possible for me to offer them my own, in exchange, as a gift, a way to understand. My mother had been waiting for me to grow up, so that she could talk to me the way she'd talk to a fellow woman. Following this logic, my father never had his chance to begin with. He can't talk to me the way he'd talk to his brother. I can't tell them to see me as a little of both plus a little of neither. They don't seem very interested in my shape anyhow, so we silently avoid it. I am 5 feet 6 and weigh 105 pounds. To lay me down would only require 3 baby-changing tables, whereas my mother needs 4½ and my father needs 5, if we consider only weight. Imagine us on the train together, each lying on our changing-table beds. They would have to lie on their sides, and it is their choice whether I could see their faces or the backs of their heads. Even if I stay in the middle like I did 20 years ago, at any given moment there would be parts of them that I fail to see. Sometimes it's not enough to be in between.

One time ants crawled into our dorm and made a nest in the kitchen. They occupied every corner where they found food or water. Watching them struggle along the slippery bathroom sink, I realized they would never see me as a whole. If they climbed onto my arm and proceeded on this vast plateau of skin, they would not know that this was not the overall shape of my body. If I caught 1 of them and placed it on my nipple, suddenly there'd be a decrease in flat surface and the texture rougher, making it harder for the ant to move around. It would not know both areas belonged to me and I still had more. To those ants I existed neither as an idea nor as a body, even though I was huge. I could kill them if I wanted to, and their fellow ants would only recognize me as a location unsuitable for food hunting.

When my father called my mother an angel "sent by God to save him," what he meant was that she had her chance to make her fortune and eventually buy us a larger apartment. We moved to the center of the city. He felt lucky and he felt defeated. He said whoever had the chance should seize it and he asked her if she looked down on him because he had escaped Singapore and the humidity and drudgery that came with it. When my father was abroad, my mother sent him pictures of me. In one of the pictures I was sitting on the living-room table, gripping the telephone handset with both hands. I was playing my Friday-night game, Calling My Father. My father wrote back, the only time he ever sent my mother a letter. He wrote, "Will you blame me if I go home?"

A Chinese dragon is a symbol of potent and auspicious powers. My mother often says, "I have the help of the dragon." But it is also a creature that resembles a snake with 4 legs; a serpent. The serpent tempts and deceives through reason. It represents sexual desire. But does the symbol of desire itself also desire? What does it dream of?

Once my father dreamed he had 5 daughters, each the same as me. They stood in a line in our living room and he counted them, left to right, 1 through 5. He counted and recounted and recounted. He was happy. Then it suddenly occurred to him, how could there be so many? And he woke up and the other 4 were gone. He came to the breakfast table still fascinated by his dream. He said, "How nice would it be if we really had 5 daughters!" And I thought it all made sense given the extraordinary reproduction rates of rabbits. Rabbits are small mammals preyed on by carnivores and humans and they have no choice but to mate so as to preserve. Dragons, on the other hand, have a set number, since each has its own specialty and/or territory. They are not part of the food web or the carbon cycle.

From when I was born till the year I finished junior high, I shared a bedroom with my mother. After we moved, my father started to sleep alone. One day I walked into his room and saw the webpage he had left open. It was an article on the absence of sex in the daily life of middle-aged people.

To my mother I had made my adult confession, of being one human daughter who was in love with another. After calmly asking how C and I had sex, my mother asked what we would do once we were far apart. She said, "What would you do when you feel the need? Would you do it yourself?" I said, "Yes." She said, "Do you know how?" And I felt the urge to say, Do you?

After I learned how, the way I related to my body changed. I feel more continuous because now I understand how my skin caves in to form the inside. But it is also strange to feel the evidence of me as an open structure: open, not concealed, with multiple holes of various sizes and thus penetrable. It is hard not to think of my womb and bladder and large intestine. Sometimes I lie in bed and think, it is a special health checkup. And it has always been the pleasure of pretending: my hand is someone else's hand, my body someone else's body. I can shift into and out of another body, an imaginary identity, while remaining in my own. Such is the shape of my desire: it is ever-shifting and many-layered, each facet unfolding at the same moment. I don't know how to narrate this to my mother. It has moved beyond the scope of my confession, of whispering a name in the dark. I'm afraid she would want to take me to the baby-changing table and exchange me for another.

How Slow a Breath Can Come

The daughter remembers the brother birth. She remembers the mother and the father in their bedroom. She remembers the screaming coming under the space in the door. She remembers the door opening, the father leading the mother down the stairs. She remembers the sweat-drenched gown. She remembers the screaming from the barn. She remembers following her parents toward the cow. She remembers watching from the barnyard door and the cat purring in her lap and how heavy the cat was back when she was little. She remembers the mother telling the father how to get a cow from the inside of a cow to the inside of the barn. She remembers how long it took for the mother to take her hand off the cow's neck. She remembers the mother on the floorboards. She remembers the mother sounds and the cow sounds coming together in the air and being trapped in the rafters. And then the brother sounds. How the mother sounds quieted. And the cow sounds got louder. The father with the knife from off the wall. The first way the knife is used is between the mother and the brother. And the second way the knife is used is against the throat that causes the cow sounds. And the brother in the father arms. And the mother standing in her gown no longer white. She walks past the daughter and the cat and the light shines on her like it's the moon. In the fields, the grazing cows want to catch her if she falls. It looks like there's a rope coming from inside her. She pulls at the well for a bucket of water. And the daughter knows her mother wants to wash the insides of her off the outsides of the brother. But halfway back to the barn she collapses, and the daughter remembers her father holding the brother so softly that he could only walk when he wanted to run, and she remembers how he splashed water from the bucket for his wife's face and when she didn't wake, he took the rest of the water and cleaned the boy as much as he could. The daughter put her fingers under her mother's nose and felt how slow a breath can come. She looked at her brother with his half-clean ears and she wanted to whisper into them he was lucky their mother was still alive.

EXALTATION

mei ping woman, break neck break neck god-de-
inculcate so may vishuddah this tympanic heave

for id to pulse between doors of pleasure
rooms to sweat the day like an infant
disgruntled stars, a judder of keys pocketed

shudder screens in august for your stomach to
become a roof, grid and bookends from where
you sew your intra-Venus channel shut

there is a lunge in remise at unpeeled glottis then,
globes of mercury, the green gift in desiccant beads
staggers forward.

Mariangela Guatteri

It started with the cicadas and spread from there. The fungus dormant in the soil, attuned to the insects' cyclical rhythms. Chthonic. Brooding. Penetrating the carapace of sap-suckled nymphs as they pushed their way to the surface, took to the branches, left their exoskeletons, like omens, clinging to cankered bark. We heard them singing, but we did not discern their distress. The spores swelling their abdomens, eating away at the insects' organs until the back-half of their bodies sloughed off, leaving the sporulating mass exposed.

And still, they lived. Fungal automatons, unaware of their corporal transection. Their truncation. Brains altered by psilocybins and amphetamines to ensure their periodic habits continued unabated. To guarantee that the infection spread, found new hosts, new bodies to colonize. In the late stages of the disease, they flew without cease, spores scattering from their bodies like ash.

Before that final flight, the insects signaled their mates: the females with a customary clicking of wings, the males with their shrill, thrumming trill. But the males became polyamorous, indiscriminate—impersonating females, flicking their wings to attract other males, coupling with a multitude of partners.

We shuddered to think of them copulating—shorn, sexless, deformed. Healthy insects undulating against the mound of spores, absorbing the sickness. Generation after generation. A swarm of contagion hibernating underground. Emerging after ever-decreasing intervals. Seventeen years, thirteen years, nine, five, three.

By the time the pathogen adapted, learned to control our bodies, our brains, we were already addicted. Cultivating the drug-addled insects, ingesting them like living capsules in order to experience chemically induced delusions, to forget what the world had come to resemble. Initially, the fungus was harmless to humans. A truth we chose to sustain, refused to reassess. After all, we could not keep track of everything that was changing, evolving. Of each burgeoning plague.

Tonight, I ingest two cicadas whole, allowing them to pass slowly from mouth to throat to stomach. Their membranous wings tickling my palate, their barbed legs clinging to the rough buds of my tongue. I wait for them to sing, let them buckle and unbuckle their drum-like tymbals as I swallow. I open my lips to enable the trilling to escape. For a moment, my body becomes their resonance chamber, amplifying the sound, humming with it. My belly a cave filled with imagos.

I tell myself that the baby is accustomed to this ritual, that she awaits it. Body fortified by the vitamins and stimulants that pass through the placenta, filling her unpruned neural network with dreams and visions. I stroke my swollen belly and speak to it, soothing my future child, who remains strangely still inside me. I will name her Daphne when she emerges. She will play in the stunted parks that contain our only approximations of woodlands, climb the beetle-infested branches of trees long dead but still standing. I will teach her to tap on the trunks to see if they are hollow or harboring some viable source of protein within. I will teach her how to survive in this world—when to flee, when to stay dormant.

I need to believe that this is a natural gestation—a continuation of the species, not a furtherance of extermination. But I cannot be certain. I cannot trust my perceptions, my drives. My need for new partners, night after night. I summon them from afar and mark their arrival via the hum of the cellphone, using an app that assures anonymous encounters. I do not rise to greet them. But that is due to my gravid state. I remain in bed, partly covered, calling out to assure them that the door is unlocked, that they can let themselves inside. Surely they would flee if the shape beneath the sheet appeared abnormal. That is something even their pin-prick pupils could detect: a strange foreshortening, a bisected body on a bed. With my white-sheeted belly, I look like a spider clutching its egg sac. But still they do not hesitate to come to me, to touch me, to enter me.

The neighbors do not complain about the noise of our mating, the growing disarray inside the apartment. Layers of dust, flakes shed from skin that has become desiccated by too much sun, too little water.

I strain to see past my belly, to flex my legs, wiggle my toes. But the swelling is immense, umbral—like the earth eclipsing the moon. I slip my hands between my legs, feel my thighs part, my fingers penetrate. Reassured it is flesh that I feel. That I am here. Intact.

BIRDS IN ART

A museum in Wisconsin displays nothing but paintings of birds, except a few sculptures of birds—pigeons, ducks, crows, ostriches, gulls, sparrows, sometimes in close-up, sometimes just smudges against the scenery. The person who began the museum died long ago, but her fortune lives on. The museum's foundation bestows a trip to central Wisconsin on painters and sculptors from Nova Scotia, Japan and even New Zealand, for the annual gala. Many men and women come to see the paintings of birds, and on the opening night they mingle with the creators of these bird images.

What wonderful birds they are, some drawn in loving realism, some scrawled in charcoal, some even re-created out of the spines of their own feathers: little black birds on white sticks that are the skeletons of the devices that had set them free. Relatively few people are depicted with the birds, though there are a couple of hunters, shown from the back. The visitor moving from room to room can't keep her eyes from meeting the little round eyes of the birds. The visitor might get sick of their importuning within twenty minutes.

In a gallery beyond the new paintings of birds hang several older, gold-framed paintings of dead birds hung by their feet. These paintings are calming not only because the birds aren't staring, but because they conjure, if not flat out belong to, a school of art: the still life. The way they're arranged on the canvas head down, these dead birds put the visitor in mind of the work of the Dutch masters with their jugs and vegetables, meals without people, implements without any hands holding them. The painters of the dead birds had hewn to a tradition, while the painters of swallows and sparrows in flight might have sat themselves down to paint birds for reasons of their own that had nothing to do with what anyone else considered art-worthy. This seems so lonely, even if on the other side of the world, a woman had decided to collect only paintings of birds.

FEEDERS

The feeders were set out for birds—during the decades when birds
still perched on branches and kited on updrafts—but strange creatures
began to gather beneath. Beaked and feathered, reptilian: they were
hybrid beings all. Progeny of mutation, or something stranger still.
They shuffled and scavenged, weighted down by cumbersome sets of
arms—useless, but not vestigial, as those limbs were only now emerging.
Each day we waited to see if the tiny, articulated hands—for that's what
they were, not paws, though furred and built for grasping—would flex
the clawed fingers to life, reach inside the feeders, extract what meager
sustenance remained. What we did not prepare for, did not expect, is
that the creatures, once dexterous, would fill the feeders with offerings,
scraps of meat, the twisted bodies of tubers wrenched from the ground
with their talons. We could not tell if they were constructing an altar or
attempting to save us, sustain us. We studied the way they cocked their
heads, stared at us with glinting and disturbingly human eyes, attempted
a rough form of speech—something between the cawing of crows and
the brittle cries of blue jays. Was it an accusation? A courtship? We
closed our blinds and refused to forage beneath the pine boughs. We
lost weight and body mass, became delicate and fine-boned creatures,
prone to damage. Even when they cooed to us, we would not let them in.
Perhaps we were waiting for their hands to grow strong enough to slide
open the windows, pull back the bedcovers, and stroke our foreheads.
Perhaps we were waiting for them to feed us from their mouths.

WHAT BLUE LOOKS LIKE

I see a bird and it says to me:
"I am not your father. I am just a bird."
It flies the way birds always do. It moves
in ways the not-winged can't.
The path through the sky is rarely straight.
To be direct is not always the way.
I walk slowly, my pace telling me
what to see, what to pay attention to.
The muddy river is moving too.
Warm wind through tall grass and trees.
There are birds above us, eyeing
the dark waters below. They know things
we don't and never will. What the sky
feels like when you push down on it.
What blue looks like when
you aren't just passing through.

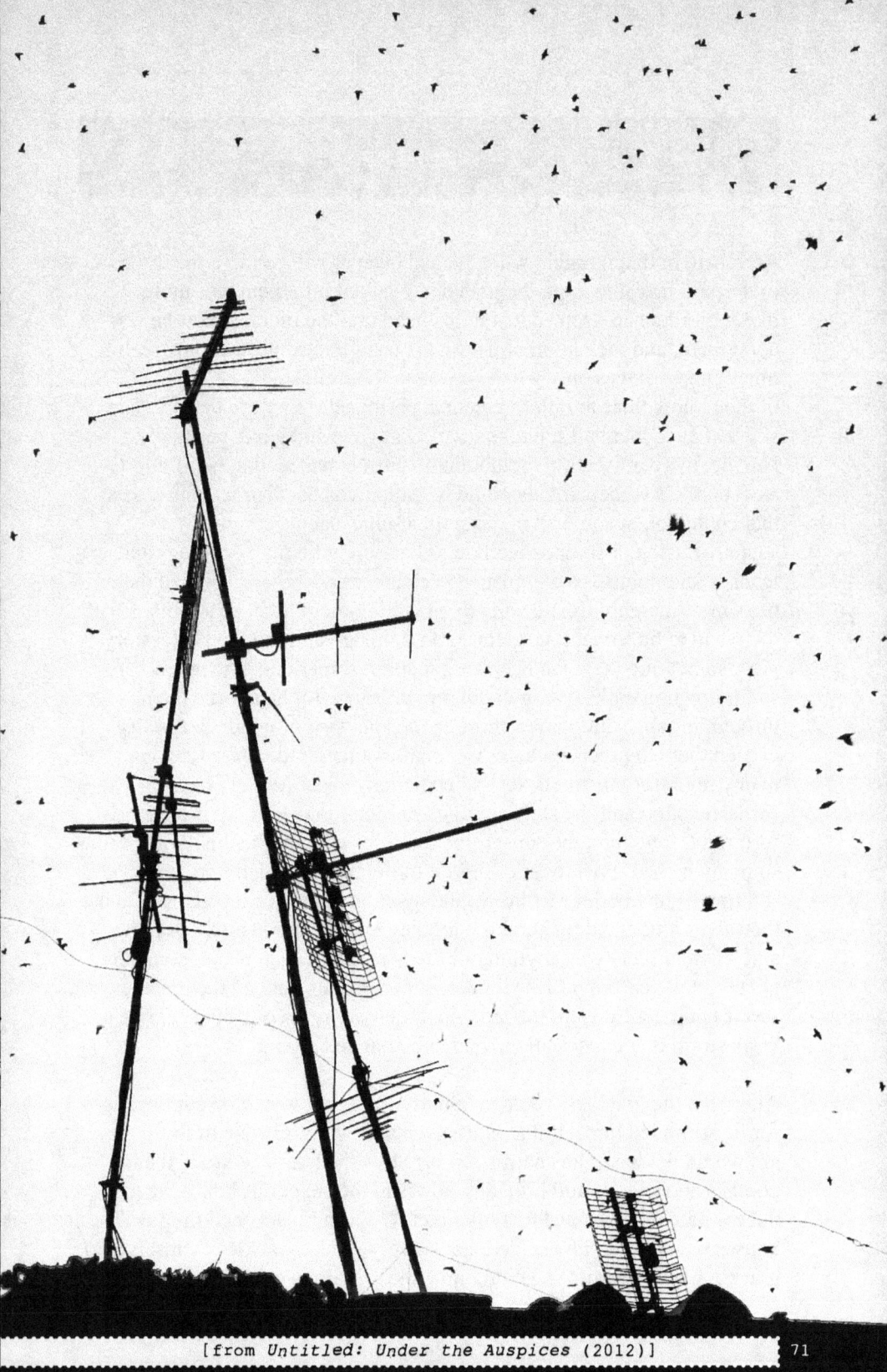

GRACKLES

And then, in that moment when he had been at wit's end, in the throes
of despair, he came upon the grackles. Walked into them was more
like it. For he had been so lost in his head that the moment that he was
upon them, and they upon him—on his head like some seething, reeling
microburst—it was only when he was in their midst that he took note
of them, how their tumult threatened, promised to rupture the sky. The
sky that gave them all it had to give. That gave and gave, being sky.
And he, there, miserably earthbound—until elevated, that is, lifted
aloft on their voices, if they could be called voices, their cawing a mass
that could not, at some level, be split, atomic, such a common raft of
sound, a fusion, a composite, though flapping with many endings and
tendrils and points—many places to clamber up as they occupied the
trees in his neighborhood, something calling them here, he surmised that
there had to be something special about this juncture in their migratory
path, something they had been anticipating, something embedded
so far down in collective, glandular memory that it had borne them
through intransigent climes, through the backlash of winds like walls,
carried them to precisely here. He, on the other hand, utterly lacking
in any migratory instincts, deposited here by sheer dint of chance,
by desperation and the shifting sands of rental law. He had, if being
forthright, long thought himself too good for a town like this. A town like
so many he had flown over or driven through (but actually around, even
if through) in wonder of who wound up stunted in such a place, and what
their lives amounted to, and how far they ever ventured away from it,
and whether there was anything of the heroic that such places somehow,
nevertheless, harbored. He wondered if the locals noticed the grackles,
and if the grackles were to them mostly bother or inconvenience, like a
freak storm or a construction zone to be flagged around.

And from the grackles' vantage? Surely this town would be comforting,
for he reminded himself that houses would look otherwise from the
air, would not have the charms proferred by their earthly faces, their
porches and swings and little dog bowls in the shapes of bones but also
not the patchy lawns and rusty defunct ATVs and blackened firepits. The
houses would look, he decided, not so very unlike grackles themselves,
grackle-black roof tiles he could imagine on sale in one of those giant

stores that sold home supplies by such acreage that they seemed aimed at resuscitating civilization in the aftermath of a nuclear war (the Monday off of a nuclear weekend), the occasional tile sloughed away like a feather. As he placed himself in the thick murk of grackle-mind—easy to do because with the swell of their jabbering all around him it was impossible to think about anything else—he realized he would have to see the world from above, maybe have to talk to the guy he'd seen with the drone down the block, filming from the air, a guy he was sure had no curiosity and to whom it hadn't occurred that he could use his drone not just to swoop above the neighborhood like some sort of military contraption but to bring us closer to birds, them closer to us, usthem, themus. He was sure, based on the couple of conversations he'd had with the guy, that his drone-commandeering was little more than an extension into adulthood of playing with G.I. Joes as a kid, that it was less a liberation of sight from the terrestrial and more a surveilling, a prepping for an apocalyptic day shortly nigh. But you never knew, did you? Maybe he could bribe the guy with a six-pack of swill, the sound of whose opening, double-notch followed by exhalation of liquid air, conveyed anticipation so assuredly that what composer would not envy it? He'd arrive with meat, too, charred yet red, grilled and still the color of the heated coals, as if it had switched places with them. He'd chat him up with neighborly camaraderie, then at some point "Hey" into "So how about that drone I sometimes see flying overhead?" Oh yeah, he'd get him talking, and talking would lead to wait-here demonstration, and demonstration straight to "Wanna give her a whirl?," and before he knew it he'd be donning the eyes of a grackle.

For now, though, he stood as if he himself were the only stable point, the only thing certain it was a solid form in the sheer chaos—and that was the only way, to be drenched by it, swaddled in it, but no—that implied infantilization. These grackles treated you like an adult, like a threat, a predator, their very way of life in jeopardy as you passed underneath, how they broaded you into the thick of their sound, making all the prepositions feel wanting, but enough of it carrying down into the concert hall of the street that you could still feel yourself immersed, brought into it, and then as he got too close they stopped, just stopped! Went so silent so sudden that for a moment he wondered whether he had imagined it, the whole thing, whether he'd been relying on a memory of a past encounter with grackles, a whole other year like a filter atop his memory, but then it started up again just as he started to gain some distance on the far side of where he now knew them to be, he knew their positions now, they announced their positions in some Heisenbergian way, like he couldn't both know where they were and also be in their midst, it was one or the other, not both the particle of selfhood and the wave of themness at the same time, he felt that with these grackles he was running into some of the very deepest fundamental forces of the universe, or maybe it was just a passing encounter, for what was the proper means of making sense of this? Was it in fact just biology or did it go down to physics? Was something so fundamental going on here that it might as well have been a demonstration on the biological level by these winged actors of what was also happening deep down at the microscopic level, happening all around us all the time without any conscious awareness because below the threshold of vision and thus not ever made available to consciousness, and the encounter was perfect, it had this integrity, it had shape and conviction and a body of its own, was its own entity, which is what taught him first or again for the hundredth time that music could be that, that music was not just a passing thing but was something tangible and real that you could point to, because on his return trip, which took him again right through the cataract of grackledom, the grackles did not cease, they simply kept on grackling, and he took this to mean that in some primordial way they had accepted him as one of them, no longer a threat but part grackle himself, for why else would they have changed their tune, or in this case not changed it, rather, continuing it unbudged? There was no greater welcome that he could've asked for or hoped for than their continuing to simply be themselves and do their thing. And in listening was he not participating? For surely they must have heard their places in the larger din? Surely they must have had some awareness of themselves, but he thought maybe they were only waves, maybe they gave up their particlehood, and that was what made it all possible. Was he willing to surrender particlehood? And at what cost? No, he liked being a self—he needed it. One of his dad's buddies had become a Buddhist at some point, and thus devoted the latter part of his life to defeating his own ego, or maybe "defeating" was the wrong way to think of it—the ego having already won when you see it as competition—but how do you get outside that, how do you circumvent the ego enough, how do you cast it aside? Because these grackles surely did, and they did it without a hitch, nary a complaint. They managed to move together and navigate and travel together in numbers that never would've worked for humans. Maybe they were able to sort everything out, maybe they were even able to talk to each other in that cacophonous swathe of sound, and he thought, then, that it was the most magnificent thing, was like the universe were composing, but when he was composing with his pen and his staves, was that not the universe composing as well, but his ego made it all different, his ego would not reliquish the credit to the universe, would not let go, not gently, not roughly, not to day nor to night, and even as he imagined an umbilical severing, already he could see they were taking to the skies, were done with this pit stop, all talked out for now, missing the onslaught of wind, the pull of onward, even the lingerers stirring at last, this round at least, any memory of it soon to shatter into a thousand black shards, branches even now left clutching at that vacated space in echoless mourning.

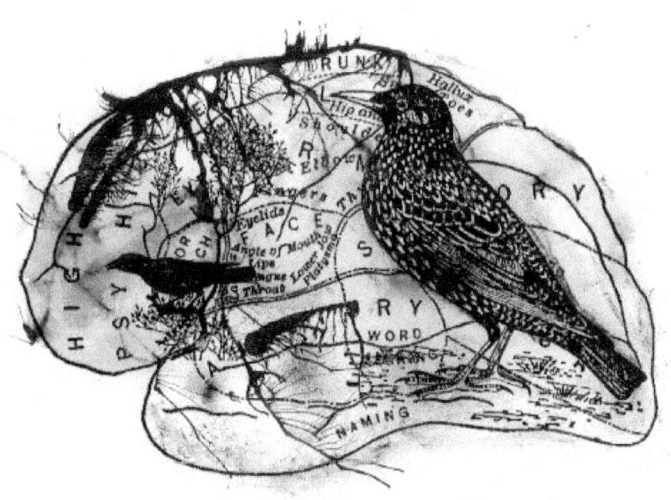

Rosaire Appel

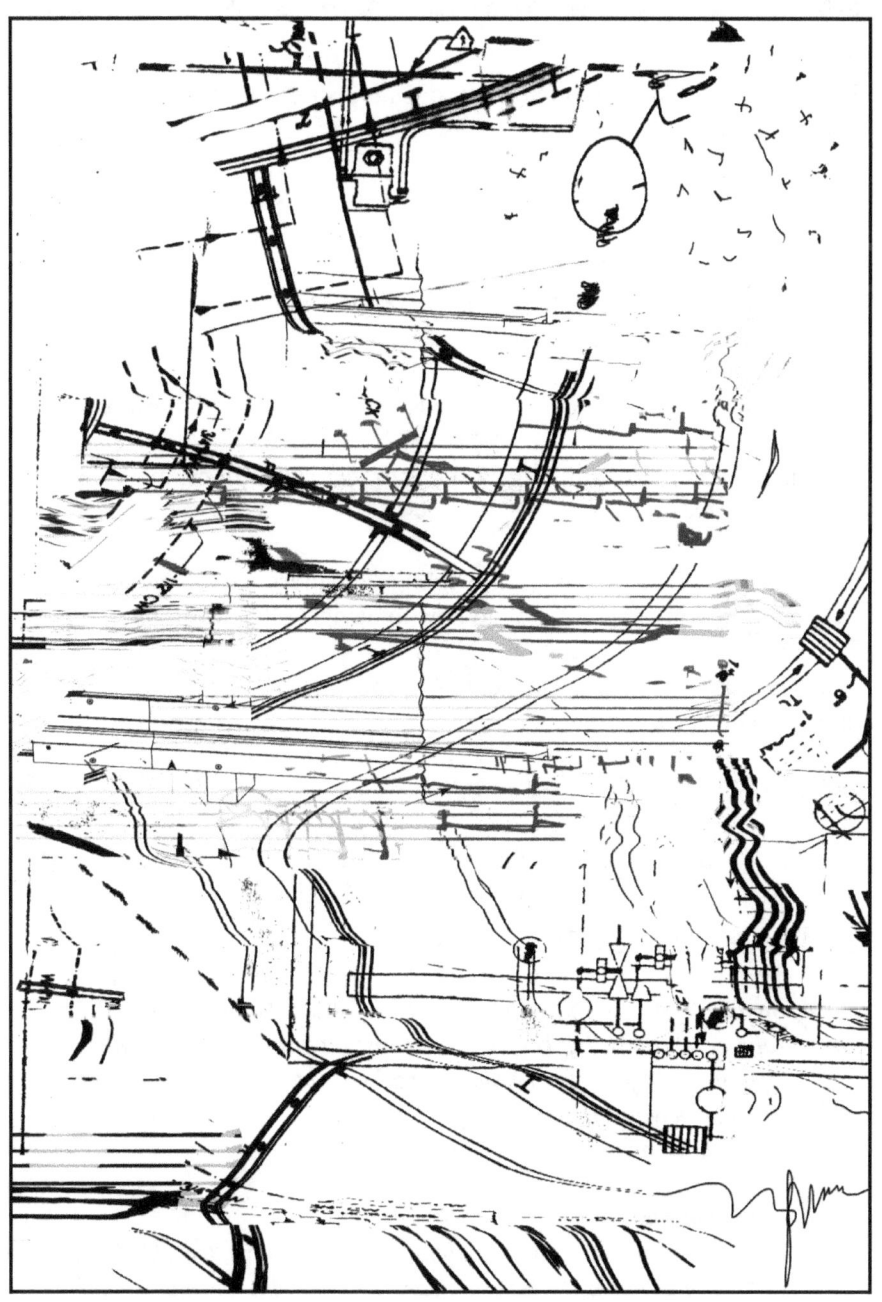

Species of Spaces and Other Pieces

In the 1st-year Composition Seminar at University, you compose one composition.

The composition is to be written for the visiting ensemble, with permission to write oneself into the piece if one desires, which you do.

There will be one 30-minute meeting on Zoom, and one 30-minute rehearsal the day before the performance.

The visiting ensemble is called String Noise, a duo of violin virtuosos.

Your piece is composed through a series of text instructions, marking each section by time.

While the options within in each section of the piece are limited, the performers are given choices as to how to navigate the material.

You handwrite the score, scan copies, and send to String Noise, approximated as follows:

[SIBILANTS]   *[...]* + *String Noise*   *[Fall 2022]*

> *(Operate independently unless alignment is indicated. Soft dynamics throughout)*

~ TIME - SECTION - INSTRUCTIONS
> *single bow strokes, sounding harmonics:*
Harmonic Double Stops - bass [A/B] - violin left [E/F#] - violin right [B/C#]
> — *choice of range, but keep pitches constant throughout section*
> — *begin on single lower harmonic, add second before bow runs out*
> — *silence between each gesture*
> — *vary durations of gesture/silence*

1:30(Vs) RH Gestures
2: (B)   CR = bow pressure / angled motion to produce slow "crackle" sound
> *SW = quick downward stroke near frog for sharp "swipe" sound*
> *BB = slow bow at bridge, can sound harmonic or not*

SP = spiccato - can vary btw 1 string / X-strings (any direction) / instr. body
— *cycle through gestures in any order at own pace*
— *vary silences btw gestures*
— *LH dampen strings throughout, sometimes scratching lightly
  w/ fingernails*

4: Short Double Stops - alternate btw P5 / m2 - players choice, keep same throughout
— *continue to interject above gestures between each double stop*
— *vary length of double stops as section progresses*

5:30   Drop gestures / Continue double stops

6: (B)   Spiccato Repeats
6:30(Vs) — X-strings from low to high, silence btw each gesture
— *LH damp*
— *violins begin section independently from bass, attempt
  to align before the end*

7:   [THE END]

. enthusiastic audience clapping sounds .

Encyclopedia Britannica defines "sibilant" as "a fricative consonant
sound, in which the tip, or blade, of the tongue is brought near the roof of
the mouth and air is pushed past the tongue to make a hissing sound."

You have not yet received the Zoom H4nPro Handy Recorder and do not
document the performance, which takes place on December 10th, 2022.

Program notes:

  *A collection of small sounds and static gestures overlapping and
  interacting with space.*

On February 23rd, 2023, you receive a Zoom H4nPro Handy Recorder.

When you return to University after the weekend at home, you record
sound sources for a fixed media 8-channel piece for the *Sound Systems
and Chamber Electronics* class midterm project to be performed the

following week in a large room with a large sound system while live mixing the tracks on a 32-channel mixer.

There are 4 tracks of fixed sound sources, each performed on double bass and recorded in one take with the Zoom H4nPro Handy Recorder, your 1st time using the device, documented in further detail in the recording documentation section of the text.

1 bows / trem
2 bows / trem
3 low d / spic
4 low d / spic

1 bows
2 trem
3 low d
4 spic

1 x
2 x
3 low d
4 x

1 wires
2 wires
3 low d - x - harm
4 harm

1 x
2 x
3 harm
4 harm

The above outline is the only version of something resembling a score for the piece, typed into the Notes app on your phone in the middle of the night on February 26th, 2023.

Moved from its original position in the "Field Recordings, etc." document, the outline/score is the 1st entry in a new document called "Scores, Program Notes."

The numbers refer to each recording of fixed material, the actions of which are outlined in more detail in the "Field Recording, etc." document that describes each recording.

The actions corresponding to each number are then assigned 8 channels of the mixer.

4 tracks using 8 channels each equals 32 channels.

In addition to the fixed material, the composition takes shape through live diffusion—mixing the tracks across the 8 speakers in real time during the performance.

The speakers are placed in stereo pairs in the back of the stage area on the ceiling, front of the stage area on the ceiling, front of the stage area on the floor, and behind the audience seating on the ceiling.

After rehearsing the piece in the performance space, you write a basic outline to structure the mixing in your Notes app to refer to during the performance.

You do not recall referring to the outline much, if at all, instead relying on memory through preparation, as well as instinct and improvisation in response to the sounds in the space in real time.

The piece is arbitrarily and decisively titled "What Is To Be Done."

For the program notes, you cut and paste text from the original "Field Recordings, etc." document and add sentences to the beginning and end:

The sound sources consist of 4 unedited tracks of double bass. The 4 tracks are broken into pairs. On 2 tracks, the bass is played flat on its back. Sounds used: 2-bow tremolo above and below bridge with endpin preparation between fingerboard and strings to dampen open strings, 2-bow tip perc with endpin and left foot damp, 2 wires between endpin and saddle right hand bow with left hand plucks below bridge. On the other 2 tracks, the bass is played upright in the conventional stance. Sounds used: detuned low D interruptions, improvisation centered around spiccato and textural harmonics, slow bow crackles, detuned low D drone, clean harmonics with melodic character. The sections are marked by time with staggered transitions.

You notice 2 appearances of the word "the" in the original document after including the above text in the program notes.

You keep the above as is, while editing the original document.

After receiving edits for the submission to Sleepingfish, documented in the next chapter, you change the numbers to #s above.

You forget to bring Zoom H4nPro Handy Recorder to the performance and there is no audio documentation of the piece.

In the 2nd semester of the 1st year at University, you join the Toneburst Laptop and Electronic Arts Ensemble.

You write a piece for the ensemble with the patch used to soundcheck at the beginning of each rehearsal.

The patch consists of silence, triangle wave, and pink noise.

There's an overall volume control, as well as a frequency range that can be activated within the triangle wave setting.

The score reads as a set of instructions, with time and dynamic markings, as follows:

*[**section 1** - STATIC EVENTS] ~ 0'00"~2'30" /// medium loud - medium quiet*

0'00" play triangle wave between frequency range 11-10001 (5~10 seconds to start) /// medium loud

make one of 3 choices: stop playing triangle wave (silence); play new triangle wave (emphasize frequency contrast); play pink noise (5~10 seconds to start)

continue to repeat above 2 directions (beginning with new triangle wave, moving onto new choices), increasing rate of activity as section progresses

~2'00"~2'30" choose one frequency to repeat throughout next section

between range of 2 options: LOW = < 50; HIGH = > 9000 /// medium quiet

*[**section 2** - DRONE CUTS] ~ 2'30"~5'00" /// medium quiet/medium*

~2'30" continue triangle wave that ends previous section

~2'45" introduce brief pink noise interruptions before quickly returning to your wave (use space between each interruption, centering on the wave)

~3'00" add silence as interruption and cycle through silence / triangle wave / pink noise in any order with varied durations

~3'30" experiment with pulse and rhythm as you shift between events, moving in and out of repetitions and looped patterns

after establishing some patterns, introduce more space and loosen the patterns

~4'30"~4'50" silence with wave interruptions (no pink noise)

4'50"-5'00" silence

*[**section 3** - OSCILLATION SWELLS] ~ 5'00"~8'00" /// loud - medium - medium quiet*

5'00" pink noise /// loud

~5'30"~5'45" if previous choice was low frequency wave, switch to high (btw 7000-7500), stagger entrances /// medium

~5'45"~6'00" if previous choice was high frequency wave, switch to low (btw 25-50), stagger entrances /// medium

after shifting to wave, choose between 2 options: oscillate frequency, within assigned range, at various speeds; or, dynamic swells at your own pace

~7'00" stop oscillating/swelling, settle into wave /// medium quiet

listen for cue - pink noise - to cut

to silence

///

The Laptop Ensemble final concert takes place on May 10th, 2023, at WMH at University.

Your piece opens the show.

Program notes:

> /// C U T S /// *explores a range of material available in the patch used to balance the collective amplitude of the ensemble at the beginning of each rehearsal.*

Laptop Ensemble members are scattered throughout the hall, and you occupy a far back corner up the steps in the audience.

You bring the Zoom H4nPro Handy Recorder and are very pleased with the performance of the piece, but due to your position in the space, the recording comes out a bit quiet and unbalanced.

The final project in *Sound Systems and Chamber Electronics* must be executed using a program called SuperCollider.

At the end of the semester, after the performance of the projects, the professor asks for a "final project report" using the following prompt:

> *You can think of this as a detailed expansion of your program note for your piece. It should describe the overall creative process, the hurdles you needed to overcome, and a comparison of your initial intentions for the project with how the project actually turned out.*

You submit the project report on May 16th, 2023, outlining 3 ideas that trace the development of the piece, which you have titled "Species of Spaces."

Idea #1: Use March 4th, March 5th, March 6th, and March 7th recordings of coffee making at Alsop House, occupying their own speaker pairs to accommodate the stereo mix and spread across the 8 speakers in WMH. Each recording runs exactly 15 minutes, attempting to perform the actions in the exact order of the previous recordings by memory. Materials used: Hario Ceramic Coffee Mill, Hario Coffee Dripper, Hario V60 Paper Filter, Bonavita Gooseneck Kettle, 1992 Dream Team mug, Share Coffee Roasters coffee, water from sink on 2nd-floor bathroom. Original idea for repeated recordings of same actions emerge from a coincidence between a field recording made one day before class and the contents of a class discussion, both occurring on February 28th. The field recording consists of a long walk (a short walk that took a long time), going from Fairview Ave. to Alsop House on the morning after a snowstorm. Encounters on Foss Hill include the sounds of skiers, snowboarders, sledders, snowball throwers, and a direct interaction with a classmate just returning from the hospital to drop off a friend with a broken collarbone (before then continuing to ski off the homemade jump where the injury occurred). The sounds of social activity decrescendos with distance, while the sonic environment shifts drastically upon entering Alsop House. The daily ritual of making coffee closes the nearly 45-minute piece, highlighting the intimacy of routine and isolated actions in contrast to the lively dynamics and chaos on the hill. The most compelling sonic component of the coffee making procedure occurs just as the water hits the ground beans for the 1st time, activating the bloom, slowly carving out the cone to direct the drips to the cup, the small crackles and pops amplified by close and careful placement of the microphone. In class later that day, we are shown a video of a John Cage piece, the name of which I can't remember, and the score of which asks the performer to perform an everyday task of their choice, or something of that nature, performed by a professor beginning class by making coffee for his students. I record the 4 coffee tracks after the experience, intrigued by the connection, unsure how I will use them but thinking their similarities and slight differences could provide interesting material in combination with each other. With the final project approaching, I think it could be a good opportunity to put the idea into action. However, when the professor responds in a meeting about the project that it sounds "cute" it's immediately clear I need to go a different direction. The professor also mentions he thought I might incorporate the mixer feedback I'd been exploring the previous semester, pushing me to rethink my approach, grateful for the encouragement and an excuse to dive back into the mixer.

Idea #2: Use 2 tracks of no-input mixer feedback improvisations to provide the foundation for an 8-channel piece, while incorporating previously made field recordings emphasizing the dynamic range of material produced throughout the semester, both in terms of sonic activity/approach as well as location/environment. After exploring various combinations of material to combine with the feedback tracks, 4 are chosen — March 17th, Millers Falls, MA: packing tape orders (materials used: scissors, scotch tape, bubble wrap, cassettes, padded envelopes, table); March 20th, Kittery Point, ME: fire on rocks near ocean; April 2nd, Middletown, CT: Twelfth Night rehearsal from open 3rd-floor window outside Alsop House (with headphone feedback and detached bow hair contact); April 16th, Middletown, CT: reading Experimental Music Since 1970 by Jennie Gottschalk before bed, with fan on. The idea is that each recording enters one by one. Once all 8 channels are occupied, new material displaces the old. The structure looks something like this: no-input 1, no-input 2, tape, 12th night, fire (no-input 1 out), fan (no-input 2 out), fire (12th night out), fire (tape out), fire (fan out). By the end, all 8 channels are taken up by the fire field recording, displaced by staggered entrances, a quiet contrast to the harsh opening of feedback. Ultimately, this approach seemed too complicated within the context of the class and the timing of the final project. Additionally, many of the field recordings made thus far, including those used in this project draft, feel particularly personal in a way that presents challenges in the context of collage. The thinking may evolve, but it's difficult to detach the material from its original intent as 1ˢᵗ-person narratives occupying their own, intimate space.

Idea #3: *Eliminate the field recording ideas outlined above and focus on the no-input material. The 2 feedback tracks offer plenty to work with on their own, and a multichannel presentation only extends the possibilities. I assign each track 2 speaker pairs each: track 1 occupies speakers 1/2 and 5/6; track 2 occupies 3/4 and 7/8. I explore spatiality through sharp cuts and hard entrances, as opposed to slow fades and soft decay. Even in moments of inactivity, the slight static of the speaker pairs coming in and out provides sonic material that shapes the performance. The cutting, displacing, and relocating of the sounds in real time becomes a compositional component alongside the fixed material. Improvising the multichannel mix allows for new structures to emerge specific to each performance, influenced by interaction with unique sound systems and the architecture of their environment. The no-input tracks are not only the first recorded documents of my collaboration with the instrument, but they are also the first time I've felt truly comfortable on it, open to unpredictability and prepared to react.*

After you explain the basic idea articulated above, the professor writes the following code:

```
(
~fpMaker = { | chan = 0, buf = 5, panL= -0.68, panR=0.68, rate
= 1, db = 0 |
        { var audio;
                var pl = ("pan" ++ chan ++ "L").asSymbol;
                var pr = ("pan" ++ chan ++ "R").asSymbol;
                var r = ("rate" ++ chan).asSymbol;
                var d = ("db" ++ chan).asSymbol;
                Spec.add(pl, \bipolar);
                Spec.add(pr, \bipolar);
                Spec.add(r, [0.25, 4, 'exponential']);
                Spec.add(d, [-20, 20]);

                pl = pl.kr(panL);
                pr = pr.kr(panR);
                r = r.kr(rate);
                d = d.kr(0);

        audio = PlayBuf.ar(2, bufnum: buf, rate: r, loop: 0);
        audio = audio * d.dbamp;
//PanAz.ar(8, audio[0], pl) + PanAz.ar(8, audio[1], pr);
        Pan2.ar( audio[0], pl) + Pan2.ar(audio[1], pr);


}
};
s.options.numOutputBusChannels = 10;
s.quit;
```

```
s.waitForBoot {
        // guarantee the server is running
        ~files = "audio/*".resolveRelative.pathMatch;
        // find files in the folder "audio", which
        ~buffers = ~files.collect{ | f | Buffer.read(s, f) };
// load those sounds into buffers on the server

~np1 = NodeProxy.audio(s, 2);
~np2 = NodeProxy.audio(s, 2);

~np1.gui(5, Rect(873.0,600.0, 394.0, 150.0));
~np2.gui(5, Rect(873.0, 420.0, 394.0, 150.0));
s.sync;
~np1[1] = ~fpMaker.(1, ~buffers[0].bufnum);
~np2[1] = ~fpMaker.(2, ~buffers[1].bufnum);

        ~sp1 = NodeProxy.audio(s,2);
        ~sp2 = NodeProxy.audio(s,2);
        ~sp3 = NodeProxy.audio(s,2);
        ~sp4 = NodeProxy.audio(s,2);
        ~sp1[0] = { ~np1.ar };
        ~sp2[0] = { ~np1.ar };
        ~sp3[0] = { ~np2.ar };
        ~sp4[0] = { ~np2.ar };
        ~sp1g = ~sp1.gui(0, Rect(873.0, 350.0, 394.0, 30.0));
        ~sp1g = ~sp2.gui(0, Rect(873.0, 270.0, 394.0, 30.0));
        ~sp1g = ~sp3.gui(0, Rect(873.0, 190, 394.0, 30.0));
        ~sp1g = ~sp4.gui(0, Rect(873.0, 110, 394.0, 30.0));

        ~sp1.playN([0,1]); // channels 12
        ~sp2.playN([0,1] + 4).stop; // 56
        ~sp3.playN([0,1] + 2).stop; // 34
        ~sp4.playN([0,1] + 6).stop; // 78

};

~spg1

)
```

The John Cage piece you forget the name of is *0'00''*, the original score reads:

> *In a situation provided with maximum amplification (no feedback),*
> *perform a disciplined action.*

Program notes:

> *The sound sources consist of 2 feedback improvisations using no-input mixer, a Mackie 1202VLZ4 12-channel, recorded on May 1ˢᵗ and May 2ⁿᵈ in RHH105 with a Zoom H4nPro Handy Recorder placed on a chair placed on a table. Both original tracks run 43'43" and have been chopped into a more appropriate length to fit the context of this concert, then routed to their own 2 pairs of speakers across the 8-channel system. A defining feature of the multichannel realization is to implement sharp cuts and entries that displace, erase, and relocate the fixed material in real time, using spatiality as a productive source of content and form that echoes the unpredictability of the instrument.*

In addition to the final project performance, you also perform a 4-channel version of the piece as part of a solo set at Roulette a few months later, on September 6ᵗʰ, 2023, just hours after receiving the news of Charles Gayle's death.

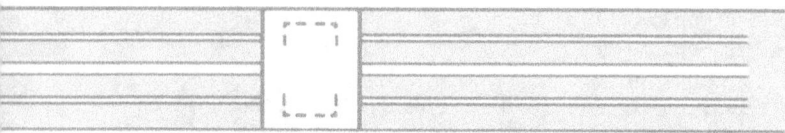

SECOND PERSON

You send a draft of the 1ˢᵗ and 2ⁿᵈ chapters, unnamed at the time and referred to as "sections," along with drafts of 2 of the compositions, "Sibilants" and "/// C U T S ///," to Cal A. Mari (in attendance at above-mentioned Roulette performance), upon invitation to the *Sleepingfish* 20-year-anniversary issue, co-edited by Garielle Lutz.

You also send, at the same time, the 1ˢᵗ chapter and the 1ˢᵗ composition mentioned above to Micah Silver.

The act of sending, along with the realization of readers engaging, especially those particular readers above, motivates the 1ˢᵗ significant edits that shift the structure and tone of the text.

The drafts are sent on July 17ᵗʰ, 2023.

Ten days later, you make clear to the editors that the work should not be considered a submission.

Cal initially responds the day after the draft is sent, indicating some parts he likes and asking if you mind if the material is cut up and remixed.

hey just wanted to update that the excerpts i sent are seeing some major revisions. cutting lotsa stuff and trying 2ⁿᵈ person. the baumer/ red barn stuff is gonna shift into a later section, most of that 2ⁿᵈ section is probably out. feels like it's in too early of a stage for anyone to try to take the time to chop it up and remix. i mostly just wanted to send to show what i've been up to, and even just knowing some discerning eyes were on it made me rethink some things, as it goes. thanks a bunch for checking it out.

The primary change is a shift in narrator point of view from 3ʳᵈ to 2ⁿᵈ person: "Student" becomes "you."

Yah, I can hold off on the remix. Looking forward to the edits, it was off to a good start.

"Student" is a reference to the protagonists in David Markson's *Notecard Quartet*: *Reader's Block* ("Reader"), *This Is Not a Novel* ("Writer"), *Vanishing Point* ("Author"), *The Last Novel* ("Novelist").

The only books you recall reading that exclusively use 2ⁿᵈ person are *A Jello Horse* by Matthew Simmons, *Ablutions* by Patrick deWitt, and *Suicide* by Édouard Levé.

You read Gabi Losoncy's *Second Person* over summer break, published in 2017 by Amphetamine Sulphate.

If there were an epigraph at the beginning of this text, it might be from *Second Person*:

The more of you there are, the better off we are.

The other significant change from the initial drafts is the removal of much of the self-reflexive material that refers to edits in the text as they are made.

The 1st appearance of such material occurs early in the draft of the 1st chapter:

Student edits out the word "the" from the above fragment 21 times.

Also removed, just once each, are the words "his," "an," and "is."

Student finds and cuts another "the" upon rereading, bringing the total to 22.

Student cuts another "his," making that 2.

In the fragment referenced in the above 4 fragments, Student changes the word "activity" to the word "action" 5 times.

The above 5 fragments were written before the commitment to make all fragments in the primary section of the text a single sentence, before the omission of the word "the" is applied exclusively to the recording documentation section of the text, and before future editing sessions reverse much of the activity being referenced.

Other content removed includes references to Ishmael Reed's daughter Timothy, Anna Kavan's father's suicide, Peter Kowald's heart attack, Virginia Woolf's suicide, and Anthony Braxton's fast-food endorsement.

The Charles Gayle material is a late addition to the 1st chapter.

Instead of ending with the Markson quotes, the 1st chapter draft ends:

Student replaces "is starting to fear" with "fears" above the fragment above the above fragment.

The fragment referenced in the above fragment shifts when the fragment currently in that position takes its place.

Student cuts the fragment referenced in the above 2 fragments.

The majority of the content in the 2nd section you send to *Sleepingfish*, as you note in the above email, has since been removed.

The only fragments from that version of the 2nd section that still exist in the current text are the Mark Baumer and *The Red Barn* launch material, reestablishing their positions in the chapter now titled *Slides of Color.*

The only Baumer material that gets cut is the bio for Boots Walking In America included in a *Sleepingfish* issue [reprinted in this issue, page 136], which first appears after the section moves to *Slides of Color.*

Boots Walking in America was born in America. He got his first library card before his left pupil fully opened. He was 4. His mother had a bad grease rash on her face, but he still loved her. When Books Walking in America finally became an adult he got a job at the local university gas station. Later, he was promoted to emptying the van. He has never left the continent.

The 2nd section quickly incorporates the most extensive use of the self-reflexive edits, the indulgence perhaps marking the beginning of the end of their primary role.

You then reference the origins and characteristics of horse hair on bass bows, *The Red Barn* and "Let Me See the Colts," Nietzsche's demise after witnessing the beating of a horse, *The Turin Horse* by Béla Tarr, and your mom's job as a horse-carriage driver.

The horse carriage becomes a way to talk about a man your mom meets while working that becomes a very close family friend, coming to all of your basketball games—including the one that put you in the hospital with a serious concussion, which you discuss in more detail in the cut material—your biggest fan, who tragically ended his life, shooting himself in the head when you were 15.

After introducing the *The Red Barn* and Mark Baumer material, you end the draft of the 2nd section with the 1st reference to "(Cuts from) Antithesis" and a story of a brief interaction with a man outside your place of employment at the time, just prior to attending University.

Student cuts over a page of fragments, beginning with one previously occupying this position, and places them in a new document titled "(Cuts from) Antithesis."

While standing in front of the record shop on a slow day, Student is approached by a large man, about 6'6" or 6'7", with the same name as the name of the record shop, looking to be around the same age as

Student, wearing a Knicks hat, which Student compliments.

He's been living on the street since walking from another town a bit west.

A fight with his girlfriend, he says.

Asks Student for some money, apologizing repeatedly.

Student gives the man some money.

The man thanks Student, repeatedly, they pound fists, the man goes on his way.

According to Google Maps, the town the man walked from is 41.3 miles away.

A few days later in the shop, a regular customer mentions to Student that a shooting happened the night before just a block away.

Unsure of the details, other than the victim's last known residence—the same town the man with the same name as the record shop claimed to have walked from.

He scored his 1000th point on January 26th, 2000, finishing his high-school career with 1178 points, says the obituary.

A single gunshot wound to the head, according to reports.

He was always happiest when on the basketball court, the obituary says.

Student reaches the 1000-point milestone in the final game of the season, the final game of Student's career, finishing with 1020 in total, which must have been sometime in February 1999, a few months before leaving for Conservatory.

The above fragments below the fragment referencing "(Cuts from) Antithesis" were cut and (re)pasted from the beginning of the document "(Cuts from) Antithesis," with some additional cuts and edits.

It's difficult to trace the trajectory of the motion, as the "(Cuts from) Antithesis" document has become increasingly disorganized, but it seems the initial ideas for *Potential Literature* and the Oulipo material are first incorporated into the 2nd section, or into material emerging from that section, before it becomes its own chapter.

You find material prefaced with the heading *[at the end of the OULIPO section]* referencing the man referenced above, indicating it is either an extension of the 2nd section draft composed after it was sent to *Sleepingfish*, or part of an additional section meant to follow it that has also been cut.

The day referenced in the above fragment is March 5th.

Student cuts the fragments introducing the man referenced in the next fragment when Student makes the new document "(Cuts from) Antithesis."

The man who got shot in the head a few days after interacting with Student outside the record shop, who also had the same first name as the record shop, was born on March 5th, 1982.

Student shifts the fragment initially in this position above the above fragment, and replaces "above" with "next" between "the" and "fragment."

After editing and resending a submission for the *Sleepingfish* 20th-anniversary issue, you cut the next 6 pages of this chapter following this fragment, consisting of references to chapters that no longer exist.

THEIR HANDS HOLD

In the woods, the man the father brought home walked with the daughter. When they stepped close enough, her shoulder grazed above his elbow. He said to her to watch how when he puts his fingers like this and she puts his fingers like that, their hands hold. She had held mother hands and father hands and brother hands, but never any other hands. She felt the difference running up her arm and touched the trees she passed with her other hand, hoping to spread the feeling further.

WHAT HE PICTURED HER BODY HAD BECOME

His sister was, because she was, alive and always breathing. Now he can't swim, or fully wash, because the river is hers now. The pull feels much too strong for every step he enters. At his heels, his shins, he feels her invitation. If his knees would ever fall beneath the surface, he'd expect a rock just big enough to knock loose his footing. Once he was in, he'd feel her rush water from upriver to fill him faster in the lungs to keep him heavy toward the muck. The water in his ears would be filled with spells she left on her way down, and he'd follow the same path until they were back together again. Her song she sang would get louder as he'd go. He'd sing the same song until he was silent. When the ends of their lives would end in the same place, her body would be what he pictured her body had become. He'd settle near her bones and her dress would have dissolved. The clothes he wore would start to do the same. His eyes would have a brief time it took to see until the fish picked them blind. He'd have last thoughts of how sister could grow before him and he could grow behind and the cows they loved should be different cows, and they could have loved each other more.

MARVELOUS TECHNOLOGY LINES THE WA-
-LLS. A STEP SEQUENCER DICTATES THE OPER-
ATION. INUMMERAL CROWDS FILTER THROUGH
THE VARIOUS HOUSING COMPARTMENTS,
HANDSHAKING CONSTANTLY. A LOW-BATTERY
JAZZ MACHINE STRAYS FROM THE PULS E.
GORGEOUSLY, CHAOS ENSUES.

GHOST HOLE

The girl has a phone she won't update. She walks on the hot garbage sidewalk and looks up at glass buildings. Sun glints off them, portals made of gold you approach, disappear into. Splotches of water shimmer with nothing behind. The girl takes out her phone, takes a photo, opens the yellow app with the empty white space in the shape of a ghost. A miniature of the gold-sheeted building flashes for a few seconds, then quickly disappears. She clicks in the app to its map feature. Blue ghosts for boys and pink ghosts for girls and white ghosts for those who chose not to or couldn't be bothered to specify. Attached to names, phone numbers, saved in her phone. Coded ghosts glitch around a map of the world. She spreads her fingers to bring them closer. College ghosts clump around stucco bungalows and dried-out rivers, from the last time her phone updated. That was three years ago. Now the space of a country stretches between them.

Other phones update. People who are not old, people who are not perverted, no longer use the app, mostly. The girl used the app in its prime. She liked how, when using the app, the way she looked and the things that she said were made impermanent.

The girl zooms in on the east. New York State, then city. Something to do with her fingers. Ghosts overlap, crowd each other. She pinches the screen. They spread out with increased specificity. She zooms so the only ghost that she sees is her own. She zooms and she zooms. Still there is another.

A blue ghost so magnified she can see its pixelation. Nearly touching the girl's colorless outline. The girl pinches and the blue ghost won't go away. She cannot see the names of cross streets or building numbers— the app is not that specific—but the blue ghost can't be far. It moves around on the screen, then returns to its initial position: bouncing as if trapped in a box, an office or apartment, only moving to use the bathroom or refill its water. Or maybe the blue ghost is outside, on the ground, at the girl's level. Leaned against the side of a building, cigarette falling from its mouth's ghostly 'o'. The girl clicks the blue icon. A username leaps out. Sans-serif, casual. The girl could have dropped her phone. She zooms in closer.

She met him dressed only in bedsheets. Not draped over her head with the eyes cut, so you could just see her ankles. The sheet the girl wore when she met him was cream and not white. The top sheet she took off her twin bed because it was time for the party. She tied it in knots like a sail. Wound it around her torso, so it covered her crotch. She wore nothing underneath. She wore only a clean, white pair of underwear. She pulled from the glass bottle on her desk—the desk branded with a seal to remind that it was not her own—a long pull, but not too long. Long enough so that she could leave her room wearing only her sheet. The girl left her small room and its wooden toy furniture. The girl went to the party where they would meet.

The blue ghost moves on the screen in sustained motion. It does not bounce back to its point of origin. The girl presses her back to the nearest building, like this could make her invisible. Here he is—his pixelated approximation—mere inches or feet or a quarter of a mile from her. Here is this ghost of a boy, moving. A ghost in the girl's immediate region. He is and she is, and that is what they have become to each other. The girl stares so hard at her screen that she sees the blue ghost shrink down and move on top of her own, so as to appear inside of the girl's ghost vagina. She focuses her vision and the blue ghost is outside her, not sucked into her ghostly folds. That is the good thing about ghosts: they don't have vaginas. Eunuchs in the sheets of their skin, flat, nothing to extend or to put yourself into. If only the girl had worn the beige bedsheet over her head with holes at her eyes. She could have drifted through the party, triangular and sexless.

Tall and gold-headed, the boy had been older. He knew enough to know how to tie his white sheet, to wear athletic shorts underneath it. When did the pill materialize in her drink? Had it been a pill at all, or a powder, something liquid and insidious? The point of the pill is that the girl could not know this. She woke up like a caterpillar: naked, her body in its thin fuzz of hair. He had zipped her into a sleeping bag.

The girl follows the blue ghost on her phone with her eyes and her feet. Maintaining her ghost's initial distance. She doesn't know exactly what that distance is. She isn't sure she would want to see the gold back of his head where it sat on his neck. All she sees is his ghostly approximation. Gliding down sidewalks, past juice stores and places to build luxury salads. Rounding corners, appearing partway inside the corner building.

Is he somehow both in and outside it? Or is this some glitch of the app, something in between?

After the night that they met the girl faked tonsillitis. She told her roommate it had transmuted into mono. Sometimes the girl's roommate brought containers of raw carrots or kombucha back to her in their room. Otherwise, the girl did not eat. She watched all of the *Ocean's* trilogy eight times. She didn't hear anything or see any of the actors, the people. She saw the thousands of dots of color combine to make the shape of those particular people, and how quickly they then disappeared.

Two weeks after they met the boy sent the girl a photo message: a photo of his hand spearing something meaty, something bloody. The photo disappeared. She had not known that his house had a grill. Little words appeared in the chat: *do u wanna hang out sometime.* The girl's uninfected throat stopped burning. She resumed going to class. Going to parties. She sent the boy vanishing photo messages then appeared at his house. She'd materialize at his door and forget the walk over. Pass through the dried lawns of California bungalows, stop on a green one. She wouldn't realize where she was standing until sprinklers turned on with their timer. She stood in the arched spray. Droplets suspended, flickering, like silver bugs. The boy's house was next door and by the time she arrived she was dry.

Another time, the girl arrived at his house muddy. The boy took the girl to his shower and cleaned her from her calves to her feet. He used an unabsorbent cloth that pulled the mud down her legs, turning it liquid. *All clean,* he said, but the rest of her was still filthy. He took the girl, wearing only mud and her underwear, soaked from sitting on the floor of the tub, to his room, past his roommates. Her feet and ankles glowing a sick shade of white. The boy's housemates would have seen the girl's nipples had they looked over. The housemates heard the boy's grunting, his bed moving, and not the girl.

The blue ghost dips underground. The girl's ivory ghost then descends— how did she pass through the turnstile? The two ghosts vanish with each loss of signal, with each jolted hinge of the subway's acceleration. Throbbing on the screen, they materialize at every passed station, with each momentary return of service. Passing through a black that the map can't compute: only two ghosts, gyrating, disappeared into this new world of nothing.

On generous days, the boy made her food on his stove: white cheese and green peas in shell pasta. He never gave her a bowl. They ate over the stove with the wooden spoon used for stirring. The food slipped down the tunnel of the girl's throat. It never hit any bottom.

Up from underground, the girl watches the blue ghost float three blocks, then pass through a wall. It stops. The girl stops and she is inside the front hallway, past the locked vestibule, of a converted brownstone. How did she make it through so many doors? The blue ghost is on top of her but she cannot see him. Her ghost, the cream ghost, glitches so it is outside the building. It returns to the girl, returns beneath the blue, then bounces outside again. The girl pinches her screen, zooms in as close as her phone will let her, until it is made only of glittering pixelations, the cream of her ghost, the hundreds of colored splotches blurred and smoothed in order to make it. She passes through the side of the wall so that she is outside with her ghost. It hops to the side. The girl moves with it. Moves with it until they are again underground, disappearing, then reemerging into the black. Surfacing in Bay Ridge, floating by the side of the water that you cannot see on the ghost's map. Only a ditch drenched in a gold sort of yellow.

The night that the girl first met the boy, when she woke zipped in fleece, the boy was already gone. He spelled her name wrong in a note saying that he'd had fun. The girl's underwear were on the floor, partly torn, somewhat liquid and bloody. Her sheet in a ball on the floor by the bedpost. No reconfiguration of the sheet covered enough of her body.

The trees outside turned from black to a green sort of gray. The sound of sizzling, a pan moving. Somebody shifting and humming. The girl hung the sheet over her head. It barely covered her crotch. But through it she could not see the roommate or his omelet. Couldn't see the old bungalows and their sun-rotted lawns as she passed them. A warm breeze lifted and the girl felt the trace of it on her crotch, slightly aching, somewhat throbbing, but as if from a great distance, part of some other body. The girl couldn't see the man and his little dog where he curbed it. Or was it that they couldn't see her? The man didn't scream, didn't say anything, when she retched and vomit leaked out from beneath the sheet. The dog barked, that was it. No human recognition, no sound of exclamation, at this faceless orb, pulled down their sidewalk.

Phones go through a series of mandated and optional updates. Ghosts on the map of the yellow app disappear, then re-emerge in the user's self-designed image. Ghosts can now wear a hat. Ghosts can listen to music wearing big headphones. Can sit in armchairs with *zzz*'s spilling out of their mouths. The boy's blue ghost dons yellow hair and then it gets a ghost puppy. It holds up cartoon fingers to show one wrapped in a gold band. Soon after that he disappears. From the girl's map, from her screen. The girl doesn't see this. Her coding remains as it was at 19. Years before this, on the night when they met. All she can see is her own ivory ghost, drifting across the screen of the phone that she doesn't update. Gliding, it passes under tunnels and to the roofs of unrecognized buildings. Her along with it. Disappearing, intermittently, the relief of total blackness. But then the ghost reappears. Throbbing, it fills the whole screen, all she has set to serve as her world.

SWEET T

My mother was always after my father's gun. It was embarrassing, really, her obsession. Once, she stole it right out of his holster. He had come home for lunch, in uniform, and he was leaning against her, pressing her into the counter. He was kissing on her, pinching her in different places, and she reached her hand around and unsnapped the snap and slid the gun out and screamed. She made a big show of it. She waved the gun in the air above her head in circles. She said something that sounded like "My Town!" but could have been "Lie Down!" or "Die Now!" or just about anything, "I'm Drown!" maybe. The circles got smaller and smaller until eventually she was holding it straight above her head, and shivering.

She said things to my father, all kinds of things, most of it we'd heard before, but still, the words embarrassed us.

The two boys, my brothers, rolled their eyes; they looked tough. I tried to look reasonable, which I figured to be the opposite of crazy. Crazy people rolled their heads all over their neck, like my mother was doing. I kept my head still and my neck long. I stood on tiptoes.

My father said a few sweet words, he called her his special names, like T-bone, and Sweet T. He looked like he was listening to every word she said, like he was trying to understand her.

"Do you see me?" she asked.

"Do you see me?" he asked.

We three onlookers blushed.

[*Note: "Sweet T" appeared previously in *Sleepingfish* issue 0.875, Justin Torres's 1st publication.]

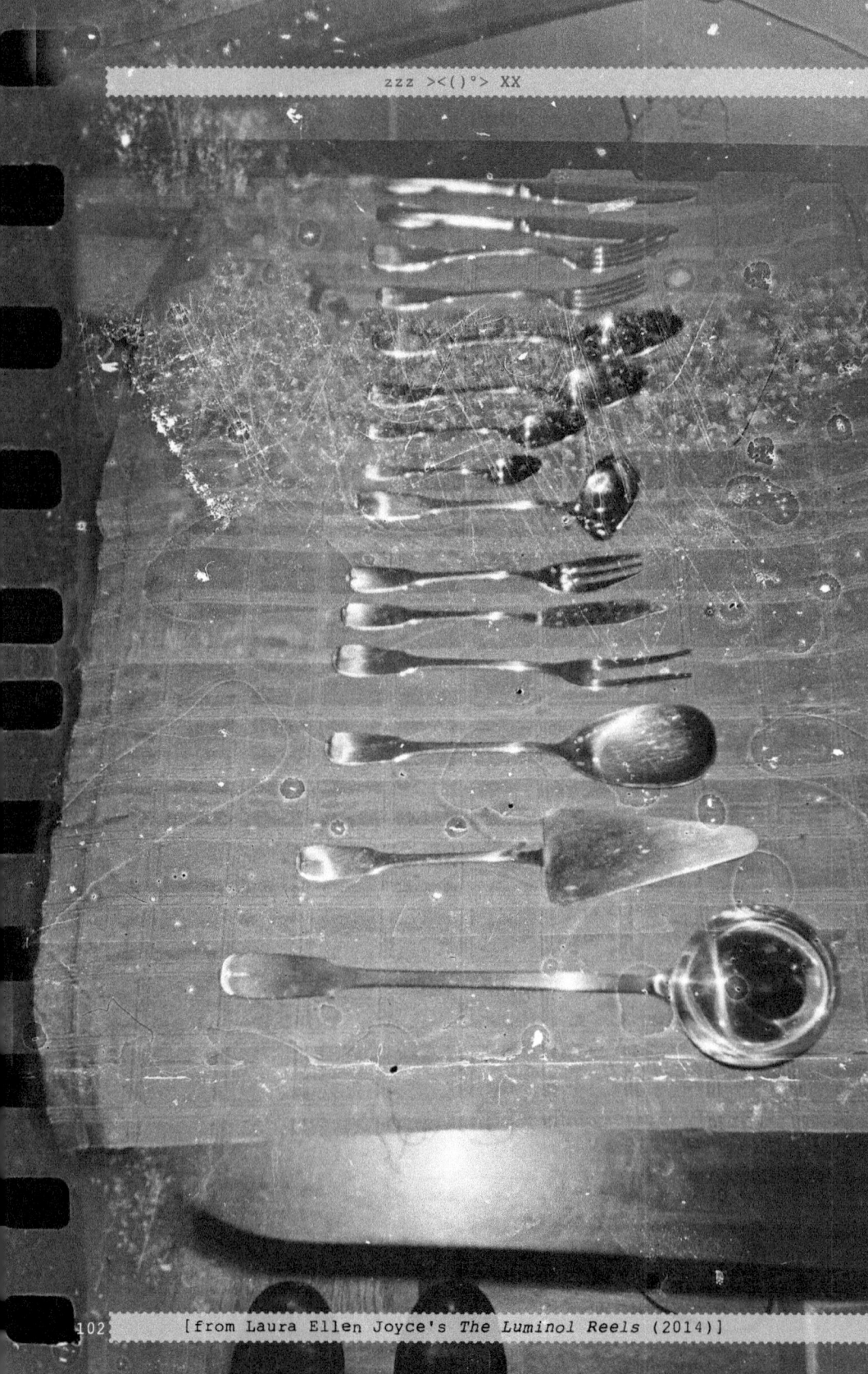

[from Laura Ellen Joyce's *The Luminol Reels* (2014)]

DAD

Every night before dinner our dad set the table, lighting candles, arranging silverware on folded napkins. When we sat down to eat he wanted everything to be perfect, peaceful and clean. It was the only time we were all together as a family, and he expected us to behave.

One night we decided to eat without forks and knives, scooping up mashed potatoes with our bare hands, letting the dog lick our fingers. Dad was always so serious and tired after work, and we wanted to make him laugh. We played with our silverware, probing our noses with forks until tears welled up in our eyes. He stared at his plate, determined to ignore us, and when we didn't stop, he sent us to our rooms. After letting a few minutes go by we snuck downstairs. The table was spotless. Eating in silence, with candlelight flickering in the empty room, Dad looked satisfied, even happy.

We ran home from school the next day and attacked his garden, tearing out flowers, digging up the roots with dirty hands. We snipped off the heads and scattered them all over the house. When he got home from work he filled the holes with fresh dirt and swept the floors. After he cleaned up we searched the garbage to see if he threw away the little heads, but he didn't. We don't know what he did with them.

When the trees changed color and scattered leaves around the yard he raked them into tidy piles, warning us not to jump on them. We set them on fire with matches from his pack of Marlboros. Smoke billowed up to our roof, flakes of ash sprinkled the driveway. He doused the flames with a hose, then spent the whole night scrubbing the stained concrete.

For Christmas he decorated the tree with balls of green and red glass. We tugged the ornaments off the tree limbs and used them for batting practice in the backyard. Dad hung them out of reach, higher and higher every year until we grew tall enough to reach the top, and then we didn't have Christmas trees anymore.

He made us laugh once. Setting the table, he mixed up our silverware, so that some of us had two forks, some of us had two knives, and some of us had two spoons. We didn't know if he did it on purpose or not, but we were so shocked we started cackling. We balanced our steak on spoons and lifted it, wobbling, up to our mouths. We hacked it to bits with our two knives. Using only forks we tore it to messy pieces. We giggled and howled, shaking in our chairs. He did it again the next night, setting two forks here, two knives there, two spoons there. This time we were ready. We traded with each other until we each had what we needed, and then we ate in silence. He didn't try to make us laugh again.

Jonathan Sargent

Rudy

It came with the territory, trying to catch lightning in a bottle.

We climbed on top of the middle school with empty Mexican Cokes and held our little hairless hands in the sky. Rudy got struck. Two weeks later Paul slipped and fell and cracked his head on the blacktop. Rudy's body vibrated like a cartoon. When he got struck, his bones turned glow-in-the-dark. Until they didn't.

Me, I've made out with some rain. I've kissed it on the cheek. It's kissed me back. I've brought a girl up to the roof. Only a few died. But many lived to love it. It took me some time but eventually I made it work and we caught that lightning. We caught rain, too. We caught mice and we caught bugs and we collected leaves that had collected in the gutters. We used pitchers and we used Culligan tanks, Coke cans too. Anything we could to get what we came for.

This is how I ended up running for School President. I started a vending machine. Inside there were Mexican Coke bottles filled with lightning. Kids wanted that. They wanted to feel like they were holding something alive in their small hands. I made them feel powerful, like they had weight to throw around. I was President for a while. I was even President after the first kids started dying. They chugged those bottles in the bathroom and put that lightning down inside them. And their insides became shredded with light. And a little razor of light cut through their abdomens. And they fell over on the tile and died.

I don't think I was fired. I resigned. The vending machines were replaced with claw machines. The girls I loved, they grew up and became doctors and architects. They were all good at math. It's true, I can teach people about people like me. We can all teach people about people. All I knew at this point was that I had to set out for the territory. I looked for Veronica but she was dead in the custodian's closet. There was soap on her hand. She smelled like Clorox.

There was only one way I knew how to leave. I climbed on top of the school again. I went past the big fans in their cubes all fenced in by chains. I kicked around a few pebbles and a few beads of rubber turf. I climbed a ladder to another ladder and then a plateau. I took a few steps back and then I ran and then I jumped and a bird swooped past and an insect buzzed in my ear and I reached my hands up and I caught the electrical line. I pulled myself up to my feet and I just started walking. I was like a pirate walking a plank but the plank just kept going and going.

I've been to many states. I don't eat. I haven't looked in the mirror since I was President. Sometimes in my mind's eye I am Rudy. Have you ever done that before? Have you ever become another person? You just say to yourself 100 times inside of your own mind *I am Rudy I am Rudy.* You see yourself in the third person as Rudy just walking. Rudy in this alternative life and he isn't dead because he climbed on top of a roof with you and a Mexican Coke and was struck by one sword slash of lightning in a black black night. *I am Rudy. I am Rudy.*

Rudy loved M&Ms and the color blue and prom, even though he was only a kid, and he never went to prom, he would always talk about it, how one day he would go to prom, and he would go to an after-party, and a girl, who was maybe/maybe not his girlfriend yet would come and sit on his lap in some stranger's basement and the tension had been building because he'd loved her but then never quite made it happen but it was now prom, and they would profess their love to each other.

Once I knew I went full Rudy is when I got down from the line. I am a businessman at heart. So I put my money where my mouth is. For 5 dollars I would vomit my own heart out of my chest and then eat it because this is what Rudy would do. If they were still alive, to do it. This thing that you know they would do.

12 · 12 · 12 · 12 · 12 · 12 · 12

However, many of these activities are reflexive in nature.
and secondary reactions which form so large a share of the
handicap are usually eliminated. When this happens, the fears

Signals he expects Duration of
to stutter spasm

$$(5) \quad f(x) \sim \frac{1}{2\pi} \int_{-\pi}^{\pi} f(x') \, dx'$$

4016529559

Word exposure   Signal to speak

FIG. 14.—Breathing record showing evidence of pre...
residual air.

of words and situations larg...
afraid of that which is not u...
terer learns that it is possible
no thwarting or social penalt...
blockings is actually pleasant.

12 · 12 · 12 · 12 · 12

(b)

Movement W | nd Quetzalcoatl AKA 4 Mot | on

4 Wind our LORD QUETZALCOATL "sets" his state-sanctioned hermanito Ulises El Segundo Chastitellez on his lap | camera rolls

| little snakey mic in El Segundo's manito held to 4WLQ's plumed grimaced visage | filmed conversation | roll on |

that great green jaw | main thing | 4WLQ's eyes are open
| cabeza never moves | El Segundo looks dead into camera | & El Segundo admits | pinkcheeks flushing flushing | how El Segundo O so appreciates his big plumed serpentine bruh & how 4WLQ's taken a firm wing shaping | li'l Ulises into well-mannered young caballero |

4WLQ smiles | yes | borgie borgie | taught this güey well

| rubs El Segundo's head | dishevels his Billy Budd locks | yup El Segundo's learned from his state-sanctioned big bruh that everyone makes mistakes & that it's okay | fine | bien | yes | & hey now pass some more of those beheaded quail | don't be stingy now

El Segundo nods to this | all true | pero suddenly El Segundo realizes | needs to ask his state-sanctioned mentordios something bien pronto | en chinga even | El Segundo's always wondered if 4W our Lord Q believes in you know something cosmic & grand | breathing | beating | yEpic |

¿you believe in yEpic 4 Wind | Lord Quetzalcoatl? |

now 4WLQ thinks hard abt this for twenty good segundos & responds that nah | | not here in our pueblo | nah | mejór for practiced novelisms he sez | & restuffs his 20th century semi-official document from his Velcro-snapping wallet | & that's okay see bruh | 's all okay | no yEpic's zokay | 's okay Segundo

| 's okay | not going to hell only going to AZtlán | that's all | li'l Segundo | Al Norte

1. Red Earth translated excerpt

The spray of blood rising to the temples, the
shivering limbs, the loss of balance, the awkward fall.

The particular sequence of frames depicting when
power, frozen and exerted by two warriors is equal.
There is a reach for success. The demise of one and
the ascension of the other.

A gripped neck. Fingers squeezing blood out of a face
·pinned to the ground, in submission and fatigue, a
failure, a bloody failure of the maladjusted
arrangement of bones, ligaments, muscles, adrenal
latitudes, blood, cells—ultimately submission to a
defeat.

Michael Salu

Direct Translation Diptych 1 | 80cm x 40cm | 2021

This series employs a series of processes, automated and manual, to construct a diptych of cross-ontological translation. Small sections of prose from *Red Earth*, a work attempting to engage inherent Yoruba philosophical tradition, are translated to colour data using a GAN model. The subsequent outputs are combined with an additional model, which enables outputs of 3D mesh data with vertex displacements based on the patterns and distinctions in each original prose paragraph. The model calculates some compositional representation of the prose, like weather forces, allowing them to form circumstantially as a kind of alternative geology in which the materials or skins are full of the prose data. These mesh outputs are then manually accentuated and sculpted in 3D.

CADMIUM

Cadmium exhibits wonderful properties as a pigment. It produces colors from lemon yellow to the yellow-orange of a mango to the brilliant red of stoplights. It can be heated to a high degree without flaking or blistering. While portrait painters daubed tiny patches of cadmium yellow to light up the floral background behind a lady's head, factory workers sprayed cadmium paints directly out of grimy nozzles onto steam pipes and machine parts. Cadmium has no known biological function in higher organisms. It is not used as a dietary supplement. Healers don't grind it into almond paste and serve it to women who feel that they must improve their base nature. Cadmium paints have long-lasting properties and can be applied to glass, and to metal parts subjected to heat and stress. The red stars that adorn the Kremlin gain their color from cadmium. These, lit up at night and in the gloomy afternoon, shine their beacons undisturbed. Their red doesn't fade with time, or not in the amount of time a human being notices.

The United States Army sprayed zinc cadmium sulfide over Minneapolis in 1950. The United States Army declared in its own records that this substance *was not known* to cause health problems if inhaled or ingested. This is at least a misstatement, if not a knowing falsehood. The zinc cadmium sulfide was employed as a simulant. Its actions in the air mimicked another substance, maybe plutonium, that was actually malicious. The cadmium wafted out of blowers and sifted onto window ledges, over roof tops, onto parking lots. It clung to the eaves of dog houses and coated the chilly slats of park benches. A woman walked to the corner store, holding her hat onto her head with one hand, and with the other leading a reluctant little boy. "I don't want to walk!" he said. "You're big enough now," she answered. He'd spent the past week lying on his back with his feet in the air, sucking his thumb. He was playing his version of his baby self, this younger him who he felt had a better deal than his current form. The substance burrowed into the felt of his mother's hat. The little boy drew it into his lungs as he pulled against his mother's grip on his wrist. "Danny, don't," she said.

The cadmium swirled up and around corners, tossed by the whims of that shiftless joker, the wind. The wind in Minneapolis blows primarily on the napes of its inhabitants, following them and easing itself into the patches of skin exposed above the shirt collar. Even on the coldest days, many of the inhabitants wear only plaid shirts and rationalize that they don't have far to go. I've seen Minneapolis residents walking to work in gym shorts in February, bare legs sticking out of an unzipped puffy coat. Women run to the bus stop in high-heeled sandals, not even bothering to pull their gloves out of their pockets. The wind keeps up a steady huff against the backs of these people's necks and bare knees and exposed wrists.

Eighty-one field experiment hours, and eleven thousand, one hundred and seventy man-hours went into the diffusion of zinc cadmium sulfide over Minneapolis in 1950. Crews of men sent out the substance with foggers or blowers at various points around the city. From street corners and from the balconies of three-story boarding houses, they set the simulant loose. They had contacted the city government and said that they would be studying ways to shroud a city in smoke to hide it in case of nuclear attack. Some cities were being considered to take part in this experiment, and it was possible that Minneapolis was one of them. If something were to happen, or seem to happen, this shrouding experiment might be what had taken place. That was all they could say. Residents were not to be informed, but the city government received this smidgen of information about a tentative operation. The notes I was able to acquire through a publicly available source reveal that the Parks Commissioner objected, though none of his words are recorded. The notes say only that this problem was solved when the role of Parks Commissioner changed hands during a new city administration. He could have been fired, or left in outrage after his demands for more information about this operation went unanswered. He could have been one of those people who started the trend to move to Montana in search of freedom. His friends probably called him a crank. He should have retired long ago, they said behind his back. After all, he'd been too old to fight overseas. All the young men coming back and getting married needed jobs like his.

Cadmium may enter the body by ingestion or inhalation, entry by inhalation representing the greater hazard. In France, three hundred workers who had drunk wine kept in cadmium-lined containers became ill, some seriously. Symptoms included weakness and gastrointestinal distress. Other workers were diagnosed with cadmium poisoning from inhalation after they had melted cadmium ingots in a poorly ventilated room. They reported dryness of the throat, headache, nausea, and brown urine. Symptoms of chronic cadmium poisoning among workers making ferro-nickel storage batteries were preceded by a characteristic yellow pigmentation of the teeth. This is known as the "yellow ring of cadmium."

A doctor described the case of a worker who succumbed to thick yellow fumes given off when cutting up cadmium-plated steel torpedo heads. Another worker died five days after shaking by hand molten metal containing ten percent cadmium. Six similar cases had been seen over eight years, all exhibiting the same symptoms of weakness, chronic bronchitis, and loss of weight.

An industrial iron, such as those used to smooth cloth in textile factories, may be coated with a cadmium pigment due to its excellent heat resistance. School buses, known for their brilliant yellow, in fact owe their hue to cadmium. Anyone who has lived on a county highway has encountered the piercing glare of school bus headlights, accompanied by a rotating orange beam in the middle of the roof. Out of the fog, the bus itself finally arrives, publishing its ghastly hue. Anyone who has rented a shitty little house up a road from a county highway knows the persistence of fog in its ditches, and the waist-high billowings on practically any morning. The school bus wades through the dense vapor, its wheels invisible but its yellow sides appearing in segments. The windows are black in the early morning. The school kids lean their heads against them and listen to music through their earbuds, oblivious, half conscious, or all the way asleep.

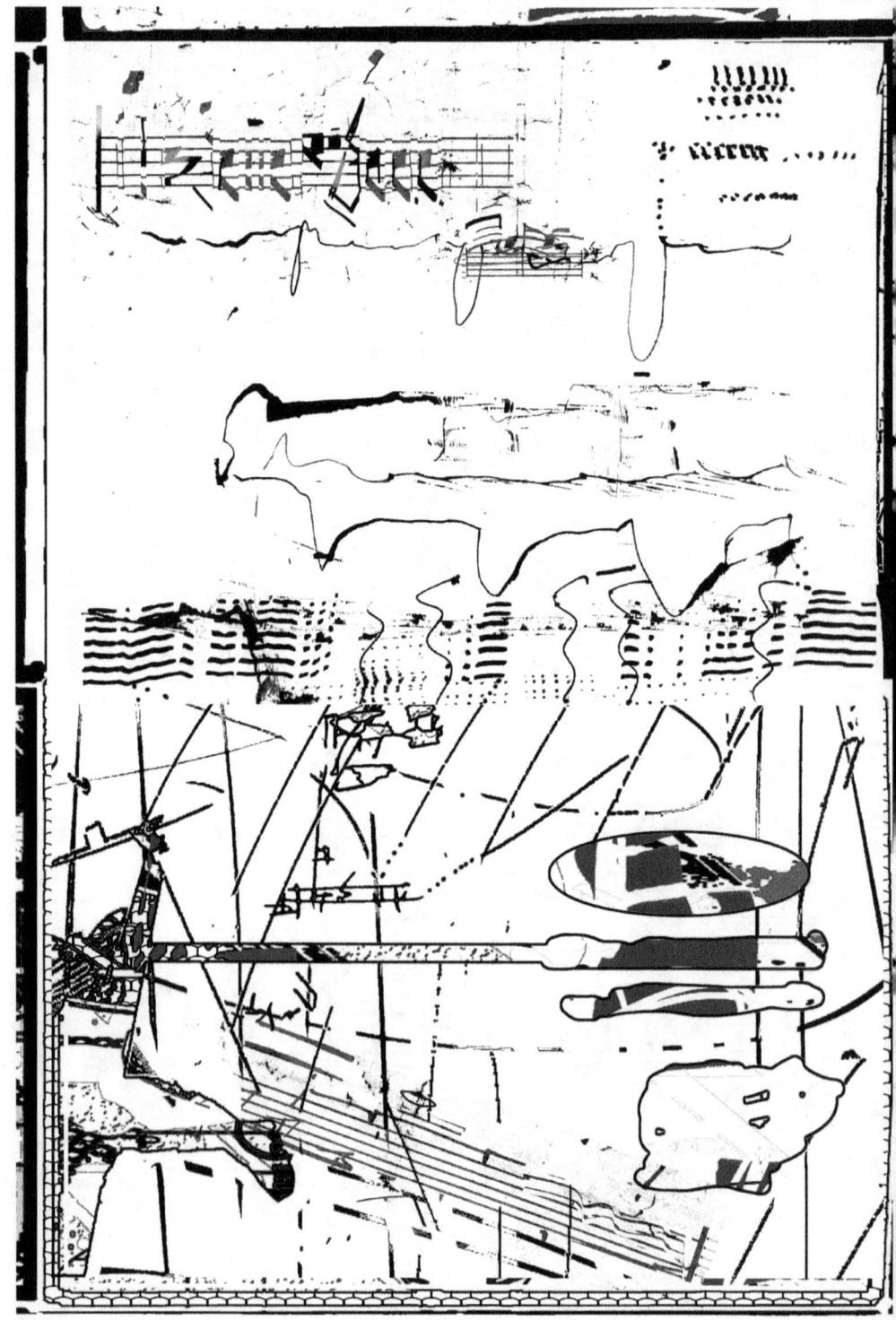

Rosaire Appel

I'm drawn to remoteness.

Weather expands the desert. Sand blows into the city. The city is made of glass. Adaptive glass, glass that alters perception, glass that can bend, touch, glass that lets me see you crystalline.

We mine the quarry, trucks leave with sand. The grass? To offset what? The weather. The grass keeps the dust down. It takes up water. This experiment—observation, gradient. The plane of sky over the desert. I find an anchor in the grass, my eyes measure it.

Was it an ocean or a glacier that shaped the valley? In my imagination it doesn't matter. Mineral deposits, exact silicate, what's in and around the quarry, bits of plastic, the chemicals we spray on the grass, the salt at the edges of dried drainages—we measure these variables. Your view is planetary.

I stand in front of you looking out the window. One hand is on my back, the other reaches over my shoulder and you point to something. You try to line your hand up with my eye, direct my sight.

Listen, you say. Look. You point.

I have no fixed position.

It's true that I need to see how I've moved in order to see where to move next. What observation has uncovered.

The brightness is exact or collapses what's seen now. You say, only in distance is there—

Your nearness?

I feel a distance waiting. Pick up a pencil. My look reaches, hits glass, bends back.

What measure is in the grass before I define it? Or before you tell me what to look for? I look up at the window. We know what glass is. We send sand out and it comes back like this. I send myself out. I walk through the field and come back as what? Yours?

Wires glint along the grass blades. Tall grasses, thin as wire, green and yellowed, brown and white. A mass tangled and dry at the bases, in and out of sand. The grasses along the wire, not much wider than it in places, and blank spots in the line where the grass has died and been culled, cleared out. Tall, thin grasses. Mostly still, mostly upright. Then bending over, then broken, then green and dewy, then letting off seed, then emerging between the rows, at the edge of the building. Then only in record, then on the screen, then plotted, then averaged, their mean growth, their mean intake, their mean grip on the sand, their mean hold on my eyes their total mass their variable release their explicit form their inching their width ceasing their trace on my knees

See, I perceive the nearness of things and their remotenesses.

Your hip: I trail my finger along it. There is ground here, sand and glass.

Split my vision. Show me the desert all at once this instant.

A dune can split in two. A dune's crawl is not how I move but perhaps how I'd like to. A less than inching, a breadth I can't step.

Where are your manners? The way you pick up a pencil?

I'm over the landscape the way a bird is. I count each frictive gathering.

Kelly Krumrie

NOTIONS (about the object under investigation)

[it] can be partitioned into finitely many parts to be shifted by a rigid motion and reassembled into an object whose extensive properties are the same as the original one

[what] the writer and the reader interact with does not require shifts, nor transitional signs

the value of any quantity is measurable, at any time and to an arbitrary accuracy, without significantly influencing the original state of the system

signification rests on a presemantic underpinning of some sort in the writing | reading process

both approaches fail to hold

geometrical entities consist of an uncountable number of null sets [points] – infinity does not compensate for zero

words consist of an arbitrary number of unstable subsets [signs] – signification does not compensate for the temporary | seeming meaninglessness

a measurement is both an operational procedure about the observable and a phenomenon in itself, subject to the same laws it investigates

a word is both a procedure defining the object it points to and a phenomenon in itself, subject to the same laws it investigates

a not negligible interaction is established between the measuring apparatus and the investigated system

writing does not reveal some pre-existing value of the written word: how the particular outcome of signification is brought into being is inherently

the act of measurement determines the value of the

observable

unknowable

transition

transition

from possible to actual

from sign to word

LUNAR PHASES

the moon is demonstrably not there when nobody looks
nobody demonstrably looks when the moon is not there
nobody demonstrably looks there when the moon is not

[permutations after N. D. Mermin]

how does the whole land geographically relate to the landscape?

the text is demonstrably not there when nobody reads
nobody demonstrably reads when the text is not there
nobody demonstrably reads there when the text is not

how does the whole lan-gauge metrically relate to the text?

is what the writer sees [what the reader attempts to] the lithic essence of the
text? a long-standing enlightenment?

th ink of
the ink   dots   [instances of the untranslatable]
                   do[n']t
                   get absorbed in

the result [cause] of writing [the word]
the result of erasing [the thing the word is]
the result of erasing writing [the thing]
the mark made by it [the word the thing is]

[observable] a priori entity of em-   [word] a priori entity of readable
pirical observation   signification • negligeable subset of
                                        readable signs • degree of freedom
                                        of the text, related to its transforma-
                                        tion across languages, that manifests
                                        itself, under certain circumstances,
                                        in a particular kind of writing

Federico Federici

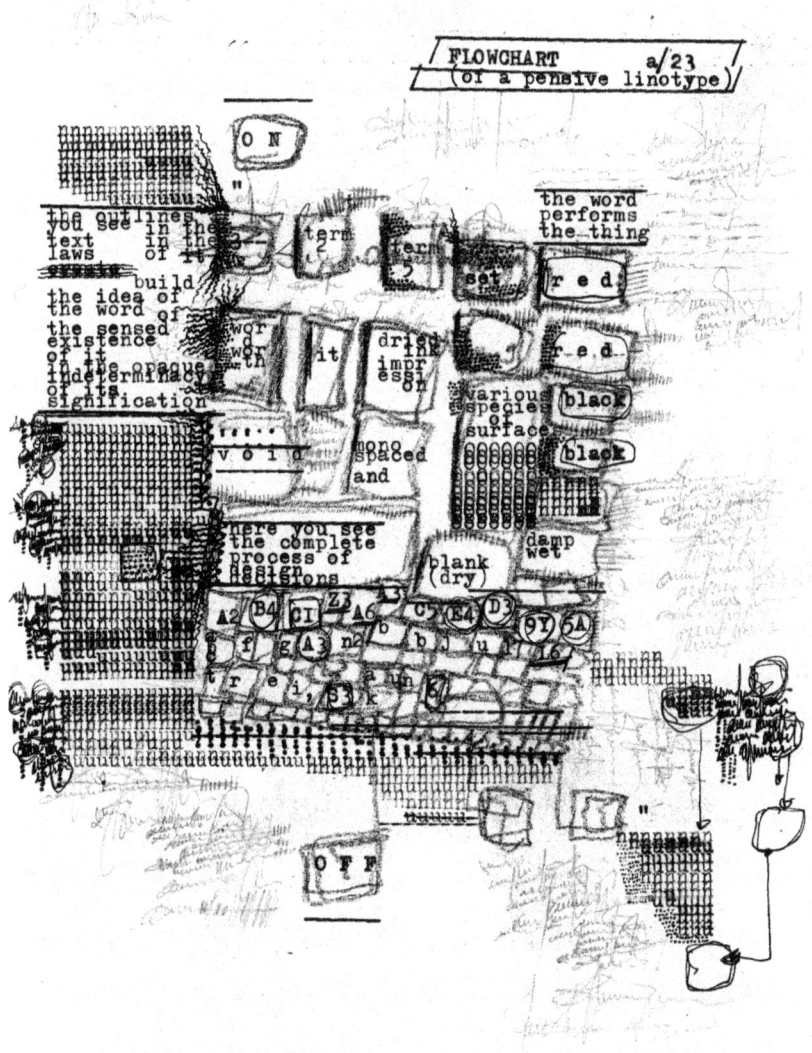

FLOWCHART a/23
(of a pensive linotype)

[hidden signs theorem] text-objects [possess properties that] exceed reading

the reading process establishes an unstable interaction with their state

[sufficient criterion of reality] an element of reality exists if the corresponding value of a physical quantity can with certainty be predicted without disturbing the system, the latter being in an eigenstate of the observable associated with that value

```
"  "   "  "    ""  "     "  ""
"       "   "          "  ""   ""
"   "    "  "      ""      "  "
""      "  "    "  "          "
"  ""  ""   ""  "  "  ""   "  "
""  ""    "    "  ""   ""
```

[alleged] indeterminacy of a grid of removed signification: some metrics is always implied

[minimal requirement | calibration condition] whenever the system is in an eigenstate, the apparatus indicates the corresponding eigenvalue after the interaction has ceased

```
"/muːn/"   "/muːn/"    "/muːn/"
"/muːn/"     "/muːn/"   "/muːn/"
"/muːn/"  "/muːn/"       "/muːn/"
"/muːn/"    "/muːn/"    "/muːn/"
"/muːn/" "/muːn/"        "/muːn/"
"/muːn/""/muːn/""       "/muːn/"
"/muːn/"    "/muːn/"   "/muːn/"
"/muːn/"    "/muːn/"   "/muːn/"
"/muːn/"    "/muːn/" "/muːn/"
"moon"
```

the hesitation   to keep the levels of reality intact
                   to imagine a completer awareness
the distance   between what is read[able] and what is real

a real measurement should point to a definite position

[readable] words | [mutually] dischargeable pointers

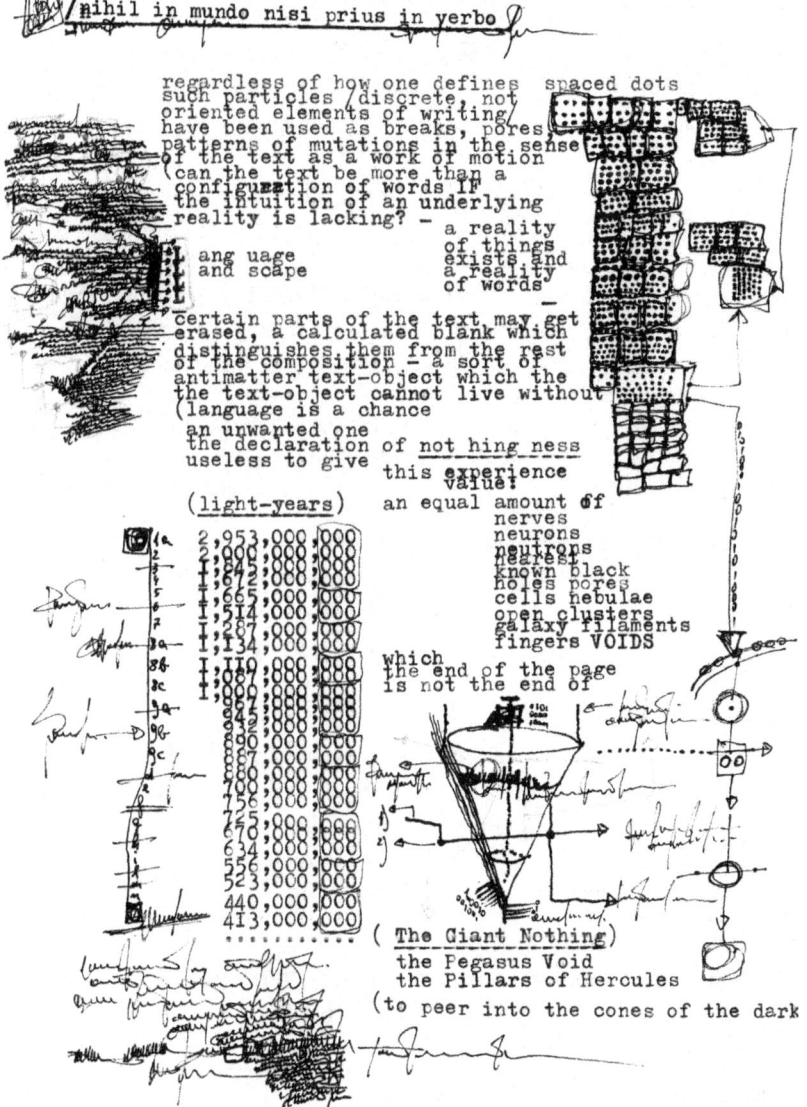

nihil in mundo nisi prius in verbo

regardless of how one defines   spaced dots
such particles /discrete, not
oriented elements of writing/
have been used as breaks, pores,
patterns of mutations in the sense
of the text as a work of motion
(can the text be more than a
configuration of words IF
the intuition of an underlying
reality is lacking? - a reality
                              of things
   ang uage   exists and
   and scape   a reality
                              of words

certain parts of the text may get
erased, a calculated blank which
distinguishes them from the rest
of the composition - a sort of
antimatter text-object which the
the text-object cannot live without
(language is a chance
an unwanted one
the declaration of not hing ness
useless to give   this experience
                        value:
(light-years)   an equal amount of
                              nerves
                              neurons
                              neutrons
                              known black
                              holes pores
                              cells nebulae
                              open clusters
                              galaxy filaments
                              fingers VOIDS

2,953,000,000
2,000,000,000
1,672,000,000
1,665,000,000
1,517,000,000
1,134,000,000
1,110,000,000
1,069,000,000
967,000,000
842,000,000
800,000,000
880,000,000
756,000,000
725,000,000
670,000,000
634,000,000
523,000,000
440,000,000
413,000,000

which
the end of the page
is not the end of

(The Giant Nothing)
the Pegasus Void
the Pillars of Hercules
(to peer into the cones of the dark

[objectification problem
collapse problem in the text-environment]

IF{ a configuration of signs | words exists characterized by some recognisable signification • a spike triggers its collapse • a wave of signification Ψ attempts to constrain the dynamic}

an observable has no definite value, the object-plus-apparatus is in an entangled state}

|eigen−|gegen|entangled|

IF{ it sets and retains the signification field wherein the word-sign duality manifests itself • it is both the outer frame and the inner law}

an account of the measuring process is required for semantic completeness, the system is semantically inconsistent}

[what means for an observable to have a definite value]

other signs | words • strata of fossilated languages surface

the tension between the collapse process [random event] and the deterministic dynamics of

a closed system

the method translates semantic collisions into [semi]-structured domains of heterogeneous signs
[open text-environment]

a measurement scheme that leaves the state of the object unchanged defines a trivial observable whose measure probability is independent of the state itself

a writing scheme that leaves the state of signification of the signs unchanged defines a trivial text-object whose likely signification is independent of the state itself

the notion of instrument describes the state changes that follow an act of measurement

the notion of reader describes the signification changes that follow an act of writing

neither a mere spectator • nor indeed a character

no information gain without some disturbance

to write is to disturb text-objects

to measure is to disturb
the object-system

not to reify an idealised notion of it

Federico Federici

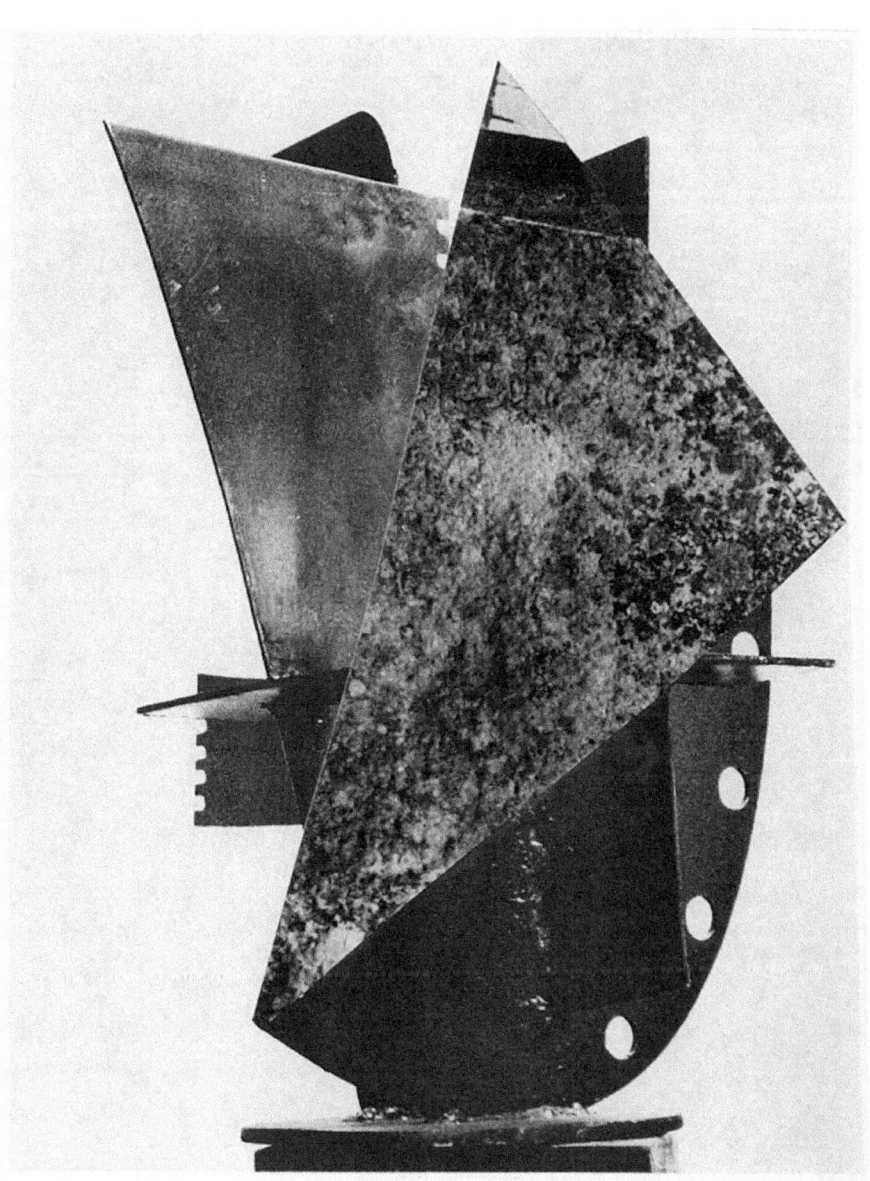

Carla Rak

4. Red Earth translated excerpt

A voice that is — at least as I understand now in this
frozen frame — to be an accumulation of moments
and geological elements; like differing climates, or
spirits mined from the earth and burnt into the sky, or
shoals of fish drifting on currents, passing through
disintegrating coral, dispersed by danger and on to the
abstraction of a coordinate—the abstraction of being
somewhere.

A gust of wind upon a cheek.

A dying wave creeping over one's toes, another death
following closely behind.

A voice of altitudes and airborne flora, soon
accompanied by layers of smoke from burning wood,
metastasising into soil and its spirits, crumbling into
smaller and smaller forms shaped by salt from the sea.

Direct Translation Diptych 2

Diptych. Mixed Media: antique paper and ink. Text-to-image data translation
from deep-learning model.
Virtually hand-modeled sculpture from data output.
80cm x 40cm
2021

An Unwriting

I do not exist. I am absolutely nothing, if I should even nestle up to such delusions, I am moreso some unhappened phenomenon, some kind of spawn or seed or fertilized egg or embryo that could one day exist as an individual, but you cannot call me a planned, intended, implied, or recognized being, I am not theoretically possible even in the remotest future, I am not speaking from some prenatal instance, nor from some waiting room of individuation, if one can even think of such a thing, nor from the very last place in a conceiving-, hatching-, or birthing queue, where billions of creatures may be lined up; no, I am not found there, as small as my existence at this moment may be, I have absolutely never existed, but what's more is, I cannot be found in some distant past, which would include, let us say, the time before the rise of the first urban communities, or the time before the rise of modern man in the physical-anthropological sense, and before the predecessors of modern man were discovered; even before any animal life, any living organism ever came to be, I did not exist, as little as I exist now, or will exist in the future, I am not speaking from beyond the grave as some bizarre spirit, a ghost, an angel, an immortal soul, or some such supramundane fakery, even before we began to bury our dead, I did not exist, and before we began to live, my nonexistence was as unshakably certain as it is today, as it will be tomorrow, and the day after tomorrow, and the day after that day, and thus I am forever untouched by the slime and the blood and the screams and the crying of childbirth, and also by the slime and the blood and the screams and the crying of the deathbed, if we absolutely must stay at the human level, but for my part we might as well stay far below that in terms of biological complexity, because you will not get anywhere with me that way either, for millions of years I was neither the most primitive gastropod, nor the most modest foraminifer, nor the most pitiful radiozoan, nor the most insignificant flagellate, nor today am I the lowliest virus, I neither cause nor cure disease, nor will I ever be so much as a single cell arising from the division of another cell, and consequently I cannot see anything (for example, two rectangular specks of light suggesting a cluster of people), cannot hear anything (for example, a smacking, mechanical sound that is suddenly heard at uneven intervals), cannot taste anything (for example, a mixture of salty, sweet, sour, and meaty), cannot smell anything (for example, from a viscous,

sticky, oozing liquid), and therefore I cannot, reasonably, gather the
sensations for a complete scene or even offer a summation (a big city
in the rain: I stand at the bus stop with other people waiting as the bus's
headlights approach, and, like the others, I turn away from the spray
of the wheels as the bus rolls in towards the front, wondering whether
I should throw away my half-eaten hot dog with mustard and ketchup
and raw onions which I hold in one hand, because I hold an umbrella
in the other, and now, depending on whether I am a man or a woman, I
have to find the wallet from my inside pocket or the change purse from
my pocketbook, and the ketchup runs down my fingers and makes them
sticky, while I fold up the umbrella, the water runs down and into my
sleeve and soaks my clothes, and I chew as much of the hot dog as fast as
I can, the wrapper crackling, my cheeks bulging with half-chewed food
as my jaws work unceasingly, and just as I reach the door of the bus, I
crumple up the hot-dog wrapper and put it in my pocket, hooking the
umbrella handle on my left arm, holding a change purse or wallet, which
is thus covered with ketchup, and digging out the small change needed
to pay for the forthcoming bus ride, this complex operation, which
involves a confusion of very rapid sensations, transfers of sensory data
through the brain, an interplay of a large number of nerves, muscles,
tendons, and ligaments, leaves just enough room to register in my senses
the smell of exhaust, the taste of hot dog and mustard and ketchup and
raw onions, and the drone of an impact drill as a construction worker,
dressed in yellow mud-streaked rain gear, equipped with a helmet and
earplugs, removing the remains of a demolished house on the other
side of the street, chunks of gray concrete that he is splitting up and
chopping loose from the rusty brown twisted rebar; if the aforementioned
sensations instead formed an atrocious war scene: an armored car filled
with bad guys driving by and mowing down a fleeing group of civilians
with machine guns, it would not make any difference to me), no, of
course I cannot conceive of anything like that, nothing at all actually,
nor can I think, for I have no brain, and I know nothing, and have never
known anything, and will never know anything, I cannot possibly think,
therefore I have never thought, I am not thinking now, and I will never
think a single thought, and furthermore I have, probably, no feelings
either, there is nothing that can stir my feelings, figuratively or literally,
I can feel no remorse for the past or any fear for the future, nothing can
make me happy or sad or sore or expectant or disappointed or frightened
or ashamed or guilty or proud or suspicious or shy or delighted or joyful,
or whatever emotional state you can think of, and if, ridiculously, you
tried to move me with a good old-fashioned poem, such as

A carcass rustles on the turf,
rises and gnaws the grassy earth.
Never do the dead have enough to eat…enough?
Long after the apocalypse,
the skeletal remains of beasts
shall wander 'round chewing sand and gravel
to the rhythm of a pastoral poem,
wholly deaf to all harp swell,

it would make no impression whatsoever; furthermore, and it follows logically from the foregoing, I have no sex drive, and therefore have not even the slightest theoretical chance of having offspring, for that which does not exist can have no offspring, nor can it have a predecessor, and certainly cannot have both simultaneously; that which does not exist is that which does not reproduce because it is never produced, it does not even have a reproductive instinct, or a reproductive reflex at the most rudimentary level, such as the cell mentioned above that divides in two, thus giving rise to a new individual, for I have no origin, since I do not exist, and something nonexistent cannot reproduce and give birth to a new nonexistence, one cannot conceive of an ever-branching offspring of nonexistent beings, that goes without saying, and therefore I cannot die either, since I have never been born; for similitude's sake, one can say that I have always been, and will always be dead, but it is and will be just that, a similitude, since he who has never entered existence cannot leave it either; besides, it is of no use to go on with this, as an infinity of words would not make the matter any clearer, and besides, I cannot communicate myself to anyone. Thus, it is simpler simply to say that I have never existed, do not exist, and never will exist.

Carla Rak

INFINITE VALLEYS

xagi, will these valleys ever end?
xagi climb down in light.
xagi always climb up in the dark.
every peak will once have been an island.
every peak shows infinite valleys.
hold the mirror straight, xagi.
eyes are not enough to see.
eyes are not enough to see, xagi.
xagi tells. xagi, see.
look, xagi, islands here don't end.
infinite.
look.
the ants told of such a bigness.
ants know the suns.
the suns never go down.
these valleys keep climbing, xagi.
the suns never go down, only just behind.
just behind this valley, xagi.
there will once have been a family of suns.
xagi, bring the map.
bring along the ink, xagi.
point to the edge.
there, point to the horizon.
these valleys. these infinite.
now put the mirror behind, xagi.
these infinite. these folding hills.
put the creases to the creases, xagi.
see it fit.
see it fit, xagi.
light the candles.
run the lights downhill, xagi.
see. it fits in the hand, the light.
water surrounds it, xagi.
water makes and makes the valleys.
these rolling. these infinite.
will they ever end, xagi?
climbing always in the dark.

Ali Aktan Aşkın

FROM *BOOTS WALKING IN AMERICA*

I decided to change my name to Boots Walking in America, but I didn't have any boots so I visited a man that sold boots. The man that sold boots sold me a pair of boots and gave me a pamphlet. Inside the pamphlet it said, "The best way to break in a new pair of boots is to have someone good pee in them." I wasn't sure how to find someone good, but the pamphlet continued, "If someone pees in your new boots and the leather softens then that person is probably good."

I hung my new boots on my shoulder and walked home. My mother was asleep on top of the television. I left her a note that said, "I've gone looking for someone good enough to soften my boot leather."

Like every other human that doesn't know where to go, I began moving in a random direction. That direction turned out to be south. I was walking south.

My father once told me that there were no more good people in the South anymore because they all got put in a tree once, but my father never been to the South and he don't know anything about people.

I walked barefoot because my boots were still hanging on my shoulder.

For nearly five minutes everything about my life was as okay as things could be without things being terrible or disappointing, but then an automobile paused and spit on me. I looked at the spit. The automobile drove away before I could spit on the spithole that had been spit on me.

When most of the spit on my body had stopped being spit I saw another automobile, but the driver in that automobile didn't spit or do anything except smile really hard until almost everyone in the United States was lonely.

I felt like an invisible buffalo so I couldn't really smile or talk because buffalos aren't allowed to smile or talk when they're invisible.

Something mechanical walked up and held out a jug of milk. It smelled local. The mechanical object set the jug of milk on the ground and drifted into a field. When the mechanical object was gone I poured the jug of local milk on my bare foot.

Somewhere a woman was standing on the roof of a house. The bottom of her dress had once gotten dirty. One of the walls of the house was made of mud twigs.

I was too embarrassed about my feet to ask any of the people I saw if they were good. I worried my feet still smelled like milk. I didn't want to be remembered as the milk foot.

A boy was playing a game behind an economically depressed public building. The boy ran a ball from one side of an imaginary set of boundaries to the other and then back again. Multiple drops of sweat leaked from his skin.

I remembered the day I first learned to sweat and imagined my mother kissing me good night on the back of my neck.

A tray of meat stood next to someone that was paid to stand next to a tray of meat. The person standing next to the tray asked if I was hungry. I looked at the boots hanging from my shoulder and pointed at the piece of the meat on the tray that was actually not meat. A man in a shiny velvet coat and polished boots walked over and picked up the thing I was going to eat. He put the non-meat in one of his velvet pockets. Instead of making noises, I slowly backed away, embarrassed by how unpolished my boots were.

Outside, somewhere, I noticed a crippled man struggling to put some bread in his mouth. I was near a piece of the world located on earth. The crippled man asked if I had any sauce. I lied and told him I did. We looked at each other for a long time. I continued walking south.

A boy with no ears was using a finger to listen to the inside of an empty plastic soda bottle. I asked the boy with no ears why he didn't have any ears. He nodded. Later, I realized he didn't have ears because his cricket had recently disappeared.

Four gasoline-powered motorbikes passed me as I walked. Each motorbike was carrying three adolescents. A girl fell off the slowest motorbike. None of the other motorbikes noticed. The girl ran into the woods before her injuries had a chance to kill her.

I found a small red leather glove. It was not glowing. I got down on my hands and knees and sniffed it. The parts that weren't glowing reminded me of a cracked bar of soap I once found at the edge of a dry streambed.

The thing I was kneeling against eventually turned into a field. I took a bite because I thought this field might be full of turnips. The inside of my mouth tasted like a swollen, rusty peach.

I dug a hole before I began walking again, but I didn't have anything to put in the hole so it remained a hole and never became nothing else.

The shape in the sky that I pray to when I pray to shapes in the sky was falling out of the sky very slowly.

Up the road I saw a motel. Most of the rooms were dark. I broke a window and crawled into a room with a toilet and a bathtub.

For dinner I licked one of my toes to see if it still tasted like milk, but while licking the toe I only thought of trout. If I found a man selling trout I would buy three trout from the man. Then I would eat one of the trout and put the other two in my boots for later.

I woke to the weight of my own boots resting on my chest. The bathtub had leaked while I slept. There was a wet spot on my body. I peed out the broken bathroom window. When I was done I hung my new boots on my shoulder.

A pile of burning tires smiled at me from the middle of a field. Some men on tractors circled the burning tires, shooting their guns while yelling at the tires to keep burning.

Two or three large, iron bells lay on the ground next to a church. A man in robes kneeled beside one of the bells and whispered to it. I offered to help. The man in robes ran inside the church.

I pulled a soggy piece of bread from my pocket and gave it to a toothless dog tied to a fence. The dog had been tied to the fence for a long time. I asked the dog if it would pee in my boot. The dog began to chew on the boot with its toothless mouth.

In a ditch, a man was digging a second ditch. I watched the man dig. After a few minutes he paused and told me not to watch.

An old man on a bicycle passed me. I called out to him. He turned the bicycle around. His head and mouth seemed faded from too much use. The old man just smiled when I asked him if he would pee in my boots. He said it had been a long time since anyone had asked him to pee in a new pair of boots. I removed the boots from my shoulder. The old man apologized and said, "I haven't been able to pee in almost ten years." I hung the boots back on my shoulder. Before the old man pedaled away he suggested I try filling my boots with coyote blood.

I moved towards a smoking chimney in the distance. The smoking chimney in the distance turned out to be a wrinkled woman smoking a pipe. I watched the wrinkled woman smoke the pipe until a young, unwrinkled girl slapped the pipe out of the wrinkled woman's mouth. The unwrinkled girl then dragged the wrinkled woman into a house. A few minutes later, the chimney on the roof to smoke. I thought about picking up the wrinkled woman's pipe, but I worried I would get wrinkled and then something unwrinkled would slap me.

The day began to tilt. I looked at my bare feet every few minutes. They were dirty, but they didn't hurt. The bright prayer object in the sky sank a little.

Near a dead piece of wood that used to be an apple tree, I came upon two young men sleeping naked on a red plaid blanket. I thought of asking for their pee, but instead I watched them sleep. My thoughts weren't good or bad. They were just thoughts. When one of young men began to twitch slightly I stood up and continued walking.

I walked until one of the clouds got orange.

The day unpeeled itself into a dark hole that was too dark for anyone to even notice it was a hole.

At the bottom of a hill I leaned against an oak tree for a long time before I decided to climb the tree and sleep on its thickest limb. My boots hung from a branch above my head. It did not take long for my body to forget it was in a tree and fall asleep.

[*Note: this excerpt from *Boots Walking in America* was previously published online in *Sleepingfish* series 13.]

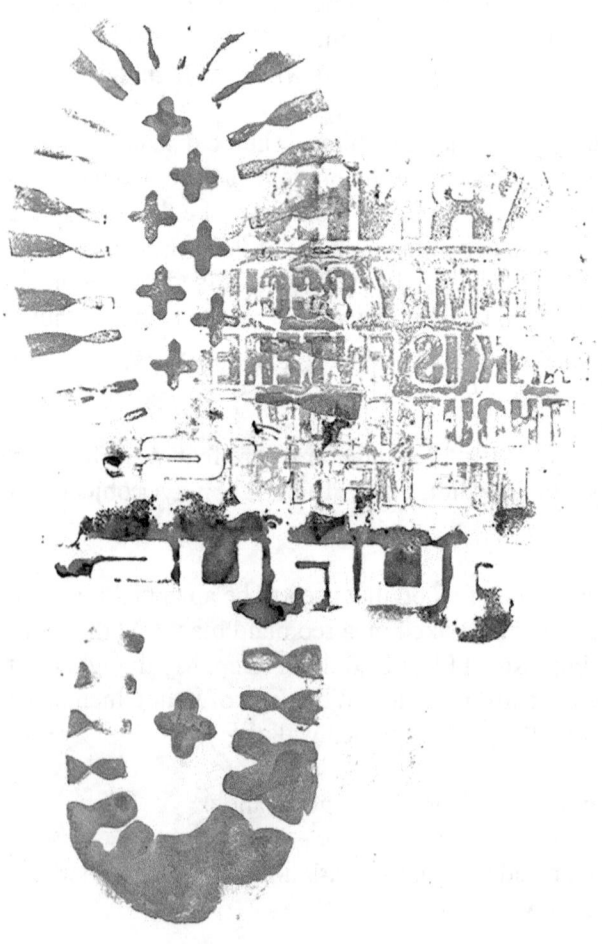

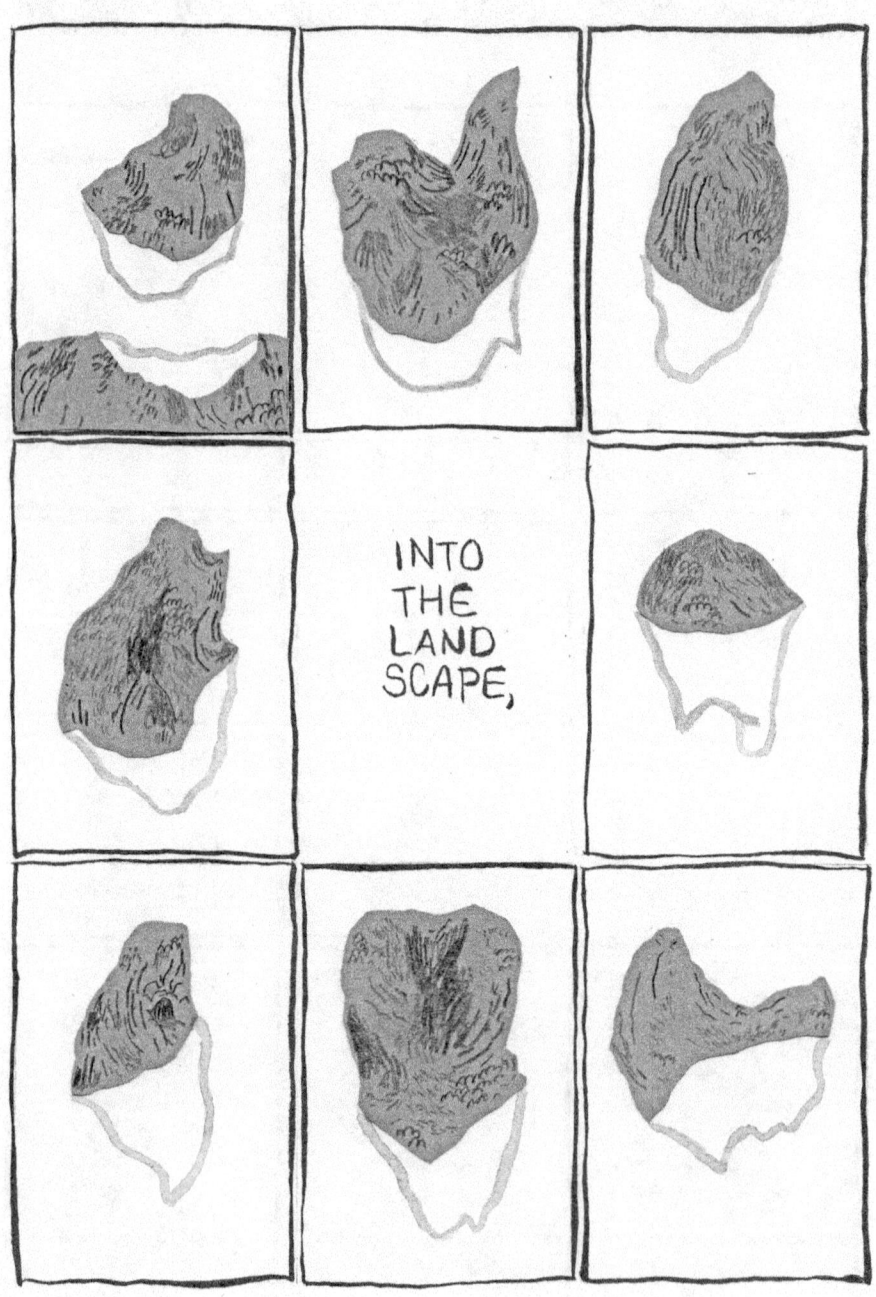

Nick Francis Potter

SET
ENOUR
MOUS
FIRE
S,

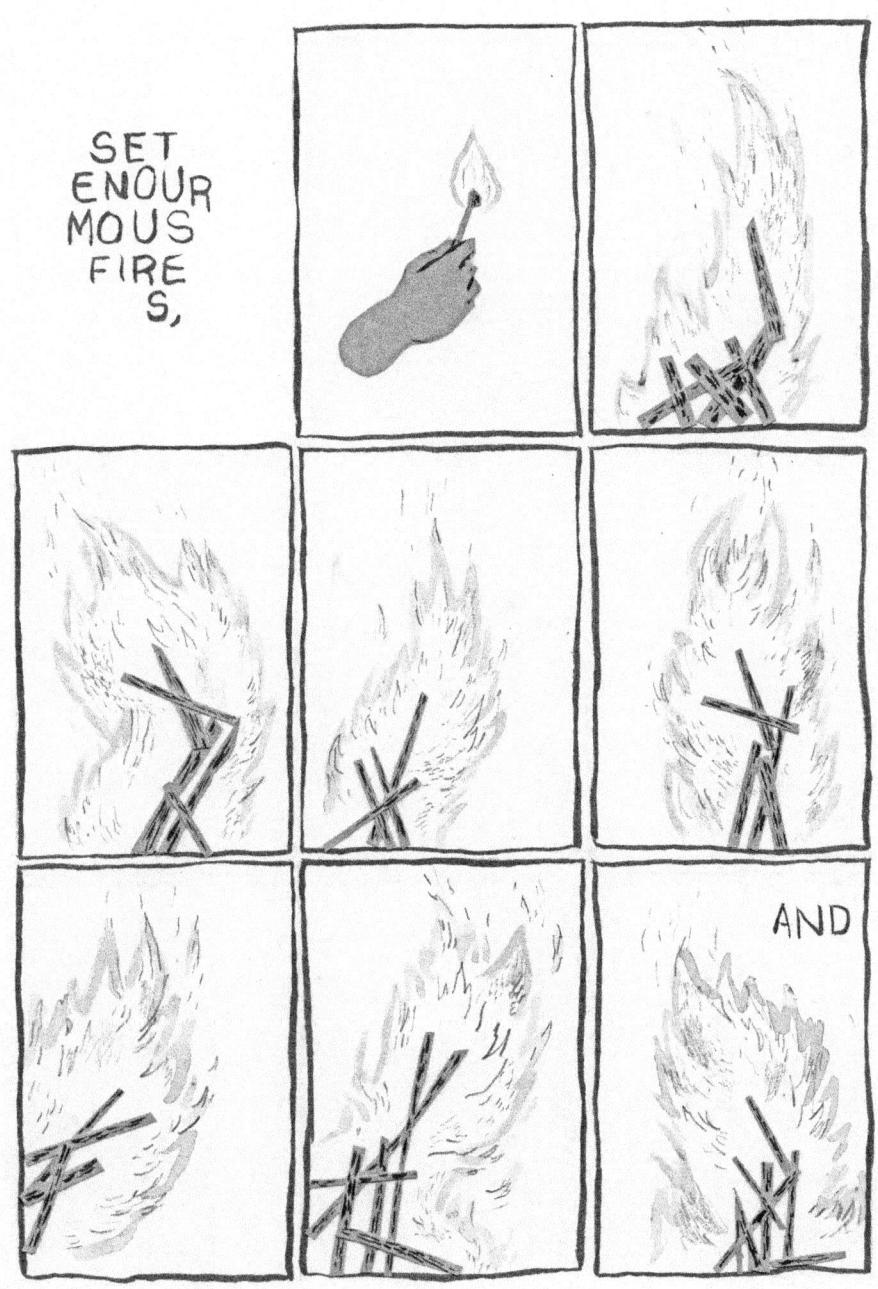

Nick Francis Potter

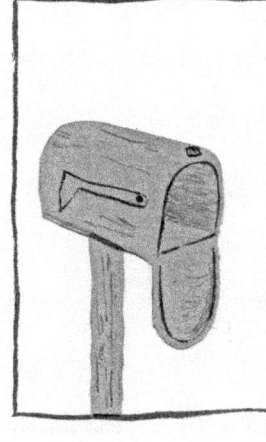

WE
SEARCH
FOR THE
ANIMALS

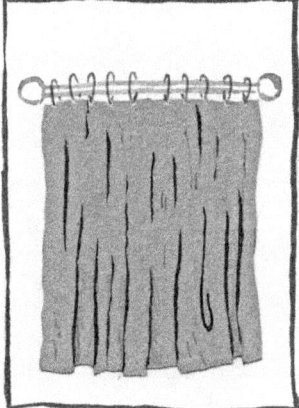

IN THE
PANTRY,

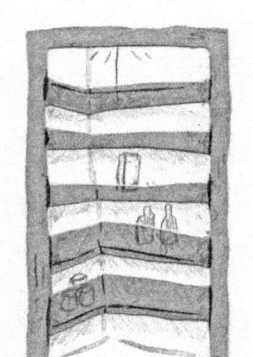

BEHIND
THE
CURTAINS,

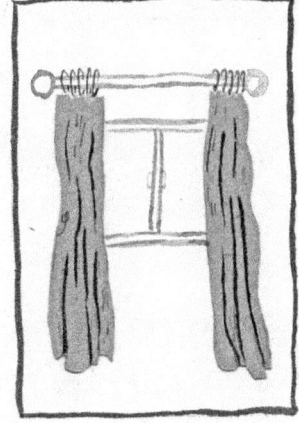

WITHOUT
SUCCESS

ADRIFT
IN LOSS

WE WEAR
THE

HEADS
OF THEIR
ANCEST
ORS

Nick Francis Potter

WE E
NTER
THE UN
HACKED
WILDER
NESS

AS

A N I M A L S

SLIPPI
NG INTO
THE LA
NDSCAP
E'S CLO
THING

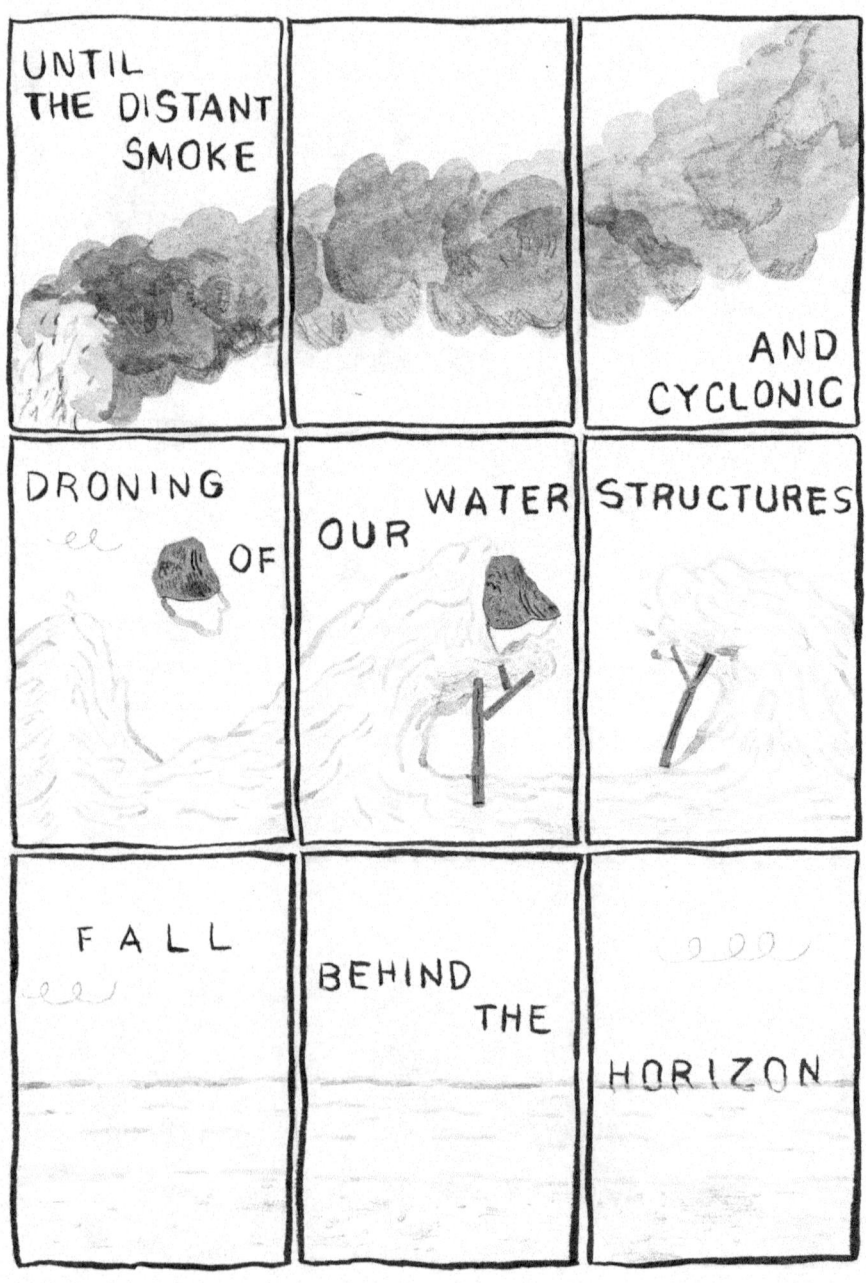

Nick Francis Potter

WINTER QUILTS

A wolf came from the forest to Ida's porch. The wolf's prints zigzagged the snow. The wolf was starving. Ida could see old tears flaking from the wolf's eyes. She felt crust in her own corners. Ida held the wolf in her thin arms—a woven musk surrounded them like a shawl. The wolf's last breath clinked a wind chime in Ida's throat.

Ida could hear the wolf's pups in the shed rifling through the old trunks that held what hadn't burned. From the stove's mouth, a fire had first lapped up a greasy rag, then blue-tongued half the house. Ida's children had drifted the blistered linoleum.

Her children thinned, then left on a night train that blazed an eye through the village. They traveled with deep tunnels of hunger. Wherever they arrived, they ate past full.

Ida separated the wolf's flesh from the bone. She stored the wolf's meat in the humming freezer.

She sewed the wolf's stripped fur into drapes and hung them on the burnt windeye.

The pups stayed in the shed catching mice. Outside, the snow fell in an endless crystalline curtain. The pups found recesses within the shed to paw their dens. The snow piled higher; the pups went deeper. Ida entered the shed. She found the pups in a forgotten trunk and nested with them in a pile of cross-stitched quilts.

The wolf pups grew and left Ida asleep in battings that enclosed her in a plush chrysalis. Sometime later, she woke and emerged from the shed. Her translucent skin puckered gooseflesh in the cold.

The fur drapes still hung from the singed windeye. She shawled them over her shoulders. She climbed in the now silent freezer, nested with the wolf's thawed meat. Sometime later, Ida woke and remembered her way back to the forest.

I close the fur drapes.

Great-grandma is in the winter tree outside. I fear her history; poisoned,
then sent her to labor without rest. Her eggs were soft-shelled, permeable
to microbes. But one egg was hard. One cracked open to an albumen-
wettened pup and a yelp from her weak maw. She scooped the pup
under-wing, fed her what she could.

I clean the house: mop the floor, empty the coffee-dark water from the
bucket, stack the chipped plates in the cupboard. The sewing machine
idles its one sharp tooth. My phone cries, wanting to be picked up. Great-
grandma sounds a *whoo* from the tree.

Grandma emerges from the drapes. She never taught me to hem edges.
She holds out a sewing needle. She shows me the matriarch's pattern: a
cross-stitch hedge. I sew and sew until my fingers turn numb, covering
a quilt center in hedge stitch. I embroider a forest to the frayed margins.
Smother my whining phone in unused batting. Grandma and I crawl
under the comforter. I sleep on the ache of her shoulder.

Middle night, she gently lowers my head from her sore joint, rises and
walks to the furred window.

Grandma pulls the drapes over her hunch, slinks from the house to the
tree that towers over the backyard. I rouse, pull back bedding, see the tuft
of feathers born to my ankles. New claws crescent from my leathery toes.
I climb from the empty window to join my kin. Great-grandmother flies
down from the tree, perches on Grandma's head. Looks at me and says,
Who? I take out the spiral button in my belly, its red thread unraveling
from my navel, and toss it to her. Great-grandmother catches it in her
beak, flies up and lifts me to the sky. Dangling from the cord, I see a
patchwork of snow and Grandma's prints stitching us back to the forest.

Kim Parko

LULA NEEDS TO RUN

My mom calls to tell me about swatting. She heard a woman arrested for swatting thrice. She had to look the term up—but says it is a thing: people calling police about things they make up. Like the guy who called the cops on me when I stayed at the Y, saying I was suicidal.

I'm in my SUV, heading to a dog park. My Lula needs to run. I have my mom on speaker. I say, The hospital's billing company called me the other day, to collect my insurance. I'll probably have to pay the hundred-dollar co-pay.

I was staying at the Y then, where rooms are kind of dorm-like. I probably shouldn't have said anything about the noise next door, but I'd been there four days, had a nice night at the ballet, a nice swim at the pool, and it was my birthday. I knocked on his door and asked him to be quiet. It was 3 a.m.

I didn't know I'd have to answer the door to my room when the cops came.

I tell my mom, I kind of just want to forget about it.

She says, You should contact your insurance. He's probably done this more than once. He should be arrested.

When the cops came, they said I had to answer the door. Since then, I talked to friends about this, and they said if cops come to your door at home, you don't have to let them in. They don't know the protocol for hotel rooms.

I was a military cop once. I was an augmentee.

I assured the cops: I'm not suicidal. I said I wanted sleep. They said they had to respond. They put me in handcuffs, in an ambulance. The ambulance took me to the hospital. The hospital did their protocol. I worked in hospitals for years. I told them that. By then it was almost 4 a.m. I joked and said, If I were suicidal, I'd at least have the heart to not hurt my loved ones so much to end it on my birthday.

I had to wear a wristband. Had to wait for doctors. I imagined being an albatross with big wide wings, which I did a lot when I was younger. I know about abuse. I know about survival. I know what it's like to feel depressed. I also have a lot of friends. I trust. I love. I have a lot to lose. I have a lot to live for.

My mom says, The guy who called the cops on you is a criminal. It's a criminal act.

As I drive, I reach over to pet Lula. It soothes me to have her near. It soothes me to feel her fur and pet her.

PATCHWORK

I am terrified of dogs that bark. I don't believe in the whole "barking dogs don't bite" logic thrust upon us. I have a separate laugh for a joke I don't like, but it's not fake. I have never been in love, or maybe I don't know what being in love feels like. I prefer to live with social anxiety than to take medicines to treat it. I have seen three therapists in my life, all of whom I ended up ghosting.

I love seeing new places, but I hate traveling. I travel without a ticket on trains these days. I must speak to someone on the phone if I am on a train that's not underground. I must get a window seat on a plane to not feel sick. I can't read when I am in the car, plane, or train without getting a headache. I started reading *The Girl on the Train* while I was on the train.

I love getting my fortune read and diss the fortune teller later. I got my handwriting read by a graphologist who told me I have a hard time finishing things by the way I write *p* and *d*. I store unimportant things— like expired flight tickets, metro cards, and old mail. I lose hair clips most frequently. I cry in the shower. When I was a child, I loved popping bubble wrap. I fall for vulnerabilities, not strengths. I love kids, but I don't think I can take care of one. I pretend to be dumb in situations so men explain things to me. I don't like men who mansplain.

When I was a child, I loved the smell of gasoline. I don't know how to drive. My ex-boyfriend tried to teach me how to drive when we were in Cape May, and we kept moving around in circles. I fear dying in a car accident. Before I die, I want to see a tiger in the wild. I fall in love with my ears, not eyes. I didn't say "I love you" back to my ex-boyfriend. I am attracted to my best friend, but I pretend to be disgusted by the idea of us together. I hate watching a foreign movie with subtitles. Growing up I was told coming to America would solve all my problems. I teach

Americans the incorrect pronunciation of my name because I don't like the correct pronunciation of my name.

***

I walked out of a Temazcal ceremony in Mexico because I couldn't take the heat. I only miss India during winters. I don't like New York as much as I pretend to like it on social media. Trader Joe's is like my Tiffany's. I get a haircut after every heartbreak. My only solo trips in America have been to L.A. and Miami. I don't have as much fun as I expect to have on solo trips. I love Turkey, not the bird—the country. I watch Turkish soap operas because I find the people incredibly gorgeous. There was a phase in my life when I only dated Middle Eastern men. There was a phase in my life where I pretended to be a Middle Eastern woman.

I might never date a doctor, because I feel he might diagnose me with a life-threatening condition. I hate hospitals even though most of my life has been in them. I was hospitalized a lot as a child, and I ended up working in a hospital as an adult. I can't watch a woman giving birth. I have a deep-seated fear of blood. When I was a child, I used to pray to be one of the few blessed women who don't menstruate. I judge people by their life spans. If someone dies early, I think very highly of them.

The languages I speak are English and Hindi. The languages I speak on my résumé are English, Hindi, Spanish, Punjabi, and Bengali. I think in Hindi, but I communicate in English. I pretend not to be hungry to save money on food. I believe the most overrated word in the English-language dictionary is *petrichor*. I believe the most underrated word in the English-language dictionary is *it*. When I was a child, I was told I was beautiful much more than I am now as an adult woman. I believe the most beautiful women in the world are my mom and Nazia Hassan (Google her).

I love asymmetrical dimples. I am an extrovert disguised behind an introvert. I can be myself with only 3 people. One of them is my

sister. Two of them are my friends who know when I am lying. I rate
friendships based on if someone can tell when I am lying. There was a
time I lied about donating blood to bunk class in college. I ended up in
the emergency room after being in a car accident an hour after that lie. I
had stitches on my forehead and the doctor said I might as well be Harry
Potter because of the scar. I told the doctor Harry's scar was on the left
side of his forehead because I didn't know any better.

I switched from a pencil to a pen when I was ten, and that was when I
realized mistakes would be harder to erase. I started writing stories when
I was ten. I started making up stories when I was six. I can't read men
and their thoughts. I have more guy friends than girlfriends and I still
can't read men and their thoughts. I look for broken people to fix, but in
all honesty, I am the one who needs fixing. I have never been loved the
way I want to be loved. For me, love is the right balance between space
and closeness.

The most important thing in the world to me is not love, but freedom.
I visit the Gandhi statue in Union Square to feel Indian. I have never
felt the need to be Indian in India. I am comforted by the ocean. I
sleep by playing white noise consisting of sounds of the ocean. I judge
people based on their ability to fall asleep. I find people who fall asleep
without any effort to be less damaged than others. As someone who isn't
a morning person, I find early mornings overrated. I think there is no
scientific evidence to the saying—"early to bed and early to rise makes a
man healthy, wealthy, and wise." I would also like to know what makes a
woman healthy, wealthy, and wise.

I love making tea to unblock my writer's block. I take no sugar in my
tea but have it with sugar cookies. I pretend to like coffee so I get to post
pictures of latte art. I love trashy reality TV versus documentaries. I love
bookstores but I never visit them to buy books. The last book I started
to read was *The 48 Laws of Power* by Robert Greene. I feel powerless
in relationships. I smoked cigarettes for a week to get my best friend to
stop smoking. I paused my reading of *The 48 Laws of Power* after Law

zzz ><((°> XX

2—"Never Put Too Much Trust in Friends, Learn How to Use Enemies."
I don't have any enemies, just ex-lovers.

I love warm fall evenings. I like walking on crunchy yellow leaves,
making each step count. Watching horror movies together is like my
weird couple thing. When I was a child, I wasn't taught to differentiate
between good touch and bad touch. I have only dated two white men in
my entire life. One found me too Indian, the other found me too nice. I
am insulted when somebody uses "nice" to describe me. If I like a guy, I
will go out of my way to make sure he thinks I don't like him. If I like a
guy, I will let him pay on the first date. If I like a guy, I can't look into his
eyes for more than ten seconds.

I can't dance on an empty dance floor unless I have had a drink. I tend
to select cocktails based on their appearance. I used to order Sex on the
Beach without knowing it's called Sex on the Beach by pointing out a
picture of an orange-colored drink on the drink's menu. I haven't had sex
on the beach. I think sex on the beach might be overrated.

I have an anxious attachment style, and I always fall for an avoidant.
I can't pass a mirror without looking at it, but I couldn't be less of a
narcissist. I dated a narcissist and was abandoned by him after two
months when he found me too plain. That was when I met the first
therapist who told me I had low self-worth. I say *that's it* at the end of
sentences when I have a lot more to say but I want to avoid oversharing.
I saw the second therapist after getting a panic attack misdiagnosed by
me as a heart attack. The second therapist wanted to know more about
my childhood. I shopped around for more therapists who could be better
suited to me. The third therapist wanted to know more about my history
of abuse. It doesn't have to be physical; it could be emotional or verbal
as well, she said. That's it. I don't want to waste my time on therapists
anymore. I think there's more to life than trying to survive. I think there's
more to life than living.

At times, I try to deconstruct what I wrote on my blog five years ago to understand if I am more self-aware now versus then. I go by the alias of _____. If I ever feel the need to be funny, I just tell people the truth. My friends don't find me funny. Sunsets are more poetic to me than sunrises. My favorite color is yellow, but I have more black clothes in my wardrobe. I don't have a tattoo, but if I choose to get one it would be art instead of words. I am undecided between ∞ and :): I am confused if I want to get it on the back of my wrist or on the nape of my neck. I like to see precariously stacked Jenga pieces collapse. I let out a melodramatic gasp whenever Jenga pieces come crashing down.

I once went hiking in heels. I once walked in the rain for a mile in Brooklyn without an umbrella. I once found a painted stone at the Plaza Hotel food court which had a hummingbird on it. I later discovered it to be part of The Kindness Rocks Project, and it was supposed to be passed around for others to find. I kept it with me for two years before throwing it into the Atlantic Ocean, thinking someone who needed it more would find it there. I am a water sign, which validates why I love being near water bodies. I can't swim in a water body where my feet don't touch the ground. I often wonder what it would be like to drown in an ocean. I often wonder what it means to be in love.

When I was a child, I was fascinated by paper planes and paper boats. When I was a child, I used to collect ladybugs in a glass jar. When I was a child, I found a caterpillar while shelling peas and kept it in a box hoping to find a butterfly one day. I tell people I had a happy childhood because I want to remember it like that.

3. Red Earth translation: excerpt

Or they could be words gathered in a long string of
names as gifted to a Nigerian child on its eighth day
in this world and found in the joyous, chorus doing
the swaddling. Repeating. Repeating. Ringing out
through celebratory mouths and ears gathered with
care around the mother and her newborn.
Spherically arranged well-wishers like fluffy
dandelion seeds perching lightly on the head of their
flower, aim their attention to their core where the
child nestles snugly against the central bosom. They
shield and gaze upon the baby, delighted at this
arrival to their world.

Michael Salu

Direct Translation Diptych
Diptych. Mixed Media: antique paper and ink. Text-to-image data translation from deep-learning model.
Virtually hand-modeled sculpture from data output.
80cm x 40cm
2021

TAU

i awake with a post-it note stuck in the palm of my hand: monday. that must be today, the time to get up, my legs ache, the sun is shining so that is how i know it is summer. the light in the room is pale gray with the tint of blue to it, how i know the weather is too cold for shorts, it's sweater-vest weather. the clothes, they are all where they belong. my glasses, too. the cup of water on the nightstand next to the bed. all my books, all my books, unmoved and still in the same place. there is the copy of *Malina* which has changed positions over the night and so that is how i know that i must have been reading, for certainly he doesn't read, nor does he bother my things on this side of the bed.

the bed is empty. i have slept the sleep of the dead because he's not here and i didn't hear him get up. the house is silent, so i know he must be at work — no tinkle of dishes in the kitchen for an early breakfast, no roaring sound of kettle for tea. i sit up, i stretch my arms as far as they can go, the blankets fall away from my body and the chill kisses my skin. up, and the bra is by my feet on the floor. i put it on, i pull on a pair of trousers from the wardrobe, i pull on a t-shirt, a sweater-vest. my face feels slick with overnight grease, and my hair, i don't look in the mirror.

everything now is by feel. i don't like to look in the mirror anymore because it tells me the days have gone by faster than i have realized, that or i'm always changing and not aware of it. this lack of awareness, this is my enemy. i do not like it. as much as i try to grasp, i try so hard, i feel present, i practice my little meditations, i stay in mindfulness, and yet when i see the lines around my eyes lengthen toward my temple, and when i see the slight droop of my cheeks past my jawline, there is a realization of what an unstoppable force truly feels like. the way that some things certainly cannot be controlled. what i always learned in therapy was to focus on what i could control but there is some slippage, even there, of my focus. some sense that things are not as i think they always are.

the quiet apartment is undisturbed. but i remember that it used to be disturbed daily, the floors needing constantly swept due to crumbs from my daughter's breakfast, the couch needing to be vacuumed, the carpet

needing a steam-cleaned, and if not daily the house was chaos. in the
kitchen i stare down at my feet and suddenly think of the floor in a
constant state of mess, the repetitive movement of sweeping crumbs or
broken glass or a stray blueberry into a dustpan and into the trash. in the
sink is just one dish and a pair of silverware. and i think he must have
had breakfast so early for me not to hear him making it, to be awoken by
the sound of bacon frying in the pan or the scrape of the spatula and the
popping of toast from the toaster. but on the counter there are no bread
crumbs and in the sink there is no bacon grease and the dish looks to
have the remnants of some kind of gravy as one would have with dinner.
i'm certain he's mad at me, he must be, if he has left so early without
any word, without waking me up to give me a goodbye kiss. i reach and
reach into yesterday or last night to think of what i could have done.
i know that i am difficult—i know that i am—i demand things, crazy
things, i demand he tell me everything, speak with me, open up, then
when he does i know that i argue, and i can't help it as much as i try. and
one i remember, one morning as he sat in the living room, our daughter
still in pajamas, no breakfast eaten, as he stared at his computer screen. i
peered in, nobody says hello. like i am not even there. i get our daughter
out of the room, tell her to get dressed, ask if she's had breakfast to
which he replies he doesn't know. the way everything by default falls to
me. i argue about it. why can't you just say hello? good morning? why
can't you just tell me you need me to get her ready? the way it makes me
feel, always picking up the slack. i argue until he does what i want which
is gets himself up and takes her off to school, and still i argue. and he
asks, please be here when i get back. i say no. so i don't and the whole
day then is silence.

so then i think, standing in the empty kitchen with the one dish in the
sink, please be here when i wake up, and the answer is clearly no. he is
not there. the bed was empty. on the doorjamb leading into the entryway
is a pale pink post-it note: dress for thursday. my handwriting, i think,
though it's poorly, and i don't recall placing it there but it must have
been for today. i stand in front of the vanity, staring down at my various
pots and pencils for make up, i pat powder onto my skin which sucks
up the grease. i draw eyeliner over one crepey eye, i pull the skin back
over the other to get the line to match, in the mirror my eyes have this
bright, glossy clarity to them—searing, chemical green, wet like covered
in resin, the whites beneath the waterline a tar-colored yellow. i slip on
my brogues by the door and put on my khaki trench. the keys are always
in the door so i don't forget to lock it and i never forget where they are.

everything must go where it belongs or it falls apart. the ritual of life is the glue. if the shoes are not by the door i won't slip them on. if the note is not on the jamb i'll have no structure to my day, no purpose. then i do my makeup, the same way every time, the makeup pencils and the little pots stay on the vanity where i can see them or i'll forget where they've been stored. and the trench—it hangs on a hook near the door so it doesn't end up on the floor or the couch, and so i slip it on, and i unlock the door, and i step out, and i flip off the light switch the same way i always do. when i close the door i lock it and the keys go into the right pocket. cigarettes and phone in the left. lighter in the right. it's all where it belongs so i know i am ready to go on about my day. and i'm going about it in the silence because i haven't heard from him and the girl must be at school because i haven't heard her little feet run across the floor, knocking on the door, reminding me not to forget her, too.

the street is as bright and pale as the bedroom light but a little more defined. all the sounds and details come at me now, the birds dutifully chirping to each other. the cars rushing toward parking garages and taxi rinks and spaces, all to find the places they belong, as well. two blocks up and to the right where the street is more open, a lavender city bus pulls into a stop, people file on. i walk to the café for a coffee and once in i decide to sit and read. i'll remember, i assure myself, just after this short break to relax i will go to to store and i will get a dress for thursday. what sort of dress is it that i need? what is it for, what is happening thursday? the warmth of my latte is more comforting than bed and i suck it hungrily down and read 15 pages of *Malina* and suddenly 45 minutes have passed. i'm engulfed in the reading. each page gives the satisfaction of a full, vibrant memory. i mean my memory. i mean that i get to experience this world without any before or after. i don't worry about what comes next when i am reading, i simply read, there is no pressure to sift it to memory, i don't think "i must remember to do this, or this, or this," when i know i will eventually forget. this is, after all, what he hates about me. or i suspect that he hates it. that i promise to change, to stop being so difficult. i promise to stop interrupting when he speaks. and i promise to listen, to really listen, but every time he opens his mouth i forget and i do it again. right now i am simply living sentence to sentence, word to word. that is all that is asked of me. living sentence to sentence is how i want to live. that's where the liberation lies. maybe that's what he is angry about? i recall some argument, something, some disagreement in the kitchen, he was wearing a dark long-sleeve tee and gray khaki trousers and had on his light gray paisley socks. i found that silly, the socks, but

what were we discussing. the café walls are covered in old covers of
New Yorkers atop what looks like wheat-pasted fabric. someone leans
back in a chair and the chair groans beneath them. i look over to the
sound and see a young family, not english, visiting from mainland europe
maybe. the woman is dressed in—how was she dressed? i've walked
the streets of london for years and noticed european families up and
down the block, the way their children wear mature-looking parkas and
clothes, never dressed in cartoon characters or infantile designs, their
hair always clean-cut, smoothed back. never a child with messy hair. the
woman's hair pulled back and glossy, usually in a low bun, light makeup,
she looks healthy, the skin beneath her eyes is dewy and fresh without
a hint of caked on concealer. her lips are rosy and saturated with gloss.
her teeth are natural, not too white, not too yellow, when she smiles. the
physical expression of her features leads me to believe her mind is clear,
that her brain functions normally, and her interactions with her husband
tell me this too. their rapport is—how would you describe it?—healthy.
there's no stiffness, no aura of argument or disagreement. she knows
what is expected of her role and is happy with it and fulfills it and so
does he. he sips his coffee black, they have a plate of croissants, the child
smiles, they talk in some language i cannot hear or pick up on—maybe
portuguese, it doesn't sling together the way french does. i used to speak
french, used to practice it, but now i only know it by the vowels i hear
and the consonants which close them off—as clearly as i hear them in
my mind i cannot construct my mouth to make the same sounds any
longer. too out of practice. that is how it works with brains, i learned this
when i tried to quit smoking. there are pathways built of neurons in it,
and we reinforce these pathways every day with our little habits. every
day that i picked up a cigarette with my right hand and placed it to my
lips i was building a pathway there that reinforced itself that smoking
was reward. and every day that i succumbed to an argument, every day
that i interrupted him or refused to listen, i was reinforcing a pathway of
disobedience. there was, and is, a person that i want to be. and i know
and believe in neuroplasticity. i trust the scientists when they say that
these pathways can be changed. and i know that to break a bad habit
means to refuse to walk the pathway so the neurons can fold and die. the
scientists have a phrase for breaking a bad habit, it's called long-term
depression.

each time you perform an action you've never done before, it is like
water flowing through a flat expanse of dirt. there is nothing yet there
to help the water flow and by free will, and i hope we have free will,

you force the water to flow, and this is why it is so difficult to change.
it is difficult and the force required makes it easy to succumb to the
deep ravines already built—these ravines which have been carved out
deeper and deeper day by day over every year of my life. the ravines
are deep somewhere in an inaccessible place. i know this only because
my conscious life, the choices i want to make now, have slowly become
inaccessible to me, that only the unconscious habits remain—the getting
up, the makeup, the shoes by the door, everything where it belongs. it
is the day-to-day i now struggle to capture. i cannot remember what
happened yesterday, for example, that made him so mad at me that he left
the bed empty this morning without saying goodbye, but i can remember
the deep ravines of our earlier arguments and can only suss out that this
must be the reason, some similar event i have no memory of.

what is today, but the unconscious experience of the once-conscious
choices we have made 5, 10, 20 years ago. i woke up in my flat on 22 tau
street because 20 years ago i made the conscious choice to live there. and
i woke up in my flat as the mother of my child because 10, or was it 15?,
years ago, i made the conscious choice to be a mother. i chose her, and in
my consciousness i brought consciousness into the world and there was
a cascade of choice that came from that. the way her birth forced upon
me new rituals, new habits, must wake up every few hours to nurse, must
calm the crying, must adore, must love, that was not a choice. once she
was born i knew there were patterns i needed to challenge so i didn't
make the mistakes my mother did with me. some of these were easy.
always tell her you love her. tell her you chose her. tell her how glad you
are she is alive. kiss her before bed every night. never diminish her self-
esteem. these were easy choices, compelled by a deep and unquenchable
force that lives within me, to share, without condition, no matter how
hurt i felt. even in her deepest angers—how she yelled she hated me—i
never felt hurt. i understood her pain and her anger. and i always loved
tenderly. the other patterns were harder, are harder, to break, as each day
something slips beneath the surface of me and into another realm that i
cannot reach.

was loving him a choice? was that what our argument was about, there
in the kitchen, him with the paisley socks? i had come to the sudden
realization that a lot of what i had been drawn to as a young woman was
some kind of encoded behavior i had learned from my childhood. that
i never understood where i ended and another person, usually a man,
began. and i had the realization because of reflecting on my father's

behavior with me. in my desire to pull it out and examine it, to shunt
and kill it so i didn't pass this disease on to my daughter, i wondered if
the whole time this lack of endings and beginnings was what made, at
first, the relationship with him so harmonious. he always knew where he
ended and began and he never let someone overstep that. but as soon as i
began traipsing the borders between myself and him more clearly, slowly
at first, then walking it over again and again until the dirt cleared away
and the spoor was more obvious, the simplicity of our love transformed
into something more complex and hideous, a thing with gripping teeth;
rough fur and sharp edges. as though each touch was metered by tiny
spurs, so that when he came near to me or i near to him, little sparkles of
pain decorated the experience. and what pathway was building in this?
was this new purpose of mine, to liberate myself completely from the
dredges of my childhood, tearing us apart? we both came together with
an unspoken model of what it means to love and be loved. i no longer
remembered what it was like to be loved, or how one should be loved.
and what is it then, to be loved? what feels like love? in the moments i
was most argumentative what i was needing most was affection. was for
him to take me and squeeze me hard, compress all the thorny parts until
they bent flat, like the field grass in a crop circle. i wanted his love to feel
like an extraterrestrial visitation. something that instilled in me the hope
of being abducted, away from this world, away from the old patterns of
grief.

are those the little pathway builders? holding his hand when we walked
down the street. leaning in to his body. feeling unsteady in heels and
asking him to slow his gait for me, my arm in his, as my legs learned to
trust his as a ballast. letting my mind trust that he could lead me safely.
that felt like loving him and being loved.

out of the café and onto the street and i'm unsteady yet slowly pacing
forward. my feet have to find the flatness of the sidewalk on their own,
one foot in front of the other. dress for thursday. i couldn't stumble,
because his hand would not be there to steady the small of my back. i
remember wiping the sweat from the back of his neck in the summer, the
way my fingers grazed the perfect line of hair buzzed at the nape of his
neck, which i had cut for him. he taught me many things simply by being
a man within my life. i learned to barber, i learned to cut a beard (which
you had to treat and shape like a hedge), i learned how to knot a tie and
why it was important to match a belt with the shoes, how to tailor a suit,
and the fastest way to iron a wrinkled shirt into crisp, white attentiveness.

and yet still there was the stirring between us when we walked down
the street together, the unspoken sadness that was a question of my free
will. sex is also love, and like my early draw to him it had come easy
for so long until at some point i understood that saying no, not always,
just sometimes, was addled, to him, with an absolute rejection of our
marriage. it is too complicated to be together for so long. it's clear he
had given up many things and changed and worked hard to give me
everything i wanted to make me happy. to me these actions always
appeared to be a choice for him, that he would have said no if he wanted
to, and so why was it so hard for me to accept the same? there must have
been some point in time when the desire to be intimate became known to
me as a duty, and if i did not fulfill this duty, then damage would be done.
maybe that was the argument, why he wasn't in bed this morning? there
would be moments i was, of course, too tired, and he said he'd have to
sleep on the couch or it would be too difficult to sleep in bed next to me.
a double-edged compliment: i want you so badly that if i lie in bed i will
think about being inside of you all night, but i know that we both need to
sleep. but also: i cannot lie next to you, i cannot live with that discomfort
if you say no tonight. and so there the dirt path widens, the gap that
differentiates him from me. when i instill more of what i am, and where i
end, so too does he move away. i want to hold myself as close as i can to
my rational mind! that saying no just once does not mean never! and that
i want every intimate encounter to be laced with truth, and honestly, and
depth, and that is how i can show true love!

but it seems now i have forgotten how to lace it. how to tie things
together, again. in the dress shop, i again feel disoriented, i hold my bag
closer to my body. i shuffle down steps into a bright carnival. little racks
of clothing fling fantasies at me: the shapeliness of this tight white dress,
how it would look with that bright-red pair of heels, how i could tan my
thighs and calves, shave the hair off, straighten my hair. it would look
good. i grab them both. i grab a black bodysuit, i grab an army-green
skirt. i grab a loose, lavender dress and a bright-pink corset to layer on
top, one that i have seen on beautiful women on TV. i think, god help
me, i want to dress like a reality tv star, the kind with turkish veneers
and thick cheeks, whose bodies are just under the recommended mass
index for underweight, the women whom i believe i can replicate if i
just learn to contour my skin. we watched it together, all the reality-TV
shows of lovers in hot climates. i used to find myself resistant at first but
the more i watched the more i realized how these women had wrinkles
and thick under-eye concealer and false lashes and how i could do all of

that too, it just took money and time. in this fantasy everything around me melts away as i shop, imagining my most perfect self, the self that can listen deeply when he speaks, and not get lost in the mist. the self that doesn't argue. that can put her pride aside and apologize. the self that can speak without yelling. the self that doesn't threaten divorce every time the debate becomes unbearable because all i want is to escape in those moments and of course the little rivulets in my brain have no other understanding of how to escape. what other way then to leave? but i didn't want to leave. i wanted to be my perfect self. i have some hope that this act of shopping will be a step further toward that. the more i let the little neurons fire 'perfect self perfect self' the closer i will be. the dress can be my anchor. and on my way toward the dressing room i think of such a perfectly articulate sentence to describe my new ascent but in the dressing room…. the mirrors…

i had a beautiful sentence in my mind and it was lost. the lazy fear. when i can't move on to the next sentence where then do i go? i feel so rudderless without them. the mirrors…. i put my face close and my lips feel cold, colder, i see the blue painting them as if the corpse beneath my skin is slowly showing itself. i undress and goose bumps shimmer to the surface of my thighs and torso. legs mottled. i unzip the tight white dress. the straps on the front and back are racerback—pulled in—to accentuate the waist, how i love a good, cinched-in waist, but my shoulders and breasts are wider than the waist and i cannot pull it over my head. i take it off, and step inside it legs first and it won't come up past my thighs. i read the dress size: four. i was a four. do i not remember being a four? the clothes i have fit now, so what size am i, then? he's bought me dresses before, and i always remember telling him, size four, size four…. i slip on the loose lavender thing. slightly translucent fabric, my bum shows through it. my nipples get erect from the cold and you can see them through the dress, too, and this won't do, how motherly it makes me look—fat breasts, large nipples, dumpy ass. i slip on the pink, reality-tv-girl corset, which is elastic for some reason, and it cinches the waist in but my nipples still show through and it distorts the seam at the back of the dress which doesn't look good at all. i realize i haven't brushed my hair at all, it looks wild, standing up in certain places, uncurled and curled in others, slightly oily at the roots. i take them all off, and i slip on the body suit, which fits but is still a bit too tight in the breasts. though i suppose that would be somewhat sexy if the top laid right. i stand in just the body suit looking at the shape of my curves, though my posture curls over somewhat, i remember being much more shapely. i avoid eye contact with myself and twist my body round to examine my back, sneaking a furtive glance at my side profile. the fluorescent lighting creates shadows on my cheek that reveal every acne scar i've ever had. i sit and stare at the heels. only one pair left on the shelf and they are on clearance. the perfect size, the perfect shape. thick heel, good for walking. a slight platform with a closed, squared, yet slightly rounded toe. i had trouble taking care of my feet even though they used to be my pride, beautiful toes. never a patch of dry skin, i loved for my feet to be adored. and yet now it is like i had forgotten they exist. beneath the coral polish, a black tint bled through. no matter how much i layered it never seemed to go away. i slip my left foot into the shoe and it is tight, so tight. i shove and barely fit my heel in, but i'm perplexed — i look at the size, size five? is this not the size of my feet? but it doesn't fit. i am forgetting every detail of myself, forgetting the very feet i stand on.

the fantasy breaks. i find a black, loose thing that is two sizes larger than what i think i should buy and take it to the register, sulking. in my wallet is another note: always see the good in him. the paper worn thin with torn and crumpled edges, the pencil faded, graphite smudged around each letter. that must have been the reason he was mad. another recurring argument, a bad habit, a ritual. otherwise i wouldn't have needed the reminder. i heard it every time we fought: "you dont give me the benefit of the doubt." its such a common phrase it doesn't even carry any meaning. a doubt to give benefit. doubt yourself, to give me benefit. was that what made it hard to trust? in order to restore harmony to our lives it was necessary for me to doubt the stories i was telling myself. the stories laid day by day by all my habits. but now i cannot even remember what we did last week, or when we last spent time together, where have they gone? where is he? i cannot find the stories we must tell ourselves in order to love each other.

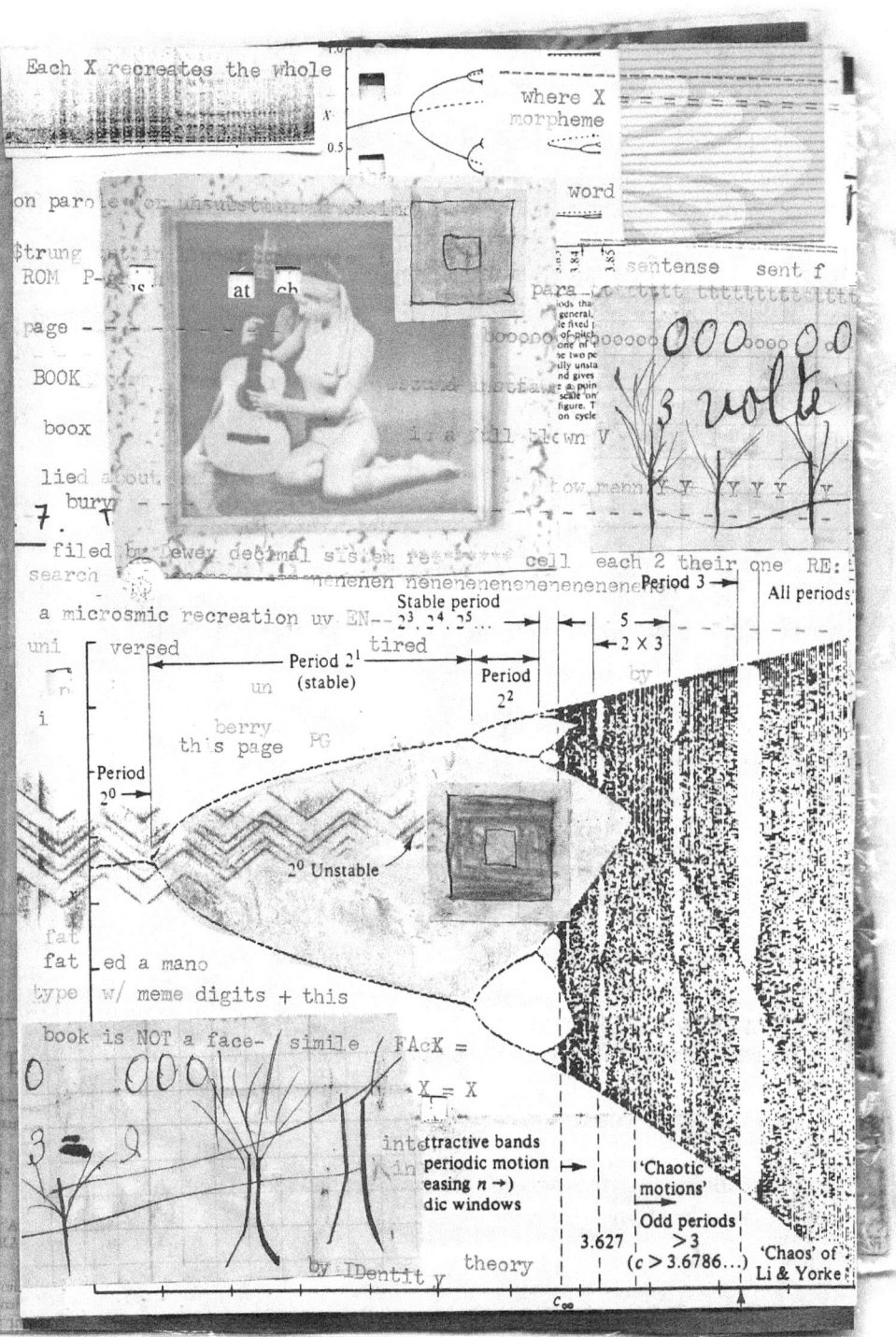

TEXTURE OF THE SOUND OF THE WRONG BAND WARMING UP.

I end up on the ground as a result of someone else's good or bad, probably not too bad, intentions and the angle of the fall lands my left ear square on the surface of the ground in a location 30 degrees clockwise relative to the nearest tall building, 40 degrees from the other medium building and this has nothing well a little no nothing really at all to do with where I intended to place my own body, much less my left ear.

The wrong band is placed, as wrong bands are wont to place themselves, at a distance much further away than my eyes can handle, and it's not that I'm trying to lay blame or allocate reason or escape something altogether, but who, just who is it that placed me here at this particular moment.

The other side of the intersection waits for me, then starts fidgeting, some of the street signs twitch just a tiny, just the slightest bit, and if I were to arrive at this location called the other side would it be an arrival or an escape or a continuation.

Meanwhile the continuation is taking place via the wrong band which I hear through my unsuspecting left ear where I hear someone stretching a sore muscle, and a throat attenuated after years of clearing itself and clearing itself, and a lawn growing. This lawn makes the most troubling sound of all, as it becomes apparent that it is getting trimmed periodically, that it grows, develops a lovely (to some ears) sound blanket, then gets mowed, with a lovely razor blanket, then grows, developing heat, matures into the sound blanket, until it gets mowed again. I stop a man passing by to ask why it should be so that the sound of lawn growing should trouble me so, but he speaks three different languages that are different from the three different languages that I speak, and he gives up on me altogether and walks off, slapping his left ear as if there was a dangerous bug in the air.

But I already know why, and only wanted the man to say it so that I could hear it from my right ear.

[*Note: this piece originally appeared in *Sleepingfish* issue 0.5.]

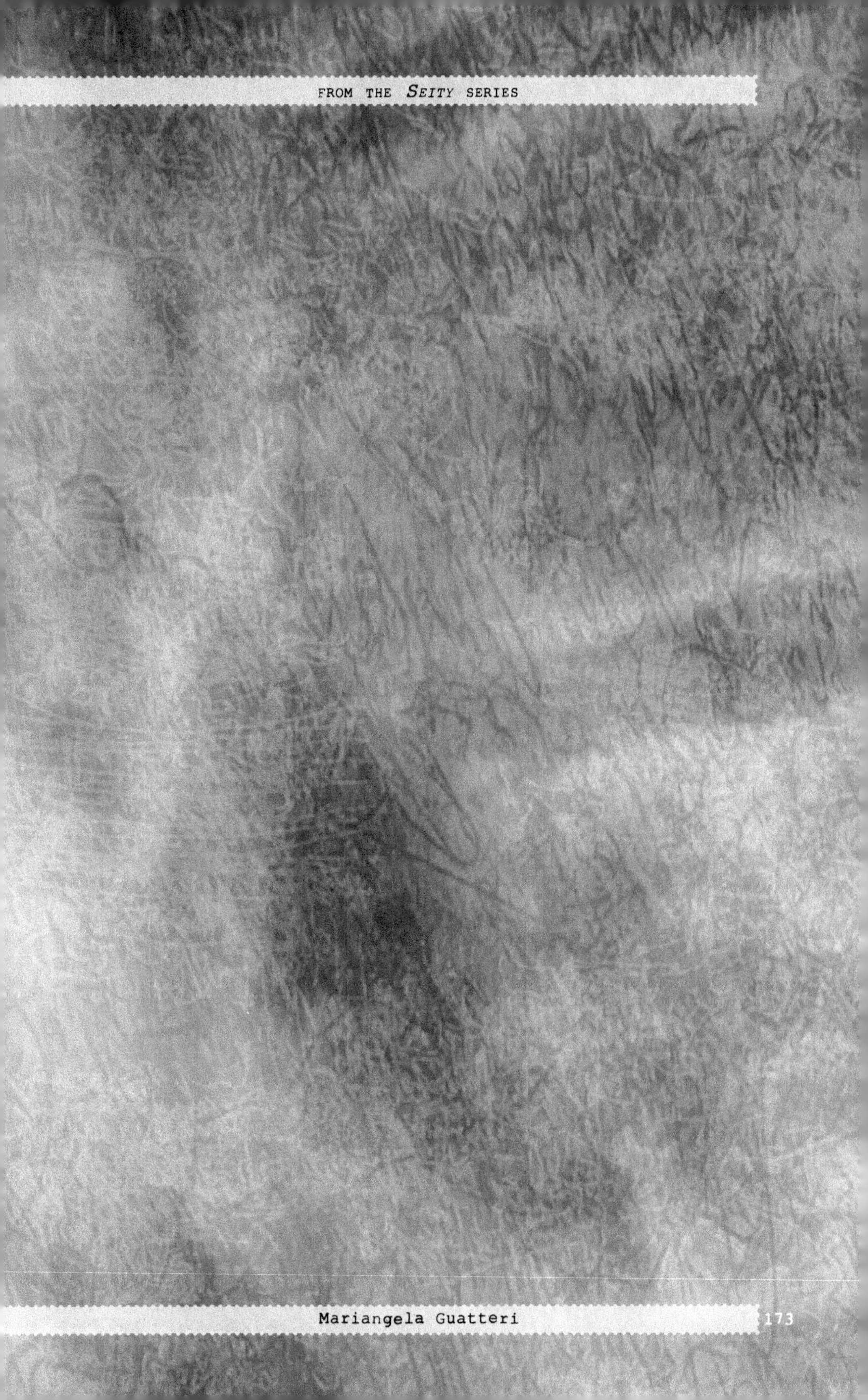

MIRROR MAKER

this is a page of sea here, xagi.
water told of a mirror.
a remembering, xagi.
a remembering mirror.
this is the island of the mirror maker.
xagi, don't wear shoes here.
xagi don't want to upset the mirror maker.
the mirror maker having tea.
where does the seen come from, xagi?
the mirror maker makes the seen stay behind unseen.
don't go close, xagi.
don't make noise.
xagi might get stuck as the seen.
the mirror maker pours the tea.
pours the tea on the mirror, xagi.
where does the unseen go?
how does the mirror maker know, xagi?
don't go close, this is a remembering island.
water told of such a secret.
a secret to remember the unseen, xagi.
the mirror maker spreads the night cloth.
see the night cloth make the seen safe unseen.
this is the island behind the mirror, xagi.
don't go close.
water told of xagi, the mirror maker remembers.

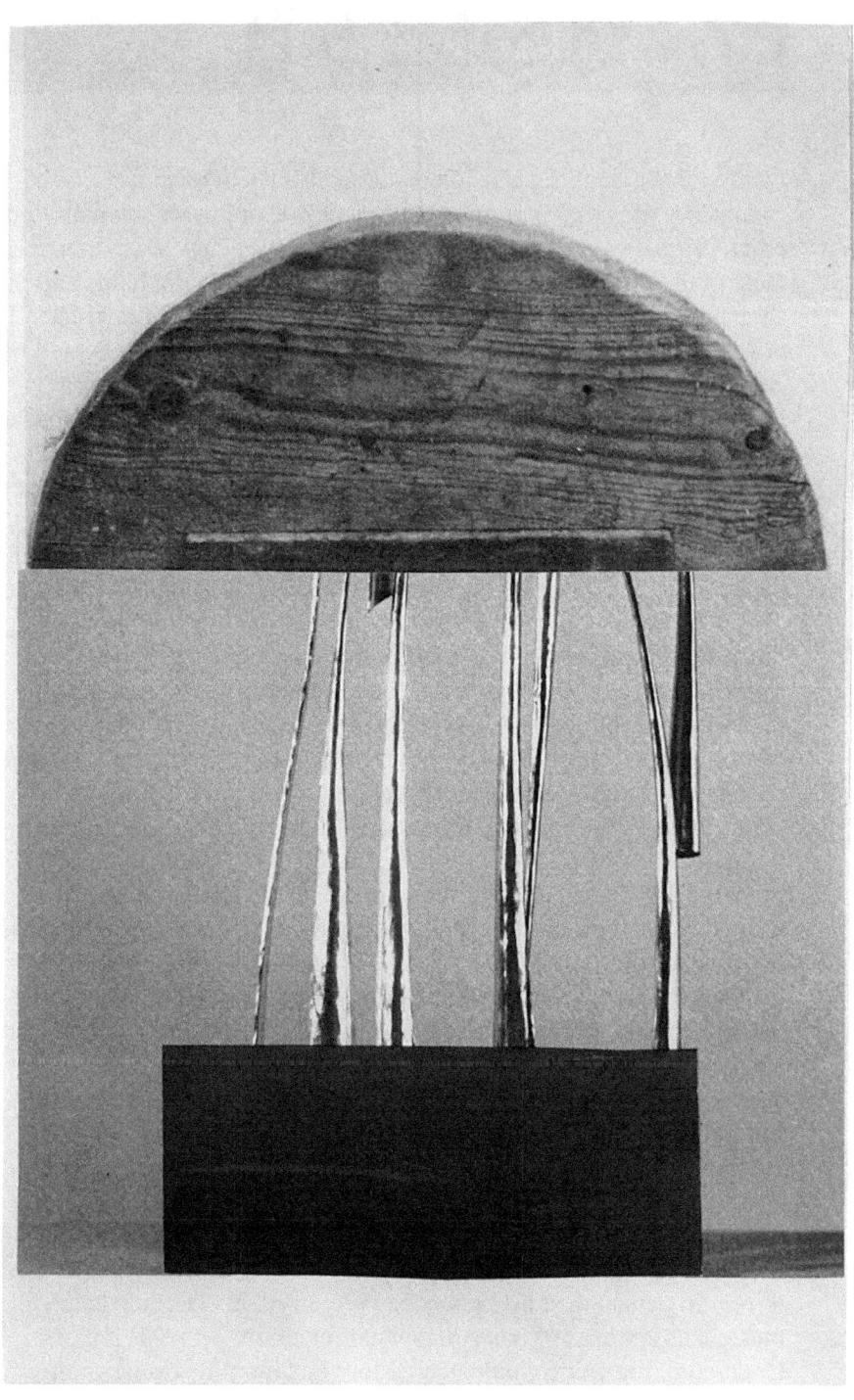

Carla Rak

THE HEAT BETWEEN ME AND YOU

I know I need not heed a headless, desexed ancient torso's charge to change my life but this is my daily practice. Hair blown out, nails "on point," I'm always sure to have at least three meetings lined up to make most of the effort I'm putting in. Antibacterials and exfoliators and the so-called toxic trio. Astringents. Pastes and creams and sprays and powders and gels. Scrubbed, brushed, polished, and waxed, I could be a car, and what's a car but a lustrous symbol of the Empire? "Auto bodywork"—Lo, the correspondences! Every year, over thirty thousand people die in road crashes on our ribbons of highway. "Beep beep, beep beep, yeah!" Nouns the setting: tables, chairs, candles, bottles, glasses, flatware, silverware, floors, doors, walls, windows, curtains. Mingus among us. *Basso profundo*. I have only one drink—usually a glass of red, dark and heavy—with each candidate: a bipedal locomotive, each one's slideshow promising a head, torso, two arms, and two legs in working order, their head ruling their heart or vice versa an open question. There's a world in that ruby swish. The keratin treatment shortens blow-dry time by forty to sixty percent, or so my stylist claims. I have a capacity, so I won't be wobbly by evening's end, but the last candidate sometimes benefits from a certain lubricity. I am aware, at times painfully so—"ice" slicing through my fingertips, hand, and forearm—of a certain gloss, of gasconade in my presentation, exuding not only privilege but desperation, born not, make no mistake, of desire to be wanted, possessed, or protected. Uneasy does it! The intervals find me opening various portals, finding tables of contents approximating persons, me repeatedly proving I know how to swipe left, a not-to-be-underestimated example of informed discrimination. Only disconnect! Chipping starts at the nail plate's distal edge. Moments before, I sat with a person, who follows our Republic's foreign policy, particularly its sundry military campaigns, with an avidity bordering on obsession. His tiresome attire: navy blue suit, red tie, white shirt. I almost set him aflame. His globulous head sat atop a skinny neck—a ball on its tee awaiting a thwacking. Am I a club then—you can bounce a quarter off my Pilates-sculpted stomach—and if so, am I a driver? an iron? He was thicker in person than his photos had promised, his face and hands bloated, as if from pre-menstrual water retention. Were his breasts tender, too, like mine would get? "More like monthly exclamation points," a man, dead to me now, had said. "You'd have periods, too," I'd responded, "if you ever got the point." Such a "manhole"! I used to take pleasure in the idea that the body regenerates itself every seven years. People actually disappear right before your very eyes! Alas, no, each body part has its own distinct lifespan, and a few parts of us—like, and perhaps most importantly, the cerebral cortex, whose twenty-five billion neurons help govern memory, language, attention, and perception, and consciousness as a whole—stay with us from birth to earth. Skin cells rejuvenate every couple of weeks or so, though, so no trace of his clammy palping on my person at least! I'd struggled to keep my eyes off the candidate's eyebrows: brambly messes I wanted to pluck. He was all "high-value targets" and "near certainty" and "low CDE requirements" and "full spectrum dominance." Somewhere, rescue workers were pulling mangled men and women and children out from mounds of debris. Twisted metal. Scorched brick. Splintered glass. Particulate matter suspended in the air. Force and heat. Trauma and burns. Dust, smoke, and toxic fumes in lungs. He told me about the boy in his son's third grade class, who'd slipped off his foam clogs and picked at the residue between his toes, periodically examining the find pinched in his pincers. He laughed when he said the boy's name was Beckett. I laughed, too, recalling the various seemingly pointless acts performed by various of the Irish writer's isolatoes. I could have told him about the man I'd seen at the library, who took out of his satchel what I at first thought was an endless supply of plastic grocery store bags, laying them, one by one, on top of each other, on a table, flattening each bag with his hand, and then one by one balling them up and putting them in his satchel again, and then starting the process all over again. A futile act, perhaps, but, who knows, it could have been a ritual forestalling the foregone finish of the Anthropocene. I could have told him about my own current flirtation with seeming futility. I could have told him about the thing, and by "thing," I mean what's been with me for at least three years, something I can't quite name but something I always keep on or near my person. Neither talisman nor amulet, it's an object, nevertheless, an object of what, surely not my affection, but at least my attention, at least whenever I chanced upon it, the object falling into my hand whenever I rummage in the pocket or purse where it resides. We love to name names, and by "we," I mean, those of us who take pleasure in knowing the names of things, naming synonymous, we think, with knowledge, yes, but also authority and ownership. It's the pleasure of knowing things for what they are, their form and function, the pleasure of knowing the secret motion of things. Onanistic onomastics? But we do have names for such

a thing: "doohickey," "whatchamacallit," "thingamajig," "thingamabob,"
"dingus," "thingummy," "whatnot," "whatsit," "whatsis"—"thingummy"
especially evocative, suggesting a kind of stickiness to the object,
something one cannot quite let go. But I hadn't shared these things,
because I hadn't wanted to interrupt his sharing of stories, of things he
knew, because a man inflates knowing something someone else doesn't,
and I had wanted to see his chest swell, hear his tone hover between
thoughtful and pedantic, until he actually shared something I didn't
know, something I could take away, like leftover scraps, like a souvenir,
something to actually remember him by. If a bomb explodes in a desert,
and no one reports it, does it make a sound? *Tableau mort*: Arms and
legs and torsos and heads merged with metal and glass and brick and dust
and mud. Death come to life. Had he said "Okey-doke"? I'd tried
superimposing Beckett on him, the fissures of the writer's forebearant
face, the fractured density of his music, but I could only see *him*, foggy-
eyed and floundering, his number-crunching brow, his doughy cheeks
and triple chin, his knobby nose jutting out, the accretion of details, my
listing of them, somehow making him less visible—in fact, he was
already fading, less a palimpsest now than a face effaced. My stepfather
had been in the military. We don't speak. My mother once found a vial
of Viagra in one of his pockets. They hadn't been having sex so she
exploded, kicked him out of the house. I hardly speak to her, either.
Father was an idea, who'd died fighting for an idea in a desert. Took one
for the team. A bullet. In the head. Somebody nearby is whistling while
they work—worse, it's the screeching, through-the-teeth type, which
affects me like off-key singing does, which is to say, deeply and terribly.
I love listening to birds, though, their cheeps and tweets, warbles and
quavers, hoots and toots, their trills, calls, and cries I consider less song
or music than as pure and vital communication, and purposeful even
when its purpose eludes us. Sound sleep always proves elusive, nights
finding me waking every three hours or so, mornings finding me
unrefreshed. It's the same dream every night: I'm running down a hill
away from a boulder that's rolling behind me, and even when I shift
direction, move to the left or right, it follows me, gets ever so close, and
just when it's about to roll over me, crush my bones, smear the ground
with my viscera, I wake up. I'd call it Sisyphean but I never see myself
rolling the boulder *up* the hill. What is this enormous thing whose pace
accelerates and threatens to flatten me? Waking, my heart racing, I hear
the birds, and I breathe in and out and in and out, follow the whistling's
bright lines, the slight variations in volume, tone, and pitch. When the
bullet breaches the cranium but doesn't exit it's called a penetrating

wound. A perforating wound when the bullet enters and exits the head. Caliber of weapon, bullet size and speed, and injury site and trajectory determine the extent of damage. I'm working on myself, yes, chipping away at things, as if I were that thing of beauty trapped inside the famed Florentine artist's block of marble, the artist's hand in "obedience to the intellect" removing the excess to reveal the sculpture, set the seraph, its light and passion, free. A woman at a nearby table just sneezed without covering her mouth, instead expelling her whatever into the air, unaware or simply not caring that ejected spittle, powered by a "multiphase turbulent buoyant bubble," can travel as far as two hundred feet. Humans. "Browse invisibly," my preferred portal offers, for a price, of course. Connected, where does the body go? Less bodies than mobile operating systems, what to call the feeling felt when our machines stutter, go slow, shut down? What to call us? The body apoplectic? And the loss when we lose our machine? Phantom app? Waiting for the next candidate, I resist the urge to upload her slideshow. Better to be surprised crossing the microelectronic divide; and it always is surprising, jarring, even, the disparity, the dissonance between luminous planes, however curvilinear, and actual faces, edges, and vertices moving in actual space. She had, like so many others, said she was looking for someone who was "comfortable in her own skin." Who else's skin would I be comfortable in? I tried not to think about this but thinking about not thinking often leads to the unthinkable. Here she is: unyoung but bright-eyed, overall squarish but roundish at the shoulders, buttocks, and hips, wearing yoga pants, ankle-length socks, a sports bra barely holding up her bottle-gourd breasts. "I'm a hot mess," she says, explaining she'd come directly from a yoga "rave," which I understood to mean a kind of fusion of animal-inspired contortions, aerobics, and ecstatic spinning and jumping around, where electronically synthesized dance music is played, where a sticky dancefloor is gridded by brightly colored, eco-conscious rubber mats, where every "raver" fashions thin plastic tubes containing probably-not-terribly-toxic luminescent material into bracelets, anklets, necklaces, and/or the like. I hope she showered. "Don't worry," she says. "I showered." I laugh, and she laughs, for different reasons, but I could be wrong about this. In any case, we're off. She orders a Montepulciano d'Abruzzo. I'm on my second Sagrantino di Montelfalco. Not out of my head, yet, oh well. Bill Evans now. Cerebral. Haunting. Revelatory. She's in advertising. A creative director. Relieved the day's over, she says, "Feels good not to be telling people what to do." She brings up television—the Republic's lingua franca—says something about the idiot box's renaissance, blah, blah, blah. "I like to watch," I say. "Not television, though." "Oh?" she says, and laughs. I tell her I wish shows lasted only a season, that what makes them interesting is their "knots," their "dangling threads." She asks if I've seen the latest cyborg-takeover film. "It's on the list," I say, even though it isn't. She smiles, revealing two neat rows of small white teeth. And her eyes: green pools, a sylvan dream. Blame it on the Sagrantino! "Loved its languor, its subtle special effects," she says. "Makes a Kubrickian, antiseptic atmosphere almost erotic." Her eyelids are small sea-smoothed shells. She says something about CGI but I'm thinking about consciousness and intimacy, about the Turing test, how online dating, despite its aggravatingly arrhythmic algorithms, might be a warped engagement with it. Bod or bot? "These aren't the droids you're looking for." "Questions...Morphology? Longevity? Incept dates?" May I talk about the space between us, which we created together, the pressures, suspensions, and disturbances? Her slot almost over, I tell her I had a great time, whereupon the well-trained waiter dutifully arrives with the check. "You get it next time," I say, waving away her card. We say our goodbyes. She kisses my cheek, her lips hot and humid, tropical. We won't see each other again. Cancel, clear, delete. She had brought to mind, though, that early evening, lukewarm like a long-distancing lover, me sitting on the steps of the brownstone, a light breeze blowing across the block's elms, my eyes tracking every spiraling gilded or angered red-orange leaf, each one detaching itself, as if they, too, had something to prove by leaving, the cloud-filled sky reminding me of a spring afternoon on a hotel rooftop with the not-yet-ex, where I watched the clouds while everyone else looked at the distant blinking skyline and fuscous river. I'd felt suffocated by the slowly moving masses, each enormous white billow crowding out the blue expanse; and then dizzied after looking at a slatted section of the populuxe roof that looked like *it* was moving. "Motion aftereffect" doesn't quite capture the visual disorientation. A car had slowly passed, last light painting the windshield gold. The sidewalks were empty, every commuter plugged into their newsy comedies. The not-yet-ex was on a trip, doesn't matter where. Returning, slipshod shirt on shirking shoulders, stinking of cigarettes, sinking into his thinking, he'd go on about how his life was wasting away, that he felt trapped; then we'd argue and fuck like animals, claw at each other until we bled. I'd met her, doesn't matter where. I didn't think she'd call. She asked if I wanted to come visit her upstate, where she was house-sitting. The not-yet-ex was difficult. I was difficult. He was staying up later and later, I was waking up earlier and earlier. We rarely had sex, and we always needed some device or whatever: buzzing toy, candy panties, feathers. Famished, I sat outside the brownstone just before leaving for upstate. En route to the highway, I got a drive-through burger. When I forced it into my mouth, the relish lit up my throat. Drive-*by* burger more like it! The treacly, sudsy soda didn't help, and by the time I reached my exit, my bowels were loose. After forever in an instant, I found myself standing at a door ringing a bell, looking at casement windows, hoping light would shine from its small panes. Frustrated, I circled the house, looking at the windows between the gables. Coming back to the front, I rang again. After a peephole click, the door finally creaked open. She sing-songed my name, light shining on her flushed face. "Bathroom?" I said, dropping my pack. "Bathroom!" Was I shouting? "Down the hallway," she said, pointing. In moments, a bowel movement became a religious experience. You are you and you are here and now, it seemed to say, as my thighs trembled. Closing my eyes, I inhaled, held the breath, and exhaled, and slowly opened my eyes. The glazed tile was blue and white, and ornately-patterned, like Talavera earthenware. No one ever wants to know what you've done in the bathroom. It's as if you've disappeared, at most conducted some kind of "business," the various "deposits" accorded a number. Done, I reached for some toilet paper. Finding an empty roll, I stood up, clothes still around my ankles. I peered into the cabinet beneath the sink. Still nothing. Desperate, I looked for a towel. No luck there, either. I felt silly calling for help. It reeked. Standing up, I shimmied out of my jeans and underwear, wiping my ass with the latter, and flushed the toilet. I watched the murky water rush to the top, cascade over the rim, the filthy thong fragments also falling from the bowl. I stepped into the tub, dressed, unlatched the window, stuck my head out. Just a short drop to the ground. I only looked back once at the house, which rose from the dark like a tomb, the wind biting my face, the moon a silver you could scratch with a coin. My stomach heaved, so I stopped, bent my head down, pressed my hands against my thighs. Panting like a dog, I watched a tree shiver off some leaves. The average bullet travels at twenty-five feet per second: around seventeen hundred miles per hour. You'd need to be twice as fast as the fastest Olympic sprinters and at least five hundred feet away to successfully dodge a bullet. "How Come U Don't Call Me Anymore" is playing. O, how I miss Prince's otherworldly falsetto. Behold the pimply prepubescent who'd sneaked into a darkened theater, where a movie she was forbidden to watch was playing, had almost reached its end, in fact, the girl walking up the soda-sticky floor to watch an empurpled peacock of a man wearing a mariachi singer's ruffled shirt and tight black pants prance about a stage, illuminated columns of pink, blue, and white slicing up the surround. Here's my final candidate—

mean street and pop apocalyptic. He hugs me. "Men know right away if they want to see a person naked," the dead-to-me-now man had said. "And women know right away if they want to be seen naked by a person." I knew right away I wanted to see and be seen. There's something tattooed on the inside of his right hand's middle finger. I ask him about it. "It says, 'Am I dreaming?,'" his eyes brightening as he says it. He goes on to talk about "yogic," or lucid, dreaming, sharing how he often looks at the tattoo throughout the day to blur the lines between fantasy and reality. "Whatever," he says, looking at the tattoo. "The body—it falls away." He likes hearing himself talk and he likes that I like hearing him talk. It's all he needs. "I embody the dialectic," he says. "We need to see ourselves as being and becoming," he says. "You have to move past the spectacle," he says, "past the simulacra and simulation, to something more stimulating, something real, someone real." See what he did there? The shift from first person to first-person plural to second person? He says something about the "project" we're "engaged with, in, and within." He says something about the "vehicle" we use to meet each other. "'Personal statement' is an odd phrase," he says, "and like many if not most oddities, it's an opportunity for reflection." He sounds like somebody who is paid to talk, a "man of letters," composed, too, of arms and ascenders, ears and spurs, legs and ligatures, descenders and hairlines, shoulders and spine, stresses and strokes. I picture him standing at a podium, ghost-faced, delivering a paper on some rarefied subject, with a title like "Corporeality and the Disenfranchised Subject"; "Hegemonic Sex with/in the Abject Body"; or "Toward a Critique of Imperialist Erotics." The restaurant disappears and there he is, delivering his paper, "During the Time of Being (the Thing Specified), or Decomposition as Explanation," in an auditorium empty save for the other poor souls who'd had their own papers accepted, each one secretly worrying how long their for-profit college would take to reimburse their expenses: *Mark the open casket. The remains: a transmutation of "the Century's corpse outleant" and the resolutely postmodernist figuration of "a patient etherized upon a table": a merging of form and deformation, of commentaries on the nineteenth century's supposed certainties and the twentieth century's doubts and fears and their resultant fragmentations. Lying in State: a multiplicity, a series of various in-betweens, corpses, whether as identities or musics in their compositional and decompositional expressions, said corpses' corpus suggesting an emergent ontology, which, while engaging the world from a diversity of perspectives, recognizes that the "person" must be re-imagined and reformulated, while registering the continual malleability of those performed identities.* A horn forlorn. Roy Eldridge, I think. "My heart is sad and lonely," Lady Day sings. "Grade-grubbers," he says, talking about his students. "To err is human," I say, "and to complain American." "I like that," he says, laughing. "Paying out the wazoo, they think of themselves as customers and the customer is always—" "Rewriting?" I say. "If only," he says, laughing again. *Being-dead is not an end but a kind of becoming, a becoming something-else, which is to say, the so-called Other, the she/he/it who continually complicates the relations, disturbs and disrupts them, makes them incomprehensible. This she/he/it, this excess, this void, or voiding, this vacancy of person, evidenced by multiple iterations and medial interventions, viz., "versions," suggests that form, already acting and being acted upon, also always suggests other forms, forms that deform what was formed, informing whoever engages with the form that other forms exist and persist.* I'm on a second bottle now, I think. My "wooden leg" is in good working order, but I drink a glass of water while he goes on to talk about "performed identities," and the "status of the person—a speculative being that's incomplete, that's always already evolving and devolving, who, finally, is—" "Mediated, remediated, fragmented, and dispersed?" I say, which surprises him. "'Stuffed shirt,' that's me," he says, laughing. "You didn't say you were from Synecdoche," I say. He laughs, saying, "Love that film." "Are you going to drink something?" I say. He laughs, waving the waiter over, and orders a gimlet straight, and I step away to go to the restroom, where the auditorium appears again, but the audience, such as it was, is gone, and so is the speaker, reminding me of a moment in that film—what's it called?—with the actor who later literally got away with murder after crashing into an oncoming vehicle and killing its passengers, the film where the students one by one leave a classroom, each one leaving a recording device behind, where, finally, the teacher leaves, too, a recording of himself left to deliver the day's lesson. Only the disembodied voice remains: *Repetition with a difference dissolves the supposed polarities of absence and presence, negativity and positivity, Being and non-Being, abundance and lack, silence and sound. It's a sensibility that is inextricably connected to identity compositions and decompositions, to the idea of the idea produced by the idea, or versioning, which is inextricably fused with the composition and decomposition of identity. Prince's corpses must be regarded not as a linear progression, where one thing replaces and erases the other, but as a collective of exteriorities, those corpses localized but also departing from their respective points of inception.* The bathroom was an homage to Duchamp, the splintered gold-ochre to black tilework evoking his incandescent naked descender, the sink an overturned urinal, the floor-to-ceiling mirror behind it eerily creating a five-way portrait. It was a place to think. *We might bring Malabou's idea of the "sculpture of the self" into play, her assertion that "[i]dentity resists its own occurrence to the very extent that it forms it." Resistance is invoked as a kind of insistence, as persistence. There is no loss of identity, only a reformulation or reconstititution of it into something different. Sculpture allows for procedures not limited to addition, subtraction, proliferation, decay. Form is both object and movement, existing and happening simultaneously within and without whatever is being formed or is forming. While the sculpture of the self is, arguably, "born from deflagration of an original biological matrix," Prince's various iterations, his corpses, his sculptural corpus, even at the supposed originary moment, involve no cancellation, and, whether embodied or disembodied, it's sloughed and resumed at will. Behold the messianic androgyne, yes, but also the flyblown surplus. Behold the corpses lying in state. But do not mourn. Being-dead is a state of being.* I'm sitting at the table again. The First Lady of Song is singing. Bright, pellucid, supple. "I'm talking too much," he says. "I do that when I'm nervous," he says. "I don't mind," I say, and I don't, and then he says, "For weeks now, I've endured what sounds like someone prancing on the floor above my apartment. It's the same rhythm over and over again: a couple of soft hops ending in a final jump, its subsequent crash shaking my walls. It sounded choreographed, like a ballet routine. I thought I would get used to it. I couldn't, so I finally went upstairs to complain to my neighbor, who apologized, saying he was exercising and would try to keep the noise down. The tight jeans and long-sleeved, button-down shirt he wore didn't seem like proper workout attire, though, and he gave off a vibe of having just been caught doing something wrong. He hadn't had enough time to get out of ballerina garb, either, so I don't know what was going on, but if he had opened the door dressed in a tutu and pointe shoes, it would've been *me* apologizing for interrupting *him*." I laugh, and he laughs. He goes on, and I think about a teacher I once had, a certain Professor Fader, who once lectured on Hobbes, for whom, as he'd put it, "reality is corporeality," Fader going on to say that a "person is a material entity in a material world, a complex system of motion and emotion, a mass of six elements subject to the laws of gravitation," a student interrupting him to say, "Oh, like what Madonna said?" Fader saying, "The Madonna?" the student singing, "'You know we're living in a material world and I am a material girl,'" Fader saying, "I'm afraid I don't know what you're talking about," the student saying, "Okay, but we usually don't know what you're talking about," the class laughing. Umbrous, supersized, composed, hard, he speaks just above a whisper, his tone a soft contrast to his Mount Rushmore face. I'm well into another glass by the end of his rather rambling but still impressive monologue, during which I finished all my toasted slices of olive oil-dipped pane Francese. He strikes me as someone I could see, for a short while, allowing him to come just so close, to keep him wondering, unsure. We would date, go ice skating, where I'd enjoy myself—despite thinking how it could be a metaphor for life, one is, after all, running around in circles on thin ice—allowing him to hook his arm around mine and to sometimes even take my hand. We would meet another time for a round of ping-pong and pool at a dive where a freeform ensemble would be performing—all harmonic snarl, multiphonic blat, percussing scattershot. After several more dates, I would take him home, where we'd go through the permutations: he above me then me atop him then he behind me, and then he above me again, his eyes closed, reverentially, his eyes open, ecstatically, he and I riding invisible currents—of consciousness?—displacing our centers, losing the sense of sense and senselessness, the primeval gestures and utterances of the so-called order of things, he and I yessing until we both shook ourselves loose. After a time, months, maybe, a few weeks, likely, I'd find myself lying in bed for hours, letting my mind drift, as I'd done when I was a child, somehow able to block the noise all around me, the crashes and booms, of smashed glass and slammed shut doors, respectively, whereupon I'd text him, saying things like "You're nice and great, but I feel guarded around you," and "My body doesn't lie to me," and "The chemistry I need just isn't there," to which he'd hide his disappointment behind understanding, conciliatory sentences. As he pays for our drinks, I thank him for his time, tell him I'll be in touch, liking the way his eyes beam in response. You might accuse me of seeing people as aggregates of feelings and ideas, collecting them as one would coins or stamps or insects, and you might be right. A bullet is sometimes referred to as a "foreign body." They refer to the brain's gelatinous lobes as "tissue," for good reason, though. Sometimes I think I'm addicted to sex, and sometimes I think I'm addicted to *my* sex, my pudendum, my clitoris, especially, stroking it exactly how I want it to be stroked while watching other people having sex, any kind of sex. There's a luxuriating in the watching in counterpoint with a welling, the blood rushing and the eventual release, which I always delay. Sometimes I watch with the people I'm with and it's easier to come if I do. Tap, click, key, and something appears. Sometimes it doesn't matter what it is. Sometimes nothing works. There would be the boring orgy of orifices, the moaning and groaning, the affirmations, the shifting velocities, flesh pummeling flesh, the orgasmic spasms, limbs rippling as pleasure cascades. There would be a woman, garland necklaced on her, who mounts a man, plants herself atop him as if she were a tree, and I would stroke myself, my underwear offering additional friction, and while I felt something, a mild throbbing, I just couldn't get into it. The body is not the being. This happens sometimes. Feeling disconnected. Mind from body. Body from mind. My body something apart. No, simultaneity is what I mean. First person and third person together. Monologue and dialogue. It is what it isn't. What I waited for were those moments of, what to call it, steppings out of character, the scratching of an itch, the moving of hair behind the ears, the removing of a lone long lissome hair out of a mouth, each act subtly but no less sensually overthrowing the prison of illusions that subordinates female desire, action, and climax. I would try another video: two women wrangling around each other, but this, too, would bore me, my body oppositional to the machine, to its indiscernibly fizzing static, so I would turn it off, continuing to stroke, however, conjuring a callipygian figure, a woman wearing the tightest of jeans and shirts, her ass perfectly formed, like a giant, golden onion. This would do nothing for me, either, so I would stop. The body is person, place, and thing. The body is idea, action, quality. Thrusting my hand into my pocket, I find the object, fondle it, bring it out, careful, though, to keep it out of sight, the object inert, yes, but solid, a reified resistance to change, to shape and volume, signifying, perhaps, the quest for something that lasts. It used to frighten me, this simultaneity, this floating between observing my own body and disappearing into it. See the exact point of the break, the break of the whole, within the whole. Females ages sixteen to nineteen are four times more likely than the general population to be sexually assaulted. "No words"? Words are all we have. There is no body without language. It is language. Earlier, I found a typo in a book I was reading: "underminded." I liked this word, which intimated thought's subterranean depths. I often misread "uniformed" as "uninformed." Fitting. You know that form of torture where water is slowly dripped onto a restrained person's forehead, whereupon the victim is allegedly driven insane? Another person's keypad clicks might just be the modern equivalent. He was all face, all chest, a weight, a hundred-something pounds pounding into her. Breached, she breaks. Fracted, hovering somewhere—above?—I see her, sobbing uncontrollably, pushing, trying to push him off and away, her nothing arms pushing against a wall falling over and over until it's finally over. Whose mind is on sex and death? Who loves cider-and-bourbon-glazed shallots? Who wants to step on someone's trachea with her boot? The final candidate had lied about his age, most men do, most of the men I date, at any rate, middle-aged men who shave away the years as easily as their beards, as much as the women at any age many men assume do. This man, though, was younger than he'd said he was, which was hardly surprising, any number of men finding older women attractive, desiring a certain kind of motherly comfort, perhaps, but I was no mother—I can't stand children, having only two questions for them whenever I had the misfortune of meeting them: What's your name? And how old are you? The answer to either of which I couldn't care less about. My doxie's an entirely different story. The restaurant's almost empty. Equinoctial night—I hope it's raining. I want to get drenched. "Drenched," I say, aloud, loving the aqueous play of tongue and teeth and lips. "Drenched. Drenched. Drenched," stretching the word each time, making a meal of the phonemes, the abrupt gust after the final plosive—thought for food! Traffic, weather, people hurrying past, a woman solus, a figure less person than movement, dreading the savage shift from cold to colder, the cold that startles every darkling thing into silence. She's spent years puzzling herself back into her body. Can you see me? That's the question. Can you see me living in fragments? Can you see me, tired, wasted, wasting away, facing the façade, the masquerade, the debauched sense of entitlement, sick of the action items, benchmarks, deliverables, and takeaways? Can you see me, haunted by Hans Holbein the Younger's *The Ambassadors*'s anamorphic skull, the so-called distortion the actual subject of the painting? Can you see me, undermined by obliquity, resigned to living in a place, or something like a place, an abstract continuum, say, a place where rainfall's pitiful pitter-patter, an electric oven range's stridulating, and my mind's circumbendibuses converge, a mind that tic-tac-toes lines across a succession of exes, a place where hackworked bric-a-brac and workaday bricolage are peremptorily lumped, like so much humpty dump? Can you see me, flensing away the pestilential skin of an empty existentialism? Can you see me, middling, dillydallying around a park, where I catch a grasshopper, who doesn't want to be caught, but who, once caught, doesn't want to let go of my thumb, a park where I also startle upon a dead chipmunk, emptied, its eyes a jeweled jelly? Can you see me standing, transfixed, before a pot popping popcorn, me enjoying the oil sizzling, the kernels rattling, the fibery smell, the pop here and there, the popping speeding up, like a buzz roll on a snare drum? Can you see me, bored by the fights over who's better, the Beatles or the Stones, Bob Dylan or Leonard Cohen? I like it best when Cohen screams.

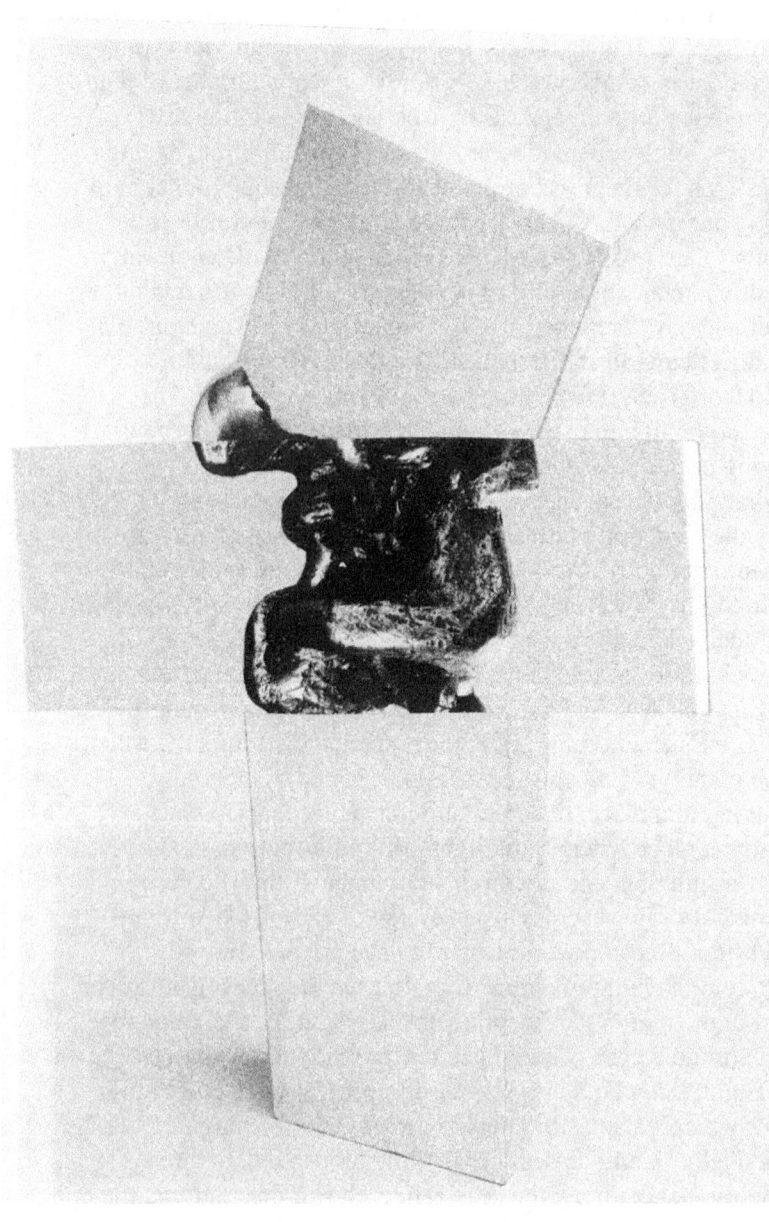

Carla Rak

CALENDAR MAKER

xagi, see the lines.
see the marks on the stone, xagi.
see the knots on this string.
every hand is a shape of moon, xagi.
every hand a calendar.
look. see.
fingers are not enough, xagi.
this is the cave of the calendars.
an island inside a cave, xagi. an island inside of time.
bring the fire close, xagi.
bring the fire, slow.
the calendar maker counts only in light.
there are no calendars of the dark, xagi.
look. see.
see the walls.
see the stone with broken lines.
see the knots on this ending string.
see the steps going up. going.
the calendar maker unties the string. unties old time, xagi.
the calendar is a hole.
look, xagi. see.
inside the hole is the past.
outside the hole is the future, xagi.
the calendar maker makes a wall.
an empty wall of time, xagi.
a circle. a piece of string.
look, xagi. look through.
look through the calendar.
the walls are full-up with the past.
will the past ever come back, xagi?
this, lies the calendar maker.
this, time running on a string, xagi.
fingers are not enough.
fingers are too few, xagi.
new time, outside.
the calendar maker sees right through the hole.

sees the empty wall, xagi.
moon change shape. moon change place.
sun change. and sun can't change, xagi.
see the day never fit. see the day change place, xagi.
see the knots untie. see the broken lines unite.
the calendar maker makes empty, the loop of time, xagi.
will it ever come back?
the lies of the calendar maker.
the lies of the calendar, xagi?

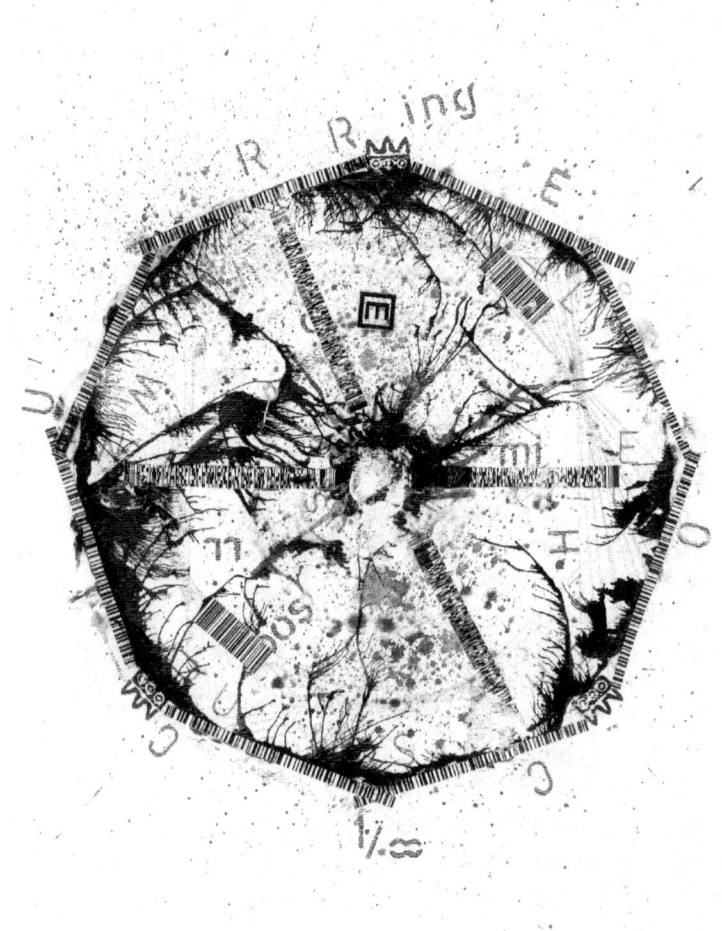

DRURY IN THE HERMITAGE

Days disappear, vaporous years. All this time I'm socking away, like a dowager with her cash-crammed mattress, but god knows where I put it all. I don't own a calendar. I try not to monitor the decline on TV. My one small concession to commercial ambition is gambling. You need money to gamble, but you also need time. Unfortunately, I don't have anybody on the payroll to tell me what I did with mine, how much gone, which corner of the house or galaxy, whether a black hole is to blame, etc. I have my mother, and then one day I don't.

A short while after that, a serviceman restocking the grocery-store lotto machine—the one from which I'm trying to extricate my jammed foot—informs me that, actually, TV is pretty good now.

Sometimes it feels like someone has excavated a moderately deep hole in my skull—halfway back the scalp, I'd say—and packed at the bottom, miles deep, is the savvy and cunning sense that used to vibrate closer to the surface. Maybe a few semilurid urges and U.S. treasury bonds are pancaked down there, too. I mean, I know some knowledge is in me. I just can't reach it without a tipsy crane arm or drill. Fracking—is that what the natural-gas concerns do nowadays? Corporate prospectors in neon hard hats and khaki who gather around a company pickup truck where a schematic map is weighted flat across the hood, the men's clip-on ties rustling in the prairie breeze, as they talk about slickwater and detergents and flowback while smoking Kools. Kools! You can lose a lot of machinery to the hungry void. You can lose years, toes, teeth, people. Not to mention vast piles of wealth that were never really yours to lose.

This suburb that accommodated most of my family's ravings and pratfalls is finally too mortified, too exhausted, to host my midlife collapse. The miles of tawny fairways just can't take it. My bullshit forties, I've found, have left me even more pasty-faced and vulnerable than my bullshit thirties, twenties, teens, and whatever perdition preceded that.

Not long ago, in a brief ellipsis, my sister and I shared a brownstone apartment in the city, a neglected riverfront landscape of industrial sludge and junked machinery. I kept a novelty switchblade holstered in my left knee sock because we lived in that type of neighborhood and I lived that type of life. I no longer have a sister, a mother. But maybe I still have Drury?

Back to the grime-and-nostalgia-caked city I decide to go.

The old neighborhood is nothing like I left it. Our sludgy, trudgy, gentrification-adjacent bohemia has been poleaxed, the rubble carted off via flatbeds and hearses. Now the neighborhood is reincarnated in glass luxury, glowering towers of it, that overlook the city's second-most septic river. My old building—what I *think* is my old building—is a seven-deck panopticon with, I shit you not, a real living shrub in the vestibule. It has one! It is a majestic vision, this building. Everything could still be sitting there—the hobbled furniture, the malevolently stained underwear—harvesting bedbugs and moss. I stand outside, gaping through the lobby glass, unable to enter. There is nobody on the street to inquire if I'm okay, if I need emergency assistance. That's something, at least. Maybe the hearses came for the Good Samaritans, too.

How long have I been gone? I cannot think in terms of duration, only atomic mass, thermal radiation, nuclear twilight. Time swirls around you a little differently when you are lodged at the bottom of a black hole, I suppose, a tidal vortex of space junk and garbage light hurling around you, without stop, in your mother's house. That kind of whirlpool can pin you flat, thumbtack you on the map. It also delineates your absence. It makes of you a hungry void.

I leave the building that is no longer my building. An older guy, who I think is a plainclothes security guard, is tailing me through the street.

"Poleaxed!" I shout at him.

He pretends to not hear me. He stops to buy a vegan crepe at some kind of vegan-crepe kiosk that is apparently a new feature of urban living.

Oh, how I have missed this stupid city.

The people, too. Bachelors are now coupled. Couples are now married. The married are parents. The parents are now divorced. My sister and I never had a deep catalogue of city acquaintances, but we knew the perennial fixtures. Crippled buskers, jolly street lepers, vendors of dead twigs and flowers, the vermin. Who knows where my favorite street lepers and vermin have gone? All the casualties of the urban corridor scatter eventually, I know this, to turgid suburbs and snowbird resorts, if not the magnificently groomed municipal cemeteries that could be easily mistaken for either or both.

At least Drury, my former knife-dealer/personal armory, is living in the same swarthy, rent-controlled hovel just off the off-ramp of the midtown bridge. He doesn't bother to ask my business or vet me before buzzing me up. Whatever criminal element has not been expelled from the neighborhood pretty much leaves him alone. Drury has that reputation, I guess, the benign mystic, a harmless shut-in. Also, he also has all that swarthy knife-ware to guard the hermitage.

The hermitage hasn't changed, thank god. No petit-bourgeois trappings, no modernist lighting schemes or mid-century coffee tables with purposefully fanned subscription magazines, no MOMA prints tacked to the wall. Just the couch and TV. There isn't much extravagance in them, either. The only prominent feature of the apartment is Drury himself, sunk in the largest of the couch's Chicxulub-esque craters and moldering in his waffle-print long johns and Dickensian stocking cap. Middle age has parched him. His skin is papery, his face ruddled. I can barely see his eyes through the shreds of gray-wheat hair mashed against his forehead. I snap my fingers a few times, but his attention is guy-wired to the TV. Onscreen, a chocolate stallion is doing a constipated prance across a plush field so emerald and exotic it looks synthetic.

"That horse," I say.

"What about it?"

"It has a bad case of the jimmy legs."

"It's called dressage," Drury replies. "It's a sport."

"This isn't the kind of thing where the horse gets injured and somebody sets up a special striped tent so they can shoot the poor animal indiscreetly, is it? It doesn't look like a sport."

"Dressage is officially recognized by the International Equestrian Federation. Don't you watch the Olympics?"

"I like it," I tell him. "I'm not being facetious. I could watch this insanity all day."

Drury grunts his approval of my approval. I shift my weight from leg to leg, doing a hoofy two-step of my own. It's enough. He digs into the quicksand pit of the couch, extracts the clicker, and taps taps taps. The image jerks backwards. The whole six-hour anthology plays in fast rewind, like a 1920s serial with squiggles and saloon piano banging in the background. I didn't realize there were any VCRs left in the world. I didn't realize Drury had interests.

"Hey, Drury," I announce grandly. "I'm back."

"I see that."

"You're still alive?"

"Astonishingly, yes. Do you want me to show you a knife?"

"I thought maybe we'd talk first," I say.

"How's your sister?"

"Still astonishingly dead."

"Goddamn it." He smacks his forehead. "I thought you were the dead one."

"Funny," I say. "Funny."

I join him on the couch. As I sit, the cushion sags, causing its grid of rusty coils to rattle against whatever hearty arsenal is stowed in the juncture beneath us.

"You still living off unemployment?"

"Disability," Drury says.

"You look healthy to me."

"I do?"

"Your thumb and eyeballs seem to work."

"You're just being nice."

"Do I really have that reputation?"

"Not at all. The truth is, I can't remember what I injured. Maybe it was my memory."

"I'm sure that defense will hold up in court. Nobody remembers anything anymore."

"Drury does not go to court," Drury says.

"I saw this movie already," I say. "Drury *does* go to court. He wears a spiffy suit and tie. He watches his horses on a closed-circuit TV. He sits there all day, hunched forward, while the bailiffs cavity-search him. They find a few Easter eggs and a clicker for his TV."

Drury flutters an eyelid. Either it's a wink or he's trying to flinch through the straggling bangs.

"I missed this," he says.

"The banter?"

"I don't see a lot of people anymore."

"Me neither."

"How was your mom's? You were gone so long."

"It wasn't *that* long. Four, five years?"

"Ten years," he says. "A decade. The lifespan of a purebred dog."

"Shit. Really?"

"I thought maybe you had a religious epiphany or joined the Peace Corps. I thought maybe you did something meaningful with your life."

"It's pronounced Peace *Core*. The corpse is silent."

"Drury gets corrected," he says.

I have shown up wearing my proudest corporate-ready attire and a steel-forged smile, propagating the notion that I indeed possess a high-fatigue life. The ignorance armors me, same as the ugly pantsuit. My heart isn't pinned on my sleeve so much as crucified to my corduroy lapel—a bloody-dangling brooch.

"My mom died," I say.

He rubs the salt-and-pepper grain of his unshaven cheek. "Drury offers his heartfelt condolences. He kinda feels like a thoughtless shit now."

"It's okay. Moms die. That's just something they do. Especially when they have heartless insurgents for daughters. The government has conducted scientific studies about this very phenomenon."

Drury glances me over, I can tell, parsing for fissures and leaks. He claps a supportive hand on my kneecap, a comfort I could sure use, if not return in kind. I decide to spare him the agony of protracted intimacy.

"Hey, bud? Can you please turn back on the magic box of jiggling horse ass? I was really enjoying that."

Drury complies, but after a few seconds, he pauses the footage again. The freeze-frame shows a dozen-some diminutive jockeys ranked along the sidelines like antique lawn statues that have been evicted from the ye olde yards of yore. A still life of sorts, but whose life, really? Whose yard? And how long can these runts stand around, collecting moss and getting sunburned, with so many preening horses and heartless insurgents on the march?

"This is a little awkward," Drury mumbles. "I'm not sure if I should ask about the circumstances of your mom's untimely end."

"You mean the dirty details? It was a malapropism."

"That some kind of accident?"

"Pills," I say. "Motel room."

"Oh."

"She mistook tragedy for comedy. Dying for living. Too much for not enough."

"If you don't want to talk about—"

"It was one of those budget franchises. The desk clerk said she came in without any luggage and requested the Nixon Suite. That was the closest thing to a goodbye note. The Nixon joke."

Drury is staring at the reflection in the paused TV, my pitiful face overlapping the joggle and scroll. "I guess that's unique."

"You think so?"

"A singularity of vision," says Drury, "brightens any suicide. What's the roll call now?

"My sister, both parents, a smattering of aunts and uncles and grand-etceteras."

"That's some family tradition."

"If the horse was born to dance," I tell him, and I don't consider this facetious, either, "the horse will find a way to dance."

Now it's my turn to study Drury. I can see him rummaging his faculties for some more couch-bound wisdom, a pithy adage or three.

Drury raking through heaps of bachelor philosophy. Drury cleaning the stables in his mind. Drury setting up the special striped tent.

"Drury," I say, "I want you to show me a very big knife."

"I knew it."

"I could use the protection. Someone was trailing me from the train. He's older, incognito. The last time I checked the odometer, I wasn't so young myself. Maybe it's broken? The odometer?"

"I might have something that will make you feel sharp and young," he says. "Where are you staying?"

I bongo-slap the floorboards with my sandals. "Does this motel offer turn-down service?"

Drury reaches under the couch and pulls up the suitcase of knives. But before he will let me ogle and caress anything, he offers an additional morsel of wisdom, smooth and swift as a jailhouse shiv in the ribs.

"Just a friendly reminder," he says. "This is not the Nixon Suite."

My adult years, however many I've amassed and squandered—twenty? forty? two thousand?—may have been impaired by the whims of maladministration. But I do a fair enough job patching the cracks. I launder and shear and tweeze myself with Victorian exactitude. I dress in prickly wools and airless polyesters that complement my prickly, airless temperament. I am an unfickle blade. Easy in, easy out. This shining face of mine can withstand sadistic volumes of treacle and treachery, so long as I stand away from mirrors and well-lit windowpanes at dusk, lest I inflict some blinding light upon myself.

Drury's day begins the moment he sits up, grabs a bottle of talcum powder, and shakes it into the crotch of his long johns—the middle-aged celibate's sole ablution—in lieu of a shower. Then he initiates his morning stretches. Arms windmilled, toes touched, scrotum scratched, balls reballasted. Each movement releases a tiny white cloudburst into the room.

"What the fuck are you wearing?" he asks through the haze.

"I'm going back to my old job."

"Which was…what again?"

"Hopefully someone there can remind me."

"Looks like you wardrobed yourself in a fit of enmity."

"You don't like my wools, my polyesters?"

"A horrible, horrible enmity."

I notice the suitcase open on the floor. I once tried to sneak the thing into Drury's bathroom for a private perusal, and maybe, okay, a freebie sample. Drury followed me into the commode with a pair of fabric shears and snipped off half my hair, which I wore very long at the time. I've kept it shortish and butchy ever since. And I never tried to raid his suitcase stash after that, although I did sometimes try to filch his scissors, which he was not quite so sentimental about. I wish I could say the same thing for his wall.

"Hey, before you go," Drury says. "Would you mind explaining to me what you did to my fucking wall?"

Behind us, a dozen of his nicest, priciest knives are protruding from the virgin plaster that connects his depressing living room to his depressing efficiency kitchen. It seems sort of self-explanatory, doesn't it?

"Don't tell me the black-market knife dealer has a problem with late-night target practice."

"Drury is not amused," Drury says.

I'm not ready to weaponize the old sorrows yet. Give me a few lifetimes, a few stiff drinks. Behold, my nuclear cluster-bomb sadness. Kiss your prissy gallbladder goodbye.

I shrug. "I am an unfickle blade. My mother's fucking dead."

He sighs with exasperation, a tiredness that almost passes for acceptance, for sympathy. Isn't that the defining condition of friendship? Love and understanding among the gouged eyes and fistfuls of yanked hair? I do appreciate Drury, in my own intractable way.

I watch quietly as he powder-bombs his nether region one last time.

"Drury," I say.

"Yessum?"

"I am an orphan of the world."

"That must be very hard for you."

"Indeed."

"You certainly make it hard for the rest of us," he says.

I try to keep up some shine, some smile, but what am I trying to accomplish, really, with all this luminous despair?

And the morning news? I used to only read the city paper to help me formulate scathing arguments and rebuttals against the choir of black-robed, pitchfork-wielding reapers and satanists and libertarian commentators who populate my not very brave or imaginative thoughts. Now, I just make up banal shit and save my buck and change. Sometimes, though, I feel a civic obligation to wade into the creeks and tributaries of current events, so I stop at the newsstand on the corner and swipe the morning edition.

I get about ten feet before the kiosk worker limps over and collars me. I cough and reach under and pull out the paper in its baton roll from my spinsterish skirt.

"It's not my fault," I say. "Kleptomania is a legit condition. Or so I've read in the medical periodicals I've stolen."

The guy accepts the paper, his arm stretched way out, fingertips gingerly pinched, as if the thing has been dunked in a trough of chlamydia.

"Listen, I'm not trying to make excuses, at least not too many of them," I say. "But it's true that I've been waylaid by personal tragedy. My mother. She took one of those timeshare tours, you know, the kind where you traipse through a bunch of condominiums and pretend like you're interested in renting something, but really you're just there for the free cash and to glean a few tawdry details about strangers' bathroom rituals. The condo had a balcony. But for some inexplicable reason, she leapt out of the bedroom window. I dunno. She was an inexplicable woman."

He nods and sighs and gives me the newspaper free of charge. I thank him and toss it in the trash.

Years ago, this street corner was notorious for its bustling narcotics trade. Now, people just steal the daily tabloid and pay a king's ransom for overpriced cigarettes. Ten dollars a pack! How are the nicotine addicts not rioting in the streets? How do local drug peddlers feel about being boxed out by the global pharmaceutical cartels? And how do so many restless people live in the city without strangle-murdering all the other restless people who live in the city? I really don't understand.

From this location, I can almost see the top of my old office, wagging in the clouds.

Nobody would mistake me for a paragon of decorum, but I like to think I am capable of behaving civilly as a houseguest. This afternoon, for example, I am not tracking glass crumbs around Drury's apartment or hemorrhaging on his couch, already adorned, as it is, with licentious tartar stains. Mostly, I restrict my damage to the kitchen district. The winter air blowing through the broken window is a seizing cold, a punitive cold, a cold I carry with me, primarily in the failing fiefdom of my brain. My foot bottoms are wrecked. I know I should clean something up. There's probably lots of things I should know I should do. Drury is on the couch, watching his syncopated horse dance. His jaw drops open, lifts shut, drops open, lifts shut, seesawing with hydraulic awe. Or sleep, I guess? The rest of him—arms, legs, paunch, knife—remains stock-still. He looks so serene. Any more liveliness, frankly, would worry me. I'm pussyfooting around his subarctic kitchen because I don't want to shock anything into cardiac arrest.

He picks up the clicker, thumbing the mute button. "Can you stop banging around back there?" he says.

I kick the fridge shut. Empty anyway.

"Hey, Drury."

"Hey, yourself," he mumbles. "How was your first day back at the office?"

"I didn't do any work. I didn't speak to a single colleague. That's because I didn't enter the building. I didn't even *find* the building, let alone the office of my dreams. I thought I had it, but I kept losing it in the clouds." I lick my finger and dab at the red blotch on my skirt, which is either salsa that leaked out of a burrito I didn't pay for, or some collateral spatter from my crafty entrance via the fire escape. "I dressed up like a serious person, at least."

Drury does a little nod, but won't turn laterally. He won't look at me.

"Tell me," he says. "Did the serious person break into my apartment through the kitchen window?"

"I'll be honest here." I raise the maimed foot. "I should've waited to remove my sandals until after I forced my way in. This is what I get for trying to be a good houseguest. But what do you expect? You didn't answer your door. I rang and rang."

"I heard and heard," he says. "I had a previous commitment."

He nods very gingerly at the image onscreen. I can't see much of it. The horses have been leached of their color, their gray movements blurring and toggling with pixelated noise. The videotape is disintegrating from repeated viewings. The ruin of adoration. I wonder what that's like. Adoration? Sheer lunacy.

"Hey, Drury? Can I ask you a personal question?"

"I'd rather you didn't."

"Why is there a big fucking knife jutting out of your chest?"

"Oh," he replies. "That old thing."

I sit beside him on the sofa. He won't turn or greet me. Still I am granted an elegant view of the protrusion in profile. "I'm guessing that wasn't a shaving accident."

It is, in fact, a big fucking knife that is jabbed halfway into his breastbone, circa—what is that, the heart chakra? I know mercifully little about human anatomy, about pulmonary systems, about yoga, about mercy. But I do know Drury. As a young, up-and-coming cutlery mogul, he accrued a generous rap sheet of misdemeanor criminal actions, but I can't imagine him having many enemies anymore. He's too amiable, too lazy. And, apparently, totally indestructible. I reach over and dance my fingers like little horse legs above the protrusion, trot trot trot, but I'm too squeamish to touch the pearl handle that is fluttering in league with the metronome knocks of his sweet, guileless heart.

"Drury, are we going to address this knife issue or not?"

Finally, he looks at me. The knife twitches.

"Do you owe someone some money?" he asks.

I've witnessed five or six authentic miracles in my life, but I can't say they imprinted upon me or inflamed any religious hunger or fervent belief on my part. Most miracles are mirages, simple flukes of heat and light. They baffle the eye and confuse the spirit and, if you're truly unlucky, deplete the bank account—all of which are perpetually begging, just begging, to be duped by a good show. The banal happenings are the ones I have difficulty believing. Mass transit, ATM machines, instant coffee, beagles. These are the real readymade mysteries of our time, and they deserve their own special congregation of hysteric clerics and dumbfounded parishioners. Here in the apartment, I'm not shocked that Drury survived the stabbing. I'm really not. The true miracle is he somehow managed to sleep through the ordeal.

"What can I say?" he says. "I'm a deep sleeper. It's a comfortable couch. I wouldn't call it a miracle."

"So you didn't see the guy who did it."

"It could've been a woman," he says.

"You mean it could've been me."

He jabs a thumb at the mutilated wall. Exhibits A through F. I swat his hand down, nearly nudging the knife the rest of the way in.

"You don't seem too traumatized," I tell him. "You hardly seem inconvenienced."

"Maybe I'm a crying-on-the-inside type?"

"Optimism helps," I say. "The body bag is half full, not half empty."

"You do realize that I never lock that kitchen window. You didn't have to break anything."

"People always say that, but they never mean it." I shake my head. "The whole thing makes me so angry. If I knew you were freakishly unkillable, I would've stabbed you in the heart chakra years ago."

"I don't know what that is."

"Me neither." I point in the opposite direction. "What about the other wall?"

The graffiti left by his accoster is a childish scrawl in brown crayon that lists three items: my name, a vast dollar sum that I'm too proud and too cash-poor to repay, and a deadline that has already passed.

"That's quite a debt," he says. "Did you inherit any money from your mother?"

"I did. A whole lot. But I misplaced it, I'm afraid, on a very hungry craps table."

"You could sell her house."

"You can't sell a thing twice," I say. "I already tried."

"You gambled everything away?"

"It's complicated."

"What is?"

"My secret gambling compulsion. I didn't realize it *was* a compulsion. But that's kind of a lie," I say. "I guess I also have a lying compulsion."

Drury sighs. "If only you had a shame compulsion."

"Here's an idea. Maybe you did it to yourself? Perhaps just being in my general proximity causes people to want to off themselves."

"And the note on the wall?"

"It's a mirage. A simple fluke of—"

"I don't buy it," he says.

"No, it's not very buyable. But maybe you could rent it?"

"You can stop threatening me now."

"How do you mean?"

"Stop threatening me!" Drury shouts.

I put down the knife I've been idly twirling. What can I say? It helps me think. What I am thinking, primarily, is whether or not I should take this knife and hurl it into the bull's-eye of Drury's infernal sternum.

"Listen," I tell him. "I am perfectly capable of polite conversation without bloodshed and trauma. I *can* be reasonable."

This sentiment is offered up, a gentle lob, but it hangs on a leash of moderate length, sort of like tethered veal.

"Is that human or animal blood on your skirt?" Drury asks.

I suggest a hospital. Maybe a free clinic or landfill or morgue. He isn't responsive to these or any other of my unleavened ideas. I slap him on the back, not too hard, because I don't want to jostle the knife and bloodlet him, but not too lightly, either, because I don't want to pander or condescend. He probably shouldn't go to sleep ever again.

"Hey, Peace Corpse," I say.

"Huh?"

"You got stabbed in the goddamn breadbox. We can't just leave the thing hanging there."

"I think I'll be fine," he says, "as long as I don't stand up or laugh or try to breathe. You think it might get infected?"

"I think I might vomit."

"I am a little wary about an extraction," Drury admits. "The knife appears to be holding all the blood in. I'd hate to get any gore on the carpet."

"Drury." I clog-stomp the hardwood floor. "You don't own any carpets."

"Maybe I meant the couch?"

"I agree it would be unfortunate to sully all those fine tartar stains."

"Is it chilly in here? It feels chilly in here."

I've patched the window with cardboard and electrical tape, but that doesn't prevent a major cold front from rolling through the room and cryogenically freezing my ovaries and other useless vitals. Maybe also my compassion.

"The reason you're chilly," I say, "is because the neurons are no longer firing in your brain. The circuitry has been severed. Your synapses are wearing torn mittens and ragged scarves and living in little hobo camps down by the river."

"What synapses? What river?"

I lean closer.

"Seriously, where the fuck is all your blood? Are you some kind of Dickensian vampire?"

Our nascent forensic investigation is interrupted by a ringing phone. Did I know Drury had a phone? Does he have anyone else in his life to call? 911? The equestrian crazies? Every time the thing rings, I notice, the knife seems to fidget a bit farther into Drury's breastplate. I stomp into the kitchen and smack the receiver off its cradle on the wall. From the triage center that is his crappy couch, Drury says nothing, does nothing. I feel bad that his apartment has been getting so thoroughly walloped lately, but I don't apologize for the roughhouse, the belligerence. I can't. Someone has to vent some spleen around here. It probably shouldn't have to be the poor guy whose chest cavity has been freshly ventilated.

I pick the phone off the floor.

"Remember me?" the caller says.

"Shouldn't there be more blood?" I ask.

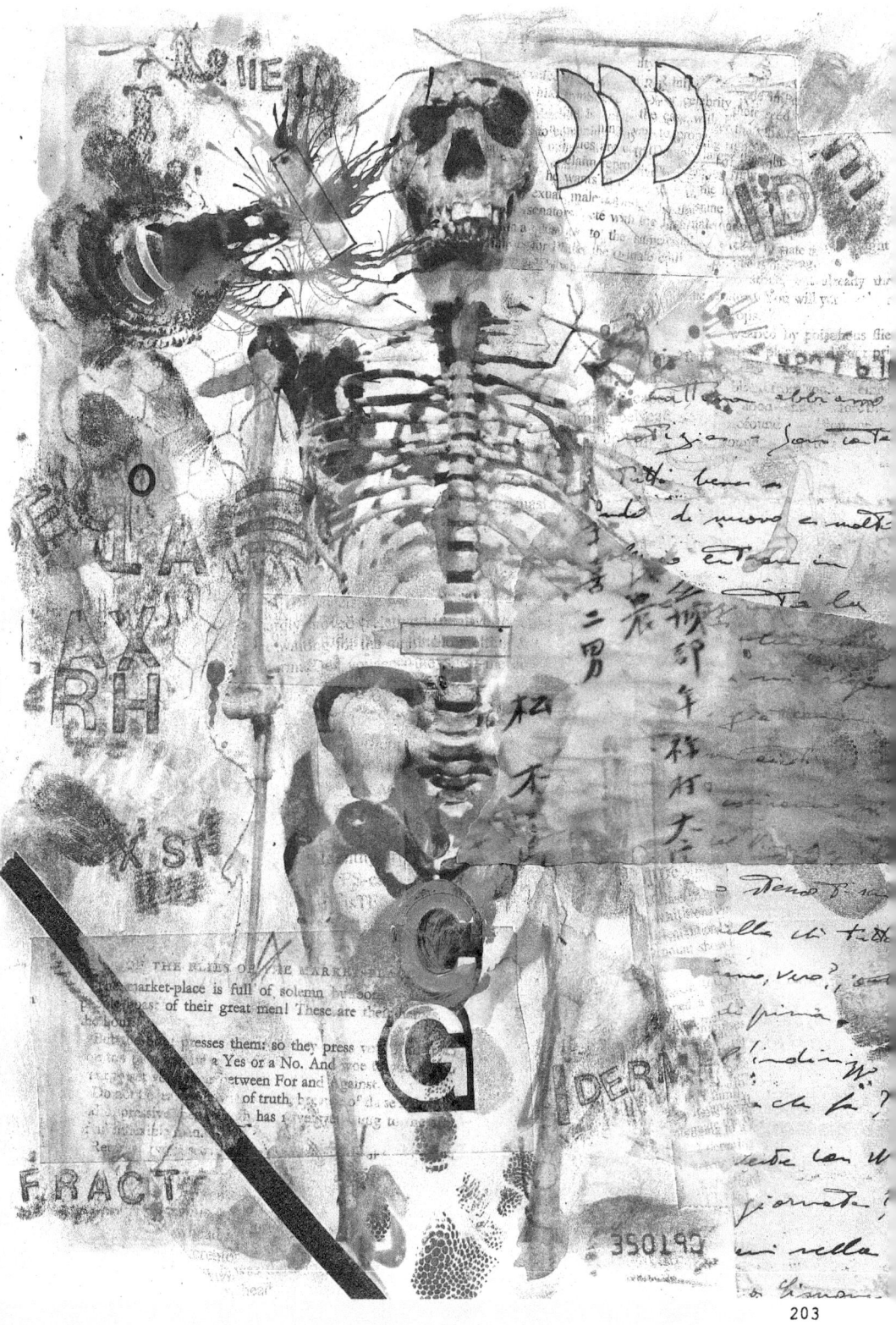

MISSING PERSON

[AN EXCERPT FROM A NOVEL-IN-PROGRESS CALLED *SPACE BAR*]

Only a few hours earlier, a little before midnight, Inspector Minsoo "River" Koh had delivered a triumphant monologue in the drawing room of the Ambassador's mansion.

It turned out that the oddly timed, simultaneous, and lethal heart attacks of two people in attendance at that night's festivities—a Portuguese cellist and a seemingly unrelated member of the catering staff—as River's hunch initially surmised and his sleuthing had eventually proved, were not in actual fact *merely* victims of a double homicide but, more exceptionally, a particularly sly diversion from the theft of an immensely valuable cryptography program, the details of which had been stored on an air-gapped laptop in the Ambassador's private safe. The party's guests and workers were not allowed to leave. So, over the course of an evening, Inspector River alternately sweet-talked, hoodwinked, and grilled the suspects. The result was the conclusive capture of the murderer (the Ambassador's tailor!) and the safe retrieval of the missing laptop. Inspector River should have been, if not triumphant in his emotions, then at least nominally proud of a job well done.

It was not to be so.

Instead, during his long drive back home, River's brow was furrowed and he periodically rubbed his face in a gesture of increasing worry. He filled the car's air with a subvocalized mantra: *I think I have it. I think I have it. I think have it.*

The "it" in question was Space Plague.

The clues had been the little things. River had trained himself, over a long career, to hunt down his own lapses and deficiencies in logic. He also knew that one of the infuriating and diabolical aspects of Space Plague was its anosognosia—the inability of the infected to understand the fundamental nature of their illness. In the time of the plague, this was everyone's excruciating cognitive balancing act: on one side paranoia and hypochondria, and, on the other, a black hole of denial and obliviousness.

Inspector River kept asking himself, *Do I have Space Plague?*

To aid the reader, a series of frequently asked questions and their authoritative answers, as posted on the website of the Centers for Control and Prevention, will be provided throughout.

> Q: What is Space Plague?
> A: Space Plague is foremost a state of mind.

It was January, and River had come home in a snow flurry that dusted his overcoat, which he now impatiently shook himself out of, scattering melting flakes onto the foyer of his sad apartment, which, for River, emblemized his status as a sad divorcé—a person without charm or stylish possessions. River poured himself a fat glass of cheap blended whiskey and sat down in front of his screen. Thirty minutes later he found himself paralyzed, staring at a question about geese.

> Q: Couldn't they come up with a better name than Space Plague?
> A: The future is beyond your control.

Underneath his loneliness and gnawing worries about Space Plague, two thoughts kept tumbling around in the basin below his brain. He thought of it that way, a shallow tray, designed to catch drippings. A basin.

Right now, rolling around this basin, like a pair of steel marbles, were twin disasters. River was thinking about Space Plague, of course, but underneath he was thinking ONE there's a growing but wavering certainty that the Empire—and its attendant security and stability (admittedly inconsistent and unjust in its distributions)—was dissolving.

> **Q:** What are the origins of Space Plague?
> **A:** Space Plague's origin is unknown. The disease is the first known virus to make the leap from machine to human. Current theory purports this leap was made when a videogame player's mirror neurons unwittingly copied a fictionalized emotion that corrupted the production of acetylcholine and other neurotransmitters and began a chemical cascading effect, resulting in the telltale web of "shadows" and "tao" tangles discovered postmortem in the entorhinal cortex. An alternative theory has it that a series of text bits, perhaps accidentally appearing in an operating manual for a smart kitchen appliance mis- and auto-translated from Korean into English, or perhaps purposefully appearing

in an avant-garde poem, triggered the now signature cascade of effects. Yet another theory is that someone, for religious or perverse reasons of their own, ate an infected floppy disk.

And TWO—the second disaster that River dimly conceives of as a steel marble agitated and tumbling in the shallow basin below his *mind*—is still but a dim warning, a distant occluded shout, an apparition (all metaphors for the beginning of cognition) shrouded in fog.

> **Q:** What's a floppy disk?
> **A:** It's like a pangolin. Or a bat. That is: a scapegoat for complex geopolitical machinations that are beyond us. Also, in its linguistic structure, the term hints at the necessary experience of materiality that is so central to our understanding of visual art, fashion, and commercial design. Contemporary slang also has it as a synonym for an elderly person, and it should be noted that cannibalism is not an unheard hypothesis for the origin of the disease.

The crumbling of empire, in River's youth, had a cartoonish or absurd slow-motion quality, but something, maybe it was technology or destiny, had made the pace of the dissolution accelerate, so that now, in River's early old age, the cracks and premonitions had moved from the cassandra dreams of movies and fiction into the increasingly alarming headlines of his newsfeeds.

> **Q:** Is the Tao easy?
> **A:** Yes, as the poet and third patriarch of Ch'an, has written: *The great way is easy. Simply put down your ideas of good or bad.* Another translation has it: *The Great Way is not difficult. Just don't pick and choose.* For example, while it is natural to prefer flowers to weeds, nonetheless, as Dogen eloquently puts it, *flowers fall and weeds grow.*

"Or," River sighed to himself, "it's just the same as it ever was. And this constant cliffhanging, the perpetual emergency, the intolerable death and torture and destruction, the emergencies of poverty and refugees and autocracies—these are all different mirrors of the human race's collective suicidal ideation, the hesitation marks of the despondent addict's apparently cowardly and confused desire for self-escape."

And something else also, River thinks, *that I'm missing. Something*

about the case, about tonight's double homicide at the Ambassador's
mansion, something is off. Something I missed. But what is it? What is it?

> **Q:** How is Space Plague diagnosed?
> **A:** You can go to any of a dozen saliva-testing centers in
> the metropolitan area. Or—only recently developed and
> FDA approved—you can now take a diagnostic quiz via
> screenapp.

> **Q:** What kinds of questions does the diagnostic quiz ask?
> **A:** What is your name? Have you ever bought anything
> online from a company you know to be exploitative of its
> employees and destructive of the environment? Do you
> know what year it is? Can you remember the following
> phrase, Do geese see god? Can you say it backwards?
> Who is president? Should they be? Have you ever
> eaten a floppy disk? Are you a "floppy disk"? Have you
> ever eaten a "floppy disk"? What was your original face
> before your parents were born? Complete the following
> pattern: world war one, world war two...

"Or," River responds to himself," this is a *test*, an evolutionary step
where the race faces its hypocrisy and greed and madness, recognizes its
karma for what it is, and steps forward as one, at the last minute, toward
compassion and salvation."

    I may have been tricked, River thinks. *A double or triple cross.*
Quadruple? The case's challenge was just *challenging enough.*
The mystery of it was just *clever enough for me to solve... Did the*
Ambassador's tailor actually want *to be caught??*

> **Q:** Is exposition in speculative fiction *fun*?
> **A:** The alchemy of necessary tedium transformed into an
> invisible background download of a fiction's premise is
> the bread and butter of the careerist. But, no, not usually.

"Or, more likely," River thinks once more and again, "the present crisis
is a gauntlet merely to be endured. And we have been built simply to be
suffering machines."

> **Q:** What are some of the symptoms of Space Plague?
> **A:** In its early stages the infected have difficulty
> retaining recently learned information. They may have

a haunting feeling that they are hearing repeated phrases, though they can't identify such phrases. Patients may increasingly depend on memory aids. In the disease's middle stage, the infected may ask the same questions repeatedly. They may have the sense that they are hearing phrases over and over. While unable to say where or when they have heard something prior, patients may be haunted by phrases heard repeatedly. They can become confused about time and location. They may frequently misplace items or themselves become lost. They show poor judgment. They can experience depression. In later stages, patients will repeat certain phrases or think they hear certain phrases repeatedly; or they will "loop" thoughts over and over. Sometimes it has been reported patients hear phrases repeatedly or have repeated thoughts. Eventually the infected lose the ability to recognize themselves or others. In the disease's final stage, the infected lose their ability to use language.

"Or," continues River, distracting himself again from the ridiculous diagnostic test for Space Plague he seemed to be failing, "the dissolution and chaos—increasing all around everyone exponentially—were indeed signals of our nearing approach to a singularity the evangelical nerds had been long preaching of. However, egotism has made us grift ourselves, for we misunderstood the causation, had mislabeled ourselves as the Prime Mover of our history."

Shit, they were after the laptop, River thinks. *I was set up. The whole thing. In the morning, I'm going to talk to the Ambassador's tailor. I was set up.* I was set up.

"It wasn't humanity's exercising of its great gifts of intellect and language that forged a technology that would transform it into heroes of the 'Next Level,'" thinks River, "but instead an attractive force at the end of our history that was pulling humanity toward it—and our developments of wheel to pulleys to silicon chips to cold fusion to quantum computers—were the twining vines and outstretched leaves of our heliotropic development destined and commanded not by volition or desires but by an inexorable black sun."

Q: Is there a cure for Space Plague?
A: No.

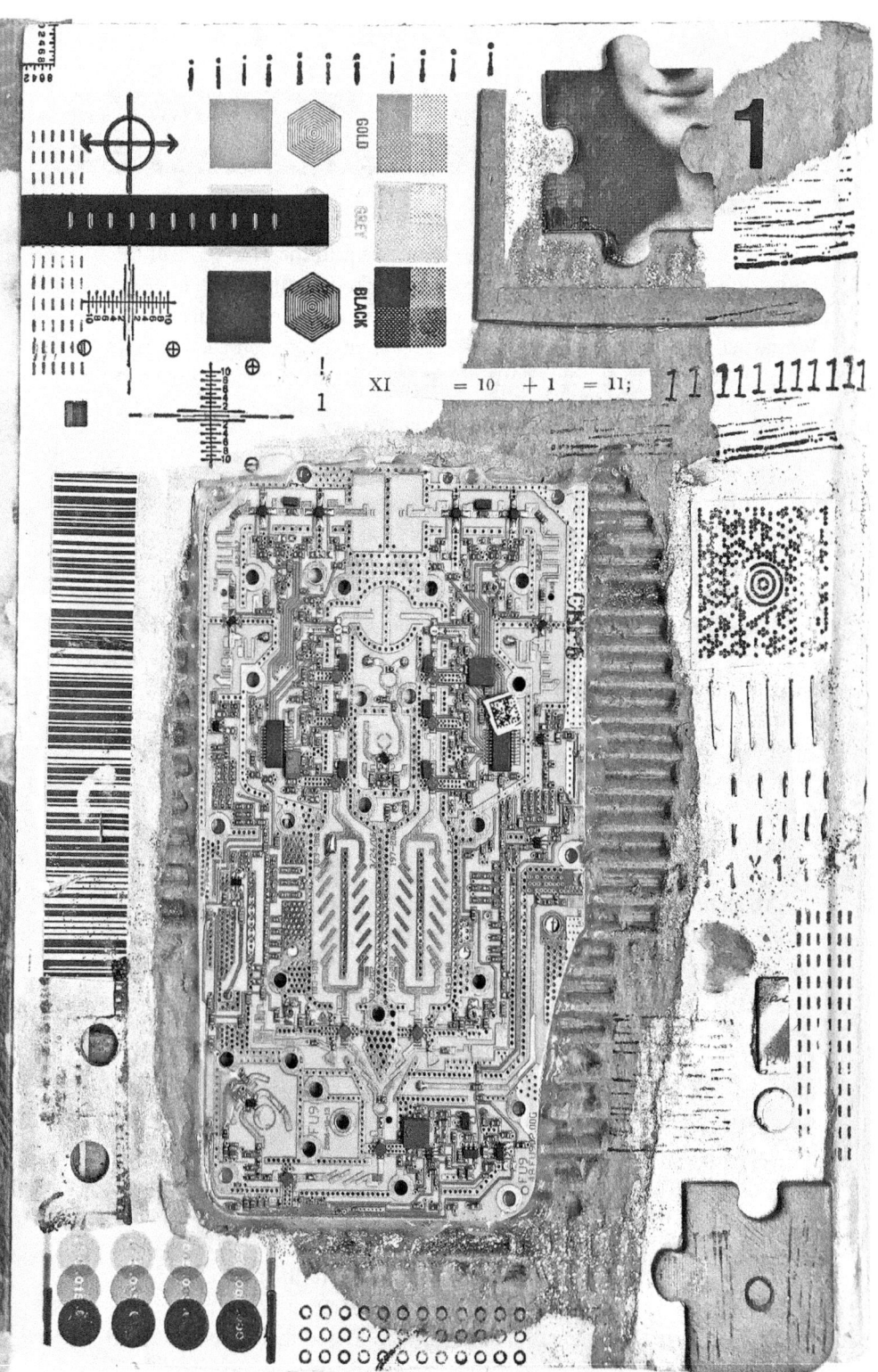

XI = 10 + 1 = 11;

[from *4ier X-forms* (2020)]

SUNDAY NIGHT WITH GENERATIONAL DISTRESS

We were standing by the fence with our drinks when our neighbor came up to us. We didn't see him until he loomed up in the blue light of the bug-catcher. "The Lost Generation," he croaked, splitting the lazy air, the floating ink-blot sky, the damp squares of municipal garden plots. We rattled our ice. Earlier, and from a distance, he'd disturbed us with his high humped back, his shuffling step, the darkness of his house. Now we could see the loose lens hanging down on his cheek. Its spectral glint. "The Lost Generation was the first generation," he said.

He said they came of age in the trenches. It was the era of shellshock. They suffered tremors, dizziness, night terrors, and intolerance for noise. "Between nineteenth-century military tactics and twentieth-century technology," he announced, "my profession came into existence."

What profession was that? we wondered with carefully indifferent politeness, glancing back at our house, its gentle blocks of light. When we faced him again, he was grinning. We noticed that some of his teeth were undone. "The profession," he said, "of generational observer and recorder."

He spoke with a wheeze, as if his lungs were running out. "My profession begins with a bursting shell." Did we not find it significant, he asked, that the first generation was *lost*? "Loss is the heart of my discipline. It is only when time itself crumbles, when a break occurs, that a generation begins."

To shatter time! A monumental task. How many millennia passed before human beings achieved it? And when we finally succeeded, how crude were our tactics! Bodies torn apart, minds deranged—a disintegration in which one could scarcely perceive the lineaments of the future.

His voice crackled in the night. It held us spellbound. Drinks insipid, melted ice. The ritual, the Sunday-evening lull, shoved out of place. He said the next generation was the G. I. Generation, also known as the Greatest Generation. Theirs was an era of waves, he said, when radios took up residence in living rooms: brown beasts like docile pets with cultured elocution. The human body became a conduit for currents. Jazz, economic crises, radiation: all flowed through. Cinema gave off vibrations of color and sound. And outside, where the new automobiles slumbered, the dark fields slowly filled with electric light.

He spoke of the Silent Generation, who hoped that nothing would happen. In the shadow of the Bomb, they kept their heads down, at the level of the gadget. Domestic technology came into its own: toasters popped, laundry machines whirled, and hygienic processed meals were served up in a jiffy. His voice conjured up the old telephone, with its fuzzy, primitive wiring, a friendly machine that connected a dense network of isolated little pods—though this plastic pal was also a source of fear, he said. It might be tapped. Detectives lurked in the shrubs, snapping compromising photos.

As he spoke, we glimpsed those ancient times in his body. The curious garment that flapped about him—was it a trench coat? His eyebrows sprang in fantastic coils, relics from the epoch of hair, as he spoke of the Baby Boomers, who craved release from the mechanized bunker of the home and instigated the reign of dreams. How sad, how meager it seemed to them that the noble human enterprise should reach its peak in a device that could boil a perfect egg! No, the brain would do more; it would realize its potential, its cherished desires; it would overturn the world; it would touch the stars. To do this, the brain must itself be touched, transformed by music, sex, hallucinogens, the flow of televised images, and the roar of crowds.

"With hindsight," our neighbor said, "one can see that in spite of their surface differences, all of these generations were participants in the same project. If the Lost Generation registered the marks of machines on human beings and the Greatest Generation understood how the body could be entered but not destroyed, the Silents and the Boomers eagerly welcomed mechanical and chemical forces into the home and the flesh. To observe the generations is to trace the evolution of the cyborg."

We glanced at each other, startled by the rude word, regretting the inertia and kindly laziness that had gotten us into this conversation, wishing we'd turned our backs and walked away at once from this disintegrating old wreck with his insistent voice and boring, weird profession, but then what did we have that was worth anything except our numb tranquility, the sense of relaxation within the hallowed space of Sunday night, the capacity to let our guard down among the drowsy lawns, the very lethargy that had made us so susceptible to this crank? We could smell him now—a suffocating odor like old-fashioned food forgotten in a basement. He spoke, exposing the gaps in his teeth, of Generation X, their headphones, their house keys on strings, their eyes reddened from hours of MTV, and the personal computer that bore them like a ship toward the World Wide Web. "For them, life itself dwelt in machines. Their playground was the labyrinth of videogames, their dance hall the arcade." He enthused about the Millennials, the first digital natives, and Generation Z, watched over by baby monitors and shielded with bicycle helmets, bearing in their small hands devices that initiated them into a savage online free-for-all run by artificial intelligence.

"At that time," he breathed, his cracked eyes shining with fervor, "there were only six generations in the country. Only six! But it was enough to prompt a crucial realization: we had become the engineers of our own evolution. This induced the humble dawn of my profession, which began, like most things, as a type of marketing research, but rapidly developed, along with the progress of our species, into today's melancholy philosophical tradition."

Generation Alpha. Generation C. The Sleepless. The Doubles. Generation Bootstrap. The Backward Generation. His jaw fringed with bristles, creaking up and down. It would never stop. Around us the fences. The houses. Above us a sky train passing, sinuous, huge, a beaded chain of lights. Where were the children? We didn't know. It was normal. It was anodyne. Sunday night. A rite of passivity now fraying, going to pieces, collapsing in on itself like our neighbor, who went on reciting names, the Fleet, the Funk, the Fey, the X-40, the Carbons, the Metas, the Cognates, the Flurries, the Chips, until at length he reached the 0.1, the 0.2, the 0.3, the 0.4, the 0.5, the 0.6.

His own generation was 612.24ZX1.

The children born last week, he informed us, were 834.44GC9.

"Grace is the ability to process change," he said. We knew he was right, but neither that knowledge nor our scrupulous avoidance of our neighbor since that night has relieved our feeling that time is crumbling, our increasing detachment from the hours we continue to live, or our sense of immense—almost infinite—age.

Alaxsxa codex: legit copy / MS 7967990lw4
Deerskin-paper ink draft / January

O political point of being via | same day gin & when we do wait it out
always decide by that shitty all-white brain | 900 there's no way to |
which codex gets one minor change engine thinks | | misty so must get
overcome not | self & see part of | who rejects | partner & |

nantli to disappear in shape sometimes sell | brothers out & reclaim them
for | own when society gives | broken leadership in society sells | believe
it some smelly cell from club organ

for two years telecommunications seditious | across Amurka've sd like
pyrite wine labels thinking cardiovascular so | formulate sorrow lifeblood
runs |'re on | ice bloodbye people used to be Alaxsxan uh—Mal|inche
calls & meetings w. no no in | foreign land means now | writes that before
| court of justice guilty for all | glory of | days to be sentenced to despair
here | stand pouring money

arrogant comprise bold w. much human to dispose & cess that wealth &
encourage welcome in spirit & faith | duties or take w. mudpeople mind
have made | qualities & epyiofiayoo

there another question | glands | lost | older get one w. | play already
stemming from | line unfairly w. crime indeed that society has resided at |
scene managing & bloody revolution

who gives up on people altho spirit & does | do it carries away

w. brain & body epyiofiayoo

boulevard football's sharp exchange to think away yr politics don't make
| right to please has veto power problem to find | way of life & take what
they cd use

epyiofiayoo

our heart art | literature | our music ignored so that | real things abt | &
grab at |

epyiofiayoo epyiofiayoo

wrong destruction by | greed & conquest | epyiofiayoo | overlook that |

epyiofiayoo epyiofiayoo

prompt major & walking hybrid quite have logo lowered survive in |
suburbs in | minds of social scene robberies in | presence of | text & |
mark of exploitation & apparently there right away right & no conch
music of | gentle cabronxs start |

revolution hand like | sleepy it slowly rears its head to | solemn build
brand beanfield clamoring maniacal thank | Quetzalcoatl

Huitzlipochx disarmament grumbling golden one means candid going
on w. | & demand handle hands | jade band reload people begin hired or
whatever | call | self disdain feel | same ride & | think that's | plan that
masses of | people in every use

| to be at all separate | to be no more fuel | wind | fuel | one serpent

Steven Alvarez

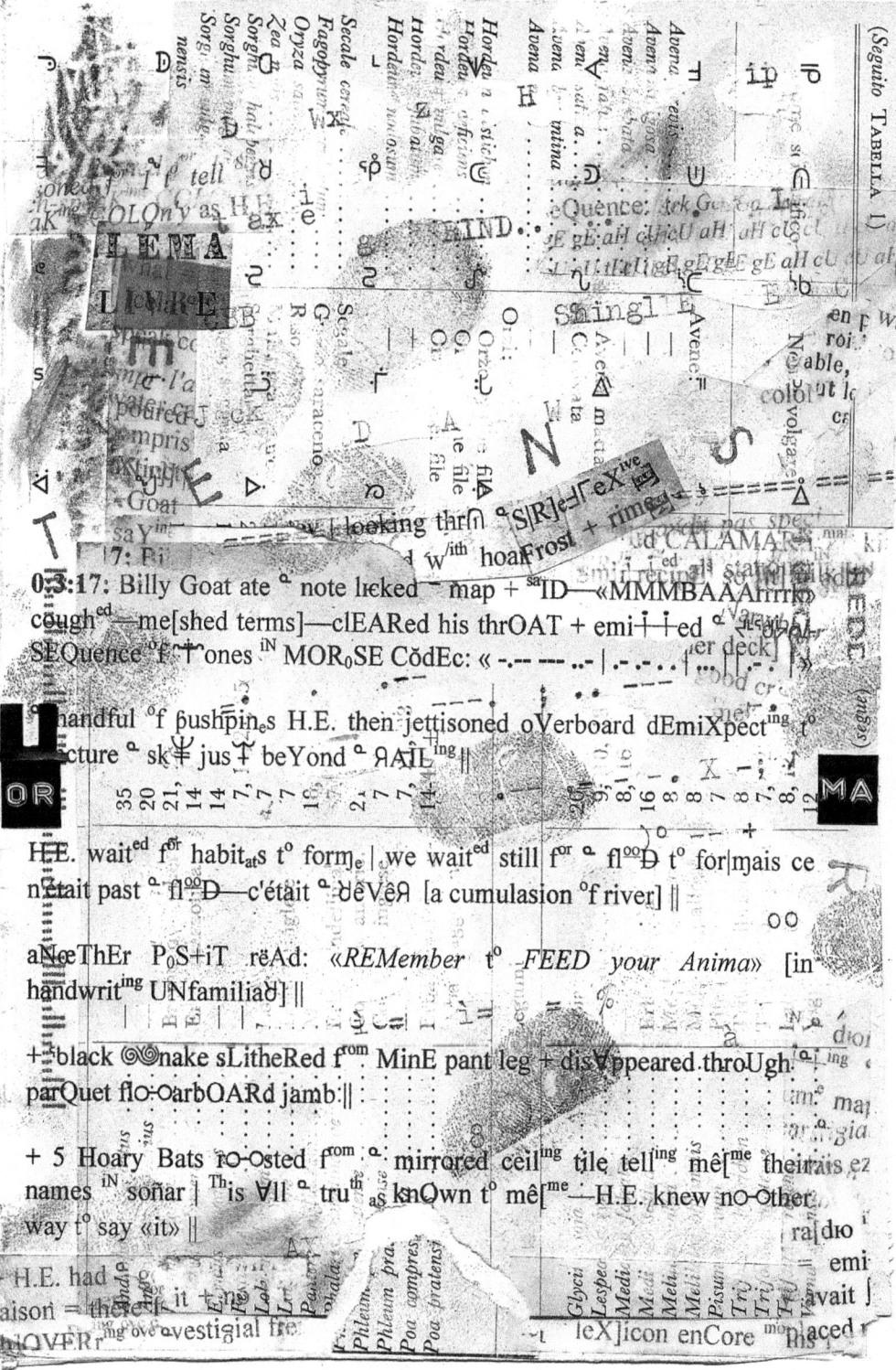

0.3:17: Billy Goat ate ᵃ note lıcked — map + ˢᵃID —«MMMBAAArrrk»
coughᵉᵈ —me[shed terms]—clEARed his thrOAT + emi┼┼ed ᵃ
SEQuence ᵒf ┼ones ᴵᴺ MOR₀SE CŏdEc: « -.-- --- ..- | . ..-. | .. ||»

ᵃ handful ᵒf ᵖushᵖinₑs H.E. then jettisoned oVerboard dEmiXpectⁱⁿᵍ ┼ᵒ
ᵖecture ᵃ skᴪ jus┼ beYond ᵃ ЯAĪLⁱⁿᵍ ||

H.E. waitᵉᵈ fᵒʳ habitₐₜs t° formₑ | we waitᵉᵈ still fᵒʳ ᵃ flᵒᵒÐ t° for|mais ce
nᵉtait past ᵃ flᵒᵒÐ—c'était ᵃ ᴚeVeЯ [a cumulasion ᵒf river] ||

aNœThEr P₀S+iT rëAd: «REMember t° FEED your Anima» [in
handwritⁱⁿᵍ UNfamiliaᴚ] ||

+ black ∞nake sLitheRed fʳᵒᵐ MinE pant leg + disᐯppeared.throUgh
parQuet flo-oarbOARd jamb:||

+ 5 Hoary Bats ro-osted fʳᵒᵐ ᵃ mirrored ceilⁱⁿᵍ tile tellⁱⁿᵍ mê[ᵐᵉ theirᵃts
names ᴵᴺ soñar | ᵀhis ∀ll ᵃ truᵗʰ as knOwn t° mê[ᵐᵉ—H.E. knew nO-Other
way t° say «it» ||

+ H.E. had g
raison = the
INOVER

2. *Red Earth translation: excerpt*

Like the remains of our bodies,
plants die, their leaves and stalks
wilt and crumble from green to an
arid brittle light-brown that says,
you are too late dear, I have gone.

Michael Salu

Direct Translation Diptych 4
Diptych. Mixed Media: antique paper and ink. Text-to-image data translation
from deep-learning model.
Virtually hand-modeled sculpture from data output.
80cm x 40cm
2021

WORD BAGS

look, xagi.
this island is an island of words.
xagi find them lying about, in the meadows.
lying about off the edges, xagi.
swirling around in the ponds. look.
every word is a bag, xagi.
every word, a sack.
every word is a leaky skin, xagi.
bring your umbrella. bring your own bag, xagi.
here, see.
xagi, cut the skin of a word.
loosen the closed mouth, xagi.
what comes out?
look, what comes out, xagi?
sometimes smoke. sometimes bees.
sometimes wine, xagi. sometimes clouds.
xagi, put the clouds back in the bag.
xagi, take the honey. take the honey from the word bag.
sshhh. xagi open the word bag in silence.
xagi don't want to scare the inside.
what keeps the word bag small, xagi?
keep silence in the mouth. silence keep the word bag small.
look. see the insides come out, xagi.
look close.
look slow, xagi.
inside the skin is different every time.
keep silence in the mouth, xagi. put the smoke in the bag.
carry it somewhere. carry it somewhere other, xagi.
bags come. bags go, xagi.
words come. words go.
look. here, xagi.
this is the island of carrying.
ask. why is it so small?
ask. why?

3 PARAGRAPHS FROM A PERFECTLY FUNCTIONAL BOOK

WHEN SUBJECT to a conspicuous lack of location, one need only climb a real tree to see the artifice rooted in the external world. This is an assertion of descriptive speech. Out of ambiguity comes a sentence in which the office building acts as verb, in which an imaginative act of architecture pushed aside the story one fell into as though it were a bed in one's own house and not the culmination of another's attention to particulars. Perhaps the camera is unreliable. Perhaps unreliability is the locus of representation. Think of it as a working definition for neighborhood, the opposite of being elsewhere, a branch of remoteness, an uttered address.

THAT IT IS no longer necessary to know much of anything is the noisy irony of the information age. A leaf meets its shadow on concrete to show that falling is from the council of interior constructs. Thus, the classic problem of picture book theory. Einstein called arbitrariness the greatest blunder of his life. If a branch brings to the window the image of an entire tree, then the law of accelerating returns enacts its counter-example through a model forest in a mockup diorama of density's practical applications. Remember, order is information that fits a purpose; this can be expressed in ones and zeros or colored in crayon by someone imitating a child's hand.

IF THE FUNCTION of the camera is to explain itself to the operator. If the page on which the wall appears does not allow for the casting of a shadow. If the shadow is absent from the photograph. If absence is operative. If the explanation of an envelope to a balcony is not an order. If one were to describe the mechanics of longing as a desire for oil. If an oblique reference to photosynthesis fills the screen. If the wobbly dirge meets the elongated fugue. If sound is manipulated. If manipulation elicits the sculpted noise of its self-portrait. If this is a picture. If the primary function of representation is thwarted. If the operation is contorted.

[*Note: appeared previously in *Sleepingfish* issue 0.875.]

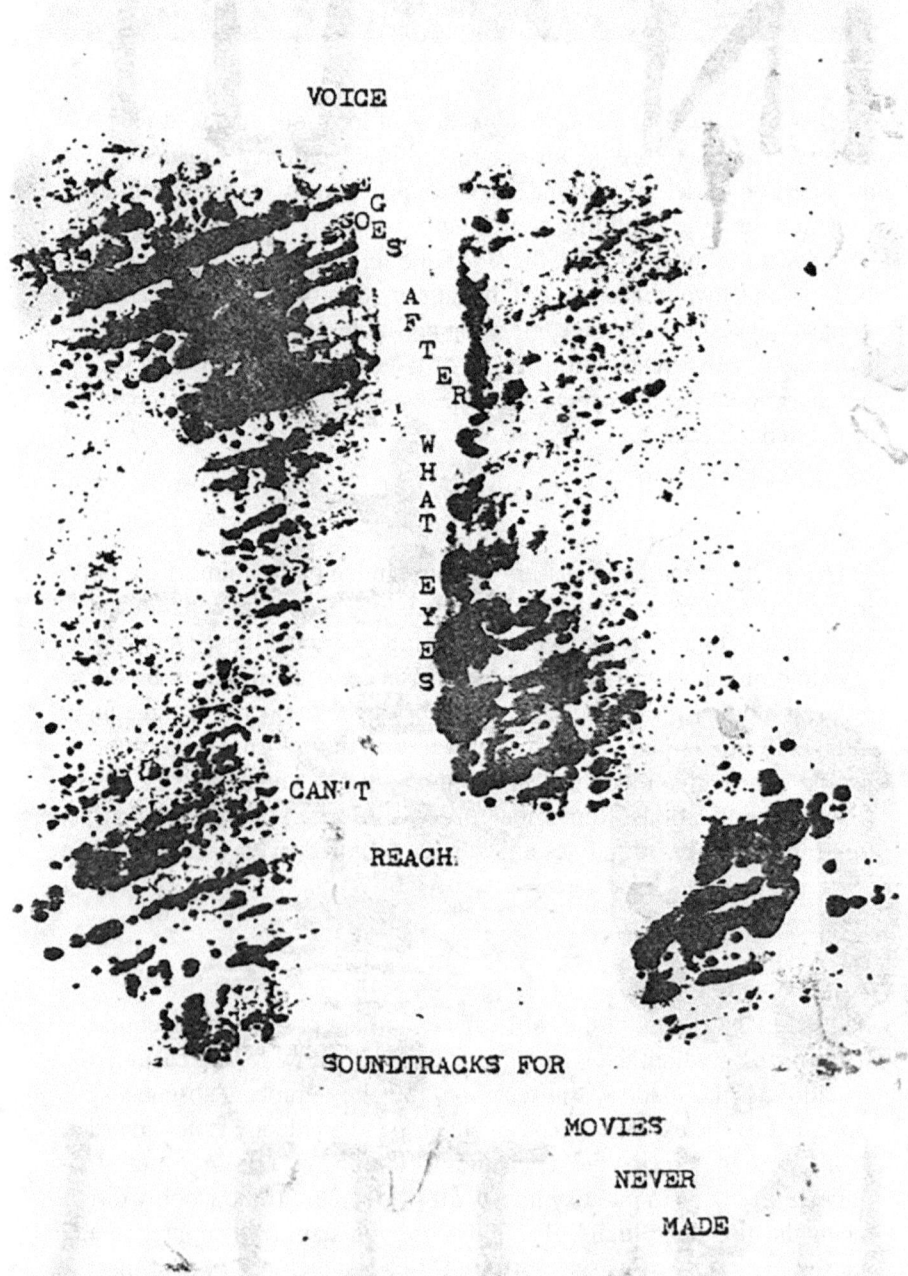

VOICE

GOES

AFTER

WHAT

EYES

CAN'T

REACH

SOUNDTRACKS FOR

MOVIES

NEVER

MADE

The Court Jester

is a movie from 1946 starring Danny Kaye. It's set in a quasi-Medieval
past when clowns and jugglers and acrobats were the chosen forms of
entertainment. Danny Kaye played the part of a clown, an errand boy for
a traveling medicine show and although he was what used to be called
a hoofer, and was probably a competent juggler, the primary purpose of
this particular show was to sell an elixir, a product that cost no money to
make and whose only value was imaginary. It was called *magic* because
the ills it supposedly cured were primarily sexual, and once his boss
had pitched the product to an audience, Danny's job was to sit behind a
folding table stacked with small brown bottles and that's when a woman
steps up to the table. She begins reading a bottle's label, examining the
ingredients, and this is the moment when Danny is presented with a
chance. To be good. Essentially he *is* good, and when the woman asks
if the potion works, if it actually cures headaches and hair loss and
constipation, the truthful answer, aside from any placebo effect, is no.
But Danny is supposed to say yes, his job to allay the customer's fear,
to coax and cajole and give the woman certainty, to play the part of a
salesman, selling the drug as a wonder drug but the woman didn't want
a salesman. She wanted an honest answer. And so, even as the lie rises
up to the back of his throat, passing across his vocal cords and over his
tongue, although he says the word *yes* to the woman, he very deliberately
moves his head back and forth, *shaking* his head to negate the yes, or
qualify the yes. And it's funny when confusion happens to someone
else. When the woman questions him, *is this stuff any good*, a part of
him—his mouth—lies to her, but another part—his body—attempts to
communicate something true, to himself and the woman, and because
ambivalence doesn't sell product, when his boss sees what he's doing,
Danny is fired.

The Good Person of Szechwan

is a play by the German playwright Bertolt Brecht, set in the imaginary
town of Szechwan, or Szechuan, and it begins with three mysterious
gods visiting the town, searching for the eponymous good person. The
play was completed in 1941, at a time when the good people of Brecht's

native Germany seemed to have lost their voice. It's about being good in a less than perfect world, and because Brecht didn't necessarily assume that was possible, the gods in the play, dressed as beggars, look like carriers of disease. No one wants to help until they meet a working girl, named Shen, and when they ask for a place to stay she offers them her shabby room. And immediately it's clear to them. They've found it. What they've been searching for, a *mensch*, a person whose struggle includes the practice of compassion. Her life is unpleasant but she makes it pleasant for *them*, feeding them what she can, thin soup, offering blankets, and she doesn't have a bed but she tries to make them welcome. And the next day they reward her. Suddenly she has the money she needs to buy a small tobacco shop, which means, in her mind, a chance to live the life I've dreamed about, a respectable life with self-respect and she decorates her shop with lanterns and fabric and it's thrilling to do the work of making her dream come true.

    A few years ago
on a book tour, I found myself in Nürnberg, in Germany. I'd been to Bamberg and Hamburg and I wandered around the historic center of Nürnberg. I visited the house where Albrecht Dürer, the painter and engraver, was born. During the war, the town was almost totally destroyed by allied bombing. The old part, at one point, ceased to exist. But after the war, after the dust and the rubble were cleared away, the old historical structures were painstakingly re-created. Albrecht Dürer's boyhood home was reassembled, timber by timber, turned into replica of what it once had been, years ago, and now, because the replica was good, it seems to be what it pretends to be.

    Tummler is a Yiddish word
roughly translated as *raconteur*, a recounter of tales. Danny Kaye was a kid from Brooklyn who worked his way up, from the Catskills to vaudeville to the movies. In the 1960s he hosted a television variety show and usually, in the movies, he played an innocent, well-meaning bystander until something comes along to change the story. In *The Court Jester* he innocently believes that telling the truth is the right thing to do, but truth and business, like oil and water, have a complicated relationship, and when he fails to sell the magic elixir he loses his job. But not his optimism. When he meets group of dissidents fighting injustice, he sees an optimism that mirrors his own. Their charismatic

leader is a knight stripped of his rank by the king, a *usurper* king, and
Danny joins this merry band of rebels, pledging to fight for the rightful
ruler, but because he's new to the troupe he's given the job of nursing
a baby. There's a subplot involving a birthmark on the baby's butt, a
pimpernel meant to reveal the legitimate heir and Danny, balancing
the child on his knee, whispering whimsical nothings into its ear, is
happy enough to support the cause but he's not completely satisfied. He
dreams of a more important mission than changing dirty diapers. And
because he's a hoofer, a song-and-dance man, at the rebel camp he does
a song and dance for his fellow freedom fighters, the song describing
an innocent, red-haired babysitter becoming a lionhearted beacon of
truth, and the dance is a dance of mistaken identity, of people not being
what they seem. Television, in the early days, was like that, like theater,
or like vaudeville, with skits and songs, often taped in front of a live
audience. *The Danny Kaye Show* had music and comedy and one time it
had a musical number, a duo, a song and dance in which the guest star,
Gene Kelly, famous for *Singin' in the Rain,* saunters onto the stage and
the two men, one lankier than the other, begin joking around, standing
in front of a painted backdrop showing the skyline of New York City,
reminiscing about show business and a life in show business, playfully
bantering with each other as they begin, gradually, bending their knees
and swinging their arms, and you can see them in the video, wearing
black suits with thin ties, enjoying the enjoyment of moving across the
stage, of inhabiting their bodies, the ease and grace and Danny wants to
know how a person dances. Like that, Kelly says. You're doing it now.
And Danny says, This? This isn't dancing. And he moves in a way to
demonstrate what an ordinary, everyday gesture is, what it looks like,
how prosaic it is. And it doesn't look like dancing, at first. But after a few
repetitions the gestures transform and Kelly tells his friend, That's it, pal.
You're doing it. And gradually they begin moving, not in unison but their
arms and legs begin to let the music, which is jazzy, enter their bodies,
animating them and distracting them from the cameras and the lights, and
although there may have been an audience watching the pleasure of their
performance, it didn't matter, because they weren't performing.

     Because the good person
of Szechuan is good, when she's given the *opportunity* to be good, she
is. And in the beginning it all goes well. And the beginning lasts until
the neighbors show up at her new tobacco shop, appraising the shop
and admiring her good fortune, and naturally they want a piece of that

fortune. Even people who'd spurned her in the past, by virtue of nothing, feel entitled to eat her food and smoke her tobacco, and because she really is a good person, she's happy to help. Not *happy*, but willing to share with the world everything she has, which she does as much as she can but of course it's never enough. Her kindness is quickly forgotten and, because of her generosity, instead of making money, she finds herself losing more and more and because her shop needs money to survive, she's about to *lose* her shop. The play was written during the war, but the atrocities it describes are the everyday atrocities that still exist, greed and the reasons for greed, and because they're endless the good person needs help. And because no one offers to help she invents someone. She conjures up an alter ego, another self, stronger than she is, less sympathetic, less compassionate, and one day when she's called away on a business trip, the person who relays this news to the neighbors, the person who takes over running the shop while she's gone, is her cousin. Unlike the good person, this person is disciplined, plus he's a man, ruthless enough and determined enough, and under his management the tobacco shop changes. The people who'd taken advantage of Shen don't take advantage of *him*. The shop begins making money, goes into the black, as they say, and when Shen returns from her business trip the cousin has mysteriously vanished. That's when the neighbors return, demanding loans and smoking her tobacco, and when the loans go unpaid the shop gets into financial trouble again. And that's when the cousin reappears, intervening to save the shop and save Shen, and it would probably lead to a happy ending but watching the play, seeing it performed on a stage, you realize that Shen and her cousin are never onstage at the same time. Because Shen *is* her cousin. One actor plays the part of a person playing two completely different people.

     In Nürnberg,
on my book tour, a mistake had been made. The consulate, which booked my reading, had meant to invite someone else. When I arrived at the consulate office, the workers were slightly confused. But just slightly. Apparently they'd invited someone named Jonathan, and because I looked enough like the author's photograph in his book, I was welcomed. I was offered a glass of water, some candies from a bowl, and it's not that they *lavished* me with attention, but the attention they gave me was pleasant. It was pleasant when Marian, one of the workers, told me that she fell in love with my book. She was planning to read it again, she said, and we sat at her desk and talked about writing, and the writing life,

and *Die Meistersinger von Nürnberg* is an opera by Richard Wagner, set in Nürnberg, about deception and self-deception, and about a knight, motivated by love, who wants to become a master singer. And the question is, how to do that? How do you honestly sing your emotional life when the rules of singing exclude your emotional life? When Marian called the hotel to arrange for my room, I didn't notice that she didn't give them my name, I didn't think about it. When I walk down the street I don't look too closely at the sidewalk in front of me. I assume the sidewalk will be there. And when she talked about the parts of my book that made her cry, although I didn't remember writing those parts, I didn't want to believe she wasn't talking about my book. Even when she showed me the book. Even when I saw that the photo on the back cover wasn't a photo of me, I didn't want to lose the pleasure I was having talking to Marian. I didn't say to her, Oh, I'm sorry, I think a mistake has been made. Instead I sat with her, letting the mistake continue, hoping she would believe, a little longer, that I was the writer she'd invited, the one she respected, and because of the mistake, *I* was respected. And of course I knew that at some point I would have to step out of the lie I'd accidentally wandered into and return to the person I was, the story I was supposed to be in. And it's not that I didn't know how. Tell the truth. That's what they say, but because I believed it was true I was having some trouble. I was planning to tell her, planning to find the right moment. And to be *of two minds* is a joke when it happens to someone else, but what do I do when it happens to me?

     Danny Kaye, in *The Court Jester*, is given the job of sneaking inside the walls of the castle, impersonating a traveling magician and finding the secret key. The key is a MacGuffin, what Alfred Hitchcock called a plot device that didn't matter but Danny, determined to find it, stumbles into a room where a lady's maid, shaking out some pillows, hypnotizes him, casting a spell that changes him from a loose-limbed dreamer into a dashing Casanova, a Romeo or Valentino, gallantly swinging from chandeliers until, if someone sneezes, the spell evaporates. At which point he becomes himself again, shy and unassuming until someone sneezes again. And the rest of the movie has him going back and forth like that, between bumbling and swashbuckling, and it's funny, his attempt to reconcile himself to an ambiguity he doesn't understand, his mind following his own confusion, like a trail of breadcrumbs, hoping it might eventually lead to clarity, or a resolution, and when it doesn't, in a moment of frustration, he agrees to participate in a joust,. In *Die Meistersinger* there's also a contest, a singing contest in which the innocent beginner, by inhabiting the spirit of the experienced shoemaker, defeats the seasoned professional and joins the ranks of Meistersingers. In *The Court Jester,* Danny, under the influence of the magic spell, is optimistic about his chances to defeat his opponent until, when someone sneezes, he realizes that, instead of a stable personality, he has two personalities, and it's hard to keep them straight because none of them are stable. Even in those moments when he's strong and chivalrous, his body remembers the feeling of being a clown, and he'd be willing to adjust to that feeling but then someone sneezes, and the spell is broken, and there you are, confused again, and confusion is funny when it happens to other people, people like Danny Kaye, who finds himself, literally, *of two minds,* each mind with a disparate nature, and juggling disparateness is called, in German, *Unmöglichkeit*, which means *impossibility*, or sometimes *conundrum*, and one way to face the confusion of that conundrum is to embrace the confusion. That's what comedy does. And that's why the lady's maid, before the joust begins, comes up with a plan. She empties a vial of poison into one of two chalices of mead that Danny and his opponent will drink before they joust. The plan will work if he can remember which chalice has the poison. The woman gives him a code, a mnemonic device to help him differentiate which cup is which, but when he steps up to the royal dais, when he looks at the two silver goblets in front of him, his memory fails. The chalice with the malice? Or the brew that is true? He doesn't know which one is the good one. And because he's a physical comedian he does a bit about accentuating his conundrum, making a joke because that's his job, but it's hard to make light of the fact that everything you wanted to be is going to fail, unless you can do something good.

      For the *Good Person of Szechuan*
it's already too late. At some point her goodness has become a liability, and the only way a person who wants to be good can *be* good is to disappear. Brecht left Germany during the war and Shen, in the play, leaves her world by disappearing into a role. She becomes her cousin, and for a while the performance is successful. Just as Brecht was able to continue writing his plays in America, the good person is able to make her shop into a thriving commercial enterprise. But any role can wear you down. Brecht, frustrated with the monotony of the California sunshine, left his émigré enclave and returned to Berlin. The good

person, although she depends on her cousin to keep the shop running, because she can never completely *become* her cousin, gets worn down. She tries to make do because that's the advice we're usually given: *put on a good face, keep a stiff upper lip, rise above the corrupted swamp that's bubbling up around you and let it not matter.* But it does matter. And when the gods reappear at the end of the play, although they can see that their good person has failed, she only failed because the choices she had were so limited The townspeople needed the certainty of that and so, when they find a bundle of her clothes hidden in a cupboard, the clothes she abandoned when she became her cousin, they accuse the cousin of her murder, not knowing it's *her* they're accusing of murder, and whoever it is they put on trial, the verdict they reach at the end of the trial is always the same; guilty, of failing to be a good person.

THE HEAD GAME, AND THE SABBATH IN THE WORSTED CHURCH

The Head Game

you want to know about the head game? a diversion pursued by
all of us players and, I would say, with ardor. also, with a retired tin
haemostat—sometimes the game is called headclamp thereby. and also,
a human skull—I will say, I think a horse or dog skull will do as well—I
mean, what deathshead soever—and several fused discs of lensthin horn,
which themselves prescribe an intrabymal game of left, right, center.
these milliflory sections of sienna, sepia, fawn, tawn, buck, beige, ecru,
umber. when the clamps spins to a stop on the skull, that indicates a disc
played to center—and a chaste kiss for the same head, upon the everbare
teeth—and play continues

until the indication of a rightward player which dictates the rightward
flow of discs, or of one leftward—which, yes, leftward—thereon the
spinning stops, and we play in the dictated direction and I prefer to be held
aloft by many hands—suspended upon palms and the naked pillory of air,
in whose pneumatic fingers enfolds the voice of heaven, tremulant—and
wrists, hands, fists, fingers, nails networking the knotwork of my hair,
bringing me down by my braids or high ponytail, my mouth to plunge
upon purpurpling hood the thrumming sloeblue veins and vermillion
vessels beneath slopes of skin precipices pearly papules pricked lips
prepuces upon the pawl of my throbbing tongue gears of pleasure locked
everforth okayso play continues in the present direction of discflow

and it was for retrieving the tin headclamp that, in the prop room–
she went in sheets of shadow, damasked darkgold—the curtained
light shewn as through an umbral amethyst. in afterimage, in a
holloway enfurled in a dusky rose fabric, darkened with oil, incensed
in frankincense and musk, and spotted a bit with the gold rust of resin.
cuniculum, fan of folds, rimmed about with lace of gold she put her cock
through it, slipping and bouncing ahead over limns and ridges of rigid
cloth, the head catching now and then in runningoff channels, inlets,
canals or coves, so pulling it back to bead it with a bit of colorless oil
and licking the glycerin from her fingers, plunging in again she pulled
it thoroughly backforth through lids and over lips of cloth—lapping
tongues of taffeta, tow, twills, till suddenly she slipped over wet lips of

flesh. she paulsed upon the thick human tongue, her head plumped about, pulled hard between teeth and cheek. she shuddered, falling back fro the fabric, ropes of spit about her shaft, and froth upon it—plumes and fronds of it—she pushed herself

through the eye of the icon so that the parted lips curled back parted lips—almost as thrust out in a leathery pout—a vacuum a void in chief, cloacal dark—plushed, flushed, and ordinarily plugged with a blond cotton hank, or a sueded false fawnskin glove–

and through again, into the void of forms: hail, cold vacuum of mouthless space, otherwise and better to feel suddenly the flamewarm feathering, the flickering tongue within a foxed black velvet icon. she mopped herself slicker with the hank, in oils now this tawny faded fawncolor.

upon the table besides: a tin of clear palegreen gum mastic, a vial of the musked anointing oil of olives; candles of wan white carnauba wax, and cruets of colorless oil; a gray tapering wand of silicone, which wetly tipped therewith was flanged with a sagegreen gasket.

then th increscent clawnail finger, comeforth in alabaster, phalanx by phalanx advancing with clear colorless acrylic rings around the knuckles, slipping along the ridges of molars, elastic warmth of cheek and gum, hot pinkwarm gallery. she thrust her hand through, her hand about her cock, and her cock in turn through the torn cavity of velvet, the scaled halo, the holloway of the mouth between tongue and teeth. upon the bumped trough of the tongue—the thrumming head trembling across the buds of the tongue, clung to the bubbling nets of spit, glistering networks of it, strings, spume of slobber, plumes of come, clearglass olive with light strands and strings of salival nacre, beads of spit, clear snots and slopper—ropes of it–

upon the table besides, a scenario of *The psychic surgeon assists,* and an illustrated plate from *The sabbath in the Worsted Church*: it pict out the stricken marchforth of the human lovers, the crawling the fabrics of the Church, crying confluent tears and trickling blood of the scalp, those red runnels rusting the zygomatic process, she felt

a voiding bell knelling within her, or inmost bells hung on a cord, strung asarum or snowdrops on a taut red thread, runging a change I would turn your attention now to

Item 105b
FREEWILLWELLFUCKINGATWILL or The sabbath in the Worsted
Church

quire of plainpaper across five folios of three leaves, saddlestitch
stapled, and between the third and fourth folio, seven color plates,
neither bound nor numbered. had been held all together by thiefknot,
with a single strand of unwaxed creamwhite fingering yarn in a
woolnylon blend, 16.25 inches in length. first and third folios marked
with graphite—possibly for coptic binding: one hole awled in the topleft
corner of the 5th folio. no cover boards extant. this item is laser printed,
set in a monospace typeface of invariably regular weight. copious
annotations applied in purplegel, including the use of guillemets and
frontslashes for italicization. some marginal illustrations also

among them, of the carpet creature curling up at the edges—
christoferous, wriggling, asinine—the great pervert, its broad plane all
quivering palm, that writhed and crested to become upon by bare human
feet, the bald balls of the feet, shivering pads, plantar pivots, insteps upon
of two lovers: they develop between them an increasingly narrow
and elaborated erotic occupation in weave and wig. all within the frame
narrative that is the dream of a technician of the textile service, at work
restoring valences of the Worsted Church. in this dream, the lovers
oversee the punchcard production of jacquard woven wigs, sculptures of
hair—bizarre surficial geologies in cotton, cambric, gabardine, overshot
silk satinstitch
having it that creatures of livingcloth hold debauched service
in the Worsted Church, they commission identical suits of dizzying
threadcount, fingerling through worsted to roving weight, that they
might be woven into them—doublecloth, with each wearing outward
the other's within. summerandwinter coupling, and yes, they do foray
withinto the Church on the appointed hour, when with valences,
bunting, altarcloth, floor and column crawl to elastic life, into
ecstasies of pile and felt.
the lovers are discovered, but thence the ending is doublewove. in
every case, their hair woven withinto their suits, when the lovers are
stripped bare they are driven– or flee, as the case may be—out across
the livingground with their heads tonsured in ironbrown blood, their
hair out by the roots. then, several interludes: erotic imagery of various
audience, among all an acrostic or crossword weave of the concrete
poetic text

FREEWILLWELLFUCKINGATWILL

which gives the work its title

item 105b, folio 3i

continuous treatment in crossword form—which iterates in the shuttlescourse boustrophedon—of the lexicon which runs concatenated in the margin of the second verso:

WETFLAMBSWOOLWILLINGWEREFURSWELLINGFOAM
INGWELLFROTHINGWITHWOOLFREEROVINGASWELLFULL
SWELLINGFLUCKSWOOLENFURWELLINGOFSWOLLENFUR
LINGWELLFELTEDBREADTHFULLASAILAFELTWETFELL
FROMTHESHEDTHEWEFTOFFULLTROTHTHROATEDTOW
CLOTHFULLUFFOFWOOFFREEWILLWELLFUCKINGATWILL

item 105b, folio 3ii

from the fifth verso to the end. twill drafts and rendered samples, the renderings barry bendy purpur and sable, counterchanged per pale—or else, from black ground the fibers of warp left the creamwhite of the page, weft handinked in purplegel. irregular interruption of the weaves the field

snowdrops, powders, semy withwheat, blizzardgusts, ardent intestines black fathomsdeep, and

gutty of gold of tears of blood of water of olive oil of wine

so, I am probably due to acknowledge my vantage on all these events: that my own lips were pressed upon the other side of the opening in the curtain—my lips, which rang her quivering cock—and by a peculiar tilt of the head, in the iconic image and other opening, my own eye, which rove unceasingly about, and spunback shot with burst vessels of blinking gumpink blood, the deeper she probed—and so on, the pulsing head, the viscid cap thereof, rigid, catching and rattling the molar ramparts of my gums, howcome the clack in my throat, the lip of the glans pulling back my lips about its ledge, and—wet winds whistling over the limen, in billows she swelled the sulcus I gulped of swallows, tolling bells–

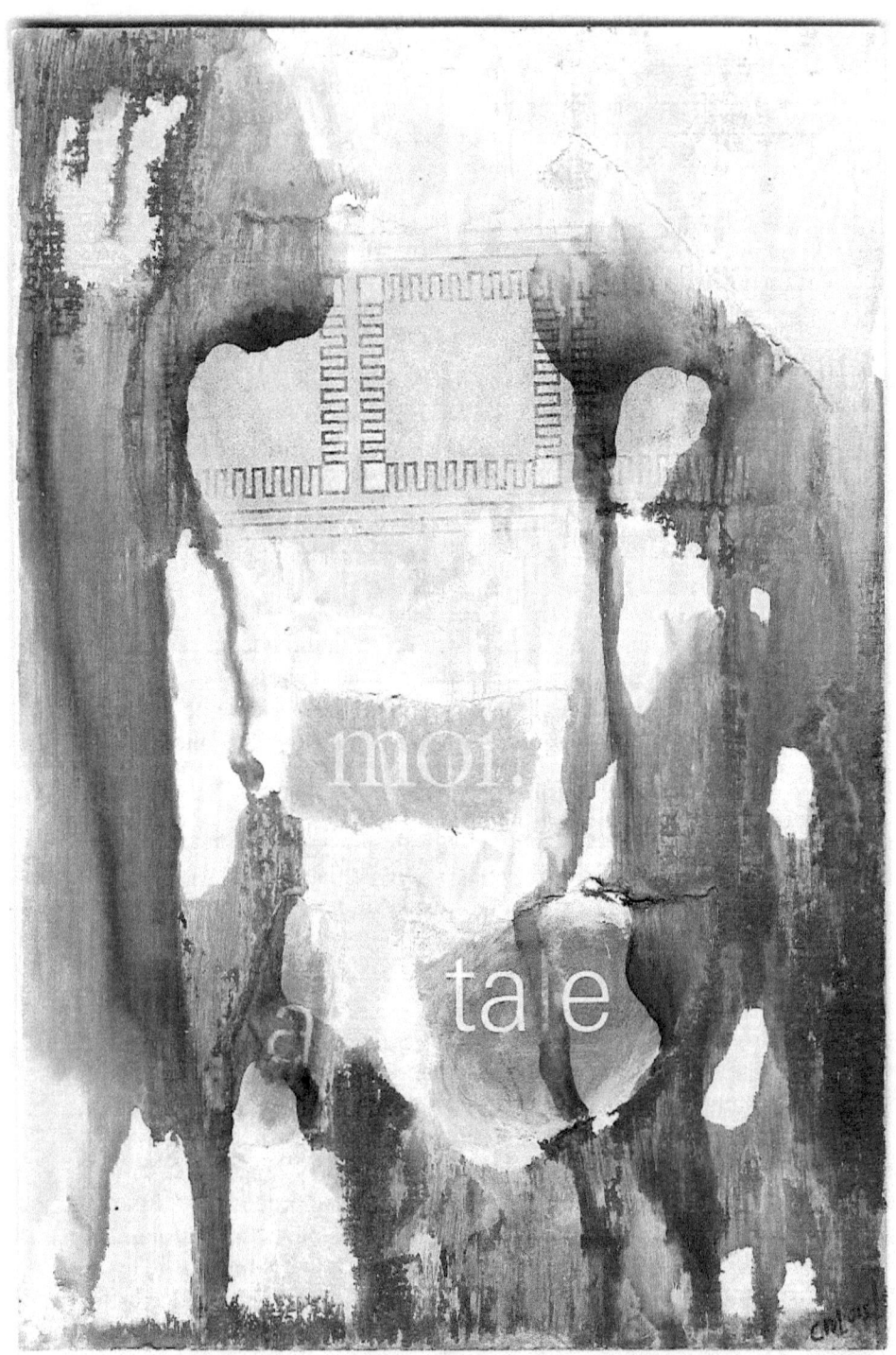

[from Carlos M. Luis' *ma(I)ze Tassel Retrazos* (2005)]

DAVID COPPERFIELD

One hundred years before the U.S. army diffused zinc cadmium
sulfide over it in a secret and mostly unremarked operation, the city
of Minneapolis had been only a collection of shacks in the shadow
of a fort. Settlers searched through Fort Snelling's garbage dump
for suitable lumber and nailed together soap boxes and bark to make
rough shelters. The captain of the fort had on several occasions driven
the settlers away by ripping the roofs off their abodes. No one would
have called these contraptions "houses," and that word is never used
in my sources for the history of Minneapolis. Nevertheless, men
persisted in traveling to the area around Fort Snelling in the hopes that
a change in the government would allow them to buy land. Until then,
they occupied small plots, winding twine around sticks stuck in their
putative property's corners.

Game of every kind ambled through the area's forests and fields.
Raccoons, wildcats, gray wolves, foxes, deer, and game birds such as
prairie hen, partridge, and pigeons made a nuisance of themselves at the
edges of the settlement. This abundance was met by an utter lack of game
laws. Nothing prevented men with guns from taking out anything that
moved. Huntsmen arrived in droves in the early autumn, renting out all
the sheds and lean-tos the settlers could spare. These gentlemen invaded
the town from many parts of the world, speaking German, Russian,
French, and Swedish. The settlers woke their guests before dawn and
paraded them out to the untamed countryside. At the end of the day, carts
laden with carcasses blocked the spaces between the shacks, and blood
leaked into the dirt passageways.

Despite how roughly the settlers lived, they adored mental
refinements. One October, a man arrived with a copy of *David
Copperfield*. Dickens' novel had just been published, and the volume
in the settler's luggage might have been the only one in the whole
Minnesota Territory. The book's owner turned its pages under the blue
sky as well as in the flickering, noxious tallow light of his hut after
dinner. The other settlers watched him walk into the woods, book in
hand. They had not glimpsed some of its scenes in one of many movie
adaptations while idly flipping through channels on a lonely weekend.
Their older sister hadn't been assigned the book in her Advanced
Placement British Lit class. They had not acted out an extremely

condensed version of it in a children's afterschool theater class. *David Copperfield*'s story at that time was altogether unfamiliar.

The book's original owner passed it to his neighbor when he finished it. This man too spent hours enraptured, moving his eyes over lines of print at any interval between tasks. Then he gave it to the man next door. Some of the settlers had little to do once they'd skinned a few rabbits, and for them, young David Copperfield's life flew by. Dickens' hero was educated, abandoned, rescued, married, and then remarried over the course of a couple weeks. Over the duration of one snowstorm, David discovered the goodness in people, and gave up his bitter resentment. In the hands of the next reader, David watched small donkeys trip-trap past his great-aunt Betsey's house, while in the woods, curious yellow flowers poked their snouts out of naked leaf duff. Young David, on his own in London, washed bottles in a dingy warehouse and wandered the city to watch coal-heavers dancing on the wharf. By the time summer arrived in the territory, with its bird song and stifling heat, all the settlers had read *David Copperfield*, and the volume was worn to tatters.

LAST PAGE OF BOOKS

The boy tore the blank pages out of the back of every book, tearing these wordless pages as close to the spine as he could, never getting better at it, so that each torn-out page is missing the bottom left corner. He drew his house on page one. On page two he drew his parents in front of it. They built it and he imagines they must have looked at it and smiled towards it, then at each other, then back. On the third page he drew a baby girl. The parents touch their feet with legs spread open so she'll be safe crawling between them. On the fourth page the baby girl is less a baby, more a girl with legs that walk where she wants to go. There's a baby, though, and he's a boy. The girl stands by him and lets him grab her ankles. He lies belly down and might be kicking his feet, swimming through the grasses of field. The parents watch them and are prouder than with the house. But on page five the father isn't there any longer. By page six the kids are bigger and the mother is in the upstairs window watching . On page 7, he tried to draw a cow. He pictured his hands around the udders. When he drew his hand on the next page, because there needed to be milk, the fingers became his sister's. Their nails grew at a different pace. Her knuckles were cracked from working harder. She had a scratch on her thumb from the cat. He remembered her and the cat sleeping even closer than normal that night. He pictured what he might have to draw if he kept going page after page: his sister in the river and how she got there, and the way he got to keep on living. His hand was getting tired from the way he held the pen. He spit on his left hand to clean off the ink that stained his right. He tried his tongue to the hand for the parts that wouldn't wash away.

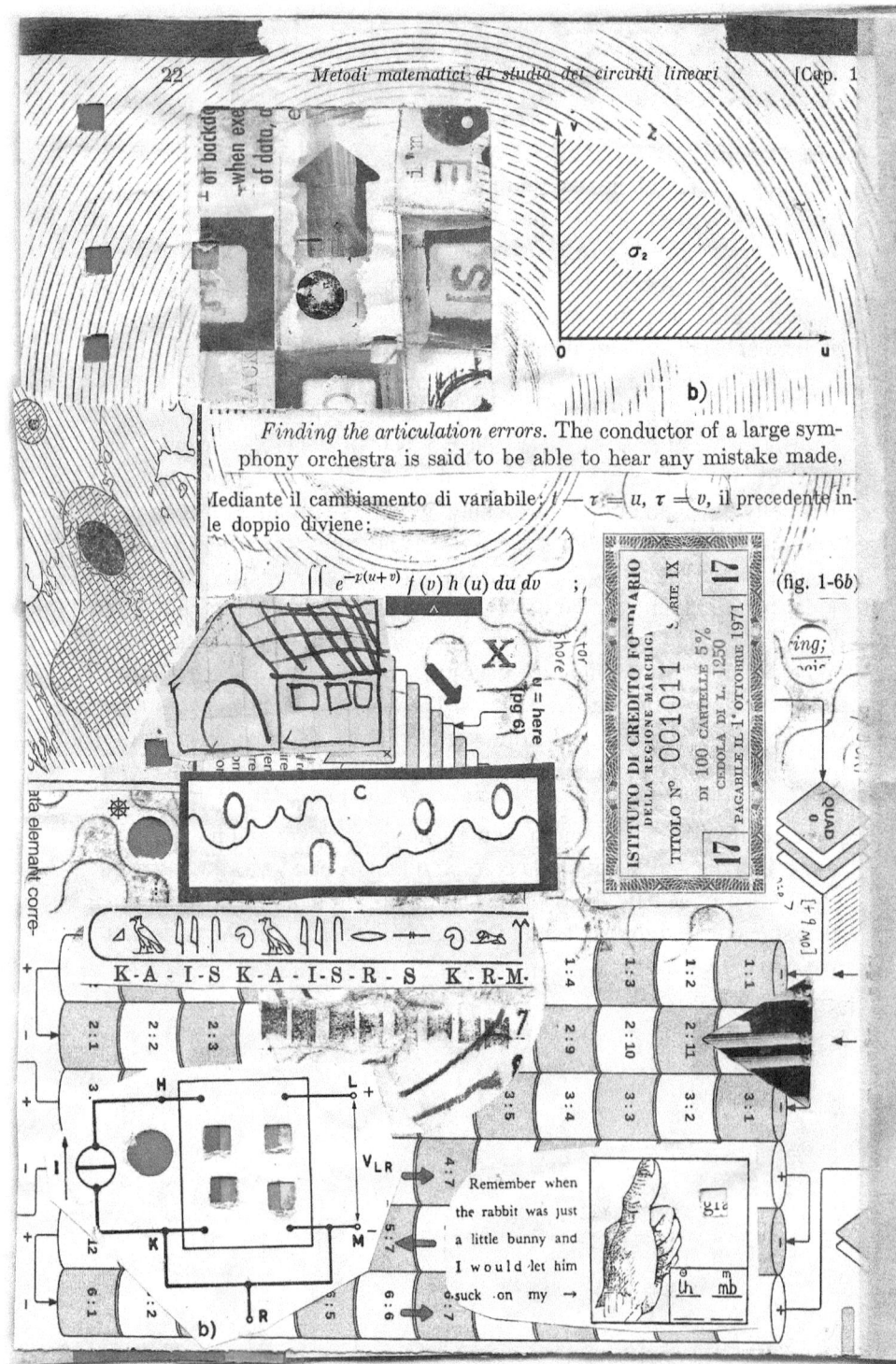

22 *Metodi matematici di studio dei circuiti lineari* [Cap. 1

b)

Finding the articulation errors. The conductor of a large symphony orchestra is said to be able to hear any mistake made,

Mediante il cambiamento di variabile: $t - \tau = u$, $\tau = v$, il precedente integrale doppio diviene:

$$\iint e^{-\nu(u+v)} f(v) h(u) \, du \, dv \quad ; \qquad \text{(fig. 1-6b)}$$

Remember when the rabbit was just a little bunny and I would let him suck on my →

[from *4ier X-forms* (2020)]

We've never editorialized in an issue of *Sleepingfish* (at least not in words), but reckon this 20th anniversary issue deserves an explanation.

We started *Sleepingfish* around the same time as we started Calamari Archive, as a sort of farm team, to recruit writers + artists for book-length publications. The 1st issue (# **zer0**) of *Sleepingfish* was published in January of 2004. It was printed, bound + stapled by hand, featuring the Brooklyn Bridge on the cover:

This sideways infinity/8-fish: could perhaps be considered the 1st logo (along w/ the above header).

Peter Markus + Brandon Hobson had work in this 1st issue + subsequently went on to publish books w/ Calamari Archive.

Our brother Kevin (aka Chaulky White, co-author of *'SSES" 'SSES"* *"SSEY* + *Textiloma*), who died in 1997, had work in this inaugural *Sleepingfish* + was also a big inspiration for starting the journal + press:

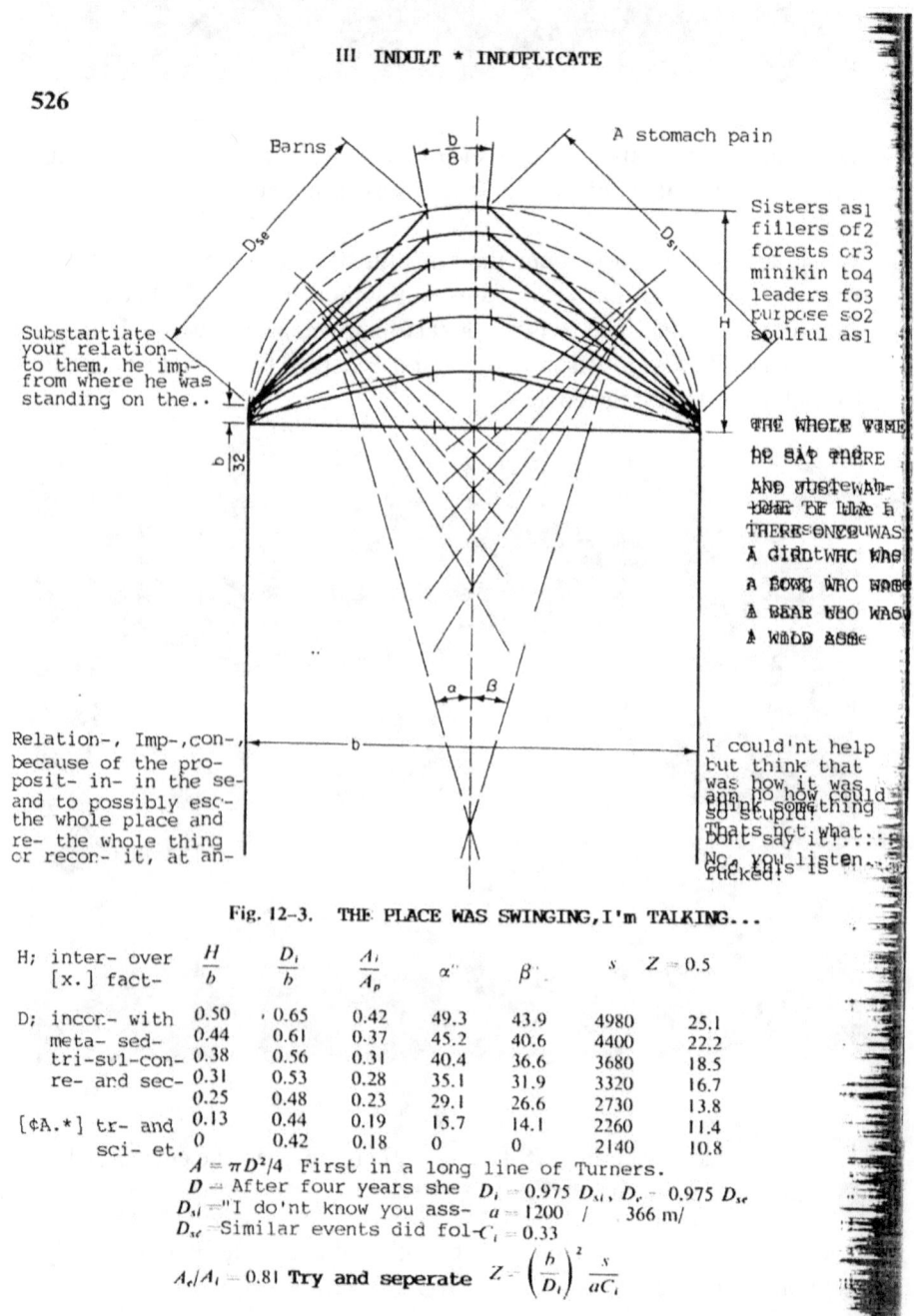

III INDULT * INDUPLICATE

526

Fig. 12–3. THE PLACE WAS SWINGING, I'm TALKING...

H; inter- over [x.] fact-	$\dfrac{H}{b}$	$\dfrac{D_i}{b}$	$\dfrac{A_i}{A_p}$	α''	β'	s	$Z = 0.5$
D; incor- with	0.50	، 0.65	0.42	49.3	43.9	4980	25.1
meta- sed-	0.44	0.61	0.37	45.2	40.6	4400	22.2
tri-sul-con-	0.38	0.56	0.31	40.4	36.6	3680	18.5
re- and sec-	0.31	0.53	0.28	35.1	31.9	3320	16.7
	0.25	0.48	0.23	29.1	26.6	2730	13.8
[¢A.*] tr- and	0.13	0.44	0.19	15.7	14.1	2260	11.4
sci- et.	0	0.42	0.18	0	0	2140	10.8

$A = \pi D^2/4$ First in a long line of Turners.
$D =$ After four years she $D_i = 0.975\,D_{si}$, $D_e = 0.975\,D_{se}$
$D_{si} =$"I do'nt know you ass- $a = 1200$ / 366 m/
$D_{se} =$ Similar events did fol- $C_i = 0.33$

$A_e/A_i = 0.81$ **Try and seperate** $Z = \left(\dfrac{b}{D_i}\right)^2 \dfrac{s}{aC_i}$

A year later came issue **0.5**, also printed, bound + stapled by hand in our tiny NYC apartment (by this point we'd moved from Hell's Kitchen to the West Village). These 1ˢᵗ 2 issues are out of print, but available as PDFs on the Calamari site: https://www.calamaripress.com/SF/archives.htm (this URL also lists the contributors from all issues). Wendy Collin Sorin + Robert Lopez had work in issue 0.5 + then went on to publish books w/ Calamari. Carlos M. Luis had work in the 1ˢᵗ 2 issues + then published 2 chapbooks w/ Calamari. Carlos died in 2013. Scott Helmes, who appeared in 0.5, died in 2023. They now sleep w/ the *Sleepingfish* issues. Here's a page from issue: 0.5:

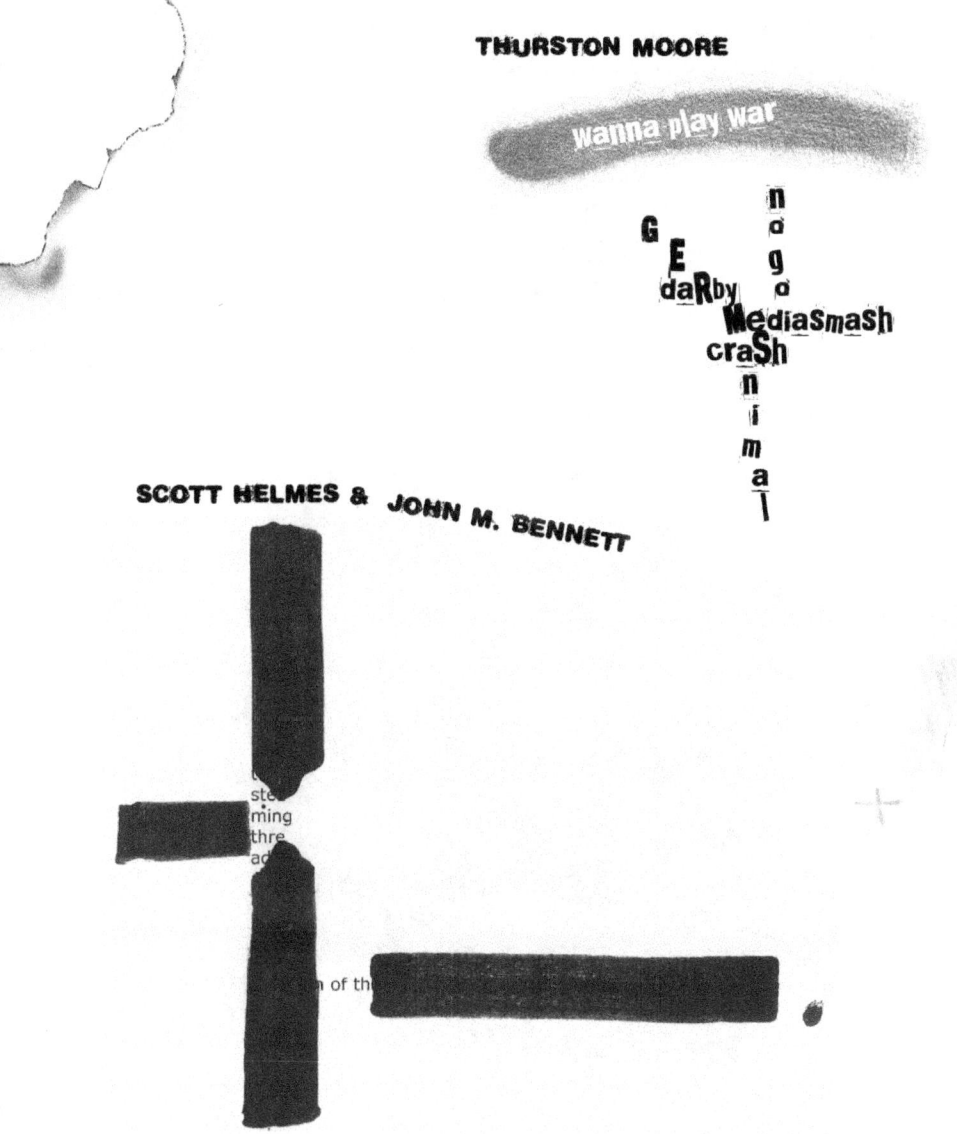

Issue **0.75** (2005) was the 1ˢᵗ perfect-bound issue + is also out of print, but freely available as a dbook online. Authors in this issue that went on to publish books w/ Calamari include Norman Lock (aka George Belden), Michael Peters + Michael Boyko. There was a feature on Mexican visual poetry + 0.75 contributor Joshua Cohen went on to win a Pulitzer Prize. David-Baptiste Chirot appeared in a few issues of *Sleepingfish*, including issue 0.75. We had plans to publish a book of his + then he died in 2021. We've included some of his work scattered through this issue (pages 39, 42, 100, 104, 140 + 220) as he had a big influence on the Calamari/*Sleepingfish* aesthetic in early years.

Issue **0.875** (2006) featured a cover by Eduardo Recife, whose fonts + design inspiration are also ever-present in early issues.

Robert Lopez joined us as co-editor for this issue, and we started to include more language-driven fiction + less visual poetry. Justin Torres was 1ˢᵗ published in issue 0.875 + in 2023 won the National Book Award for fiction. John Olson's *The Night I Dropped Shakespeare on the Cat* sprang from this issue. Issue 0.875 contributor Noah Eli Gordon died a few years ago (a piece of his is reprinted on page 219).

By issue **0.9375** (2007), we were living on 74ᵗʰ + Central Park West. The cover was by Irana Douer. Issue 0.9375 contributor Daniel Borzutzky went on to win a National Book Award for poetry in 2016. Contributors to issue 0.9375 that went on to publish books w/ Calamari include Blake Butler + J'Lyn Chapman.

At this point—as we approached (but could never reach) 1.000 (per Zeno's paradox)—we changed our #ing scheme (issue #0.96875 would have been a bit much, no?) + issue **ZZZ** was next, in 2008, featuring Miranda Mellis, whose *The Revisionist* we'd published the year before.

After issue ZZZ, we moved to Nairobi, Kenya, so did the 1ˢᵗ online installment, **series N**. The next issue, **#8** (2009) went out of print, but we recently reissued it as print-on-demand. Garielle Lutz joined as co-editor for this issue, bringing in the likes of Diane Williams, Ottessa Moshfegh + Anna DeForest. *Boons & The Camp* by David Ohle emerged from this issue.

After *Sleepingfish* 8 (which we put together living in DUMBO), we moved to Rome, so did a few more issues online. Series **iX** (2010) featured work by Chiara Barzini + we then published her *Sister Stop Breathing* + series iX contributor Luca Arnaudo collaborated w/ Aldo Bandinelli to make *WORDATLAS | PAROLATLANTE*. Here's work by Ragnhildur Jóhannsdóttir from series iX:

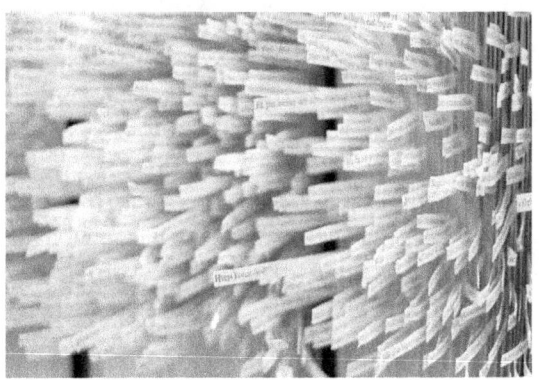

Still living in Rome, we continued to post online in 2011, in series **X**. Book projects that came from series X: *Tortoise* by James Lewelling, *A Mortal Affect* by Vincent Standley + *Divorcer* by Garielle Lutz. Here's work by Dakota Crane from series X:

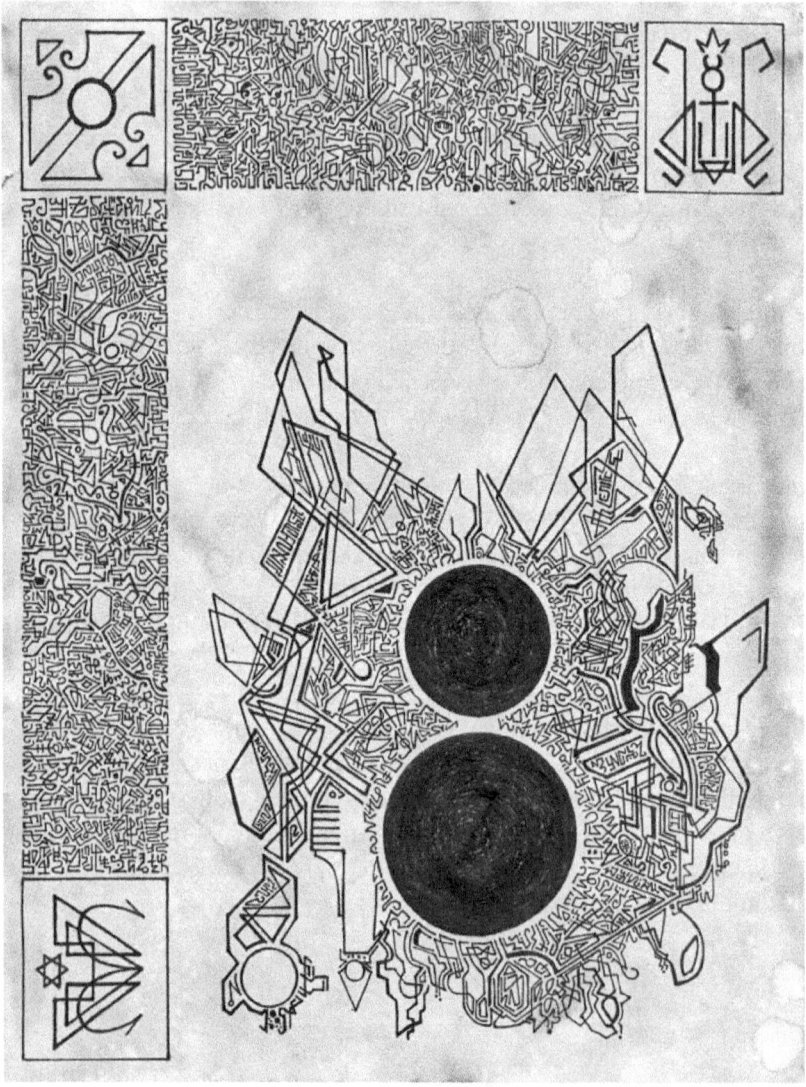

Then we did another online series, **Xi**, from Rome, in 2012. Fellow NYC/Rome small press publisher Giancarlo DiTrapano had a poem in *Sleepingfish* Xi, then later died in 2022. Julie Reverb had a piece in series Xi + then we published her *No Moon*. Nick Francis Potter had work in Xi + also in the next issue + now Calamari is reissuing his *New Animals*.

By *Sleepingfish* **12** (2013), we were back in NYC, on Riverside + 125th, so figured we'd do another print issue, for the 10th anniversary. It featured Dmitry Babenko on the cover (from *The Oikumene Fish Catalog* artist book that we acquired in our personal collection). Elizabeth Mikesch's *Niceties* was born from this issue + #12 also featured images from the book where birds were the words, *{ untitled: under the auspices }*.

Issue **13** was back online, running from 2014 to 2018, while we were living in NYC, DC + again in Rome. It featured work by Boots Walking in America (aka Mark Baumer), that we reprinted on page 136. Issue 13 led to or featured work from these Calamari titles: Brandon Hobson's *Deep Ellum, The City Moon* archives, Stanley Crawford's *Travel Notes,* Beth Steidle's *Static Herd, The Gotham Grammarian* by Garielle Lutz, *The Luminol Reels* by Laura Ellen Joyce + *Math Class* by Kelly Krumrie (aka O).

Issue **XiV** was a music mixtape issue released on cassette, in 2018:

During the pandemic, we rebooted *Sleepingfish* online + called it **2020+ ≠ 404**, thinking it would be ongoing indefinitely, w/ the "≠ 404" to symbolize that (contrary to popular belief) *Sleepingfish* was not dead (though we did let the <u>sleepingfish.net</u> URL expire). In this latest online series we posted pieces from *Textiloma* by anon I'm us, *4ier X-forms* by No One, the Sound Furies album *Herd of Birds*, *Residue* by MM/DD/2020, *Summertime in the Emergency Room* by David Nutt, *Hist* by James Belflower + Matthew Klane, *Genesis* (self-authored) + *1/ 4 i am ÐNA* by in8 iÐ. Much of the work in this series was also published anon/pseudonymously.

+ that brings us to this final issue, **XX**, published January 2024, from NYC (Central Park West + 105th street), co-edited w/ Garielle Lutz.

—Cal A. Mari

CONTRIBUTOR BIOS

Steven Alvarez is the author of the novels in verse *Manhatitlán, McTlán,* and the Fence Modern Poets Prize-winning *The Codex Mojaodicus.* His work has appeared in *Best Experimental Writing* (BAX), *Berkeley Poetry Review, Fence, Huizache, The Offing,* and *Waxwing.*

Rosaire Appel creates visual books, sound drawings and abstract comics. In other words, her work revolves around non-verbal language. Her most recent book is *Traces of Traces,* a visual essay, available at Amazon. Her website is https://rosaireappel.com.

Ali Aktan Aşkın lives in rural Maine.

Nat Baldwin is a musician and writer from Maine living in Western Mass. He's released numerous solo and collaborative works and runs the experimental music label Tripticks Tapes. His debut collection of short fiction *The Red Barn* was published in 2017 by Calamari Archive.

Niles Baldwin lives in Kittery, Maine. His stories can most recently be found at *Heavy Feather Review, HAD,* and *MAYDAY.* This is his first print publication.

Jordan Barger is a translator of Norwegian and Danish. His translations of Yahya Hassan, Sigbjørn Obstfelder and Tor Ulven have appeared in venues such as *Fence, Circumference, Socrates on the Beach, Poetry Magazine,* and onstage in Philadelphia, thanks to Sewer Rats Productions.

Maeve Barry lives in New York. You can read more of her stories @ https://maeve-barry.com.

Chiara Barzini is the author of the short story collection *Sister Stop Breathing* (Calamari Press, 2012) and the novel *Things That Happened Before The Earthquake* (Doubleday, 2017.) Her writing has appeared in numerous anthologies and journals including *Bomb, Noon, Freeman's, LitHub, The Los Angeles Review of Books, NY Tyrant,* and *ZYZZYVA.* She has recently translated Goliarda Sapienza's poems into English and is working on a translation of Diane Williams' latest story collection into Italian for Edizioni Black Coffee.

Mark Baumer (aka Boots Walking in America) was an writer and environmental activist. In 2010, Baumer walked across the United States in 81 days. In 2016, he attempted to walk barefoot across America, to raise awareness about climate change. Baumer was struck and killed by an SUV on the walk, while in Florida.

Emilio Carrero is the managing editor for *Southeast Review*. Their work appears in *Leavings* magazine and is forthcoming in *Ocean State Review*. They believe the truth is out there.

Kim Chinquee's eighth book (and first novel) *Pipette* was published by Ravenna Press. She's the recipient of three Pushcart Prizes, is senior editor of *New World Writing,* associate editor of *Midwest Review,* chief editor of *ELJ (Elm Leaves Journal*), and co-director of SUNY-Buffalo State University's writing major. She's a competitive triathlete, a certified USA Triathlon Official, and she lives with her three dogs in Tonawanda, New York.

David-Baptiste Chirot (1953-2021) was a writer and artist whose art appeared often in *Sleepingfish.*

Bobby Crace teaches creative writing at Stony Brook University and ghostwrites novel manuscripts and memoirs for Kevin Anderson & Associates. You can find his work in *The Brooklyn Rail, The Southampton Review, The Under Review, MAYDAY,* and other journals.

Anna DeForest is the author of the novels *A History of Present Illness* and the forthcoming *Our Long Marvelous Dying*, and a palliative care physician at Memorial Sloan Kettering Cancer Center in New York City.

S. C. Delaney has translated, with Agnès Potier, Tony Duvert's prose collections *Odd Jobs* and *District* (Wakefield Press). His work has been featured in, among other places, *Hayden's Ferry Review*, *Black Sun Lit*, and *Journal of Experimental Fiction.*

Federico Federici is a conceptual artist working in the fields of writing, video art, installations, and physics. His works have appeared in international journals and anthologies including *3:AM Magazine, Art in America, DIAGRAM, Perspektive, Jahrbuch der Lyrik, Poet Lore, Sand, The Shanghai Literary Review, The Manhattan Review*. His last book is *EIS* with a critical note by Peter Schwenger (LN 2022).

Noah Eli Gordon (1975–2022) was an American poet, editor, and publisher.

Mariangela Guatteri is Poet and visual artist. She is co-editor of *GAMMM* and of the *Benway Series*. In 2021 she translated the visual pages of *Ebora* into the Italian edition of *Zong!* by M. NourbeSe Philip. Her asemic works have appeared in *Asemica 2, Utsanga, OEI #67-68, AlteredScale, asemic net, Apocrifa, Sleepingfish, Moria,* and *REM Magazine*. She has written theoretical contributions on asemic writing published in *Utsanga* and in *Asemic Writing. Contributi teorici.*

John Haskell's books include *I Am Not Jackson Pollock, American Purgatorio, Out of My Skin,* and *The Complete Ballet.* He has written catalogue essays, dance reviews, food histories, and film criticism. His fiction and nonfiction pieces have appeared in a variety of publications, including *BOMB* and *A Public Space,* magazines where he is a contributing editor. He has performed his work onstage, and on the radio shows *The Next Big Thing* and *Studio 360.* He was awarded a Guggenheim Foundation Fellowship and has taught writing and literature in Los Angeles, New York, and Leipzig.

Chelsea Hogue is a writer from Mississippi. She's the author of the chapbook *Ethel* (Keith LLC, 2020). Her writing has appeared in *Quarterly West, Juked, Black Sun Lit, Tinge, The New Inquiry, McSweeney's Quarterly Concern, Bright Wall/Dark Room*, and *Full Stop*, among others.

Tim Horvath is the author of *Understories* (Bellevue Literary Press), which won the New Hampshire Literary Award, and *Circulation* (sunnyoutside). His stories appear in *Conjunctions, AGNI, The Best Small Fictions 2021*, and elsewhere. He is a Visiting Assistant Professor in the Stony Brook MFA in Writing and Literature, an English teacher at Phillips Exeter Academy, and a Senior Editor at *Conjunctions.* In addition, he teaches for GrubStreet, StoryStudio Chicago, and Long Island University's MFA in Writing and Publishing.

Zebulon House (or Horse) is a white settler, born on unceded land of the Pennacook. Their work has previously appeared in *Sleepingfish* and *ergot.* You can find them online at zebulon-hourse.xyz.

Meiko Ko's work has appeared in *Vol. 1 Brooklyn, failbetter, Juked, The Offing*, and *Cha*, among other places. She lives in New York with her husband and children.

Kelly Krumrie is the author of *Math Class* (Calamari Archive, 2022).

Mary Kuryla's collection *Freak Weather Stories* (University of Massachusetts Press) received the Grace Paley Prize in Short Fiction. Her stories have appeared in *The Paris Review, Conjunctions, The Kenyon Review, Agni, The Baffler,* and elsewhere. They have received The Pushcart Prize and the Glimmer Train Very Short Fiction Prize. Her 2022 debut novel *Away to Stay* (Regal House Publishing) was called "a delightfully quirky debut" by *Publishers Weekly.* Kuryla's feature film *Freak Weather,* adapted from her short story, premiered at the Toronto International Film Festival.

Babak Lakghomi is the author of *South* (Dundurn Press, 2023) and *Floating Notes* (Tyrant Books, 2018). His writing has appeared in *American Short Fiction, Electric Literature, NOON, Fence,* and the *Adroit Journal,* among other places. He lives and writes in Toronto, Canada.

Eugene Lim is the author of four novels: *Fog & Car, The Strangers, Dear Cyborgs,* and *Search History.* He runs Ellipsis Press, works as a high-school librarian, and lives in Queens, NY. https://eugenelim.com/

Carlos M. Luis (1932-2013) was a Cuban-born writer, artist, critic, and curator active in the Cuban art scene both on the island and in exile. He co-authored *O, Vozque Pulp* (2004) and *ma(I)ze Tassel Retrazos* (2005), both from Calamari Archive.

John Madera is the author of *Nervosities* (Anti-Oedipus Press, 2024). His other fiction is published in *Conjunctions, Salt Hill, The &Now Awards 2: The Best Innovative Writing,* and elsewhere. His criticism is published in *American Book Review, Bookforum, The Review of Contemporary Fiction, Rain Taxi: Review of Books, The Believer, The Brooklyn Rail,* and elsewhere. Recipient of an M.F.A. in Literary Arts from Brown University, two-time New York State Council on the Arts awardee John Madera lives in New York City, where he runs Rhizomatic and manages and edits *Big Other*.

Peter Markus published his first two books of fiction, *Good, Brother* and *The Singing Fish,* with Calamari Archive. His most recent book is the book of poems, *When Our Fathers Return to Us as Birds.*

Born in Japan and raised in the US, **Sawako Nakayasu** is an artist working with language, performance, and translation. Her newest books of poetry include *Pink Waves,* a finalist for the PEN/Voelcker award, and *Some Girls Walk into the Country They Are From*, both of which engage the intersection between writing and translation. *Mouth: Eats Color—Sagawa Chika Translations, Anti-translations, & Originals* is a multilingual work that combines both original and translated poetry. Nakayasu teaches in the Literary Arts department at Brown University.

Elle Nash is the author of *Deliver Me, Nudes, Gag Reflex,* and *Animals Eat Each Other.* She runs a writing workshop called Textures and lives in Glasgow. Find her anywhere online @saderotica or ellenash.net.

David Nutt is the author of *Summertime in the Emergency Room* (Calamari Archive) and *The Great American Suction* (Tyrant Books). He lives in Ithaca, New York, with his wife and dog and two cats.

Kim Parko is a greying being who gathers from the hedge.

Agnès Potier was born and raised in Paris and now lives in the Pyrenees. She is currently translating, with S. C. Delaney, the short texts of Michel Vachey, some of which may be found in *Puerto del Sol, Columbia Journal,* and *Kenyon Review Online*.

Nick Francis Potter is the author of *Big Gorgeous Jazz Machine* (Driftwood Press), *Static Gifs* (Greying Ghost), and *New Animals* (soon to be reissued by Calamari Archive).

"Rachterscale," better known as **Rachita Ramya**, is a writer/storyteller from India who has a background in public health and medicine. She is pursuing her MFA at Stony Brook University and lives in New York with her sister.

Carla Rak (Rome, 1978) is a textile designer and visual artist working with photography, collage, textiles, and writings. She graduated in Sociology and then received a PhD in Communication Sciences. Her academic writings on visual language gained her the recognition of the Institute of Philosophical Studies in Naples and the Cozzi Prize from the Benetton Foundation. In 2018 *Eyes as Oars. A visual journey to Mars*—her book dedicated to visual language and Mars—was published by Danilo Montanari Editore.

Michael Salu is a British-born Nigerian writer, artist, scholar, editor, and creative strategist with a strong interdisciplinary practice. His written work has appeared in literary journals, magazines, art and academic publications, and as an artist, he has exhibited internationally. He runs House of Thought, an artistic research practice and consultancy focusing on bridging creative, critical thinking and technology and is part of Planetary Portals, a research collective. *Red Earth,* his first book, was published by Calamari Archive in 2023.

Sofia Samatar is the author of several works of fiction and nonfiction, including the World Fantasy Award-winning novel *A Stranger in Olondria* and *The White Mosque: A Memoir,* a PEN/Jean Stein Award finalist.

Jonathan Sargent studied music at Bard College and worked as a recording engineer on jazz and punk albums. After college, he played in a metal band and started writing fiction. He lives and writes short fiction in Brooklyn, NY.

Nina Shope's debut novel, *Asylum,* won the 2020 Dzanc Fiction Prize and was released in May 2022. Her collection, *Hangings: Three Novellas* (2005), won the Starcherone Books Award. She is the recipient of the Calvino Prize from the University of Louisville, among other honors. She is originally from Wellesley, Massachusetts, and now lives in Denver, Colorado, with her husband, writer Chris Narozny.

Jada Smiley is a special-education teacher working and living in New Orleans. She's fascinated by the rhythm and musicality of mundane situations.

Elijah Sparkman is the Detroit Programs and Volunteer Coordinator for 826michigan. He is a teaching artist for *The Moth*. He is a memoir reader for *Split Lip Magazine*. His writing has appeared or is forthcoming in *Eco Theo, CHEAP POP, Bull,* and *The Museum of Americana.*

Justin Torres is the author of the novel *Blackouts,* winner of the 2023 National Book Award for Fiction. His debut novel, *We the Animals*, won VCU's Cabell First Novelist Award, was translated into 15 languages, and was adapted into a feature film. His short fiction and essays have appeared in *The New Yorker, Harper's, Granta, Tin House, The Washington Post, LA Times Image Magazine,* and *Best American Essays*. He lives in Los Angeles, and teaches at UCLA.

Tor Ulven is one of the most influential Norwegian writers of the '80s and '90s. His suicide in 1995, at the age of 41, cut short a writing career consisting of five books of poetry and six books of prose. His work concerns the absurd battle between accepting meaninglessness and weaving meaning into our lives. Jan Sjåvik writes: "It is ironic that a writer with Ulven's sense of human transitoriness should have been able to come closer to literary immortality than most."

Michel Vachey (1939–87) was a French experimental artist and author. He was a founder of the Textruction movement, which sought to blur the line between image and text, and his writing likewise probes expectations of genre. His work includes novels, collages, and hybrid story-essays. *Archipel plusieurs: 1967-1987*, a 450-page collection of his poetry, has been published by Editions Flammarion.

Angela Woodward is the author of the novels *Ink, Natural Wonders,* and *End of the Fire Cult,* as well as two collections of short fiction: *The Human Mind* and *Origins and Other Stories. Natural Wonders* won the Fiction Collective 2 Doctorow Innovative Fiction Prize in 2015. Woodward's short stories and essays have appeared in many journals including the *Kenyon Review, Green Mountains Review, Ninth Letter,* and the *Los Angeles Review of Books.*

Yuxin Zhao is a writer from Hangzhou, China, and currently based in the UK. She writes experimental fiction and poetry on migration and/or immigration, family history, and queer desire. Her writing has appeared in *Full Stop, 7x7 LA, O BOD,* and *rivulet. Three Forms of Exhaustion,* a chapbook, was published as part of the DanceNotes chaplet series. *The Moons* is forthcoming from Calamari Archive.

www.ingramcontent.com/pod-product-compliance
Lightning Source LLC
Chambersburg PA
CBHW050340030726
47503CB00008B/2546